The
Exiled
Seven

Blake Renworth

Inglenook Publishing House
Grantham, Pennsylvania

ISBN-13: 978-0-9970903-1-4

Library of Congress Control Number: 2016940292

For Josh, who encouraged me...

...and really ought to have known better.

CONTENTS

To Andrea —

Stories are adventures we undertake together, reader and storyteller, arm-in-arm. I will supply the words. You must supply the imagination.

Ab initio.

BR

1

A Foul Disposition

If you will, please imagine the tallest and most beautifully handsome man you can, the complete and perfect embodiment of classic male beauty, charm, and chivalry.

Now—cast this image far from your mind. For this tale is not about him. Many of such tales have already been told, and to tell yet another would be a great disservice to the other heroes of the world.

The hero around whom this tale revolves—and a hero I assure you he was, even if your faith may waver during the events that follow—was a hero of a different sort. Though it would be altogether unfair to say that he did not entirely look the part. He was as handsome as dwarfs come. Strong, in both physique and demeanor, and clearly one who commanded respect. But his jaw-length, dark blonde hair, the color of wet straw, and not even five-foot stature are not what you and I are accustomed to seeing in our mind's eye when we think of the heroes of tall tales. Nor his slightly crooked nose or angular jawline, for that matter.

What about his personality, you ask? For, of course, looks are not all that matter in a champion. And I applaud your depth of character. But sadly, I must disappoint you and your commendable optimism. For this hero was not charming, or dashing, or gallant, or really very pleasant in any way at all. In fact, he could be downright *un*pleasant to be around when in one of his all-too-frequent foul dispositions. And unfortunately, it is in such a disposition that we find Alariq as we join his story.

As disagreeable as Alariq was, I am sure you will find his demeanor quite understandable. You see, his story is an unfortunate one. We find him, and his six loyal companions, banished from their city-state, Alariq for a crime he did not commit, and the others for their loyalty to him and their faith in his innocence.

Seven dwarfs they were, exiled and alone.

And they were also wet. And cold. And hungry. So you see, Alariq's rather nasty disposition is forgivable, at least in the present instance. At this particular moment, Alariq was thinking how he wished they were *six* dwarfs, rather than seven, as one member of his company was nattering away yet again about their intended destination.

"It might be possible to stay in the mountains near Ishtara," said Callum, the youngest of the group, for the third time in as many days, as he picked his way down the narrow mountain path. "We would be in familiar territory and maybe our families could visit." He spoke with the optimism of youth.

"You know we can't stay on Ishtar lands, Callum," said Brimir gently. "And you know it would endanger our families to contact us. They would be exiled too. Or killed." Brimir, the oldest of the company, spoke to Callum with the warmth and understanding that often comes from age.

But Alariq had had enough. He was tired of Callum's constant talk of Ishtara, their home. Of course all of them would rather be there than here. But that wasn't an option. And it was time Callum understood that. Time he understood the price of his loyalty.

Alariq flung the water skin he had just been about to drink from to his feet. He turned around and stepped directly in Callum's path, his broad, muscled chest bumping against Callum's small, almost concave one.

"Enough, Callum! Get your head on straight! They believe us

to be traitors. Me by fault and you by association. We are lucky we weren't executed on the spot." Alariq felt blood rushing into his face and tried to calm himself. "You need to accept, right now, that Ishtara is not our home anymore. Nor will it ever be again."

Alariq looked into the young, innocent eyes of his cousin. Callum was his only living relative who had the same eyes as Alariq, a light, but rich, honey color, so unlike the steel grey of most Ishta dwarfs. It was a trait they had both inherited from their beloved grandfather, which is probably what had drawn Alariq to Callum, a relative who, in every other way, was his polar opposite.

Alariq took a step back, feeling dry brush and twigs crack beneath his feet on the parched path.

Alariq had to make Callum understand the true nature of their situation, or his young cousin's romantic nature would only continue to cause everyone angst, to Callum himself most of all. Callum had always been soft, which is why Alariq had gotten him a job in the scrollroom, exempting him from mandatory military service. Alariq told himself he'd done it to keep Callum from being a liability. But the truth was he knew Callum could never handle the realities of war.

Alariq thought he'd been protecting him. Well, his young, naïve cousin needed a different kind of protection now.

"Our family made their choice. They could have stood by me. By us." He kept his voice firm and cold, hoping it would get through to his cousin's rational side, assuming there was one. "They think we betrayed our city, betrayed them."

"No, I don't believe that." There was a note of pleading in Callum's voice. "They just didn't know what to do, how to help—"

Callum's forgiveness, so easily granted, only enraged Alariq. Forgiveness was an expensive emotion and not one any of them could afford living in the wild. Alariq grabbed handfuls of his cousin's shirt, damp from sweat.

The other dwarfs leapt forward. Three of them pulled Alariq away, while another steadied Callum from behind as Alariq released him. Brimir stepped between the two, facing not Alariq, but Callum. Alariq stared at the back of Brimir's head, at his thick, wavy, ice-white hair falling to his shoulders, gently moving with the mountain breeze.

"I know you don't want to hear it, son, but Alariq is right. Why your kin sided with Haamith is irrelevant. All that matters, right now, is that they *did* side with him."

Brimir turned to Alariq, who stood completely still, except for his involuntarily flexing muscles and deep, ragged breathing. Brimir fixed him with a pointed stare. Alariq looked back at the eyes he'd seen an uncountable number of times before, at Brimir, the dwarf who was like a father to him.

Brimir spoke as if he were talking to the group, but Alariq knew the words were meant for him alone.

"But it's time we decided where to go. Wandering aimlessly like this isn't accomplishing anything except making my old joints ache. So, when we set up camp tonight, let's settle the matter."

Alariq recognized the care with which Brimir had phrased his order. And an order it was, although only Alariq recognized it as such. Brimir hadn't insisted they make camp then and there, but rather left control of the situation to Alariq. He was grateful for that, even though he didn't appreciate being backed into a corner, no matter how gently he was maneuvered into it. Did Brimir really think he didn't know they needed to find a new place to call home? It was all that had consumed him since the huge, wrought-iron gates of Ishtara clanged shut behind them three days ago. It was his military training, always thinking of the next step. The minute they became homeless and concurrently, unprotected, Alariq had been evaluating their situation, weighing their options.

But he had come up empty. Every time he tried to think of a place to settle permanently, he just thought of Ishtara. So he delayed the conversation he knew the others wanted to have, especially sentimental young Callum. He remained silent while they had repeatedly attempted to open a line of communication to him. Well, he couldn't remain silent any longer.

"I want to make it out of the mountains today. We'll stop then." Alariq picked up his pack and water skin and continued down the uneven mountain path without another word.

For the remaining hours in the mountains, Alariq tried to make a decision, as he wound his way down the rocky road. He was grateful it was only wide enough for them to pass single file, knowing his despair must show on his face.

He knew the others were looking to him to know what to do. He had been First Authority of Division Three, the highest commander of the division. Even though only three of his current companions had been his direct subordinates, he outranked all of them. Gideon, balding and bespectacled, had worked in the scrollroom as the official historian of Ishtara, and had never served in the military. Nor had Callum, who had been his lone assistant. Brimir had achieved the rank of Third Authority, the lowest class of officer, when he had served decades earlier. The other three, Blainn, Fordinand, and Asher, all served under Alariq.

But there was more to it than who was the highest-ranking officer. Alariq had the gnawing feeling in his gut that they were all looking to him to make it right, not because of his military status in the dwarfish army, but rather because it was his fault that they were all here. It was he who had been exiled for treason. They merely chose to stand with him, believing in his innocence, and were exiled as a consequence.

Far too soon, the path began to widen and straighten, and the trees began to thin. He could put this off a bit longer, wait until the mountains were truly behind them.

No, that wasn't a good idea. They should make camp just inside the mountain range's edge. Mountains were familiar to them, their natural habitat. They would be safer here, too, still within the borders of Ishtar territory. When a small plateau just off the path presented itself, Alariq couldn't pass it by, even for the sake of buying himself a bit more time to think.

"Stop. We'll camp here tonight." He pointed at the bend in the path that concealed a small flat area surrounded by brush and rocks.

As they unpacked their supplies, Alariq recognized their good fortune that he, Blainn, Fordinand, and Asher had just returned from eastern border patrol with the rest of Division Three. Tanith, the king of Ishtara, had read the charges before they could so much as remove the packs from their backs, which meant that the four of them were already equipped with basic necessities.

Brimir and Callum had stood up for him there on the spot, so the two of them had left the city with almost nothing. But Gideon had stayed behind, collected a few more things he knew they would need and then, to Alariq's surprise, caught up with them in the mountains.

And that was how Alariq learned that he had six friends. Well, maybe not friends, but six dwarfs who believed in his innocence. He wasn't sure he had any friends. But then again, he wasn't sure he'd ever been interested in making any. Nonetheless, he now had six dwarfs for whom he must take responsibility.

Alariq directed the others to set up camp and start cooking a rabbit he'd shot earlier that day, while he entered the woods alone with his crossbow to hunt for something bigger. As he walked into the sparse, empty woods, he wished he had his full armor too. He felt naked out in the mountains without it. Instead, he and the other three soldiers wore only thick leather vests and thigh-sheaths over their normal clothes, which provided only a thin layer of protection. The others wore nothing but the usual dwarf attire: a linen tunic, wool coat and trousers, and boots.

As he hunted, he let his mind go blank, refusing to dwell on the ugliness of their situation. He returned an hour later. At the sound of his footsteps they looked up and several grinned appreciatively at his catch, a large elk. Gideon and Brimir immediately went to work on it.

"What did you do to this thing, son?" Brimir asked him, examining the elk's crushed hip.

"That's how I found him," Alariq replied.

Gideon looked sharply at the dead animal, his tiny eyes narrowing into almost nothing, his glasses digging into his cheeks as he squinted. "Well something big had a hold of him, that's for sure."

Alariq saw a couple of the others glance around nervously. Callum stood and walked over to get a better look at the elk.

"What could have done that? I don't even see any teeth marks."

"The only thing I know can do damage like that is an ettin." Blainn looked almost accusingly at Alariq. Although the shortest of their group, he was also the most muscular, and a menacing

6

look from him was generally met with cowering and muttered apologies.

Fordinand snorted. "Don't be ridiculous. Ettins haven't been in these parts since the Ettinwar over thirty years ago. I don't even think they've bothered villagers for leagues around here, at least I haven't heard say so from them or the knomes. Tanith's division decimated their army."

Fordinand had been Second Authority under Alariq. Those who were fond of him, which was pretty much everyone, called him Ford. He was classically handsome, with rich dark brown hair and eyes that were the identical color, with a smooth face and strong jaw. He was the tallest of all the dwarfs, here or back home.

Home. Alariq supposed he had put off the discussion of home long enough.

"Ford's right. It could have been any number of things, including falling from a height in the mountains. But it doesn't matter, we're well out of sight and still technically in Ishtar territory. Nothing will attack us here." He turned to Brimir. "Cook the meat well so it keeps."

Brimir nodded and focused his attention on the animal's crushed hindquarter.

Alariq sat down on one of the smooth rocks that had been moved around the fire in his absence. For long minutes, they all just stared into the flames at the rabbit, slowly browning on a makeshift spit.

Alariq knew the others were thinking of Ishtara, just as he was. Most would think it a harsh place, ugly even. But Alariq had never thought so. It was a huge, open mine, yes. And although it was referred to as "the Pit" by the knomes, the migrant workers who did the mining in Ishtara, Alariq always thought it had an industrial beauty about it. The mine was carved artfully into the largest mountain in the Brackish Mountains, making it look as if the peak had caved in on itself, becoming inverted. There were circular levels that descended gracefully lower into the earth. Various paths and streams led outward and downward, twisting, turning, cutting through the rocks and trees of the smaller mountains around the mine, like roots of a hundred-year-old tree.

Ishtara was primarily an ironstone mine, which gave the mountain a bluish tint. And the constant working of furnaces made the whole place glow. It could be seen even from the foothills. If their camp wasn't surrounded by tall rocks and trees, they would have been able to see it then, glowing blue in the night.

Alariq caught himself gazing intently into the fire, imagining he was a bird looking down on Ishtara, alight in her manufacturing magnificence. He quickly looked away and realized the only one of them not doing the same thing was Brimir, who already had the hindquarter removed, skinned, and ready to put over the fire. Alariq removed the rabbit and checked to make sure the juices ran clear. He silently passed it over to Gideon to cut up and distribute.

The moment had come. He could put it off no longer. "Alright. So, we've all been thinking about it for the last four days. Any ideas?"

No one needed to ask what he meant.

Blainn spoke first. "What about Karxana?"

There was immediate backlash. Gideon dropped the rabbit back into the fire and looked at Blainn, his face frozen in shock. Ford, Asher, and Callum started yelling about loyalty. Brimir just shook his head and looked at the ground.

Alariq had thought about Karxana too, but only for a second. It was the only other dwarfish city-state on the Continent, which gave it immediate appeal as a new home. But based on the others' reactions, he was quite glad that he had already dismissed it.

"No. Karxana is out. I won't be disloyal to Ishtara, even if Ishtara was disloyal to me." Alariq did not need to raise his voice. The minute he'd started speaking, attention was given to him. "Besides, they'd probably kill us as soon as they found us on Karxani lands. And even if they gave us asylum, it would likely be on the condition that we give them information on Tanith and Ishtara. And I won't do that."

The others looked relieved for a second and then turned to glare at Blainn for even suggesting they take up residence with Ishtara's enemy.

Blainn looked uncomfortable, but not at all apologetic. He had always had a harshness about him, both in manner and appearance, but it seemed even more intensified now. "Well, you may not care that Ishtara was disloyal to us, but I do. I don't owe them nothing after the way they treated you. Treated us." He pointed his thumb at himself and Ford. "Like our testimony counted for less than nothing."

The others looked slightly less accusatory, but no less resolved against such an act of betrayal.

Callum broke the angry silence. "What about Knaba?"

Alariq remained silent. He had been wondering about Knaba as well, but before he could voice his concerns, Gideon spoke them for him. "The knomes have a good thing going with Ishtara. They won't risk upsetting the king by taking in a traitor. If Tanith knew they had offered Alariq asylum, their protective agreements would all be in jeopardy."

"We could try." Asher's voice was hopeful. "Knomes are very empathetic creatures. If we explained that Tanith is mistaken, that Alariq is innocent...they would probably believe Ford. He gets on well with them." As Ford's younger brother, Asher well knew the effect the handsome dwarf had on others.

Gideon shook his head. "They've worked hard for this arrangement. They might be empathetic, but they're not risk-takers. Even if Ford could convince them of Alariq's innocence, they'd be too afraid of the consequences. They depend on Ishtara for protection."

"And I'm not sure I want to put them in that position anyway." Ford looked contrite, but firm. "They're good creatures, gentle. I don't want to cause trouble for them."

Alariq momentarily bristled, wondering if that was an insult meant for him. But no, this was just Ford being Ford, noble and self-sacrificing, always thinking of the well-being of others, especially those less able than him.

"I agree," Alariq said. "No Knaba."

He waited for one of them to say it, but no one spoke. "I guess that only leaves us with Dirnovaria. It has no official race and all kinds live there, so we shouldn't feel too out of place. It seems like our only option."

The silence continued, stretching out behind Alariq's statement like a road disappearing into the horizon.

Finally, Brimir looked up from his wrinkled hands and spoke in his mild, thoughtful way. "Then that's that. I guess we're going to Dirnovaria."

"It'll never feel like home," mumbled Asher dejectedly.

Alariq stiffened, but before he could suggest that if Asher didn't like it, he could just toddle right back to Ishtara, Brimir, sensing the argument coming, said, "So now we just need to decide how we're going to get there."

Alariq continued to glare at Asher for a minute, who looked very much like his brother, just younger and a little less striking, before turning his attention back to the group.

"Right, well we've got the Seven Gateway Cities we can go through. Ishtara is obviously out, as are Karxana and Knaba. And we can't get anywhere near Ettinridge. So that leaves us with Prienne or Lysette on the river, or Eridu up north."

"Let's rule out Eridu, too," said Ford. "It's the farthest away, we'd have to travel through the desert, and the Utu are a treacherous people."

"Agreed?" Alariq asked, although he didn't really need to. Everyone nodded assent. "Alright. Well, Prienne is closer," he began.

"But the road there takes us through the Wayward Hills, which means ettin territory."

Alariq understood well the fear in Gideon's voice. Ettins were huge, vicious creatures, about three times the size of dwarfs. Destruction was a game for them, although they were much smarter than they looked and highly militarized. They were sometimes hired as mercenaries because of their ability to follow any order without interference from their consciences.

Alariq, Blainn, and Ford knew well what happened to the enemies of ettins. Ishtara's most recent war was against the creatures and the atrocities committed were too horrible to think about. When they'd captured dwarfs, they tortured them, not for information, but as a scare tactic. When Division Three began to advance and take ettin camps, they found more than a few limbless fallen comrades. Not all ettins were like that, of course, but the ruling class killed off any of the weaker members of their species.

"It also takes us back through Ishtar territory and Tanith said we had one week to get off Ishtar lands or we'd be killed. There's no way we could make it that far north in three days." Brimir said it matter-of-factly as he stoked the fire, but Alariq thought he detected a note of accusation in his voice. Perhaps for not having the foresight to pick a destination sooner? Or was it because he already resented standing by Alariq in general?

"Lysette is much farther though, especially if we take the southern route around August Sound, which is the only way we'd avoid Ishtara and the ettins," said Ford.

Alariq's voice was harsh and rough when he spoke. "Well it's not as if we have anywhere to be, anyone waiting for us."

Everyone looked away from one another. Alariq wished he could take the words back. Instead, he said, "So Lysette it is. We'll backtrack just a bit and take the mountain road south. Then we'll go under August Sound and follow its edge until—"

Gideon cut him off with a shout. "Dendreya!"

Brimir made an excited noise in his throat, but the others simply looked confused.

"The old charter town? Where they made glass?" Callum asked, brushing his blonde hair off of his forehead.

"Right." Gideon was talking more animatedly than Alariq had ever seen him. He was the second oldest of their group, but he'd always had a childlike look and way about him, which was even more apparent now, his round face, slightly deflated with age, practically glowing with excitement.

"It was founded back when the knomes refused to work and we weren't getting any ironstone out of the mountain. We needed another way to sustain our city, so we established a large settlement on the edge of Loraheem Forest. But it's empty now. We could live there." He seemed genuinely happy at this prospect.

"Everything is dwarf-sized, so we would feel more at home, and we'd have everything we need to sustain ourselves," added Brimir, who likewise looked brighter than he had since they left Ishtara.

The dwarfs perked up, glancing around at one another.

"It's the size of a large village, though, right?" Asher asked. "Would we really want to live in a place that big all by ourselves?"

The others were silent for a moment and then Callum spoke quietly and hesitantly, as if each word were risky to say. And they were.

"Maybe we could persuade our families to join us there, you know, once we're established."

Alariq stood up so quickly he kicked one of the logs in the fire and sent sparks all over himself, showering his legs, arms, and torso with red and orange flecks of molten ash. His contorted features showed his rage, but his complete disregard for the smoldering ash burning holes in his clothes and singeing his blonde arm hair made him look deranged.

When he spoke, however, it was with a low, deadly, barely-restrained tone. "Stop being a naïve child, Callum. Our family doesn't want to be with us. If they did, they would have walked out of Ishtara right behind us." Alariq turned and started to walk for the edge of the clearing. Before he reached it, he turned back and said, slightly more gently, "It's better if you accept it now, Callum."

Alariq took the opportunity to do a quick sweep of their perimeter. He took longer than necessary returning to camp; he was still angry with Callum. Maybe it was a mistake to let him come. He would probably always mourn for home, for the people who chose to believe Haamith's testimony and accept Tanith's decision to exile without further proof or other witnesses. He supposed that was to be expected when the king's own son put the finger on somebody, even a high-ranking officer like himself.

He knew he was being hard on Callum, especially when the situation was already hard enough. But his constant hopefulness and adolescent optimism wasn't productive. And dwelling on the impossible would only increase his pain in the long run. It would only increase everyone's pain.

Upon Alariq's return, the others, who had been speaking in hushed tones, immediately fell silent. Ford, Asher, and Brimir looked at him, while the other three looked at their feet or into the fire. Alariq didn't relish the idea of living in another dwarfish city, with a thousand things to remind him of home, of a life he could no longer have. But he'd made the decision to make the others happy. After all, they were homeless because of him.

"We'll go to Dendreya," he said.

Brimir smiled softly, but Gideon's lips broke into a wide, toothy smile.

Alariq held up his hands. "I'm not saying we'll stay. It's been abandoned by our people for centuries. We have no idea what condition it's in or even if it's still unoccupied. Local villagers may have moved in. If it doesn't seem like a viable option, we'll continue along the river and head up to Lysette, and from there, into Dirnovaria."

The others all sat back, content, and exchanged looks with one another. Hopeful looks. Alariq laid down without another word. As he laid there, trying to fall asleep, he couldn't help thinking that all of them probably thought he was wrong, and that once settled in another dwarfish city, their families might consent to join them. *Fine,* he thought to himself. *Let them learn the hard way. Maybe then they'll realize what a mistake they've made, following me.*

In the morning, they wrapped up the remaining elk meat, which was dry from cooking overnight. Then they ventured back into the mountains and down the road leading south. They crossed over the Austri River, the canal that flowed out of August Sound eastward to the ocean, and finally said goodbye to their mountains a week later. From there, it was much easier passage, across gently rolling hills and large plains. But despite the fairer footing, they were all much less happy. The mountains were their home, the uneven, rocky terrain familiar.

After a few days, they reached the southernmost tip of August Sound, a massive lake, nearly a hundred leagues across at its widest point, situated almost halfway between the two coasts of the Continent. They made camp on the beach, a wide strip of tan sand surrounded on one side by the blue lake and the other by rolling dunes, punctuated by tufts of tall grass. They fished to reprieve themselves of the chewy, nearly-spoiled elk meat.

Blainn took the first watch and the others fell asleep without conversation. Even Ford and Asher were too depressed to engage in their usual brotherly comradery. Alariq lay on his stomach, eyes closed, thinking about how different his life was going to turn out, how boring it would be living out his days in a long-deserted city that would just remind him of the life he would no longer have. He thought about leaving the others in Dendreya and heading out on his own.

Then, as if to remind him of the risks of being alone in this world, they came.

Alariq's eyes snapped open and he noticed a ripple in the lake's surface, although he heard nothing. But his ears were humming and skin tingling. Before he could even sit up, he felt something sharp press against the back of his neck.

2

A Most Unwelcome Overture

Now, in a situation such as this, you or I might be screaming, begging, seeing our lives flash before our eyes, remembering our loved ones, or thinking about all the things we never got to do. But Alariq's keen senses, cool head, and military training prevented him from doing any of these things. Instead, he pretended to sleep. Being as all of the other dwarfs, including Blainn, who was supposed to be keeping watch, were *actually* asleep, they didn't need to call upon any such inner strength to pretend to do so.

The weapon on the nape of Alariq's neck felt jagged. He judged it to be some sort of spear, probably made of bone or rock. Whoever this was had come from the lake, and Alariq knew there must be more of them, as he could see ripples in various places on the lake's black surface, though how many more, he had no idea. He could hear them moving around and they clearly were not as adept on land as they were in the water. They were surrounding the dwarfs.

Alariq took deep, even breaths, the cool night air rushing into his nostrils, still pretending to sleep. Like most military men, especially those in the wild with only six companions, he slept

15

with a weapon, a small, but extremely deadly knife, smooth and sharp at the tip, but serrated at the base.

He waited until the creatures had stopped moving, when he figured they were just about to make their move. In one swift motion, he unsheathed his knife, rolled away from his foe, and was on his feet in less than a single breath.

Some of the others had clearly awoken as the creatures approached them and were waiting for Alariq's instructions, trusting that he was also aware of their condition. At the first sign of aggressive movement from him, they similarly leapt into action.

Ford drew his short sword and put his back to the fire. Brimir kicked out at the closest adversary and pulled two small throwing knives. Gideon, who didn't generally have use for weapons, grabbed the iron spit that lay next to the fire and brandished it like a sword, its tip aglow. He tossed a frying pan to Callum, who was also unarmed. Asher, who slept with his bow inches from his fingertips, dove through the fire to give himself time to nock an arrow. Sparks flew everywhere. The dwarfs, who were used to heat, didn't even flinched as bits of fire and ash hit their skin, but these lake creatures screamed and struggled to brush the hot cinders from their almost-naked bodies.

In the time it took them to recover, the dwarfs realized the fire would be a powerful weapon and they put it between themselves and the creatures. They were surrounded, on three sides by their foe, and on the fourth by the lake. The creatures started advancing on them. There were twelve or so, by Alariq's estimate. Some of them looked similar to men, but Alariq could tell they were something else entirely. Most were far more beautiful. Their skin was perfect, pale and smooth with a sheen to it that made them glow. The females' hair fell to the waists, sleek and silky. The males had shoulder length hair of similar quality. Their bodies were like carved marble. They were scantily clad in outfits made from what looked like green seaweed. But it was their eyes, hands, and feet that really set them apart. Their hands and feet were very slightly webbed, although they appeared less so as the seconds ticked by. There was no white in their eyes. Instead, they were almost totally black, with a ring of silver around the outsides, which shimmered, even in the dark. It was strange, but exotically beautiful at the same time.

The lake creatures were slowly advancing on them, but seemed reluctant to attack. Alariq turned his attention to the largest of them. This creature was as ugly as the others were beautiful. There were only a few others like him in the pack. They were bald, with loose, green-grey skin, hanging in folds all over their bodies. Their hands and feet were fully webbed and their eyes completely black.

Whatever they were, they clearly didn't want to get too close to the fire. They were still slowly advancing, but not directly toward them. The creatures were slowly flanking them. It wasn't until his foot found the wet sand behind him that Alariq realized they were angling them away from the fire, so they could drive the dwarfs into the lake. Into *their* territory.

"The lake," he hissed to the others. "They're trying to drive us into the lake. Stay close to the fire."

They all stopped moving and held their ground near their camp. The creatures gestured to one another, contorting their hands into strange shapes. Alariq didn't like the look in the eyes of the female closest him. She was one of the beautiful ones, with shimmering white hair, the color of pearls. Her unwavering gaze bored into him like a screw into soft wood.

There was a single moment of complete stillness, the dwarfs staring unblinkingly at the creatures, the creatures staring menacingly back. Neither wind nor water made a solitary sound.

And then, all together, the creatures lunged forward.

Those closest to the dwarfs had spears, while a few farther back were armed with harpoons. Those with spears charged, carefully avoiding the fire. The dwarfs formed a tight-knit ring, back to back. To Alariq's right, arrows and metal flashed in his periphery, as Asher fired at those farther away, while his brother protected both of them with his sword. Brimir fought two at once, one with each arm. A small group circled Gideon, who kept them at bay with his white-hot weapon.

Three turned their spears toward Alariq. They weren't very quick, but they had the advantage of numbers and they clearly knew the terrain better. He slashed out with his knife, felt it rip one of the creature's skin, and heard a high-pitched scream. It was the female who'd been eyeing him a moment ago. He'd cut her from shoulder to elbow. He kicked out and connected with another one's leg and heard it break. He reached toward the closest one and wrestled the spear away from him. By the way the creature recoiled and clutched its forearm, Alariq judged he'd done some damage to its wrist too.

The other dwarfs were fairing just as well. These creatures, whatever they were, clearly weren't expecting the dwarfs to be such formidable adversaries. The dwarfs maneuvered them around so that the creatures were between them and the lake, swords and spears clashing, arrows flying. The faces of their foes were flushed with anger and their eyes were narrowed, flashing with hatred and darting from dwarf to dwarf. But the white haired female Alariq had wounded was the most grievously injured, and she only had eyes for him.

The lake creatures studied the dwarfs for a moment more and then, with a signal from a large, muscular male, they backed quickly into the lake, fluidly dove into the water, and were gone. Within seconds, the lake's surface was smooth once more, as if the whole thing had been a dream.

Alariq and the others stood looking at the dark, tranquil water for a few moments. Alariq had just taken a step toward the water to see if the creatures were still there, just under the surface, when they heard frantic grunting and struggling behind them.

Blainn was at his watch post at the edge of the beach, his wrists and ankles bound with seaweed and tied to a tree. Ford and Callum ran over to him, while Alariq and the others continued to patrol the waterline, looking for any disturbance in the lake. There was no sign of the creatures.

"How is he?" Alariq shouted.

Ford cut Blainn free, while Callum examined the knot on his head. "He looks alright," Callum answered. "Just a small lump on the head." He turned his attention back to Blainn, who had just removed the seaweed gag and was spitting on the ground and wiping his tongue with his shirtsleeve. Callum's mouth turned down and his nose wrinkled, but he didn't say anything.

"I'm fine. My own fault. Fell asleep." That last part was barely intelligible. Alariq didn't dwell on it. He hadn't been expecting trouble either, not here.

"I don't know that it would have made much difference." Alariq kept his gaze on the water, searching for any sign that their enemy was returning. "If I hadn't been looking right where one of them had just surfaced, I wouldn't have seen them either. As it was, I barely had a second's warning." Alariq had more concerning things on his mind than Blainn neglecting his duty.

"What were those things?" Callum asked.

"I don't know. But I'm more interested in knowing what they wanted from us." The details of the encounter replayed in Alariq's mind. "They seemed hesitant to lethally attack, and they tied Blainn up, instead of just slitting his throat. They had harpoons. If they'd wanted to, they could have killed us without ever getting close. But they never fired, not even when some of them were in danger. Why?"

Gideon stepped away from the shore and into the firelight, his thin, grey and blonde hair mussed and glasses slightly askew. "They're finfiends. And we should move. They'll probably be back, and in greater numbers."

"How do you figure?" Blainn rubbed the back of his head and flexed his thick fingers to get the blood circulating again.

"And how do you know what they are?" Alariq demanded.

"I'll explain once we get moving. But they weren't here to murder us in our sleep or like you said, they would have just done it. That only leaves one thing they could've wanted."

"Us." Asher ran a hand through his brown, shoulder-length waves. "But why?"

Gideon stopped rolling up his bedding and looked at Alariq for backup.

Alariq considered for a moment before giving the word to start packing.

"I think he's right," he said. "I got the feeling that the white-haired one was after me specifically, the way she kept her eyes locked on me. And the fact that they tied Blainn up..." he didn't need to finish. "Let's move. Get some distance between us and the lake."

Everyone quickly packed. They left the fire burning on the beach, more out of spite than for protection, and headed out in a diagonal, away from the lake but still moving west toward their destination.

Once there was a satisfactory amount of separation between them and the lake, and the terrain turned back to flat grassland, Alariq slowed their pace. "Alright, Gideon. What were those things and why were they after us?"

"I told you, they're finfiends. Lake creatures. They live in August Sound."

"They live in the water?" Callum asked, clearly both intrigued and disturbed.

"No. At least, I don't think so. Nobody knows much about them. I've heard there's an island out in the middle of the lake and that's where they live."

"How do you know all this?" Alariq asked. "I've never heard of finfiends. I didn't even know anything intelligent lived in August Sound." Alariq tried not to sound doubtful, but it was hard. He'd been on campaigns near the lake before. Why had he never seen them before?

Brimir spoke up in Gideon's defense. "I've heard of them too. Not by name, but I remember my mother talking about them after we had returned to Ishtara."

Gideon's voice was stiff, but calm. "I grew up in Dendreya. I was born there. So was Brimir, though his family moved back to Ishtara before mine did. But I remember that no one was allowed to go to the lake alone. When I was old enough to ask why, my father told me it was because the men and women living in villages near Dendreya often went missing and they said it was the work of finfiends, lake creatures who captured young men and women and took them back to their island."

Comprehension dawned inside Alariq. He had forgotten that Brimir and Gideon were born in Dendreya. That's why those two, much more so than the others, had been so excited at the prospect of setting up their new lives in Dendreya. It really was a second home to them. He knew he should apologize for his critical tone, but instead he kept moving and asked, "Are these finfiends going to be a danger to us in Dendreya?"

"I don't think so," Gideon replied. "Dendreya is nestled just inside Loraheem Forest. We never had any attacks there that I can remember."

"Well let's be cautious nonetheless. When we get there, no one goes to the lake. We'll all go as a group and check things out first." Alariq thought about the white-haired finmaid. He definitely believed Gideon was right. That she wanted him alive. For what, he could not imagine.

"They seemed surprised they couldn't easily take us out." Ford's voice broke Alariq's thoughts.

"That's true," Asher responded. "There was this one red-headed female who kept coming back at me, even though I'd hit her with an arrow and Ford kept taking swipes at her. She seemed determined to get to me, despite the fact that we easily drove her back each time. That just made her angrier. Like she was desperate."

"Maybe they've never encountered dwarfs before," Brimir said thoughtfully, scratching his white hair. "We mostly keep to the mountains and them to the lake. It seems unlikely our paths would've had reason to cross."

"Plus, we're smaller than them and humans. If they're able to handle kidnapping men and women just fine, they probably thought capturing us would be easier than falling off a log," Callum said, surprising everyone. Military psychology wasn't exactly his strong suit. Or anything military really.

Callum just shrugged off everyone's amazement and kept walking.

Alariq, still in the lead, moved along slowly. He knew they were all tired. The sun started to rise and the foliage was green and lush. It helped. It made the eeriness of their failed kidnapping on the beach seem less real. But he still couldn't shake the feeling he'd gotten when the white-haired finmaid's eyes had locked onto his.

3

A Different Life

In nature, a tactic known as mimicry is employed by animals, usually to deceive predators or gain acceptance into a stable environment. In more intelligent beings, this takes the form of behavior mirroring. This often creates a perceived sense of belonging, aiding in the bonding and attachment between people. The uglier side of this phenomenon is that it often blurs the lines between individual members in the group, who can start to take on the characteristics of another member, often whoever has the most dominant personality.

Why do I mention it? Well, because it explains why Alariq's sullenness was acting as an emotional contagion, spreading through the group like fire through dry brush and turning them all into sulky curmudgeons, who had only spoken to one another a handful of times since their discussion of finfiends three days previously. In fact, no one had spoken at all since the night before, when they had camped on one of the few pieces of firm ground they could find.

The group of dwarfs plodded along slowly. Their detour to avoid the finfiends took them south, into gently rolling plains, filled with bushes and small trees and mud pits in unexpected places. It wasn't a swamp, exactly, but it wasn't easy going.

Alariq thought of how they might've arrived at Dendreya by now, if not for the white-haired finmaid and her starkly contrasted friends, both unnervingly ugly and disarmingly beautiful. Something else was nagging at him, but he couldn't put his finger on exactly what it was.

Then Ford put his finger on it for him. His outburst was particularly startling because no one had spoken for so long.

"I can't believe they dared to attack us!"

And that was it. A few of the dwarfs responded to Ford, but Alariq wasn't paying attention. He was too consumed with what he now recognized as insult at the audacity of those finfiends. That they had dared to even try and abduct them. Then Brimir's words broke through his mental rant.

"We're not on Ishtar lands anymore, Fordinand. You are accustomed to being an officer in one of the best armies on the Continent. The kind of security we had, we took for granted, I think. That others would just leave us alone because of who we were and who we had behind us. We don't have that anymore. It's a rare thing to have in this world. We're like everyone else now."

Alariq sped up, crashing his way through a bramble bush so that he didn't have to hear Ford's response. Brimir's words had shaken him. He was right, of course. Security was rare in this world and he *had* taken it for granted.

Although the Continent was enormous, populaces were mainly consolidated into eight cities. Dirnovaria was far and away the largest and housed many different races. It sat on the eastern coast of the Continent and was surrounded to the north, south, and west by the Seven Gateway Cities, which formed a large semicircle around Dirnovaria. Each of the Gateway Cities had outer settlements, which supplied food and other resources to their city. People there enjoyed a certain level of protection from their city-state. Then, there were numerous other tiny villages and settlements scattered across the Continent, but life in those places was particularly difficult and unstable. Living in one of these eight cities meant protection and respect, as the city-states tended to look after their own and were generally suspicious of outsiders. Alariq, not only as a citizen of Ishtara, but also a military commander of one of her eight divisions, had enjoyed every privilege afforded by such a life.

Except the benefit of the doubt, he thought grimly to himself.

But all of that was gone now.

They made their way to the top of a large, grassy hill. From there, they could see the lake in the distance, stretching into the horizon in an unbroken sea of bright blue. And a little farther west, they could just make out Loraheem Forest, lush and green. It was time to start heading north again, back toward August Sound.

As they got closer to their destination, Callum asked Gideon questions about Dendreya. What did it look like, were the homes comfortable, was the forest safe, what did he remember about his time there? Callum kept tripping on rocks and tangles of dead grass because he was so focused on Gideon's answers.

"What I remember most was making glass with my father. Sometimes he'd take me to watch them blow the glass. It was amazing."

"Why glass? I mean, that seems like such a leap from the metalsmithing they do in Ishtara." Ford joined the conversation, seemingly almost as interested as Callum.

"I'm not sure." Gideon pushed his way through the tall grasses that now made up their terrain. "Times were tough and everyone was desperate though. After the last war with Karxana, one of the terms of Karxana's surrender was that they would have to do their own mining and leave the knomes to Ishtara. There had been pretty stiff competition for the knomes' labor up until then. Without such competition, I'm ashamed to say that Ishtara, under King Brennus, didn't treat the knomes very well. They refused to work. And we depend on them to do the mining."

The other dwarfs tightened in toward the old scholar, to better hear him, with the exception of Alariq, who simply plowed ahead through the chest-high grass.

"With no ironstone to smith, we had to turn to other crafts. There were some who were quite skilled at woodworking and glassmaking, but we didn't have the necessary supplies near Ishtara to do it on a large scale, because the trees there are thin and tall and mostly softwood. And for glass, you need sand and seaweed. So they set out to the lake. Worked their way around the whole northern half before they found the perfect spot. The beach is huge there, which means plenty of sand, and the wood in the forest is some of the best quality there is. You won't believe the size of the trees there, and all hardwoods too."

Their pace had slowed with everyone listening, enthralled, to Gideon. Alariq was about to say something to hurry them along, when his own words came back to him: *Well it's not as if we have anywhere to be, anyone waiting for us.*

"I always knew about the charter town, but what I could never figure out is why we didn't just do the mining ourselves?" Callum said, more in question. "Dwarfs are natural diggers too."

"True, but we're not as good as the knomes. And the mines were built with knomes in mind. The shafts are uncomfortably small for dwarfs. But mostly, the dwarfs of the time considered it beneath them. Knomes do the mining and dwarfs do the smithing. It was just the way it had always been done."

"So obviously things got worked out though?" prodded Ford. "I've never heard the knomes complain and Dendreya was abandoned."

"Right," Gideon continued. "Brennus realized that we could eke out a frugal life on wood and glass, but that the real money was still in metal, especially weapons. Although, the dwarfs of Dendreya made some amazing longbows."

Gideon paused to take a sip from his water skin before continuing. "Anyway, the king realized the value of the knomes and they signed a treaty. More of a contract, really. The knomes would mine for one season out of the year. They're so adept that three months' worth of ironstone is enough to keep us busy all year. And they got accommodations in Ishtara while there, too. Before, they had to camp in the mountains. There were also provisions about using some of the ironstone to make beams to support the mineshafts, to make for safer working conditions."

Gideon paused, his brow furrowed in concentration, remembering. "See, the knomes don't *need* to mine in Ishtara. Knaba is a gold mine and they make a good living there. But they're small and weak, so what they *do* need is protection and weapons. We could provide that. So, they work for us for one season each year. In exchange, they get to keep any gems or precious metals they find in Ishtara and are considered officially under our protection."

"I never knew all that," said Ford, looking at his feet. When he noticed some of the others looking at him peculiarly, he said, "I don't know, I'm just surprised they never mentioned it. I mean, I thought we got on well, you know?"

"It's not exactly a proud moment in our history." Brimir spoke in his usual, gentle way. It was a tone that always made those with whom he spoke feel like they had been truly listened to and understood. "For those who think we were right to treat the knomes so poorly, like Brennus, the treaty showed weakness. He considered it his biggest failure as King of Ishtara. And for those of us who feel guilty about how we treated them, well, we're embarrassed and ashamed of our behavior after the war with Karxana."

"I should think so," grumbled Ford, kicking his feet slightly as he walked. It was rare of him to speak ill of Ishtara or her king. But Ford was a true defender of the innocent. "I can't imagine going down in the mines without those steel beams. There would probably be a cave-in a week."

"You're probably not far off," said Brimir sadly. "But we had just fought an incredibly bloody war the generation before, and it took us a while to recover. We had been fighting with Karxana for as long as anyone could remember. This is the longest peace with them since the clans split millennia ago. We were finally unencumbered by the constant threat of war. For the first time, we were able to focus on building our city-state, bolstering the quality of life for our citizens. We were finally able to prosper. It went to even the best dwarfs' heads."

After that, they were quiet for a while. They made camp burrowed in a rocky outcropping. It had clearly been used for this purpose before, probably many times, as there was a well-defined fire pit and some rocks had been moved to make the natural shelter more enclosed. But, just as clearly, it hadn't been used in some time.

Before everyone retired, Alariq handed Callum the knife he

usually slept with, instructing him to keep it close. He wondered if there would be any weapons left behind in Dendreya. Their group wasn't exactly well equipped for defending themselves against a formidable foe.

Alariq was on watch duty for the first shift of the night. He held his crossbow lightly in his lap. It had been a gift from his grandfather, who had taught him to hunt with it, but Alariq preferred it so strongly to any other weapon, that he used the bow in his military occupation as well. In fact, it was Alariq who had created a special group of highly-skilled archers in his division. Asher had been one these Deadeyes, as they were nicknamed.

Asher used a standard wooden longbow, but Alariq's crossbow was made of a special Ishta alloy, called starmetal. Starmetal was created by combining ironstone mined in Ishtara with fragments of fallen stars. Smelted together in an open-hearth furnace, wrought by the dwarfs, and cast into forms at exactly the right temperature, starmetal was the single greatest innovation in dwarfish history.

The bow had been in his family for generations, but whoever had crafted it could clearly work magic with metal. It was a work of art. Most dwarfs were good craftsmen in general, but it seemed that metalsmithing was a true calling for some.

Alariq heard a noise with his keen ears, a gift from nature to dwarfs in exchange for living half their lives underground. It was just a frog, however, so he relaxed his grip on his bow.

Unfortunately, Alariq had never been one for the usual crafts. Which is why he had become a career military man, unlike most dwarfs, who served their mandatory twenty-five years and then went back to crafting and creating. Alariq recalled how many had complained when Tanith had moved the term from twenty years to twenty-five. Alariq personally thought it should be fifty. To him, with an average life expectancy of 300 years, twenty-five seemed so trivial. In fact, the kings long ago had lived to be 600, although that hadn't happened in generations.

Alariq had joined the dwarfish army when he was thirty, the youngest age permitted in the service, and had served for exactly ninety years. It was hard to believe it had been that long. Dwarfs were required to serve their minimum service sometime between the ages of thirty and one hundred. Most put it off, but Alariq had not only joined on the day he was eligible, but had never left, even though he'd served far longer than was required. He needed to feel like he was of use, needed to be productive. And he was a good soldier, and an even better commander. He always knew he was more valuable using the weapons than making them. Now that was gone too.

By the time Alariq handed over watch duty to Blainn, he was thoroughly homesick. He had been closest to his grandfather, who had been dead over a century, and his father almost as long. But he thought about the others he'd left behind. *No*, he corrected himself, *those who stayed behind.* He couldn't blame them, really. Haamith, the king's son, had apparently given very convincing testimony. As much as he would like to fault Tanith for blindly believing his son, he couldn't. He would probably believe his son above all others, too. If he had a son to believe.

Alariq tossed and turned for the remainder of the night, with dreams of sons he'd never had and a life that was now gone. He woke up, more tired than when he'd laid down, and more depressed than he'd ever been. He knew he should snap out of it, pull himself up by his bootstraps and kick himself in the breeches. But he couldn't. So he just ate the breakfast Gideon prepared, grunted out one-word responses to the others when necessary and for the most part, stayed away from contact with the others.

"We should be there by the end of today," said Gideon, who alone seemed unaffected by Alariq's mood.

A thought crossed Alariq's mind for the first time. *What if Dendreya was destroyed?* He'd figured on going to Dirnovaria in the beginning anyway and wasn't as bothered by the idea as the others. He'd love to just blend in, disappear. He wanted to fade into the fabric sewn by the hustle and bustle of other faceless people, people who did not know his past and would not be a constant reminder of it. But the others would be crushed if Dendreya wasn't an option. He knew it was because they were all still foolishly nursing the hope of calling their families over.

None of the others were married, which surprised him now that he thought on it. He'd never really considered it before.

Brimir had been married, but she had died several decades ago, and Gideon had always been a bachelor. Callum was too young, having only just turned thirty a few years previously, but Ford and Asher were just the right age. Although they both did look considerably younger than their years. Maybe that was why they were still single. And many male dwarfs did wait until after their term of military service to settle down. Ford, at seventy-five years old, had served his time and said he only stayed in because his brother still had another eight years left to serve. But there was that rumor about Ford and the king's daughter. Alariq had seen the two of them together often and had heard from more than one source a betrothal was in their near future.

And then there was Blainn, about thirty years Alariq's senior, another career military man who was Alariq's Third Authority. He always said he wasn't the marrying type. Whenever dwarfs didn't marry, it always caused a stir. Dwarfs generally wed for practical reasons and failing to do so always set tongues to wagging. Most of the time, the gossips came to the conclusion that unmarried dwarfs were holding out for some nonsense like love, but Alariq had known Blainn long enough to know he was much too utilitarian for frivolous things like love.

Not unlike someone else I know. At these thoughts, Alariq's mood worsened. He just kept walking without thinking of where he was going, just kept moving forward so that he wasn't standing still.

Callum and Gideon sustained a constant stream of exchanges on various topics, mostly centered on Dendreya, Loraheem Forest, woodworking, and glassmaking, but also discussing the knomes and the wars with Karxana, known across the Continent as the Dwarf Wars. Brimir joined in occasionally to fill in areas where Gideon could only provide scholarly testimony, telling of his own experiences in Dendreya or with the knomes.

Asher was tossing rocks over his shoulder and Ford was hitting them with his sword. Blainn was humming a butchered version of a song Alariq's beloved grandmother used to sing. The conversation between the others was punctuated by occasional off-key high notes, the cracking of metal on stone, and sporadic yelps of pain from Asher when Ford would accidentally send the rocks right into the back of his head.

They were a strange bunch. And Alariq felt he was being exceedingly kind to use such terminology, even if only in his head.

It was early afternoon when Gideon began to recognize their surroundings. He began pointing out landmarks and telling stories about playing in the area with other dwarflings and children from the villages whose parents came to trade with the dwarfs.

Around midafternoon, they reached the top of a particularly steep hill. From there, they could see it.

It was a beautiful sight. To the east was August Sound, blue and infinite. The day was bright and the sun shone down on the water and then bounced back on the world, making everything seem twice as bright as it should be. All around the lake was a smooth, white beach, unblemished by rocks or grass. To the west, the beach quickly turned to forest. The tree line was abrupt and consisted of mostly gnarled trees with roots protruding from the weathered terrain. But it quickly transitioned into a dense, hardwood forest that stretched west and north as far as Alariq could see.

Loraheem Forest. It was the greenest green Alariq had ever seen. Even from far away, he could tell the trees were enormous and much healthier than those that surrounded Ishtara. He could smell them from the hilltop. As the breeze swept the countryside from north to south, sweet, earthy air pushed itself into his face. There was no other way to describe it except for crisply clean. Fresh. It was like he was smelling pure nature.

"There." Gideon exhaled the word slowly, a soft smile on his face.

Nestled just inside the trees, but still visible and over a thousand paces from the water's edge, was the city.

Well, it wasn't really a city. Alariq thought it looked more like a town-sized arena. Back in Ishtara, there was a wall-sized mural of Dirnovaria and one of the images was a great stone amphitheater, which looked similar to the sight before him. A coliseum, he thought they called it. But this was much larger.

It was an oval shape with three stories. It looked like an enormous bowl. The bottom level was made from some kind of tan-colored stone, but the upper two levels and huge gates were made of a gray-brown, weathered wood.

"It's hard to see, but there's a courtyard on the ground in the center, open to the sky. It's where all the trading took place. And once a season, they would open the gates, and people from all over would pour in. Sometimes there would even be a fair of sorts, with food and music and dancing." Gideon's eyes were misty.

"I remember my mother talking about that," said Brimir. "She said the music was the best she'd ever heard."

Except for his grandmother, joined very occasionally by his grandfather, Alariq could not recall ever hearing a dwarf sing in Ishtara. He'd never really thought about it. His grandmother was an oddity in many ways and her singing and humming just always seemed like something else that was unique to *her*, not something normal dwarfs would enjoy.

They stood looking at the small city a little longer and then headed down the hill. The trees started to thicken and soon the town was obscured from their view once more.

"There are three stories, counting the ground level. Then there are also some rooms underground. That's where they made the glass," said Gideon, gesturing at the city as he spoke. "There's the forum in the center and shops and woodworking stations all around that. Then, the upper two levels are row homes."

He paused before continuing hesitantly.

"Would it be alright if I had my old home? It's larger and...and nicer than a lot of the others because our family was one of the first to go and last to leave, so I understand if you want it, Alariq..." Gideon's voice trailed away.

Alariq had hardly been paying attention, lost in thought about his grandmother's other peculiar habits, and hadn't realized Gideon was addressing him, asking him permission to have his own home in Dendreya. It took a moment to register in the conscious part of his mind. Is that what they thought of him? That he'd want the nicest house?

"Of course, Gideon. It's yours. I don't care who lives where." He thought about it for a second more. "Although, we should probably stick together the first few nights. And then let's try to settle into adjoining houses. We don't want to spread out in case we're attacked."

The ground leveled quickly and the path turned, dumping them suddenly on the beach. Having no time to prepare himself, Alariq was immediately uncomfortable. But the lake and surrounding beach seemed unoccupied. In fact, the sand looked as if it hadn't been touched since the last rainfall.

Alariq forced himself to relax. He hadn't realized he'd stopped until several of the others passed him and headed off to his left. He turned and followed them. He could make out slivers of the town arena through the thin layer of trees, but it wasn't until they entered the forest that he got his first up-close look.

The trees around him were the largest he'd seen, but they didn't prepare him for the gates. What he'd thought must have been gates made from wood, were actually two solid, vertical slabs of trees, cut from what looked like the same tree, based on the knots and color patterns. They were enormous, almost the height of the entire coliseum. And underneath decades of dirt and wear, they were glossy. They were old and battered, but they had clearly been expertly polished and parts of them still shone. He felt humbled in their presence, knowing that they came from a single tree that would have been literally thousands of times bigger than him.

They all looked up at the gates until their necks hurt. They didn't hear anything, so they tried to push them open. They wouldn't budge, even a hair's width.

"The last dwarfs might've locked them before leaving," said Gideon. He sounded nervous, but determined. "There are several other entrances though. Let's try the side." He made his way right, following the wall until he reached a much smaller door. It was also locked.

They all exchanged looks. It seemed naïve now, to think that a readymade, fortified city, complete with homes and the supplies necessary to engage in a profitable trade, would have remained empty for all these years. But still, they heard nothing from inside and saw no signs of recent comings and goings outside.

Gideon led the way around the back to a set of small, wrought iron gates, probably brought from Ishtara. Also locked.

"Maybe the locals moved in," suggested Callum. "They'd probably be happy to let us join them. I mean, we'd offer a good deal of protection and could certainly help with the woodworking and glassmaking, if they're still doing that."

Callum, the innocent optimist. Alariq could tell how much this meant to him. To all of them. Maybe it was his sudden feelings of affection, brought on by thoughts of his grandparents, but Alariq couldn't bring himself to shatter Callum's hope without cause. He owed it to them to exhaust every possibility.

"There is one more option." Gideon paused to look around, getting his bearings. He mumbled something to himself and then kept walking, looking at the ground. "When the city was first founded, there were some deaths in the glassmaking rooms from fires and suffocation from the thick smoke. So they dug some emergency exit tunnels." He kicked aside some brush.

The others all started looking at the ground too, nudging brush and tall grass aside with their feet. Finally, Alariq's toe connected with something hard and he bit out a swear.

"You found it." Gideon was clearly relieved. He pulled aside a sheet of branches that had fallen right over the entrance. It was a circular stone doorway with a solid metal door that led underground.

Alariq grabbed the handle and pulled, revealing a steep and narrow stone staircase. Gideon led the way down a few steps and then pulled another door open. He entered and the rest followed, listening for sounds of life. They were underground and it was quite dark, but their eyes adjusted quickly enough for them to see where they were going. Gideon led them through two more rooms and then up a flight of stairs.

Alariq knew the place might be in some state of disrepair and expected an overgrown city in need of patching up. He was not prepared for the sight that met him.

The forum was barren and the entire town ransacked. Doors were missing on the ground level, even the frames were in tatters. It looked as if a battle had occurred, but had been kept completely within the confines of the town's walls. Fires had been made carelessly and parts of the buildings and earth were scorched and blackened.

He approached Gideon and spoke in a low voice over his shoulder. "I assume it wasn't left this way?"

"No. I mean, I don't think so. My family wasn't the very last to leave, so I can't be sure, of course, but—" he stopped speaking, unable to form a single word more.

"Alright." Alariq addressed the group now, motioning them close. "We need to figure out if whatever did this is still here or if this is old damage. Let's start at the entrance we came in and work our way around, one level at a time. Weapons ready and everyone stay tight."

Alariq turned left and headed around the ground level of the arena.

Callum smelled them first.

"What is that? Ugh, it smells like something rotting."

It took Alariq and the others a moment to catch the smell. Brimir and Gideon wrinkled their noses and pulled their shirts up to their eyes, looking just as confused as Callum.

But Alariq exchanged looks with Blainn and Ford. This smell was very familiar to them. They had spent five long years smelling it thirty years ago.

He could tell by the looks on their faces that they recognized the scent as well, although they were clearly just as surprised as he was to be smelling it here. Only one thing was certain:

Dendreya was occupied.

4
Twice in Trouble

Ettins.

It was an attacking, rancid smell that one would think only putrefaction could bring. Whether it was their natural scent or a consequence of their eating habits and poor hygiene, Alariq had no idea, but it was a scent like no other.

Alariq immediately transitioned from fellow traveler to commander, his features hardening and military training taking over. He tried the nearest door and the latch yielded. He grabbed the shoulder of the dwarf closest to him, which turned out to be Callum, and pulled him into the nearest shop, gesturing the others to follow.

The shop was in shambles. There were gaping holes in the walls, bones picked clean on the floor, and a heap of dirty blankets, straw, and leaves in the corner. And it reeked of ettin. The sight and stench was so revolting, the seven of them, having all crammed themselves inside, stood staring in disgust, despite the fact that they were in a very dire situation.

Alariq stuffed down his revulsion and addressed the others quietly. "Everybody be quiet."

"Why?" Callum asked, his eyes wide. "What is it?"

"Ettins," Alariq said, checking his crossbow and cache of arrows.

"What would they be doing here?" Asher peered out of the dirty window. "Are you sure?"

Alariq shot him a hard look. "I spent years fighting ettins. I know an ettinden when I see one."

"He's right," Ford said, more gently. "Nothing else smells like this. Or does this kind of damage."

Blainn nodded over Ford's shoulder. They, along with Alariq, were the only three of the group with experience fighting ettins. But the others knew enough from war stories to be frightened.

"We need to get out of here."

Alariq's statement, which he had intended as an order, was met with a hushed mutiny.

"And just leave Dendreya to those beasts?"

"Where will we go?"

"We don't know how many there are. There might only be a few."

The whispered protests bombarded Alariq. This was what happened when soldiers got emotionally involved in something. He should never have agreed to check out Dendreya.

"Enough." He spoke slightly louder than he'd meant to. Everyone quieted and looked around, their eyes and ears (and noses) alert.

Detecting nothing, Alariq continued. "You're right, we don't know how many there are. Which is why we need to leave quickly and quietly. It's probably just a few who got separated or cast out from their company, but we can't take that chance." He held up his hand to stay the continued objections he knew were coming.

"I'm not saying we're leaving for good. But we need to get a handle on the situation. This is their territory now. So we need to fall back, gather more information, and make a plan." He didn't need to tell them that the plan would probably be to forget Dendreya and move on to greener, cleaner-smelling pastures.

The six, placated, gave Alariq their full attention and cooperation.

"We'll leave the way we came. If they were back near where we entered, we could have smelled them before now, so the way out should be clear. We need to be quiet. We don't know how many we're dealing with, so let's just focus on getting out without them knowing we were here."

Alariq paused to make sure everyone was on board. "Gideon, lead the way. Blainn, stay close to him." Alariq wanted a strong fighter who knew how to fend off an ettin up front, and Blainn was deadly even when he didn't have the sword and knives he had on him now. "Brimir and Callum stay in the middle, near me, and keep your heads down. Ford, Asher, stay in back and cover us to the rear." These two always worked best as a team and Ford's strength, swordsmanship, and experience with ettins, combined with Asher's archery skills would give them the best chance if they were discovered and chased down.

They filed slowly out of the room. It seemed like the smell was worse, but Alariq wasn't sure it wasn't just a horrible transfer of scent, now coming from themselves, just from spending two minutes in that filth hole.

Gideon started back toward the entrance to the underground rooms, Blainn seemingly attached to his back. They crept silently, focused on the exit and getting out without detection. They stayed as close to the shop fronts as possible, but the debris made it difficult to stay out of the forum, where they were much more exposed.

"Just a couple more," Gideon said, his voice almost inaudible. He paused in front of an archway and waited for the others to catch up.

They all stood at the door leading to the passage that would take them outside the town walls. Gideon pushed.

Nothing happened.

He pushed again and when it still didn't give, he tried pulling.

Alariq didn't like it. While Gideon, Callum, and Brimir quietly tried to coax the door into opening, Alariq and the others turned and looked out into the forum, their eyes quickly darting from one potential ambush to another.

Alariq's fingers tingled as he gripped his crossbow tighter. He reached back into his quiver and pulled one of his all starmetal arrows, replacing his wood and metal-tipped shafts currently in his crossbow. He'd carried a small cache of the much deadlier bolts ever since the Ettinwar. They penetrated the tough ettin hide better. He hadn't had cause to use them in thirty years.

"I'd take it off the hinges, but they're on the other side," whispered Brimir, whose voice didn't match what Alariq felt was the appropriate level of concern for their situation.

"Stop," he hissed at the three. "We need to move. I don't think that door is locked by accident." He kept his voice low, but firm, trying to stress the urgency of the situation to them.

Brimir, Gideon, Asher, and Callum had never fought ettins before, but Alariq and his two subordinate officers had spent five years doing just that, and Asher had heard the firsthand accounts when he entered the service. And this felt wrong. Ettins' foes often underestimated them, taking their bald heads, huge frames, comically large arm and neck muscles, lumbering gates, and destructive behavior to mean they were also slow and stupid. Alariq himself had made such a mistake once. But he had quickly learned that ettins are in fact quite smart when it comes to ensnaring prey, getting the drop on their enemies, and other military tactics. And although they walked slowly and hunched over, they were capable of striking out extremely quickly. As they usually ran around shirtless and spent most of their time outdoors, they also tended to have extremely thick skin, tanned and leathered from the sun, which gave them yet another advantage. And all of that was in addition to their immense size.

His tone must have communicated something of his thoughts, because Brimir, Gideon, and Callum finally looked appropriately worried. They glanced around in every direction, including above them.

"I can't smell them, can you?" Alariq asked the others and they shook their heads, though Alariq could tell by the lack of sneers on their faces that they couldn't.

His voice was barely a whisper. "This doesn't feel right. We have to find another exit. Gideon?"

"Well, there are the other three entrances we tried when we arrived."

Alariq didn't much like that idea. If the ettins did know they were there, they probably locked the door to drive them toward one of the main exits.

"There's no other option?" he asked Gideon.

Gideon grimaced apologetically. "Not that I know of."

"This place is pretty wrecked," said Ford, looking around. "There might be weak spots in the exterior walls."

"I doubt it," Gideon said. "At least not on the lower level. It's all stone. Only the upper levels are wood." Gideon glanced upward. "But we can try up there. Maybe there's a tree we can access from the upper levels that we can use to scale down the outside."

Alariq exchanged looks with Ford. It was the best choice available to them, and they both knew it.

"Alright. How do we access the upper levels?"

"Follow me." Gideon took off away from the front gates. They reached what used to be a staircase, but it was collapsed half way up. The bright side was that it appeared to have been that way for some time, with vines creeping in and out of every crevice, and was not part of an elaborate plan to herd the dwarfs toward a trap.

Gideon paused for only the slightest of seconds. Then he turned to Alariq. "We have three options. There's another staircase in the same location on the opposite side of the forum, and then another one near the front gate—"

Alariq cut him off. "No, we need to stay on this side of the courtyard and away from the front gate. What's the third option?"

"Some of the shops have ladders that access the homes above. For the dwarfs who lived right above their shops. But it's random, I don't know which ones have second floor access and which don't."

"No choice," Alariq said. "That's our best bet."

He didn't waste any time and opened the closest door to him. This room was in a similar condition to the one they'd just left. Gideon followed him inside and together they looked around. He heard the others opening door after door. They were being louder than they should, but the situation was getting desperate.

They looked for a few seconds and, seeing nothing, turned and tried another door. Nothing there either. It also smelled of ettin, but was in much better shape. Maybe the stink permeated walls.

Brimir ducked his head inside their door. "Got one! Two doors down, let's go."

They followed him inside and found the other four waiting, the ladder to the second level pulled down from the ceiling, waiting for them to climb it.

Alariq went first, quieter now. He didn't want the ettins to know they'd found a way up. The others followed behind him. They barely fit in the tiny room, which was just big enough for a table and a bed for two. The room was perfectly preserved, with decades of dust. It looked untouched, probably since its original inhabitants left it.

He moved to the door and peered carefully out. Once all of the others were up, Callum and Blainn standing on the bed to make room, he opened the door and headed away from the front gates.

They moved quickly, looking around for signs of damage to the walls, weak spots that they could exploit, but the whole second level was in almost perfect condition.

"Wait," Ford held up his hand to stop those behind him and grabbed Alariq's pack to hold him up. "The ettins haven't been up here. They're too heavy."

Alariq realized at once that he was right. The walkway was made of wood and quite sturdy, but probably not strong enough to hold more than one ettin. Plus, the rooms were tiny compared to the shops below and the ceilings were lower. His stomach lurched. There was no way out from the second floor.

"So we can't get out this way. But we still might be better off up here," said Callum. "I mean, if Ford's right, then we're out of their reach up here. Plus, we might get a better look at what they're up to."

Alariq, who'd just been about to propose they head back down, recovered from his surprise and then smiled at Callum. It was his first smile in weeks. Then he took off to a point directly opposite the front gates.

They lined up along the railing at the end of the oval opposite the front gate, looking out at the walls curving away from them, searching for any sign of ettins. Alariq thought he saw movement on the ground to his left, but that side was caved in and it was difficult to see much.

They had only a second's warning. The smell. It reached them before the ettins did, but not soon enough. They looked to their left and right and out into the forum, but the cracking noise came from directly below.

The floor fell out from underneath them. Alariq plummeted into the wreckage below.

There was quiet for the briefest of moments. Then Alariq was pulled cleanly from the rubble like a piece of fruit being plucked from a basket. An ettin held him off the ground by the back of his shirt and coat. He could hear the fabric tearing.

The ettin examined him for a minute and Alariq stared back into its tiny, pale gray eyes. Its taupe, leathery skin was stretched tautly across its face as it contorted its mouth into a sneer, revealing gray-blue teeth the size of Alariq's thumb.

The ettin seemed to be considering what to do with Alariq. After only a second or two, he was clearly done considering, because he pulled back his barrel-sized hand, ready to take a swipe at Alariq.

An arrow hit the twelve-foot beast right in the shoulder. The ettin yelped and dropped Alariq. He fell on something soft and wriggling, and breathing hard.

It was Callum, struggling to free one of his legs from a huge beam that had once supported the floor above. Alariq heard struggling all around him. But he focused on the task in front of him: digging Callum out. Between the two of them they pushed the beam aside and Callum pulled his leg out from under it.

The slender dwarf stood and put weight on his liberated leg. "I'm good," he said.

Alariq turned to look for the ettin that had him by the scruff just a few moments ago. It was hunkered down under the undamaged portion of the second floor, trying to pull several arrows out of its neck, but blood was running down onto its chest, and it was having trouble finding the arrows, now just listlessly swatting at them.

Alariq looked up and saw Asher firing at the other two ettins. He briefly wished he'd had the younger archer under his command during the Ettinwar, before turning his attention to the rest of the scene.

Blainn and Gideon had also managed to stay up on the second floor. Blainn had barely caught hold of a doorknob, the floor missing beneath his feet, and was dangling right over the largest ettin. Gideon disappeared through a doorway.

On ground level, Callum had joined Brimir, who was fighting a small, barely eight-foot ettin with one arm. He wielded the knife Alariq had given him awkwardly, but Brimir, an able fighter, was holding his own.

Then Asher hit the one-armed ettin in the ear, and next turned his attention to the last, and largest, of their opponents, who was currently exchanging blows with Ford. Alariq reached over his shoulder for his crossbow, but it had abandoned him in the fall. So he pulled his sword from its scabbard on his hip and bounded over the debris, landing at Ford's side. An arrow struck the ettin once in the shoulder, but buried only a thumb's length deep. Asher didn't have Alariq's starmetal arrows, so a shot to anywhere other than the eye, ear, or neck was unlikely to do much damage.

Ford managed to get close enough to stab the ettin just above the knee, but the blood merely trickled from the tiny wound. Alariq lunged forward to join the fight.

Alariq and Ford took turns defending, then attacking, but their enemy was simply too fast and too large, easily twice Ford's height. The ettin backed under one of the few areas that remained of the second floor, shielding himself from Asher's arrows.

It swiped at Ford and knocked him to the ground, and Alariq was momentarily alone with their foe. But then Gideon appeared out of the doorway right behind the ettin, wielding a skinning knife in one hand and a cast iron skillet in the other. He hit the ettin square in the small of the back with the pan and then drove his knife deep into the back of its calf. The ettin pitched forward into the open.

Several things happened at once. The ettin crashed through one of the few support beams that still had anything left to support, causing what remained of the second floor walkway to come crashing down. Asher, who had been waiting for a clear shot, let loose an arrow. Blainn reached his limit and lost his grip on the doorknob above. And Alariq leapt through the air, both hands on the hilt of his sword.

The result was a dead ettin, topped by a very upset dwarf, with an arrow in his rump.

Blainn had fallen right on top of the ettin and into the path of Asher's arrow. Alariq missed Blainn's leg by a hair when he delivered the fatal blow to his enemy's chest.

Alariq turned to look for Gideon, but could find no sign of him under the rubble. Callum and Brimir, who had dispatched with the short, one-armed ettin, ran over and gingerly pulled Blainn from the tangle of ettin limbs and debris.

Brimir surveyed the damage to Blainn's rear-end. "It's not bad. It glanced off your scabbard, the arrowhead isn't even fully buried."

Alariq began shifting fallen wood and stone looking for Gideon and Ford, neither of whom had emerged. But over the racket he could hear Blainn cursing up at Asher and Asher barely restraining laughter.

"Ford!" Alariq called out.

"He's here," said Callum, who had stumbled over him. "I think he's okay, he's coming around."

Asher wasn't laughing anymore, but rather trying to find a way down to check on his brother.

"Gideon!" Alariq redoubled his efforts to find him in what was left of the second floor walkway.

"Up here," Gideon replied from above. Alariq looked up to find him hailing from the window of the house above. Like a much younger dwarf, he climbed deftly through the window and swung over to safety. He looked down at them from over the railing. "Everyone else alright?"

"It looks like it," Alariq replied. "We were very lucky there were only three of them."

He surveyed their group. He, Brimir, Asher, and Gideon, were unharmed. Callum, limping slightly, but otherwise fine, had successfully roused Ford and was assessing his senses. Ford seemed to be having a little trouble focusing on Callum's finger as Callum moved it across his field of vision, but when Ford stood, his stance was steady. Blainn was livid, his face red and his teeth clenched. He glared up at Asher, who only had eyes for his injured brother, while Brimir tried to remove the arrow from his hindquarters.

"Stay still, son, or you'll be yanking it out yourself." Brimir grasped the arrow near the protruding head, his brow furrowed. "I'm going to remove it now, so hold on to something."

He jerked out the arrow in one swift, smooth motion. Blainn grunted and his body clenched. He turned to look at the small slit the arrow had left, which was bleeding, but not badly. Then, he glared at Asher once more. Asher, who had assured himself that his brother was alright, fought hard to look contrite.

Alariq found his crossbow where he'd hit the ground and gathered up the arrows that had fallen from his quiver. "Does everyone have all their weapons?"

The others checked their bodies and indicated that they did.

"So what now?" Callum asked, tentatively testing his leg. He winced, but was able to put his full body weight on it.

Alariq didn't answer immediately. The three ettins were dead, the third having bled out from the arrows Asher put in its neck, but Alariq still felt unnerved. He looked around at the courtyard, grassless, with deep gashes in the ground and littered with bones and rubbish. He saw other sections of the second floor were collapsed and doors and shutters missing from ground floor shops. Dendreya looked like a war zone. Like a war zone he'd seen many times before.

Alariq heard the words in his own head just before Ford said them.

"There's no way only three ettins could do this kind of damage."

5

Misplaced and Displaced

"You think there are more?" Callum asked, fear making his voice high and unsteady.

Alariq sought to reassure Callum, who had never been in so much as a fistfight before leaving Ishtara, but who had been twice in mortal peril since. "Not here. They would have ambushed us by now," he said, trying to keep his voice light, but confident.

His reassurance's had the desired effect. Callum's entire body relaxed and he slumped forward in relief. Alariq continued, "But Ford's right. Three ettins alone wouldn't cause the state this place is in."

They all looked around nervously. Alariq could tell the others were thinking about their future in Dendreya. He, on the other hand, was far more concerned with their immediate survival.

"We should get out of here," he said, reaching behind his back and securing his crossbow to a leather belt of sorts that he wore diagonally across his body. His quiver was attached at a point high on the back of his shoulder, while the bow sat lower down, attaching at a point between his shoulder blades. "We need to figure out which way they went so we don't run into them returning to the city."

"I don't think that'll be necessary," said Asher.

"Why not?" Alariq stiffened. He didn't like his orders being questioned.

Asher's face was turned toward the forest. "Because they've already returned."

Alariq quickly climbed a pile of debris. He reached up and locked hands with Gideon, who pulled him through the railing. From the second floor, he could smell it on the wind, the unmistakable stench of ettins.

The smell of ettins, mixed with the scent of sweat and blood around him, pulled Alariq out of the present, backward over thirty years. Alariq had been in other battles before, but the battles of the Ettinwar knew no equal. The utter lack of conscience permitted the ettins to take every attack much farther down a road than anyone else would dare to tread. The atrocities had been too awful to dwell on, but they came back to him now, unbidden.

He shook himself. "We need to go, now! Let's get to the front gate."

The four below turned to run across the forum, but Alariq stopped them with a hiss. "No, up here. We'll never make it that way. We need to stay on the upper levels, out of sight."

Brimir helped Callum up the path Alariq had just taken and Alariq pulled him up. Ford brushed off Brimir's help and scaled a beam instead. Blainn followed up the pile, more slowly, his movements awkward as he futilely tried to minimize the use of his injured rump as he climbed, finally reaching the top with a mighty heave of his arms. Alariq and Gideon had each just grabbed one of Brimir's hands when they heard the yells.

The other ettins had reached the front gate and were shouting to be let inside the city. There was no way of knowing how many enemies there were. But Alariq would have bet all the gold in Knaba that it was more than three.

The dwarfs looked at one another, their eyes wide and their faces pale. Alariq and Gideon pulled Brimir up. They still had to get Asher over to them from the other side of the gaping hole in the walkway. They all considered the situation a moment longer, as the yelling grew louder and more impatient. Asher secured his longbow through a small, but sturdy loop of leather on his quiver, threw his pack across the hole to Ford, and then jumped up, grabbing the narrow overhang that jutted out over the doorways. There was barely enough to grab onto, even using only his fingertips, but he made his way steadily across.

Just as his feet hit solid wood, the ettins' voices changed. They no longer seemed impatient. Now they sounded alarmed.

Then there was quiet. Alariq and the others remained completely motionless, their ears alert. The sound of dozens of heavy, synchronized footfalls slowly increased, like drums in a slow crescendo. The ettins were on the northern side of the city, between the city and the depths of Loraheem Forest.

The dwarfs looked to Alariq for orders, their hands on their weapons.

"They're headed for the side entrance!" He motioned them closer and said in a whisper, "We'll go around to the side, wait for them to get in the forum and then sneak out that way behind them." He looked at Gideon. "You'll lead the way?"

Gideon nodded quickly.

"Then let's go. Quietly." Alariq waited for Gideon to pass him and immediately followed. The others fell in lock step behind them.

As they made their way around the arena, Alariq listened to the sounds of the ettins approaching the city walls. It felt reckless to be headed right toward them, but it was their best bet. The ettins would be drawn to the site of their fallen comrades. Then, hopefully, they'd assume the attackers had already left, or they would fan out in the city looking for them.

The ettins reached the side door, just as the dwarfs reached a gap in the walkway, no doubt also courtesy of the city's current inhabitants. Ettins weren't usually the type to fight amongst themselves, especially because there were strict punishments for doing so. Alariq had witnessed, secretly of course, more than a few executions during the war for such an offense. But then ettins were usually at war with someone, having been hired as mercenaries, or spread far apart from one another in the Wayward Hills outside their native city-state, Ettinridge. Alariq imagined them cooped up in Dendreya. It seemed like a strange decision, one that would lead to a lot of infighting.

But whatever the reasons for their current choice of abode, he couldn't think about that now. Alariq jumped across the gap. It posed no trouble for him, Ford, or Asher. But Gideon and Brimir were older and barely made it across. And Blainn and Callum were both injured. Alariq had to grab Callum's shirtfront to keep him from falling backwards into the first floor below. Blainn barely made it far enough to grab hands with Alariq and Ford, who managed to pull him up just as the ettins started pounding on the door.

The dwarfs hurried along, dodging small holes made by missing floorboards, quicker now that the hammering provided cover for the sounds of their movements.

Gideon, back in the lead, slowed as they neared a staircase. They heard wood crack and the banging ceased. Alariq tried the closest door and, finding it locked, threw his weight against it just as the ettins broke through the door below. The dwarfs filed inside and quietly closed the door behind them. Alariq peered out of a small window, the glass almost completely opaque due to a couple hundred years of dirt.

Seconds later the first ettin appeared in the forum. His chest, back, and crown of his head each bore a black tattoo, a diagonal line, intersected at the top by the outline of a semi-circle and at the bottom by two short lines. Alariq recognized the symbols. This one was the commander.

He was large, twice Alariq's height, but certainly not the largest of the horde. His eyes quickly locked on the wreckage and the dead guards. Those that filed in behind him ran straight for their fellow soldiers. But his eyes scanned the arena. He looked back at the battle zone, took in the collapsed second floor and the open doors. He immediately looked to the second floor.

That's why he's in charge, thought Alariq. *He's shrewd. He knows we were on the upper levels. He's just not sure whether we're still in the city.* The commander grabbed an ettin passing him and muttered something Alariq couldn't hear. The ettin grabbed a few of his subordinates and exchanged quick words. They hurried off across the forum. The commander walked toward the very center of the courtyard and began surveying the entire city.

Alariq turned to the others, all scrunched together in the tiny room. "We cannot use the stairs. He's looking for us. He knows we're on the upper levels. Look for a trap door."

Luck was with them and they found a ladder down to the shop below. Alariq went first. Ensuring that the door and window were both closed and locked, he signaled the others to join him. He peered through a crack in the grime-covered window. Most of the forty-or-so ettins were gathered around the three dead, but a handful of others had taken up positions at the front gate and underground entrance. And the one in charge was still scrutinizing the whole city from the very center of the forum.

Alariq's breathing quickened and he drew his crossbow. "We won't have much time, but we need to go now. Before they start searching the place. Gideon, how far is the entrance?"

"Only two or three steps to the archway, and then another twenty paces or so down the hall to the door."

"Alright." Alariq turned and did the best he could in the close quarters to raise his arm and point at the commander. "See that one there? With the tattoos? He's the leader. And he's smart. He's got lookouts at the other exits and he might've left guards by this door too. So weapons ready. Asher, you and I will go out first and cover everyone else. Gideon, lead the way and Ford, stay close to him. Everyone else fall in. Move as quickly as you can. Keep your heads down and just worry about what's between you and that door." Alariq indicated Asher and himself. "We'll worry about your backs. Ford, once you're outside, just pick a direction and run. We'll follow you. If we get separated, we meet back at the hilltop where we first saw Dendreya. Clear?"

Everyone nodded.

Alariq moved toward the door of the shop and slowly slid the lock. He leaned over and peered out of the window. As soon as the ettin in command turned his back to examine the other side of the arena, Alariq pulled open the door. He and Asher rushed out. Asher stood in front of the exit of the shop and Alariq stood in front of the archway leading to the exit. They both held their bows at the ready and waited for anyone to notice them.

All five of the remaining dwarfs were out of the shop and almost through the archway before shouts rent the air and heads turned this way and that, looking for the location of the intruders. The ettin commander pointed at the dwarfs and signaled attack. Alariq and Asher loosed their arrows and hit the two ettins closest to them. Then Asher disappeared behind Alariq, who managed to load another arrow and fired one final shot before he too, turned and ran through the hall and out of the door. Two ettins lay dead at the doorway, one nearly decapitated and the other hit in the eye with one of Brimir's throwing knives. Alariq grabbed the knife as he leapt over the beast.

Ford and Gideon were helping Blainn. Brimir and Callum had passed them and made it to the trees. Alariq didn't see Asher, but he ran after the others, placing his foot in the stirrup of the crossbow as he took a step to cock it.

Behind him, he heard an ettin crash through what was left of the door. He loaded an arrow, turned, knelt to give himself quick stability, rested an elbow on his knee, and fired. He hit the closest one in the chest. It stumbled and then fell to its knees.

Alariq cocked the bow again, nocked an arrow, and let it fly. He missed the ettin he was aiming for, the one that was almost upon him, but managed to hit one that was just coming out of the door in the leg. The ettin he hit fell and blocked up the entrance, delaying the others for a few precious moments. Alariq wavered only for a second on whether to reload his bow or draw his sword. But before he could decide, an arrow hit the ettin that was only a few steps away from him square in the throat. Alariq pulled his sword and ran toward the woods, barely registering Asher jumping skillfully down from a tree and falling in behind him.

The woods were thick and even just a hundred feet inside them, the light had dimmed considerably. Alariq and Asher quickly caught up to the others. Alariq tossed Brimir his throwing knife. A few ettins who had gotten ahead of the horde received arrows from Asher. They could hear the commander issuing orders behind them, but the dwarfs couldn't make out what the orders were.

They kept running, having no idea where they were going. It was late afternoon, but inside the forest it was almost as dark as night. The trees were enormous and they all looked the same. Even Gideon was turned around.

Alariq could hear the ettins gaining on them, the sounds of branches breaking and footsteps falling growing closer behind them. Then they could hear the enemy encircling them. They drew their weapons, knowing there was little use.

Then, as if the very air around them spoke, they heard a whisper, "Quickly, in here!"

They all desperately looked around, but it was Asher who saw it first: a small opening in the roots of a huge tree, from which a head protruded. As soon as Asher pointed to the hooded figure, it was gone.

6

Hiding and Finding

Now, you may think it imprudent to dive into a small, dark, unknown place, after an unknown hooded figure, and you would be quite right to think so. But faced with the choice of a *possibility* of death in a tree trunk and a virtual *certainty* of death where they were currently standing, the dwarfs chose the former and scrambled quickly, one after the other, into the hole at the base of the tree. Once they were all inside, the hooded figure appeared behind them, blocking their exit. There was a sudden movement and they were plunged into complete darkness. The hooded figure, which Alariq judged to be a human by its shape and proportions, had obscured the entrance with a curtain of leaves and sod behind them.

Their hideaway was clearly created for precisely such a purpose. A circular hole, almost the width of the large tree above was dug out from underneath it. Roots branched outward in every direction overhead, but the dirt floor and walls were smooth and stray roots had been trimmed away and cleared out.

No sooner had Alariq taken in his surroundings, when he heard the footsteps that belonged to a small army, coming from all directions. Small clumps of earth rained down on their heads from the vibrations.

But the only thing their would-be captors found, was the other group of their company, who had circled around to close in on the dwarfs from the other side.

"Where are they?" shouted one of the ettins.

"They're gone!" yelled another.

"They can't be, look in the trees." Alariq recognized the commander's voice, clipped and in control.

At this directive, the dwarfs tried to ready their weapons, but as the space was barely large enough for eight, they could do nothing more than elbow one another as they tried to move their arms.

"Quiet!" hissed their rescuer, though at the time, Alariq was not altogether certain they had been rescued.

But, to their great relief, the ettin had meant to look *up* into the branches of the trees. They heard footsteps move from tree to tree, punctuated by branches being shaken or broken, and calls of "all clear" and "nothing here." The dwarfs stayed like that for a while, cramped, hunched, and smushed together, barely daring to breathe, much less talk.

After ascertaining that the dwarfs had not escaped into the limbs of the trees, the ettins began yelling at one another, one group accusing the other of letting the dwarfs slip past them.

As, of course, this wasn't true at all, the other group leveled the same charge against the first group, and a good amount of arguing ensued. Finally, at the order of their commander, they fanned out to search the immediate area.

The dwarfs and their rescuer stayed that way for what seemed like hours. The hooded figure peered out of the earthen curtain for a few minutes and finally motioned the dwarfs to follow before it exited through the concealed gap in the twisted roots.

"Follow me quickly and quietly," came a whisper from beneath the hood. "Be cautious, there will still be patrols."

They followed the hooded figure as it deftly ducked from tree to tree for what had to be at least an hour. It was dusk, and the light was almost gone. Alariq hadn't believed it to be possible for the forest to grow any thicker or darker, but the trees were woven so closely together that Alariq couldn't take a single step without his foot catching against a root or his shoulder brushing against a massive tree trunk.

He doubted there would have been any light by which to see, even in daytime. The blackness was suffocating.

Alariq stayed just behind the hooded figure, but it was more sound than sight that allowed him to follow. All dwarfs had sharpened senses, including eyes that adjusted quickly to light and dark conditions. They also had unparalleled senses of direction. Without these skills, Alariq was certain they would have been lost in the forest forever.

Finally, the hooded figure slowed and allowed the dwarfs to catch up. The full moon shined down on a small, almost perfectly round clearing, at the center of which stood the most bizarre sight the dwarfs had ever witnessed.

The clearing was guarded on all sides by tall trees, the tallest they had ever seen, taller even than the watch tower in Ishtara. The trunks were smooth from the ground to a point far beyond the reach of even ten ettins, standing on one another's shoulders. Near the top, branches finally jutted out and weaved together with those of neighboring trees to create the forest canopy. This natural ceiling did not extend over the clearing however, allowing moonlight to illuminate what Alariq soon came to realize was their intended destination.

A massive tree. Not as tall as those around it, but still larger than anything he had seen outside Loraheem. It was as wide as a small cottage, with colossal branches as thick as a normal-sized tree, protruding from all sides of the enormous trunk. Alariq could not tell by the moonlight exactly how high it went, but what he could tell was that it served as a residence. The residence of the hooded figure, apparently.

The trunk had a door at the base, and there were various rooms higher up, built on top of the massive branches and adjoined to the thick trunk. A staircase wound its way around the outside of the tree, connecting the levels to one another. In the moonlight, it looked ethereal, as though they had walked into a dream.

The hooded figure crept forward and opened the door, gesturing the seven dwarfs inside. They followed tentatively, all glancing around, ready for an ambush. But once inside, Alariq no longer feared whatever it was that had brought them there. The other dwarfs visibly relaxed too. Alariq could think of no other word to describe the interior of the tree, except...warm. Not in temperature, but in character. He knew that nothing evil would live like this. The cottage was well-ordered and clean, remarkable given that it was the inside of a giant tree. There was a rectangular, wooden table with a bench on each side and a chair at each end. On the other side of a large support beam, which separated the room, was a small sitting area and a few books on shelves carved into the inside of the tree. Pale green curtains hung over the window by the sitting area.

Alariq turned around as the others struggled to make room for one another. To the right of the door was a kitchen, complete with shelves holding neatly-ordered dishes and utensils, a water pump under another window, with a stone basin and counter beside it, and a large cast-iron stove with two doors, one on top of the other.

The stove stood out to Alariq, its metal contrasting harshly with the wood and cloth textures in the room. Alariq had seen many stoves like this in Ishtara, where metal was common, but he never expected to see one so far outside civilization. The bottom compartment was where the fire was made, using wood. This served both a heating and cooking function, as the top compartment was where food was usually placed to be smoked, baked, or roasted. Getting it all the way out here would have been no easy feat.

Alariq had never entered a place that felt so welcoming, an extremely ironic fact considering the circumstances. He had felt instantly at ease upon entering, but he forced himself into alertness once more.

A suspicion crept into the corner of his mind, one that was confirmed when he turned around just as the hooded figure closed the door behind the last dwarfs to enter, Ford and Asher. Seeing their rescuer close up made it clear that it was in fact a human, as he had previously judged, but as it stood an inch or two shorter than Ford, there was no way the person was a man, as he had previously assumed.

Asher, who stood closest to the person, was staring at the figure in the darkness with a look of complete incredulity on his face, staring at the *woman* who had just saved them.

She lit a large oil lamp and turned out the wick, so that the glass-enclosed fire illuminated most of the room. The rest of the dwarfs ceased looking around at their surroundings and looked at the source of the light. She removed her hood and a long braid of golden, wheat-colored hair fell out and over her shoulder. The rest of the dwarfs made audible noises of shock.

The woman, who was taller than all of them except for Ford, stared intently back at the dwarfs. The light from the lamp cast a warm, orange glow onto her alabaster skin. She wore long, beige doeskin pants, a well-worn white shirt, and a long dark traveling cloak, which fell to her calves.

Without a word she turned and made for the door.

"Wait," Alariq spoke, and it came out more of a command than he meant it to.

Asher made to block her path to the door. She moved more quickly than any of them could have guessed possible, and before a single one of them had time to draw a weapon, she had Asher on the floor with an intricate, curved knife at his neck. He stared back up at her with a mixture of fear and...something else. Reluctant admiration, perhaps. Alariq glanced around at the other dwarfs and knew they understood that they were to follow his lead.

"I did not mean to stop you from leaving. I only wondered where you were going," Alariq said in his calmest and most innocuous voice. The other dwarfs removed their hands from their weapons and assumed more relaxed poses.

The small, slender woman considered him for a moment and then withdrew her knife and returned it to its equally intricate scabbard on her hip.

"I need to cover our tracks. The ettins will send out trackers at first light and I need to make sure they cannot follow you back here," she said.

Her voice was soft, but a little deeper than he'd expected, given her tiny stature. Even more surprising was the authority and confidence with which she spoke.

"We can help you with..." Alariq began, but she interrupted him.

"No. I'll be faster on my own. You can sleep down here tonight. There should be room enough for all of you." And with that, she opened the door and disappeared into the night, her cloak flowing out behind her.

They all stared at the closed door for a moment. Asher, still on the floor, made a low whistling sound of relief and amusement.

Blainn spoke first: "We can't let her go alone. How do we know she hasn't gone to get the ettins? One of us should follow her."

Gideon peered out the kitchen window and said, "I think that ship has sailed. She's gone and I don't think a single one of us could follow her in this blackness."

"So what are we supposed to do?" Blainn answered back, "Wait for her to offer us up in a golden chalice?" His small, almost black eyes, flashed, and his wide, muscular chest rippled.

"Enough." Alariq spoke quietly, but silence fell immediately. "This is clearly her home. I cannot believe she would want ettins to discover it, regardless of any price they might offer for our heads. She saved us from them. We shall be cautious, Blainn, but I do not believe we are in immediate danger. Get some sleep."

And with that, all of the dwarfs laid down, except for Asher, who had never gotten up.

Alariq stayed awake until he heard the sound of creaking steps. He intended to keep guard all night, despite his reassurances to the others. But the atmosphere was simply too comfortable, and he drifted off to a peaceful sleep.

Alariq awoke the next day after the sunrise, a rare occurrence for him. He felt well-rested, his muscles loose and relaxed. Before he had even opened his eyes, he could hear whispered bickering amongst the others. He cracked open his lids and saw his six companions gathered around the stove.

Brimir: "Why would she cook it if she didn't mean for us to eat it?"

Callum: "She could be making it for herself."

Asher: "Did you see her? She's tiny! She couldn't eat an entire deer."

Gideon: "Maybe she's making stew."

Blainn: "It doesn't matter, we're not eating it anyway. She might've poisoned it." He was standing with his weight on one leg.

Callum: "I really don't think that's likely."

Ford: "Yeah, if she wanted to kill us, she could've in our sleep."

Asher: "Or not rescued us in the first place."

Brimir: "Well I think she means for us to eat it. And I'm starving."

Callum: "It's rude. She hasn't offered it to us yet."

Ford: "Rude? You're kidding? You're seriously worried about *manners* right now, Callum?"

Blainn: "*I* think it's rude to cook an entire deer right in front of a bunch of hungry refugees and not offer them any."

Asher: "I thought you said it was poisoned and you weren't eating it."

Blainn: "She still could've *offered* us the poisoned meat."

Gideon: "I thought we decided it's *not* poisoned? Do you think it really could be?"

Asher: "No, that's not the point. If Blainn *thinks* it's poisoned, it shouldn't matter either way whether she offered us any, since he's not going to eat it anyway."

Brimir: "So are we eating it or not?"

Callum: "Not until she comes back and offers it to us. My mother always said that a good hostess makes it very clear what is expected of her guests."

Ford: "Okay, first of all, we're not guests. We're exiles. And second of all, we slept on the floor. I really don't think this was the hosting your mother had in mind. And third, your mother..."

But Alariq didn't wait to hear what Callum's mother could do and instead rose from his sleeping pallet and headed for the door.

Once outside, he took a deep breath of the same clean, fresh air he'd first smelled up on the hilltop. It was the forest, the trees, the sheer volume of greenery, that made the air so pure. It was a warm day already, but the unsoiled air felt cool as he breathed it in.

He turned to look at their temporary abode for the first time in daylight. Alariq wanted to think it comical, the way the rooms were so randomly bulging from the knotty and crooked tree, like mammoth mushrooms, but it was simply too beautiful a sight to give it such a label.

He remembered thinking last night it looked otherworldly, but seeing it in the warm sunshine, he decided "whimsical" was a better descriptor. The upper levels were all built on platforms, supported by the huge branches. The second floor was left open on all sides other than where it was connected to the tree. It was clearly an outdoor dining area, as the only thing it contained was a long wooden table and two matching benches. Further up, and on the other side, was the largest of the exterior rooms, which even had two glass windows, which were boarded up from the inside. Glass was a rarity in Ishtara, but he supposed it was more common here.

From there, the stairs continued to wind their way up and around the tree to a smaller room, which was carved almost completely into the tree. It also had a small glass window. The encircling staircase then led up to the final story, a petite room built completely out on a branch with large windows on three sides.

He heard a rustling in the trees behind him, at the edge of the clearing. Not sensing any danger, he simply looked over. The golden-haired woman was climbing down from one of the neighboring trees. She dropped almost silently to the ground and turned to look at Alariq. He had the feeling she had been watching, waiting for one of them to come outside.

Today, she wore dark brown doeskin pants, which cut off just below the knee, a less-worn white shirt, loosely laced up, and brown leather boots. Thin leather straps crossed over both of her shoulders and across her body, which held a small quiver of arrows and an unstrung bow. The quiver and bow, darting out on either side of her shoulders, looked like wings.

She studied him for a moment and then said, "These trees around this clearing are some of the tallest in the forest. I can see

Dendreya from here. Most of the ettins are holed up inside, but they've sent out scouts. They've never ventured this deep into the forest before though," she added as he looked around, alarmed. "I doubt they'll risk it either. They barely fit between the trees and it's too easy to get lost. They're mostly searching the beach and the hills to the south."

Alariq supposed it was a good thing they hadn't gotten separated, or the hills to the south was exactly where they'd be right now. He knew he should say something to the woman to whom he now owed his life, as well as for the six other lives for which he was also responsible. But what was there to say?

She continued to assess him. Finally, "Did you think it was empty?"

Alariq was thrown off by her question. He'd expected something along the lines of *who are you* or *what are you doing here.* "We didn't know. We came to find out."

"Why?" Such a simple question. But one that required much more explaining than Alariq was willing to do.

But he was saved from answering by the others' exit from the cottage, still bickering.

"Alright, damnit, I'll find her and ask." Even gentle old Brimir, who hardly ever swore, was disgruntled. "Oh." He stopped short and was immediately rear-ended by Callum, who had been looking over his shoulder, speaking to someone behind him.

"Sorry, Brimir, I—" started Callum, but he stopped when he saw Alariq and the woman around whom their argument had just revolved.

"I'm sorry, we didn't realize you were out here," said Brimir, his cheeks pink. He was clearly concerned she had heard their conversation about the deer, complete with the accusations of a planned poisoning on her part.

Alariq came to his rescue. "She just climbed down from one of the trees. She says the ettins sent out scouts, but not this way."

At the sound of conversation, the other dwarfs came to the door, all trying to exit at once, in an effort to get a proper look at the woman who'd saved them.

Brimir nodded. The eight of them, the other dwarfs having

untangled themselves from one another, just stood in the clearing, occasionally glancing around, alternatively at each other, their surroundings, and their feet.

Alariq kept his eyes on their hostess. At the emergence of the others, she looked less like a cornered animal, ready to strike. Alariq thought this ironic, considering there was now more of them and still only one of her. But instead, she just looked amused, a tiny smile tugging at the corners of her mouth.

Finally, she spoke. "There's deer in the oven. It should be ready. Help yourselves. Plates are on the shelf beside the wash basin."

Without a word, Blainn turned around and walked, limping slightly, inside. No sound issued for a moment. Alariq could imagine him standing in front of the stove, hunger battling paranoia. Alariq couldn't hold back a small smile as he heard the clinking of plates.

"I guess he decided it wasn't poisoned after all," said the woman, smiling as well.

The dwarfs all blushed and squirmed uncomfortably, except for Asher, who chuckled. "Or decided he doesn't care."

Brimir made an attempt at an apology. "We didn't realize you were listening, we didn't mean to imply—", but she casually waved off his apology.

"It's fine."

Callum and Gideon decided to join Blainn. Ford and Asher ventured further into the courtyard to join Alariq and Brimir. She glanced at them, but continued to study the old dwarf. Alariq didn't like the way she was inspecting him, sizing him up.

His suspicions were confirmed when she addressed her next question directly to Brimir. "What did you want in Dendreya?"

Alariq's jaw clenched. She was smart. She had already detected Alariq's hesitation to tell the truth and thought Brimir was her best chance at getting it instead. *And she's not wrong,* Alariq thought warily.

Brimir glanced at Alariq, who looked steadily back. The woman watched them both with quick, piercing eyes, narrowed in attention.

Too late, Brimir said, "We wanted to see if it was occupied." It was clearly the safest thing he could say without communicating with Alariq.

"So I've been told. Why?" She had chosen wisely. Brimir squirmed under her unyielding gaze. Alariq knew Brimir better than anyone still living. He was the most honorable dwarf Alariq knew, except perhaps Ford. He had been a very close friend of Alariq's grandfather and had taken Alariq as a surrogate grandson when he'd died, and then a surrogate son when Alariq's father had died soon after. Of course kind, honest Brimir would feel guilty lying to the person who had just saved their lives. Alariq, who was far more concerned with their safety than with the purity of his soul, was not afflicted with such a softness, and as such, had no problem answering accordingly.

He interjected. "We were sent by our king to determine if Dendreya is still a viable center of commerce."

Her eyes met his. They were almost the same color as her hair, but a tad darker, with a slight orange hue, the color of amber. He'd never seen eyes that color before. He'd only seen his own a few times. Mirrors weren't common in Ishtara as dwarfs had little time for vanity. His light honey brown eyes were also an uncommon color, but nothing like hers. Hers seemed almost on fire, like twinkling embers.

He had the feeling she didn't believe him. But she let it go. "Well I guess you have your answer."

Alariq nodded. They needed to discuss things, alone. He, Brimir, and Ford made to go inside.

But Asher didn't move. "Not really," he said, his tone serious. "Where did the ettins come from? When did they take over the city?"

What is he doing? Alariq thought desperately.

She locked eyes with the young dwarf. They were almost exactly the same height. She considered him for a moment before she answered.

"Let's go inside. We can eat while I tell you what I know."

7

A New Plan

It was a strange sight, you can be sure. Seven burly dwarfs crammed awkwardly on one side of the table and one short and slender woman sitting alone on the other, clearly amused at her guests' discomposure. None of the dwarfs had felt comfortable enough to go and sit next to her, so they had done their best to pack themselves together. After quite a few elbows connecting with various body parts, they finally gave up. Asher and Callum joined her on the other side and Alariq stood at the head of the table.

The mistress of the house seemed perfectly content to eat her plate of venison and wait for him to speak first. It was a power play. Alariq recognized it because he'd used the tactic himself. When one of the men in his division came to him and he suspected he was dissatisfied with something, Alariq would simply wait for the other dwarf to speak first. No *how can I help you* or even *what do you want*. It reminded his subordinates that *they* were the ones asking *him* for something. It reinforced their proper place. As Alariq was already very aware that this was not his house and that it was *he* who was asking *her* for help, he found her refusal to speak to be a bit below the belt. But then again, maybe that's how his subordinates felt. Maybe he'd ask Ford sometime.

He waited until she'd finished her meal. She looked up at him and smiled ever so slightly. Alariq's jaw involuntarily clenched and a muscle in his cheek ticked. Of all those around the table, he alone was standing, and at the head of the table no less; but it was abundantly clear who was in control of the situation. He wondered briefly why this tiny female didn't feel more ill at ease with seven male dwarfs in her home, crowding around her.

There was no getting around it. Alariq took a deep breath. "What can you tell us about the ettins and Dendreya?"

Those that were still eating stopped and put down their utensils. They had looked up at Alariq the second he spoke, but now their attention was on the woman.

She continued to look back at him for a moment. Then, without a word, she stood up and carried her plate over to the stone basin and set it on the counter next to it. Callum rose and did the same and then proceeded to collect the plates of everyone else who was finished. The amber-eyed woman walked over to an ornately carved chest, which sat next to a plush, comfortable looking arm chair. She pulled out a variety of books, looked through several, and then, finding the one she wanted, returned to the table with it.

Upon closer examination, it wasn't a real book, but rather a homemade journal. Alariq suspected she had made it herself. It was made from a supple, worn hide of some kind, stretched across something rigid. It was basic, but well made. There weren't many books in Ishtara. Alariq had only seen a handful in his lifetime. The manuscripts in Ishtara were mostly scrolls and loose papers. Both Gideon and Callum made excited noises at the sight of the book.

Gideon couldn't hold in his curiosity. "Did you make that yourself?"

The woman appeared surprised at the question. She clearly thought dwarfs were illiterate. Alariq was offended for the briefest of seconds before he realized she was right. Most dwarfs couldn't read and had no interest in literature. Only high-ranking soldiers learned to read in order to communicate with other division authorities. And oddballs like Gideon and Callum, who spent hours poring over what little script Ishtara had to offer, even before either of them were employed in the scrollroom.

"Yes. It's a hobby of mine."

"What did you use for the binding?" Gideon asked, craning his neck, his fingers twitching, clearly desperate to get the treasure (well, for what passed as treasure in Gideon's mind) in his grasp.

"The board is made from a thin slice of wood and then it's wrapped in sheepskin leather." She was looking at Gideon strangely, her eyes narrowed, but a smile on her face.

"And the writing? Is it on parchment?"

"No, actually. Though I do have some parchment scrolls here. But I purchased those. No, my books are written on paper. It's made from tree bark and hemp."

"Ooh, I've heard of that."

Wonderful, Alariq thought, rolling his eyes. Now Callum was involved. His cousin, face alive with interest, turned to Gideon. "It's that stuff the trader was talking about last time. The stuff that's soaked and then pounded into sheets. He said it was half as expensive as parchment. I didn't think he actually knew what—"

Alariq cut him off, his patience gone. "As thrilling as it is, could we table the bookbinding discussion and get back to the ettins?"

Gideon and Callum shrank sheepishly, but both kept their eyes on the book, which its owner flipped through casually. Finally, she stopped, read for a moment, and then consulted a scroll in a wooden case, secured to a support beam.

"They came thirty-one years ago. There were about seventy of them then." She sat back down.

The dwarfs looked at one another sharply.

Brimir made the observation first. "Thirty years? That would have been right around the end of the Ettinwar."

"They must have come here after they lost," Asher said.

"But there can't have been seventy of them." Ford looked perplexed, his brow furrowed. "I mean, the final battle was bloody. Almost all of Division One died; only our king and a few others came back. If there were seventy ettins left, why didn't they just finish the last few dwarfs off?"

"Are you certain about that figure?" Brimir asked the woman.

65

"Yes, give or take ten." She appeared disinterested in the dwarfs' conversation, but Alariq could tell she was taking in every word.

"There were only forty or so yesterday." Alariq could tell Asher's comment was not meant as a challenge to her statement, but more of a question.

The woman opened her mouth to respond, but Alariq cut her off. "That wouldn't be unheard of. Ettins only live for fifty or sixty years, so I'm certain some died from old age. Ettins reach maturity swiftly, at about eight to ten years. Then they remain almost unchanged for the majority of their life. But then once they start to age, they age swiftly. And cooped up like that? I'm sure they've killed a few of themselves off. We saw evidence of fighting in the city. And besides, even if she's wrong and there were only the forty we saw yesterday, Ford's question still needs answering. Why did the ettins come here instead of killing Tanith and what little was left of the king's division?"

"Perhaps these aren't the same ettins." Gideon's brow was wrinkled with confusion, already thinking his statement through to its logical conclusion, which Ford spoke for him.

"That's an awful unlikely coincidence in timing then."

"We don't know what went on in Ettinridge. Maybe this group was exiled for some reason related to the war. Maybe they refused to fight or mutinied or something." Callum's voice was strong and he spoke directly to Ford. Alariq was surprised at his cousin's uncharacteristic courage. Then he remembered how badly Callum wanted to stay in Dendreya and his pride turned to irritation.

"So you do not know why they came to Loraheem?" Brimir asked the woman.

"No, I'm sorry," she said, and she looked it, although Alariq could tell she was quite adept at schooling her features.

"I do not like it." Ford squared his shoulders. "Why here? Why an Ishtar city?"

"Again, it could simply be that an abandoned city was available and they took advantage," Callum argued.

"It was not abandoned."

Everyone looked to their hostess.

Alariq's eyes narrowed. "What do you mean?"

"Some villagers from one of the Sudri River settlements had moved in. The ettins killed them." It was said matter-of-factly, but Alariq wasn't fooled by her casual tone.

The dwarfs didn't know what to say to that. They sat in awkward silence.

Alariq knew his next words would cause a small mutiny against him. "It does not matter. Dendreya is not a viable option. We must go to Dirnovaria."

Out of the corner of his eye, he saw their hostess move ever so slightly. He realized he had just exposed his previous lie about their purpose for coming to Dendreya, but it didn't matter at this point. They'd be leaving this place anyway.

To their credit, none of them said anything outwardly against him, but their eyes flashed defiant. The woman got up and walked over to the wash basin and began pumping water into it.

Alariq placed his hands on the table and leaned toward them. Mimicking his stature, they all leaned in as well, tightening their circle. He spoke in a low, but firm voice, "Look, I know this is not what you wanted. But the choice is no longer ours to make. Dirnovaria is our only option."

"So we are just supposed to leave dwarfish lands to ettins?"

Of the dwarfs in his company, it was the one Alariq least expected to challenge him who did so. Alariq stared directly into Brimir's eyes without blinking.

He spoke the words he knew none of them wanted to hear. He felt as though those were the only kind of words he spoke lately. "It is not our concern anymore. We no longer belong to the city of Ishtara and as such Dendreya is not ours to defend."

No one spoke. Some looked down at the table, while others stared back at him, waiting for him to change his mind, willing him to change his mind. He could feel their resentment, their accusation. Alariq could not stand the weight pressing in on him, suffocating him with guilt and regret. He turned and walked out the door.

He sat for a long while at the edge of the forest, his back to the treehouse and the others. He stared into the dense trees. He could only see a few paces past the tree line, before the darkness of the forest engulfed everything. But instead of being afraid of the unknown in the dark, Alariq felt secure.

There was something inexplicably comforting and neutralizing about the forest. He looked up at the unblemished, blue sky above the clearing. He hated how much he already liked it here. It felt like everything would be easier here, like getting out of bed would never be a struggle or that chopping wood would be as pleasant as a walk. The only thing he thought would be difficult in this place was leaving it.

Alariq shoved the thoughts from his mind. They *were* leaving it. That's all there was to it, and there was certainly no sense in getting attached to this place.

He heard footsteps behind him and knew it was Brimir before he sat down beside him.

"You were not there when Haamith gave his testimony against you."

Alariq didn't turn, but raised his head slightly to let Brimir know he was listening. The old dwarf continued, his voice heavy.

"The king was leaving the counselroom after a meeting with the Idra. Haamith spoke from the High Bridge down to him. He announced your betrayal to all of Ishtara. Anyone who wasn't down in the furnace rooms or the mines would have heard it.

"He said he had been visiting the tenant farmers in the outer settlements and had seen you meet with Karxani scouts. That you had talked with them for a long time and then they gave you a package and left."

Brimir ran his hand through his white, glossy hair. "Before Tanith could even respond to his son, Callum had already come out of the scrollroom and was denying it. He stood within paces of the king and called his son a liar. If your division had not returned at that moment, who knows what punishment the king would have handed out to Callum. He probably would have ordered him to be executed on the spot."

Alariq looked down at the almost too-green grass, unable to form thoughts, only able to picture the scene in his mind.

"The rest you know and I do not need to remind you of the events. But apparently I do need to remind you of what this means for you and for the dwarfs in that house behind us."

Brimir paused, choosing his words with the utmost care.

"They stood by you, when no one, no one out of thousands in the city, and a hundred of your own soldiers, would defend you. When no one even of your own blood, save for Callum, would support you. And their defense of your honor has cost them their home, their lives, their safety, and their families.

"Fordinand and Blainn were on watch with you when Haamith said you were meeting with the scouts, and therefore knew of your innocence in their heads. But the rest of us felt your innocence in our hearts."

Brimir paused and Alariq could feel his eyes boring into him. When he spoke again, his voice was low and filled with emotion.

"Dendreya is all they have left, the only link to their past. Is the faith they had in you not deserving of more than a casual dismissal of the one shred of their old lives that they have left? Is it really so easy for you to crush the one hope of your most loyal defenders? This is all they have now."

Brimir rose slowly and stood beside Alariq for a moment.

"They owed you no duty when they stood with you, but they did it anyway. What duty does your conscience tell you is now owed to them?"

He turned and left without another word.

Alariq continued to sit, hunched, head down. He thought he was doing the others a kindness, pulling out the arrow in one swift motion. He thought he was forcing them to confront their situation and in doing so, saving them from dashed hopes in the future. He didn't understand this desire of theirs. He wanted to get as far away from the life he used to live as he could, wanted to lock all reminders of Ishtara in a box wrapped in chains and throw it into the depths of August Sound. Why did they cling so desperately to their old life when it was gone?

But Brimir was right. It was because of him these dwarfs were crammed in a tiny room around a tiny table with finfiends and ettins behind them and a great expanse of nothing in front.

He did owe them something.

What were they asking for? A home. A home that felt familiar, if only vaguely. He could not say their desire was unreasonable. Alariq resisted because he wanted the opposite.

He didn't want a home. He wanted a place to live. There was a difference.

But they had stood by him, regardless of the cost. It was his turn.

He stood, his decision made. A light breeze danced through the clearing. It brought with it more of that glorious forest smell, and whisked away the rest of Alariq's doubts.

When he reentered the house, he expected them to be talking in hushed tones about what could be done to retake Dendreya or to convince him they should try. But no one had moved. The scene looked exactly as he had left it. The depression and sense of loss was almost tangible, as though a heavy brown tapestry hung over everyone in the room.

Except over their hostess, who had curled up like a small animal in the arm chair by the window on the other side of the room. She had the nerve to be quietly reading, as though her home were not currently occupied by a small contingency of dwarfs. As though there was not an intense internal storm raging inside each of her guests.

Alariq had planned to resume his private discussion at the table away from her shrewd gaze, but the sight of her reading without a care in the world made him change his mind. Alariq spoke more loudly than was necessary, partly to command the attention of his peers because none of them were looking at him, but mostly out of spite.

"I have been thinking."

He was not disappointed. She turned her golden head to look at him, slight annoyance showing in her crinkled nose and furrowed brow. He felt a jab of satisfaction and returned his complete attention to the table. "Dendreya may not be completely lost to us after all."

Hope spread across the faces of Callum and Gideon. Brimir's face revealed nothing, but his eyes shimmered with approval. The other three, the three who had followed Alariq's orders so many times before, looked back at him, expressionless and unreadable, already resigned to accept whatever decision he made.

"Three of us have experience fighting ettins. Perhaps there is a way we can oust them from their stolen den. We're outnumbered, but maybe we can pick them off a few at a time. They must leave occasionally. They cannot stay shut in there, they would have killed each other by now."

Alariq meant to continue, but he was interrupted.

"They sometimes venture into the outer edges of the forest and they occasionally leave to raid local villages. They take most of the horde, but generally leave a small contingency behind."

Everyone turned to look at their hostess.

Alariq weighed his gratitude at the useful information with his annoyance at being interrupted. He was leaning toward gratitude when she stood and walked over to the table and spoke as though she were in charge. Then, he went right past annoyance and on to anger.

"They are highly militarized and their movements are very regular, and therefore predictable. But they already know of your presence and your interest in Dendreya, and will be on their guard. After your first attack, they are likely to hole up behind their walls. What will you do then?"

Alariq's voice was deathly calm when he spoke. "They cannot stay behind the walls forever. They have to come out for food." Alariq turned his face decidedly away from her, clearly indicating the matter was closed.

"Actually, they can." Her tone had changed ever so slightly, but Alariq recognized the note of warning behind her words.

He turned to face her fully now and simply looked at her. No one spoke for a long moment.

Brimir broke the standoff. "What do you mean?" he asked, his tone polite and inquisitive.

The woman stared at Alariq for a moment longer before turning her attention to Brimir. When she spoke, her voice was warmer and her eyes had softened.

"I have never seen them farm, nor do I know if they possess the patience for it. They occasionally hunt, but certainly not often enough to feed a group that size. It's more for sport, you see. The corpses usually come back in barely edible condition."

Contempt showed clearly on her face.

"I do not know how they sustain themselves, but their ventures outside the city are by choice, not by need."

"They must be getting supplies then." Asher addressed his comment more as a question to Alariq.

"From other ettins?" Callum asked.

The woman opened her mouth to respond, but now it was Alariq who cut across her. "I doubt it. Why would the ettins be here, just dying off, if they were welcome back home?" He fixed her with a stare. "You must be mistaken."

"You are welcome to believe that, if you are so inclined. It makes no difference to me. You will learn the truth soon enough from your own observations." Her tone was lighter than before, but Alariq knew better than to trust that. He studied her.

"We appreciate your help last night and the hospitality you have shown us today..." Alariq meant to continue with an admonition to mind her own business, but once again she had the audacity to cut him off.

"I find that to be very interesting indeed, seeing as the greatest show of appreciation you have so far mustered is to glare at me."

Callum started to mutter something about him clearing the plates, but Gideon quieted him.

"*You* came into *my* forest needing *my* help." Her amber eyes flashed dangerously.

Alariq took a step toward her. "In point of fact, we did not ask for your help."

"Well then next time, I shall let your incompetence carry you to its natural conclusion!"

Alariq's next step in her direction was blocked by Ford and Asher.

Ford spoke quietly, so that only Alariq and Asher could hear him. "She's not a threat to us. And she clearly has information we need. About the ettins and the forest. I doubt even I could find my way out of here, and we all know I'm the best tracker of the lot of us."

Alariq glanced briefly at Ford's trusting face and Asher's stony one before he backed away and retook his spot sitting at the head of the table. He mustered the most polite expression of which he was currently capable, and gestured toward the table.

She tested his patience immediately. "I have no need for your invitation, as it is my table and I shall sit whenever I like."

Alariq gritted his teeth as she stood opposite him at the other head of the table and addressed him.

"I believe you are right. I believe it is possible for the ettins to be ejected from Dendreya. But you will need my help," she said.

"And why would you help us?" Alariq could not keep the accusation from his tone.

Her face tightened slightly and the color in her eyes seemed less bright. She remained silent, looking at him, and then out the window. When she finally spoke, her voice was quiet, but steady.

"When the ettins first came, they kept to the city and the beach. But they have become bolder, more out of boredom than courage, I believe. They have started venturing into the forest and local villages. I have seen the destruction they bring. They raid and ransack with no purpose, save to seemingly expend their energy and find a target for their violent proclivities. I do not know why they settled here, but they were not meant for such a life. While their race is naturally aggressive, their confinement within Dendreya and lack of outlet for their hostility has created a pack of beasts so cruel and uncontrolled, it is hardly to be believed."

During the war, Alariq had seen ettins in action and they were often needlessly violent, but it always seemed utilitarian in nature, not out of pure cruelty. If she was right, and their decision to take up permanent residence in Dendreya, instead of out fighting wars like they usually did, had transformed their aggression into something more sinister...well, he hated to think of the many atrocities of which such powerful creatures with no conscience would be capable.

She continued. "I have been to the villages after a raid, found the pieces of animals strewn about the edges of the forest. I myself have only narrowly escaped their notice on more than one occasion."

Her voice caught and she paused, looking out the window again.

But then her features hardened and her voice steadied. She squared her shoulders and said, much lighter now, "I do not like having my freedom to come and go as I please in my forest limited, nor do I wish to see my main source of supplies destroyed."

Alariq could think of nothing to say. Her sudden change in tone had not escaped his notice, nor did he believe the new blasé attitude for a second. He merely nodded curtly.

"So we are agreed then? We are fighting for Dendreya?" Callum's voice was filled with barely restrained hope.

Alariq looked around at the dwarfs who had given up everything for him. And he gave the only answer he knew he could.

8

The Treehome

You may recall that at the beginning of this tale, I warned you that Alariq's disagreeable moods were quite frequent in occurrence. At that time, his unpleasant demeanor could be pardoned, or at least overlooked. But the mood in which we find him now was inexcusable in the extreme. In fact, it was so indefensible that even he knew it, which, as I am sure you guessed, only made the mood fouler still.

What made this particular mood so intolerable is a combination of the childlike sulking to which Alariq was given and the reason for said sulking, which is so typical, it borders on cliché.

You see, Alariq was cleaning.

And there were very few things in this world he hated more than cleaning.

After their resolution to reclaim Dendreya the day before, the discussion had shifted to the most pressing concern: what to do in the meantime. The eight of them decided that the best place for them to stay was in the treehome, as it was called by its owner. Alariq admitted the name was appropriate, for it was certainly far more than just a house.

Although, he thought to himself, *one would think she would take better care of the place she so lovingly calls a home.*

He was currently scrubbing decades' worth of dust and grime off the window he had had just unboarded, in the room that made up the third floor. Apparently, their hostess slept in one of the upper levels and, as she lived alone, this room had fallen into disuse. It was certainly big enough to sleep three, which is exactly what it would be doing for the foreseeable future. He, Ford, and Asher had taken this room. The other four would be sleeping in the cellar, which, they were told, was actually the original main bedroom of the house, but which its current occupant had converted into a seldom-used storeroom.

There were six stories to the treehome. The main floor and four upper levels Alariq had already noticed from outside, and the cellar down below, which none of them even realized existed until the golden-haired woman showed them the door in the floor. The room Alariq was cleaning had been an early addition onto the home, before its current owner's time. She had added the top two stories, however, which quite frankly, Alariq found overly wasteful as there was a perfectly good bedroom in which he now stood. Well, perfectly good excepting the ages of dust and a leaky roof. He could hear Ford and Asher up above patching a few worn spots, chatting and even occasionally chuckling despite their menial task.

Alariq finished cleaning the window and turned his attention to the sill, which had dead bugs and other debris inside. *How nice it must be to have free labor to do those tasks you've been putting off,* Alariq thought resentfully.

When she had said they could stay with her, he had been immediately against it, but all the others seemed quite pleased. He had to admit the home definitely had appeal. It was comforting, which was strange considering how very different it was from their home city. Ishtara was industrial and harsh, but Alariq had always enjoyed the sounds of metal on metal, the dry heat of the furnaces, and the sweet smell of the wax that was applied as a finish to many of the items smithed in the city. There, he felt useful and productive. It was hard to describe the way he felt here in Loraheem. *Soothed.* This was the best he could come up with. But there was definitely something else, some feeling he had not yet identified.

But his reluctance to stay in the treehome had nothing to do with the accommodations, and everything to do with who they would be sharing them with. He could not explain his animosity toward their hostess, except that he didn't trust her. There was something else unidentifiable about her too...but unlike the forest, whatever it was, did *not* put him at ease.

He returned his attention to the task. Upon his acceptance of their hostess's offer, she had made it clear that she had not been expecting company (*Does she ever?* he thought now, looking around in distaste) and that the two rooms in which the dwarfs would be sleeping needed considerable preparations to make them habitable.

He had suggested they just continue to sleep on the floor in the main room. Based on her laughter, she apparently thought this was a joke, and had simply walked away, a chronic habit of hers, he'd quickly learned.

He finished the first window and moved on to the other. He heard Ford and Asher laughing louder now. The looks of despondence he had seen on their faces yesterday were ones he had seldom seen before. In fact, the last time he could remember it was when Tanith had returned from fighting the ettins with only his son and four other soldiers. There had been a lot of good dwarfs in the king's division. That had been a grim day for everyone.

It was a day fixed in Alariq's memory. Tanith had left with his soldiers to secure the southern perimeter and check on the outer settlements in the area. Most of the fighting was contained to the north and west of the city, as Ettinridge lay northwest of Ishtara, so almost all of the eight divisions of Ishtara's military was committed in these regions. But the ettins were preparing a surprise attack from the south, which likely would have been successful. Tanith's division, however, spotted them before they could amass their full forces and attack the city. The ettins attacked anyway, trying to keep the element of surprise. Tanith's division defeated them, but narrowly. *Too narrowly.* All but a handful of the division had been annihilated.

But Ishtara had been at peace ever since, with only minor incursions by a stray ettin or uprising between the outer settlements. Alariq's division, Division Three, had taken care of most of those. Everyone said Alariq was the best First Authority, and with Ford and Blainn as his Second and Third, not to mention the Deadeyes, there was never any debate as to who should lead the defense of the city. Alariq thought that would have bought him a little more loyalty. Or at least a chance to defend himself.

Alariq snapped out of his reverie and realized he had been standing in front of the boarded up window for several minutes, unmoving, lost in memory. He gave his head a quick shake and started removing the boards. There was no use dwelling on it. It wouldn't make what happened any less real.

He looked through the gaps in the boards and saw Callum and Blainn down in the clearing below beating out an old mattress. Alariq had always thought Callum had blonde hair, but in the sunlight it looked reddish. Alariq tried to remember a time he'd seen Callum in the bright sunshine, instead of inside with his nose buried in something only he and Gideon considered interesting. He couldn't think of a single time, save for when his cousin was a very small dwarfling. Callum was chattering away, which was not in the least bit surprising. What was surprising, however, was that Blainn was letting him and politely (albeit a bit transparently) feigning interest. Alariq couldn't remember the last time he'd seen that happen either.

The others seemed more than willing to help clean the treehome and all appeared genuinely happy to make the place their temporary abode. At Alariq's protests that cleaning would use up valuable time, the woman had pointed out the ettins would likely be out patrolling for several days to make sure the dwarfs did not return.

"Plus, Blainn needs to heal," Asher had said, as innocently as he could.

So, Alariq was cleaning.

After he finished opening the window back up, he wiped the

glass, *which had probably been* made *by dwarfs too*, he thought. He had just finished and was dropping the latch into place when he caught a flash on the ground to his left. It was their rescuer slinking off into the woods. He watched her slip deftly through the trees, but in an instant the thick growth swallowed her. Even her golden hair, which seemed to shine as though it had captured the light of the sun, was invisible to him.

He waited a few moments, to ensure she was out of earshot, and then reopened the window he had just closed and quietly called up to Ford and Asher. "Get down here. Meet me on the main floor."

Alariq closed the window and headed out the door and down the stairs. He heard the other two lightly hitting the landing in front of their door as they leapt down from the roof, but did not stop or look back.

Once back inside, he saw Callum at the wash basin wringing out rags that were as black as soot.

"Get the others up here."

Callum immediately dropped the damp cloth back into the murky water and made his way toward the cellar door, calling the others up. Ford and Asher entered, closing the front door behind them, and the remaining three emerged from the hole in the floor moments later. Alariq made his way to the table and they all followed.

Once seated, he addressed the group. "Did she say where she was going?"

Brimir answered him. "We were all down in the cellar. We didn't know she left."

"Well I don't want her left alone anymore. When she's here, someone needs to have eyes on her at all times. If she tries to leave, follow her. We'll take shifts. Youngest to oldest."

Callum looked uncomfortable. "I'm not certain this is necess..." He trailed off at the hard look Alariq gave him.

Alariq glanced around at the others. All of them except Blainn seemed to be of the same mind as Callum. Alariq didn't like how quickly she had won their trust. The ease at which she had persuaded the others that she was a harmless bunny rabbit made him all the more suspicious that she was really a fox.

None of the others spoke, but he could tell protests were all forming behind their tongues. Asher opened his mouth to speak first, but Alariq held up a hand to stop him.

"She may have saved us, but that does not mean we should hand her our faith blindly. We know nothing of her, including why, or how, she lives alone in the middle of an impenetrable forest. We do not know what her true motives may be. We do not even know her name."

The voice was soft, but it startled them all, even Alariq, who froze, not turning and looking at the open doorway like the others, knowing what, or who, he would find if he did.

"My name is Tianna."

9

The Labyrinth of Loraheem

Alariq was one of those lucky beings possessed of a very rational mind. He thought out all of his decisions and rarely did anything impulsive. As such, he generally believed he was never wrong. He arrived at each of his decisions through logic and reason and typically stood by them. As you can imagine, this means he was very unaccustomed to feeling embarrassed or guilty. And because these feelings were so foreign to him, he reacted very poorly when they bubbled up inside him. And bubble inside him they did. Well, not so much a bubble as a rolling boil. He regretted that Tianna had overheard his remarks about her. He told himself he didn't regret saying them. Regardless, his gut gnawed and his conscience nagged.

And he hated it.

Everyone else seemed to be just as miserable. Tianna had taken to acting as though he didn't exist. That was fine with Alariq. She was slightly nicer to the others, but to say the atmosphere had been tense over the last few days was an understatement.

None of them were sure if she had heard Alariq give the order not to leave her alone. And they certainly were not enjoying their new assignment. Try though they may to comply with Alariq's directive, so far they had all, including Alariq, failed miserably. She had slipped past them on numerous occasions since Alariq had given the order to keep tabs on her. Her ability to disappear and her penchant for doing so made Alariq's anger and mistrust grow every time it happened.

It also made him resentful toward the other dwarfs. And sensing their resentment directed back at him, and their displeasure with his order, did not improve his mood. Despite the fact that she had also outmaneuvered him (twice), he still could not help but wonder if the others were really trying their best.

After she had walked in on their conversation and told them her name, she had waited for Alariq to turn around and face her. She had given him a look that might have turned his blood to ice before turning and ascending to the top floor of the treehome. Gideon and Brimir prepared dinner, a stew made from the last of the deer she had killed on their first morning there. She seemed to thaw slightly toward them when she came down for the meal, clearly expecting to have to cook it herself.

They had eaten in silence. Afterwards, as she was about to leave, Callum finally worked up the courage to ask her about her books.

Gideon whipped his head around so quickly, he knocked it against one of the pots hanging from hooks on the ceiling. Brimir nodded to Gideon to indicate he would clean up and Ford fell in to help, while Gideon followed Tianna and Callum over to her sitting area.

Alariq watched through narrowed eyes as she pulled out a few books and sat in the one chair. Gideon's and Callum's eyes were as wide as saucers. And damnit if the two of them didn't sit on the floor right in front of her, like two children being told a bedtime story by their mother!

She showed them one she had just completed and started explaining the process. Alariq, having no interest in her books, and even less interest in watching two of his company fawn over the thorn in his side, left to take a walk.

After taking about twenty steps to the edge of the forest, he remembered he did not know Loraheem and would have no hope of finding his way back. Tianna would likely have to come rescue him again and lead him home like a little child.

Alariq wasn't going to give her the satisfaction. He stood, looking into the blackness, trying to reign in his temper.

In the military, control over one's emotions was vital, and he had always prided himself on being a master at it. He experienced emotions, of course. Especially anger and fear. But he never let them show and he certainly never let them affect his behavior.

But ever since his exile, he felt as though his emotions ruled him. It seemed as though every time he got them in check, something new challenged him yet again.

Something...or someone, he thought bitterly, grinding his teeth.

He bent down and picked up a smooth rock and turned it unthinkingly over and over in his hand. He had to get these emotions under control. Just like grieving the loss of Ishtara wouldn't serve a purpose, neither would showing his displeasure with his current roommates.

Except maybe to drive one of them to smother me in my sleep.

He heard movement behind him and turned in time to see Tianna exit the front door. She started to climb the stairs, but stopped and looked directly at him.

"Later I will show you a map of the forest and the nearby landmarks."

He nodded once and took a step toward the treehome.

Tianna started back up the stairs, but called over her shoulder, "That way, next time you want to stomp off and sulk, you can do so in the privacy of the trees."

Alariq's jaw clenched involuntarily and he fantasized about throwing the rock at her retreating figure; but he remained still and did not say a word in response. He didn't have a choice but to do so, as he had nothing to retort.

Over the next days, Tianna showed the dwarfs numerous maps, most of which she had clearly drawn herself. She pointed out landmarks and explained the distances between her home, Dendreya, the beach, the creek, the nearest village, and various other key places. She also took them out in small groups of two or three to show them around.

Most of the forest was dark, but some portions were downright black. Even the dwarfs had trouble seeing in the abyss of darkness. Alariq quickly came to the realization that the biggest danger facing anyone in Loraheem was not ettins or finfiends, but rather the labyrinth of the Forest of Loraheem itself.

On their excursions, she pointed out distinctive markers, such as a particularly gnarled tree trunk, a sandpit, and a thicket of berry bushes. There was also a huge colony of honey bees in one of the trees and the buzzing could be heard from several hundred paces away in any direction. She showed them a variety of rock formations she had formed at various places, all of which gave them clues to their whereabouts relative to key places in Loraheem.

After the first few trips into the trees, she started having them lead her to various places. She would ask them to find the creek or where the beach was or how to get home. They were all fast learners and under her guidance, they quickly felt assured in their ability to navigate the forest.

They had been at the treehome for almost two weeks when Alariq suggested it was time to go back to Dendreya. The others seemed in agreement.

"You are overconfident," came the soft voice that had come to grate on Alariq's nerves like no other sound, and that included Blainn's horrible excuse for singing.

"Have we not passed all of your little tests?" Alariq responded as evenly as he could. He was actually quite impressed with his restraint. He certainly had had ample practice over the last week.

Without responding, she exited the tree.

They discussed plans for a few minutes, deciding whether they should all go or whether they should gather information in small groups first.

"What if an opportunity for attack presents itself?" Blainn asked. "We should all be there to take advantage of it."

"We no longer have the benefit of surprise. They might be expecting something like that," said Ford.

"He's right." Alariq ended the debate. "No attacks until we've learned more about the ettins."

The next day, Alariq, Ford, and Asher prepared to leave the treehome and make their first attempt at getting close enough to

Dendreya to glean some useful information about their enemy.

They had so far not ventured that far from the treehome, but they had studied Tianna's maps and the various landmarks that would guide them back to the town. They took only their weapons and some water, as they intended to return by lunch.

Tianna merely continued to eat her breakfast as they left, not even bothering to speak to them.

They headed into the forest, passing the beehive (and giving it a wide berth) and two of Tianna's rock formations in the ground. They were looking for a dead tree that had been struck by lightning, but so far, were not finding it. First, they strayed too far west and had to backtrack to the last formation before continuing in a more southerly direction. But then, it turned out they had gotten turned around in the darkness and had headed back toward the treehome instead.

They retraced their steps once again back to the last marker and headed south. The tree still wasn't where they thought it should be. So they headed backwards once again.

Only this time, they couldn't find the last marker. Alariq wasn't particularly worried. He was confident he knew which way was east and as long as they kept heading that way, they'd hit the beach eventually. He was far more concerned with having to return to the treehome (and a certain golden-haired know-it-all) after getting lost.

Fortunately, he did not have to do any such thing.

Unfortunately, the reason he didn't have to do any such thing was that Tianna materialized out of the darkness behind them.

She didn't speak at all and he was grateful for that. But there was just enough light to see the look she shot him. A small smile and a slightly raised eyebrow. Then she turned and headed in the exact opposite way he had just been about to suggest they go.

He was sure he heard her mutter "overconfident" as they fell in behind her. He just balled up his fists, gritted his teeth, and followed without a word.

The four of them managed to get within a few hundred paces before they caught smell of the ettins. They scaled two of the much smaller, though still mammoth, trees near the edge of the forest and listened as two patrols passed through their intended path about two hundred feet in front of their hiding spot. Even near the edge of the forest, it was much lighter, like the world just before dawn. But the trees were still quite dense and so they caught only the briefest of glimpses of the creatures.

After the ettins had passed and they had heard nothing for about ten minutes, Alariq made to climb down. He felt a small, but firm hand on his shoulder. He turned to Tianna, who briefly made eye contact with him and then looked pointedly in the direction from which the ettins had come. He waited a few moments, but hearing and smelling nothing, he looked questioningly up at her, but she just continued to stare through the trees, eyes narrowed in concentration.

In the tree beside them, Alariq could see Ford and Asher looking at him, asking with their eyes what they were waiting for. Alariq held up a hand and then looked pointedly at Tianna.

A few more moments passed before he heard them. Two more ettins marched through their path. Another fifteen minutes after that, another pair passed by. Then a fourth pair after the same period. With perfect precision, the original two ettins crossed their path almost exactly one hour after their first appearance.

After this pair passed, Tianna leapt from her spot in the tree, bending her knees when she hit the ground to avoid jarring them. Alariq followed, but the distance was more than he had anticipated and his knees gave out under his weight. He righted himself in time to see Ford and Asher climbing down, having decided not to imitate Tianna.

Tianna paced around, looking at the ground. She picked up several rocks and placed them exactly in their path in a jagged line. She looked at the three of them to make sure they all saw what she had done and then without a word headed back toward the treehome.

Upon their return, Ford explained what they had seen.

No one remarked on the fact that what left as a threesome, was now a foursome.

"This is great!" Callum was jubilant as he dried the dishes Gideon handed him. "We can pick off eight of them in one day. Tomorrow even!"

He handed Brimir the plate to put away a little more carelessly than he should have and Brimir had to scramble to avoid it falling to the floor, but Callum just continued, "With eight down, that's almost a quarter of them out of the way."

"You would be foolish in the extreme to attempt such a thing." Tianna spoke quietly and kindly, but her voice was reproachful nonetheless.

Wishing he did not have to take her side, Alariq joined the conversation. "She is right. We do not yet have enough information to attack."

After that, the dwarfs continued to spy on the ettins for almost a fortnight. Tianna accompanied them every time. Although after several trips, Alariq was sure he knew the way, he didn't dare say anything to her after having been wrong last time. If she was put out by the daily trips through the forest, she did not indicate it.

Alariq almost always went on these surveillance tours, but occasionally remained to speak privately with the others while Tianna was out either with some of the other dwarfs or just having disappeared again. Although he had to admit she was of immense help and had applied herself to the task with complete commitment, both of those things made him nervous. He didn't like the idea of depending so much on someone they knew so little about. That just didn't seem like good sense. And her quick and total commitment to their quest aroused his already heightened suspicion.

Why is she so willing to help?

He recalled her words about the ettins. How her face tightened and eyes glazed. It had seemed genuine. *Still...* Alariq decided it was far better to be overly cautious than overly trusting. Trust was expensive.

During these moments without Tianna, he questioned the other dwarfs about her movements and if they learned anything about her. Callum and Gideon always had nothing but praise and useless information about ridiculous things such as papermaking and bookbinding to offer. Brimir generally refused to participate in the conversations and Alariq had thus far overlooked it, trusting that if anything truly suspicious had occurred, Brimir would report it in a heartbeat.

Blainn, Ford, and Asher were reluctantly forthcoming, reporting that she spent a lot of time holed up in the top floor of the treehome, although she slept on the second to the top. She disappeared frequently into the forest, usually at night and often without them noticing her absence until she returned.

None of them recognized her accent, although that was unremarkable as few of them had encountered anyone outside of Ishtar lands, other than ettins and knomes. She spoke Dirni, just like the rest of them. Though that too was unremarkable as most city-states had adopted the trade language of Dirnovaria ages ago. It had been a necessity to learn it because pretty much everyone traded with Dirnovaria. Then it just became easier to fully adopt Dirni than maintaining two separate languages.

A few places still did though. Eridu was known for its isolation and had always refused to use the trade language altogether. It was rare indeed to find an Utu who spoke anything other than Eridian. At least that's what Alariq had always heard. But she clearly wasn't a desert dweller anyway, so that didn't help much.

Then there were the knomes, who spoke a bastardized version of ancient dwarfish, adopted into their own knomish through the centuries of interaction between the two races. But to Alariq's knowledge, everyone else generally spoke the trade language, so this information about their hostess wasn't terribly helpful.

On top of the lack of helpful observations, none of them had been successful in getting her to reveal any personal information in conversation. These nearly useless reports infuriated Alariq, making him all the more suspicious of their hostess and frustrated with his squad.

Clearly sensing Alariq's frustration, Brimir joined the conversation for the first time. "What would you have us do? She is simply more cunning and knows the area better than us. We cannot make her talk, short of torturing her. Though we'd have to catch her first and quite honestly, I do not know if such a feat is possible."

At Brimir's sarcasm, Alariq's rage reached its boiling point. "Maybe if you were all a little more motivated and a little less infatuated, you could come up with something more useful than the details of her hobbies!"

But Brimir wasn't to be cowed.

"Do you truly believe she is a threat?" he asked.

"That is not the point! I made it abundantly clear that she was not to be trusted. But you have all fallen in line with her as if she were your dearest kin!" Alariq was shouting and in the small quarters of the main floor, it sounded like a roar.

"We are doing our best." Ford looked awkward, but resolute. "As Brimir said, she is evasive and knows the forest better than us. But none of us are acting intentionally against you."

Alariq stood, breathing heavily, his hands clenched and his broad chest rising and falling swiftly. Blainn and Gideon were on watch with Tianna, assuming, of course, she hadn't snuck off again. He looked around at the other two present, Asher and Callum. Callum's head was down, his cheeks red and his hands worrying at a patch on his breeches. Asher looked stonily back at him. Alariq had always been able to count on Asher to do his bidding flawlessly and unquestioningly. He'd expected this out of Callum and Gideon, who would probably give a Karxani dwarf the benefit of the doubt if he could make books, but it was in Asher that Alariq most sensed defiance.

Alariq calmed his anger and forced himself to speak rationally.

"I do not like these frequent disappearances. Nor am I willing to simply accept her help when I cannot see a motive. She is risking her life for us. Why? It does not make sense."

"She gave you a reason," Asher said curtly. "You just choose to think it's not enough."

"I do not choose anything!" Alariq retorted. "It is not smart to believe everything you're told. If you approach the world with such naïve faith, you will be sorely disappointed in life."

Callum mumbled something down toward his lap. Alariq couldn't make it out and in fact, had barely heard any sound at all.

"What?" he asked, more gruffly than he'd intended.

Callum took a deep breath and then looked straight at him. Still quietly, but clearly this time, he said, "I think she's bored."

No one said anything. Of all the reasons for someone to risk their lives for a bunch of dwarfs to whom they had no obligation or even relation, boredom was the stupidest. It was also the last one Alariq expected anyone to offer in explanation of Tianna's behavior.

"And..." Callum spoke again, quieter still.

"And?" Alariq asked, more gently this time.

"And I also think she's..." Callum trailed off, his eyes returning to his lap.

"Yes?" Alariq prodded.

Callum looked over at the reading area before responding.

"Lonely."

Alariq was wrong. Loneliness was the last explanation he'd expected.

"She seems perfectly happy cooped up by herself to me," he responded tersely. "She doesn't exactly appear to enjoy our presence does she?"

Callum reddened and mumbled again. All Alariq caught was the "never mind" that came at the end.

Brimir, who was sitting right next to Callum, smiled slightly and let out the smallest of chuckles.

"What?" Alariq asked again.

"He said she doesn't appear to enjoy *your* presence."

Callum was the color of a hot branding iron. He glanced up at Alariq apologetically.

Alariq thought about it and he supposed Tianna did seem somewhat more pleasant around the other dwarfs.

"I think the youngster's on to something," said Brimir. "She's very isolated out here. And she's clearly been living this way for a long time. Her books alone would have taken her years. Not to mention she added on those top two stories of this home herself. And I've never heard her mention anyone else."

"She's too young to have done all that by herself," Alariq said. "She must have been living here with someone else at some point. Parents maybe."

"But where would they have slept?" Brimir asked. "You said yourself the main bedroom had clearly been unused for decades. And the basement was the same."

"A husband then," he answered brusquely. This conversation was purposeless. "And he slept with her upstairs."

"I don't think so," Asher said. "I went up to let her know dinner was ready a couple nights ago and there was just a tiny bed, built into the top of a branch. Certainly not big enough for two."

"What difference does it make?" Alariq snapped.

"The difference it makes is that living things, no matter the race, aren't meant to lead existences like this, in utter isolation, with no one to share them with," Brimir said, his voice soft. "It's not natural and it's bound to have taken a toll on her."

"So?" Alariq couldn't see Brimir's point.

"So, it's the explanation you've been looking for," he replied, in that wizened tone Alariq had come to associate only with Brimir.

Only right now, Alariq failed to see the wisdom in Brimir's words. It didn't explain anything at all. At least not satisfactorily.

"Loneliness and boredom? I'm supposed to simply accept she is out in the woods right now, traipsing around with Blainn and Gideon, spying on ettins, and taking in and feeding seven dwarfs, all because she hates her spinster life?"

The others looked at one another. Alariq's arms tingled and his muscles involuntarily clenched. He felt heat flush his cheeks.

"Listen–" Alariq began.

But Callum cut him off, "No, *you* listen. You asked us to give you information on her. Well this is my information. I'm telling you she's lonely and she's got a lot of time on her hands. She's a doer and people like that don't like to be idle."

Everyone in the room stared at Callum in shock. Ford's mouth was even slightly ajar.

"And she hates those ettins," Callum added as an afterthought.

Silence reigned.

"He's right," Brimir said gently.

When Alariq made to argue, Brimir held up his hand. "He may not be right about her motives and you don't have to believe him if you don't want to. But you asked us to tell you what we know and what we think. This is what we think. You don't have to accept it as truth, but you should accept that it's all you're going to get from us because it's our honest opinion on the matter. If my perception of her changes, I will let you know. As I am sure the others will do as well."

Alariq locked eyes with Brimir and studied him for a moment, before finally nodding and dropping the subject.

The surveillance of the ettins was faring significantly better than the surveillance of Tianna. They had discovered that the ettins on patrol checked in with a guard as they circled Dendreya. This meant an attack on the patrols as Callum had recommended was out, as the ettins would know they were under attack as soon as a patrol group failed to check in.

"What if we attack just after the checkpoint?" Blainn suggested one day, during one of their many discussions. "That way, we can get all four pairs before the guards at the checkpoint are the wiser."

"The checkpoint is too close to the city." Alariq pointed to the map on the table in front of him, where Tianna had marked the checkpoint and the patrol path. "If they call for help, they will likely be heard, and then we will have an entire ettinhorde on our tails."

The discussions continued in the same vein, with possibility after possibility being shot down.

The biggest problem they kept coming up against was how to attack the ettins without the enemy thinking they were under attack. If they sensed an onslaught coming, they might hole up inside Dendreya, which was too well-fortified for a direct attack by the dwarfs.

It was Asher who came up with the answer. "The finfiends."

Out of the corner of his eye, Alariq saw Tianna's head snap up from her breakfast, but kept his attention on Asher.

"What if the ettins thought the finfiends were attacking them? We might be able to draw them to the beach somehow and attack them there."

Alariq rolled the idea around in his mind, but it already felt good in his gut.

"We can use the stream," Gideon said and all of the eyes in the room collectively turned to him. "It's how the ettins get their water, right? Let's dam it up, block it somehow. They'll send out a group to fix it and we attack. We can put the blockage in a spot that gives us an easy advantage."

"And do what with the bodies?" Alariq asked. "We want them

to think the finfiends are taking them, so there can't be evidence that the ettins have been killed, namely their bodies. We can't move them ourselves without leaving tracks."

"We'll have to attack on the beach then." Ford came to sit at the table as he spoke, holding a steaming bowl of breakfast hash, a specialty of Tianna's. Even though Alariq had already eaten two helpings, his mouth filled with saliva at the smell. He hated that.

Ford continued, "We can tie rocks to their arms and legs and sink them. Then we can cover any signs in the sand."

"We'll block the creek right at the mouth of the lake then," Gideon said.

"It will not work."

Everyone turned to look at Tianna, except for Alariq, who had been waiting for her to add her thoughts to the conversation.

"And why not?" he asked without looking at her.

"They have lived here for three decades without so much as a single attack. Why now? They won't go for it."

Alariq finally turned in her direction, looking Tianna directly in the eyes.

"How do you know they've never been attacked?" he asked snidely. "You said there were seventy when they arrived, what's to say some of them weren't killed or captured by finfiends?"

"They weren't," she said simply, holding his gaze.

Alariq laughed. "You accuse *us* of being overconfident, but you act like you know about every dropping a bird makes in this forest."

Tianna rose and walked over to the table, her face hard and eyes flashing. "Actually, I accused *you* of being overconfident. And it's an opinion you have done nothing to change."

They simply glared at one another for a moment.

As usual, Brimir broke the tension.

"How do you know the ettins have never been attacked by finfiends?"

Before she could answer, Alariq interrupted her.

"And how do you even know when they arrived and how many there were?" he demanded. "That would have been before you were even born."

Tianna, who had been about to answer Brimir's question, snapped her mouth shut and stared at Alariq with mute ferocity.

Finally, she spoke through clenched teeth.

"I told you. When the ettins arrived, they killed the people who had moved in from the Sudri River settlements. Everyone around here knows about it."

Normally, an answer like that would have satisfied Alariq. But she had responded too slowly. As if she had to come up with an answer.

He opened his mouth to voice his suspicions and demand a truthful answer, but Brimir cut across him.

"And what about the finfiends?"

Tianna took several deep breaths, her narrowed eyes never leaving Alariq, before turning to Brimir and answering.

"I have heard of finfiends attacking humans before, mostly near August Sound or in the river settlements close to the mouth of the lake. But I have never heard of them attacking any other race before."

"And because you haven't heard of it, it can't be true, right?" Alariq shot at her. "Well, they attacked us on our way here."

"They did?" Tianna's eyes widened for a moment and then snapped together, as her lips pursed.

"They ambushed us on the beach near the Austri River. About twenty of them."

"And they tried to capture you?" Tianna asked, her voice disbelieving.

"Yes."

Tianna opened her mouth, but then closed it once more. Alariq sneered spitefully back at her.

Nothing to say? his eyes asked her and he saw her mouth tighten.

Brimir interrupted their silent argument. "Even assuming you are right, Tianna, and the finfiends wouldn't attack them, the ettins might not know this. They might still believe them to be a threat."

"And the fact that they have lived here for thirty years without an attack? That would not provide them a clue? Ettins are not as stupid as many believe," she answered.

Alariq's restraint broke suddenly. He rose from his chair, knocking it backwards. He pulled himself up to his full height and stood there, staring at her, fists clenched, but his voice was low. It probably sounded calm to an ear unfamiliar with Alariq's temper.

"First of all, you have given us no proof that the ettins have not been attacked by the lake creatures before. And second, do not dare lecture *us* on ettins. Dwarfs have fought them for millennia. We know better than any other of what they are capable. You have lived near them for a few paltry years and done nothing but avoid them and make little notes about them in your books."

Tianna looked as though she wanted to say something, but instead, shrugged her shoulders and said, "Fine. Do as you wish. I said I would help you and I will. If this is your plan, so be it."

Alariq had not been fully committed to the idea yet, but now he had no choice.

"This is the plan," he said resolutely.

Once again, Brimir tried to diffuse the tension. "Do the ettins ever go to the beach?"

"Rarely," Tianna answered. "At least according to my *paltry* observations." She looked sideways at Alariq. "They have no reason to."

"So when should we do it?" Callum asked Alariq.

"We should wait for a storm. That way it might seem that the blockage was a happenstance rather than by nefarious design," he responded to Callum and then addressed Gideon, "Does it storm here often?"

Gideon shot an uncomfortable look at Tianna, who was clearly the better person to ask. She nodded slightly, but only Gideon and Alariq noticed. "Yes, I think so," Gideon answered.

"Then we wait."

10

A Plan and a Dream

They did not have to wait long. Over the next three days, they scouted out the creek and the beach, discussing how best to block the stream and looking for the most advantageous place to attack. Alariq always had two dwarfs watching Dendreya and two keeping watch on the beach while the remaining four of them planned the attack.

Tianna drew a detailed map of the relevant area of the beach and the creek and they spent every meal scrunched around it. Far into the evening hours they debated and discussed, coming up with weaknesses and potential counterattacks.

The beach was too far from Dendreya for the ettins to call for help, so that was not an issue. The real problem was whether the ettins would suspect an ambush and send a large group, or worse, perhaps two groups, one to check the creek and the other to provide defense.

But despite all the threats to them from outside their group, Alariq was most concerned about one from within. He worried the other dwarfs were determined to execute this plan no matter what the circumstances, because failure likely meant the abandonment of Dendreya. None of them had dared to mention the idea of calling their families over again, but Alariq knew they were all thinking it. All thinking Dendreya was the key to salvaging a portion of their old life.

And he was worried they couldn't see the forest for the trees. They were too emotionally invested in this fight. And emotionally invested soldiers often fought harder, but less smart. He normally preferred flexibility on the battlefield and to trust his subordinates to use good judgement, but he felt this group was somewhat short on that of late.

Instead, he set a hard and fast rule. If more than eight ettins arrived, they were to abandon the plan. Normally, a one-to-one ettin-to-dwarf ratio would mean certain death for the dwarfs, but the ettins would be very exposed out on the beach. Moreover, the dwarfs had the element of surprise and planned to take out several of their large foes from a distance, before even leaving the cover of the trees. Alariq had lost a few of his starmetal arrows in the skirmish in Dendreya, but, if the plan worked, he'd be able to retrieve any he used on the beach.

On the third evening, they felt a breeze on the beach. That night, the forest was an orchestra of the rhythmic sound of leaves dancing in the wind, punctuated by the offbeat creaking of the trees. Alariq drifted in and out of sleep, his dreams mixing with his waking thoughts.

The rain started in the early morning hours. At first, it was a gentle, but steady downpour. By the time Alariq rose, it was clear this was the storm they needed. The forest still looked as though it were nighttime, so black was the sky above, though Alariq's head (and stomach) told him it was morning.

Alariq dispatched Ford and Asher to keep watch over Dendreya and sent Blainn and Callum to stand guard at the beach, in case the creek really did get blocked in the storm and the ettins came before the dwarfs were ready for them. The treehome was quiet while they were gone, except for the sound of the wind and rain. Tianna removed herself to her tower as she often did after breakfast, while Brimir cleaned and Gideon poured over the many volumes in Tianna's collection. Alariq sharpened their weapons, going over the plan again and again in his mind.

By the time the others returned for lunch, the rain brought

visibility down to less than an arm's reach. As they ate, they heard the thunder begin. They smiled halfheartedly at each other over their meal. Alariq well knew the conflicting emotions competing for their minds. They were grateful the storm they needed had come, glad to get the fight they knew was coming over with, and nervous all the same about the impending encounter with their enemy.

Alariq saw no use in sending out scouts when they could barely see past their noses, so they stayed inside that afternoon. Gideon and Callum were talking quietly in the corner. Beside them sat two matching short swords, which were clearly part of a set. Tianna had given them to her two greatest admirers, so they would have something more substantial than a knife and a frying pan to fight with. When they'd asked her where she'd gotten them, she said they used to be hers, before she acquired her current weapon. Callum had tried to give Alariq back his knife, but he'd refused to take it. Callum needed all the extra defense he could get.

Brimir had gone to the cellar bedroom to take a nap and the remaining four, the four soldiers, sat around the table discussing the plan, the terrain, and the enemy. But no one having anything new to contribute, they quickly fell into silence, staring at the map Tianna had drawn, their minds all turning inward. Soon, Ford and Asher decided to head upstairs.

Through the window, Alariq watched as Asher stood, a few steps up the staircase, unmoving, under a branch, blocking the stairs while he stayed dry and the rain drenched his brother behind him. A great deal of pushing and playful yelling occurred, before Asher went tumbling over the railing. Ford continued up the stairs and a few seconds later, Asher passed through Alariq's view through the window, now covered in mud, but a grin on his face.

Alariq returned his attention to the map, but his eyes glazed over. The plan was sound. They would block the creek near the mouth, where the water flowed out of the lake west to Dendreya. Brimir and Callum would wait in trees near the creek, closer to the city. Presumably, the ettins would follow the creek from Dendreya to the lake, to find the cause of their water shortage.

Brimir and Callum would give a signal when the ettins arrived.

Alariq, Asher, and Tianna, the three archers, would take up positions in trees near the blockage, while the remaining three would hide behind boulders farther down the beach. The archers would attack first and then call for the ground soldiers if needed.

Then they'd sink the bodies and hide any signs of a fight. Hopefully, the ettins would believe the finfiends pulled them into the depths of August Sound.

After dealing with the first group, everyone was to get back into position, in the hopes that the ettins would send a second group when the first failed to return. Then they'd repeat the plan and leave. Alariq was sure when *two* groups did not return to Dendreya, the ettins would come to the beach ready for a fight.

Alariq felt good about the mechanics of their plan. But the speed at which all of this was unfolding made him uneasy. The exile itself had been sudden and unexpected, and then he had been forced to make a decision about their destination before he'd been fully prepared to commit to a new life.

Then there was Tianna. The others treated her like one of the group, but her incorporation into their company was troubling to Alariq. It seemed...awkward. Her presence never failed to unsettle him.

And now this plan. Alariq was used to making snap decisions. Such quick thinking was a vital necessity in battle. But this felt different. It felt...

...*desperate*, Alariq thought.

Of all the motivations—fear, jealousy, desire—desperation was the one Alariq would have chosen last.

Desperation makes people frantic. It overwhelms them, Alariq thought as he looked around at the others. *And frantic, overwhelmed people make mistakes.*

He pushed himself back from the table, intending to go upstairs to the covered dining area and spend some time watching the rain, thinking where he did not have to constantly guard his expressions. But as he turned, he saw Brimir's head and shoulder poking out from the cellar door. Brimir jerked his head slightly to the side and disappeared below.

Alariq followed.

The cellar was large and dry, and well-lit by several wall-mounted oil lamps. The perfect quarters for dwarfs. A rectangular wooden frame lay in the corner. Alariq saw some fabric heaped in a pile inside. He realized it was a bed frame, meant to house a straw-filled mattress. Noting some sewing supplies, he supposed the others were in the process of repairing it.

Good. He hated thinking about old Brimir sleeping on the floor, with his aching joints.

"It's not so bad," Brimir said with a small smile.

Alariq chuckled. Brimir always had a knack for knowing what he was thinking. Alariq wished he could say the reverse was true, especially lately.

"I'm glad she had somewhere underground for us to sleep. It feels like home." Brimir paused, his eyes darkening. "I mean, it feels like Ishtara."

Alariq opened his mouth to say something, anything, about how sorry he was that Brimir was not back home, in his soft bed, with his people. But there were no words. So he closed it again.

"I'm just sorry the three of you have to sleep upstairs," Brimir said.

"We don't mind. I think Ford and Asher actually prefer it. And I'm used to it, being out on border patrol all the time," Alariq responded.

"Yes, that was always what I hated most about the service. The sleeping above ground. I never could get used to it." Brimir looked awkwardly around the room.

It was very unlike Brimir to engage in small talk when something was on his mind. And something was clearly on his mind. Alariq started growing suspicious, knowing that whatever it was, Brimir didn't want to tell him. Which meant Alariq wasn't going to like it.

"What's on your mind, Brimir?" Alariq asked.

Brimir met his eyes. "She's going to be risking her life for us. For you."

Alariq met Brimir's gaze, his expression even.

"She deserves to know the real reason she's risking it." Brimir fixed Alariq with the stare he'd become so familiar with over the past decades. It was the kind of stare a father gave his son when he was trying to get his son to do the right thing on his own, without having to issue an order.

Alariq couldn't say he hadn't thought about confessing the real reason for their presence in Loraheem to Tianna. Brimir was right, of course. She deserved to know that she was fighting a battle for a group of dwarfs accused of treason. It was only his mistrust of her that held him back.

Though honestly, what could she really do with the information? It is not as if they were fugitives from Tanith or in hiding from some enemy...other than the ettins, and that was of their own making. He'd thought about it many times over and could not see a way in which she could use the information against them.

Yet, something still held him back.

Alariq nodded curtly to Brimir before turning and ascending the ladder. He walked out into the rain without speaking to any of the others, not even bothering to hunch his shoulders against the weather.

He found Ford and Asher sitting in the dining area on the second floor, feet kicked up on the table. So instead of stopping there as he had originally planned, he continued up to the main bedroom, soaked. He took off his shirt and hung it on the bedpost. Each of the four soldiers had a change of clothes in their pack, and Gideon had brought along several for himself, which he had been sharing with Callum and Brimir. Alariq stared at the shirt. What would they do when they wore out? He'd never even thought about such a thing before. And it was still hard to believe he had to think about it now. Alariq couldn't take his eyes off the stupid shirt on Tianna's bedpost.

There were two beds in the room, but Tianna, without anyone noticing, had brought down a mattress and laid it on the floor. He suspected, now that he thought about it, that it must be her own. Asher slept on it, in the corner, behind the door.

Finally, he tore his eyes away from his shirt and sat down on the edge of his bed, looking out the window, not caring that all he saw was the deluge of rain, for he wasn't really looking.

Telling Tianna the truth. He had to admit he was worried she would refuse to help them if she knew they were exiles. And he hated that he was worried about it. Because it meant he depended on her. He hated depending on others. It gave others power over him. And now, more than ever, the thought that someone had power over him made his stomach ache worse than any impending battle. Especially someone he didn't trust.

But in all honesty, he did not really believe she would turn them away. Alariq couldn't say why, exactly. He only knew that his gut was telling him the truth wouldn't change her mind about ousting the ettins from Dendreya.

But still he sat. He did not rise and ascend the stairs to her room and simply tell the truth. It damn near ate a hole through his stomach to admit, even just to himself, why.

I care what she thinks about me.

He did. Alariq did not trust the tiny golden-haired vixen. And he certainly did not like her. But he did respect her.

She had saved them. More than once. And she was smart. And she lived out here all alone, managed without help from anyone, without depending on others. He had no choice but to respect her. If pressed, he'd have to admit he was even a little envious of her and her situation.

He took a deep breath and pulled on his still-damp shirt, seeing no need at getting the other one wet too. He exited the room and ascended the stairs to the top floor. He stood outside the door, grateful that the denser branches provided more shield from the rain up here.

He knocked lightly on the door.

It swung slowly open and Tianna's slightly surprised face stared back at him.

He had meant to sit down with her and explain it slowly. Explain how the king's son had accused him of consorting with the enemy, but how it wasn't true. And how much Dendreya meant to the others, who were the real victims of the whole affair. And then he meant to implore her to please continue to help them, because the others deserved a place that felt like home again.

But he didn't say any of that.

In his defense, he started to. "We did not come to Loraheem to see if Dendreya was still a viable commerce center," he said.

But Tianna held up her hand.

Alariq stopped.

When she spoke, her voice was calm. "Does your purpose here endanger me or the neighboring villages in any way?"

"No," Alariq said slowly, his voice deep.

"Then I do not need to know."

She held his gaze for a moment more and then closed the door in his face. He wasn't sure, but he thought she smiled just a bit at him first.

He stood there for a moment, rainwater dripping off the leaves above onto his head and shoulders, completely at a loss. He simply could not make sense of their hostess.

Back on the main floor, Brimir was preparing an early dinner. Tianna came down shortly after Alariq and fell in to help the old dwarf. She gave no indication of their conversation. If one could call their brief exchange a conversation.

They ate in silence. It seemed to Alariq as though everyone was moving in slow motion, even their chewing. After dinner, he expected Tianna to disappear upstairs, as usual, but she stayed on the main floor. She prepared a hot, sweet drink she said was made from a mix of leaves and herbs found in the forest and sweetened with honey from the nearby beehives. Alariq almost refused it, but at the last second nodded when she silently offered to pour him a cup.

The drink appeared to perk everyone up. Ford told the story of Asher switching one of their sister's tea for hot laundry water, in which their mother had just cleaned their breeches, when he was a young dwarfling. Callum recounted a classic, well-known comedic tale of a baker and his troubles with the fairer sex, which Tianna had never heard before, and appeared to find delightfully amusing. It was one of those stories that was still funny, no matter how many times one heard it.

It was not long before all of them were laughing and exchanging stories and jokes. Tianna told one of her own, a children's fable about a rabbit eluding capture by a comically incompetent duo of predators. Alariq found the corners of his mouth twitching more than once.

Things turned slightly more solemn as Gideon and Brimir sang an old dwarfish folk song, part of which was in the ancient dwarfish language that was only ever uttered in songs such as these, most of which had been long forgotten.

They all sat, quietly, reverently, afterwards, just enjoying one another's presence. Alariq was even glad Tianna had chosen to stay. He had faith in their plan, but whenever there was combat, there was always a chance of death. This night could be the last for any one of them and he was glad they had spent it happy and together.

Alariq retired to his shared bedroom shortly thereafter. Ford soon followed. The storm was so loud, he almost did not hear Asher enter the room a while later. But then he slept. Deeply and contentedly. His last thought was how grateful he was that Tianna had not required an explanation. He thought he might still tell her the whole story someday...but he was glad it hadn't been today.

The only thing that kept the night from being perfect was a strange dream he had.

He was walking alone in the forest outside of Ishtara. He had no weapons or armor, or even the thick leather vest he often wore. He wandered the woods, taking notice of how much smaller and sparser the trees and other foliage were here than in Loraheem.

He came to a path and although it was not familiar to him, he knew going right would lead to Ishtara and left out of the mountains and away from the city. He turned right. But as soon as he stepped on the path, a person appeared before him. It was a dwarf. Haamith, the king's son. Rather than feel rage at the one responsible for his exile, however, Alariq walked over to him calmly. And then he embraced him briefly before turning and striding in the opposite direction.

He awoke in the same position in which he had fallen asleep to the sound of gentle rain. He walked to the window, trying to make sense of the dream, its strangeness making him feel askew.

He looked out through the slightly fogged glass. The worst of the storm had blown itself out and the forest was much brighter today. He could see to the edge of the clearing.

He hunched his shoulders against the light, cold rain as he

exited their bedroom and headed down to the main floor. He heard footsteps above him and Tianna rounded the corner. They did not speak, but he waited for her to catch up to him and they walked down together.

Brimir, as expected, was already making breakfast.

Soon joined by the others, they ate breakfast and listened as the rain slowed. They would need to leave right after the meal. The ground was thirsty and the creek should dry fairly quickly once the rain stopped, so it needed to be blocked by then to make it look as though it had been blocked by debris during the storm. Alariq did not know what kind of stores the ettins kept, so he did not know how long it would take them to check the creek. They would just have to wait.

They set out toward the beach, all armed, including Tianna, who carried her small bow across her shoulder, the intricate knife she had almost used against Asher that first night, tucked in a small scabbard strapped to her calf, and a long, but delicate looking sword at her hip. Alariq did not think it would stand up to battle, but had learned better than to needlessly pester their hostess, especially considering she was about to help them take on a bunch of ettins.

He suddenly realized he did not know if she even had fighting experience and what an incredible oversight this was. He'd been too busy thinking about whether he could trust her as an ally to determine whether he could rely on her as a fighter. Though to be fair, she'd handled Asher easily enough that first night.

Alariq slowed his pace and allowed Tianna to catch up to him. "Are you ready?" he asked her quietly, so that only they could hear.

She smiled that tiny smile that came when she was amused. "Are you asking me if I know what I'm doing?"

Alariq did not answer, disconcerted that she knew exactly what he had been thinking.

Tianna apparently wasn't expecting an answer because she continued anyway. "I can take care of myself." She stopped and turned to face him, looking him directly in the eye. He did the same. "I won't be a liability," she said seriously.

"So you have fought before?" he asked.

But Tianna had said all she was going to and she turned and walked after the other dwarfs with brisk, determined strides.

Alariq felt a flicker of annoyance, but supposed he should be grateful she had reassured him at all. He fell back in with the group, trying to clear his head for what was to come.

When they reached the beach, they followed the edge of the forest to the creek, so as not to leave footprints in the wet sand. It was still drizzling, but only just. It was more of a mist that seemed just barely too heavy to stay afloat in the air. Blainn, Ford, and Asher patrolled the tree line while the others began pulling debris from the forest, beach, and water.

Alariq and Callum brought over two large tree branches with which they formed an X a few paces beyond where the lake poured into the creek. Then they moved a large rock under the branches. The flow from the lake slowed.

Tianna brought a variety of small, smooth rocks and shells from the beach and filled in the gaps under the water line created by the round boulder. Gideon and Brimir waded a few paces into the water and pulled up armfuls of seaweed and stuffed it around the branches. They stuck handfuls of clay from the creek bed into the remaining holes. The flow became a steady trickle.

They all grabbed some sticks and leaves and threw it on top to make the debris look more haphazard. The deed was done. Some water was still getting through, but it was considerably less than before, and what did find its way into the creek was very murky.

The rain stopped. To get rid of their tracks, Tianna and Callum, who were the smallest and lightest filled two buckets they had brought with them with water and obscured the tracks in the wet sand, backing slowly toward the tree line, while the others got into position.

It was a long wait. Noon came and went. Alariq, Asher, and Tianna, sat perched in trees at the edge of the forest overlooking the creek. Everyone else was also in their respective planned position.

Alariq looked through the branches of his tree, sizing up Tianna's bow. It looked very similar to Asher's, the same dark wood, but was considerably smaller, with slight backward curving at the ends.

Alariq looked at his own bow. It seemed much less elegant than Asher and Tianna's bows. It was a dark, but sparkly gray, beautiful in its own way. He'd never seen another starmetal crossbow before. Arrows, yes, lots of armor, and even swords and daggers. But as far as he knew, his bow was unique. Not because starmetal itself was rare. Showers of the fallen stars occurred regularly in the Brackish Mountains, usually preceded by some sort of pageant of light in the sky, which warned everyone to stay indoors. Rather, it was the labor and highly-specialized knowledge required to create items made from starmetal that made it extremely valuable. The dwarfs of Ishtara had created the forging technique and as far as Alariq knew, the knowledge behind starmetal remained a secret kept by his people.

Alariq was growing stiff, his muscles were tingling from remaining in such a constrained position. He stood up carefully in the branches and stretched himself out. The hours slid past achingly slowly. The uncomfortable position and what lay ahead made time stretch out seemingly without end. He felt bad for the other four in the trees and envied the three on the ground, though he knew they would be only slightly better off.

Alariq remembered once, during the Ettinwar, when he'd been keeping watch on an enemy camp. He'd been concealed in some bushes beside a road. He'd watched as a tiny snail slowly made its way across it. He remembered thinking about how enormous the road must have seemed to the snail, when to him it was only a few steps.

He felt something small hit him in the outer thigh. He looked over and saw Asher motioning silently to him. Alariq was immediately alert, but then he noticed Asher was smiling. On further examination, he realized Asher wasn't just smiling, but actually barely restraining himself from outright laughing. Asher motioned to the tree on the other side of Alariq. Alariq had to adjust his positioning to see it, but once he did, he saw what was causing Asher so much mirth.

And it was definitely not funny to him.

In the tree beside him, Tianna was sleeping.

She had hooked her bow over a short branch and looped her arm through it, nestled into a curve in the trunk, and was fast asleep. She looked completely at peace, as though this was no different than sleeping snuggled in a comfortable bed.

Alariq was furious. She was putting herself, all of his fighters, and the mission in danger. *And it's not even nighttime!* Alariq thought. It was barely dusk.

He glared at her, willing his stare to wake her.

And then he heard it. The signal from Callum, a native bird call that Tianna had taught them.

If Alariq had blinked, he would have missed it. Tianna was instantly awake and in one fluid motion swept the bow from her arm and off the branch and notched an arrow Alariq hadn't noticed was in her lap.

His awe must have shown on his face because Tianna, who glanced over at him, shot him one of her smirks. And before she returned her eyes to the place where the creek met the forest—she winked.

Suppressing the variety of emotions that quick exchange had aroused, Alariq checked that his bow was cocked and looked over to make sure Asher was likewise ready. He was. Alariq positioned his crossbow, using a branch as a brace, and turned his full attention to the same place on which Tianna and Asher were hyperfocused.

He waited. He could hear them. Then he could smell them.

The game was on.

11

A Call Too Close

Alariq saw a giant foot before anything else. He was strung so tight, he almost let his arrow fly right then, but he managed to hold on to his composure. He took a deep breath, held it for a moment, and let the ettin walk out onto the beach. Three more followed.

Alariq's stomach fluttered and sank at the same time. Getting rid of four ettins would not make much of a dent in the enemy forces, but, on the other hand, Alariq knew their own odds of all surviving were a lot better with four adversaries instead of eight.

Alariq kept his eyes completely focused on the tallest ettin, his target. Asher was to take the shortest, and Tianna, any of the others, preferably the most threatening. They needed to draw the ettins all the way out on the beach, so they could not run for cover in the trees.

The ettins caught sight of the blockage in the creek and headed toward it, completely focused on the water. They reached the creek and two of them bent over the obstruction the dwarfs had put in place.

Now was the time. Alariq fired his arrow directly at the tallest ettin, who was gazing out over the lake, clearly not suspecting any kind of attack. Before it even hit its mark, which it did, Alariq heard two more arrows loosed on either side of him.

Three arrows struck three ettins. Alariq's hit the tallest in the side and it howled in pain, immediately reaching across its body and ripping the arrow from its midriff. Asher's arrow hit the shortest ettin, which unfortunately had bent over to unblock the creek, in the back of its upper leg. The ettin was driven to his knees in the sand. Tianna's arrow had been truest. It had hit the other standing ettin, which had been looking almost exactly at them, directly in the eye. Its body lay on the ground, twitching.

Well, she certainly lives up to the namesake of the group, Alariq thought, thinking of Asher and the other Deadeyes, hoping, and knowing at the same time, that her shot wasn't just lucky.

Alariq loaded another bolt. Asher and Tianna had already sent two other arrows at the ettins, both of them hitting the one remaining ettin who had not yet been shot. It seemed to have just determined the direction from which their attack had come and started to charge, giving them a perfect target. One arrow hit it in the stomach and the other in the neck. The tallest glanced down at one dead and two wounded comrades, gripped the wound in its side, and ran for the trees.

Just before it reached the cover of the tree line, Alariq's arrow buried itself in the ettin's back shoulder. Alariq gave the signal to the ground forces and within seconds Brimir and Callum appeared at the edge of the forest, cutting the ettin off. Alariq could hear Ford, Blainn, and Gideon making their way up the beach, but he kept his attention on the fleeing ettin, trusting the others to take care of the remaining two by the creek mouth.

He reloaded his crossbow again just as the ettin reached Brimir and Callum. Alariq hit his foe in the upper arm, which wielded an ax. It dropped the ax and used its right arm to pull a large kr.ife, clearly meant for utility, not fighting.

Alariq started to reload, but two silver streaks flashed through his vision. Brimir's two throwing knives buried themselves in the ettin's shoulder and forearm.

The old man can still fight, Alariq thought with a smile.

Brimir was now weaponless. Callum stepped up and jabbed at the creature fruitlessly. Alariq loosed one final arrow, striking the ettin in the back, and then dropped his bow on the beach and pulled his sword. The ettin turned toward Alariq.

Callum used the ettin's distraction to his advantage, lunging forward and stabbing his sword into the back of their enemy's thigh. Blood spurted over the young dwarf.

Alariq was about to rejoice, knowing Callum had hit something vital, but the ettin wasn't done yet.

It let out a feral roar and then turned back toward Callum swinging its enormous fist with the force of a catapult. It struck Callum directly in the chest and he went flying backward several paces and slammed into a tree trunk.

Brimir picked up Callum's sword and charged the creature, who was already starting to weave around, disoriented from blood loss. They easily avoided its feeble swats and two blows each from Alariq and Brimir ended it.

"See to Callum," Alariq said to Brimir and he took off back toward the others.

Only he needn't have worried about the rest of his group. Asher and Tianna's onslaught of arrows had been incredibly efficient. They'd hit the ettins in just the right places, the eyes and the neck. Ford and Blainn delivered a few final blows, but Gideon didn't even need to fight.

"Everyone alright?" Alariq asked, though he knew they were all fine.

No one even bothered to answer him. All of them were smiling widely.

Then they noticed Brimir and Callum.

Alariq stopped running toward the others and reversed course yet again back to the forest's edge, where Brimir was still trying to rouse Callum.

Out of the corner of his eye Alariq saw Tianna hit the ground and fall in behind him.

When he reached his cousin, he dropped his sword and knelt.

"He's breathing," Brimir said, unnecessarily as Alariq already had his hand to Callum's neck, feeling his pulse.

Tianna showed up at his side.

"Water," he barked.

She immediately obeyed.

The others joined them at the tree line and all gathered around Callum, their faces creased with concern.

Alariq kept his hand on Callum's pulse and his eyes on his chest, feeling his heartbeat and watching his breathing, reassuring himself his cousin was alright.

Tianna returned with water in her canteen.

Alariq took it and poured some into his hands and then splashed it gently on Callum's face.

A noise in the forest drew his attention. He looked around for any sign of more enemies, but saw nothing. But it brought him back to his senses.

He handed the canteen to Brimir and turned to the others.

"Gideon. Blainn. Go take up the watch post down the creek. Give us the signal when more come. Once means they sent another small group and twice means it's the whole ettinhorde."

They obeyed immediately. Alariq looked at Asher, Ford, and Tianna.

"We need to get the bodies into the lake." Alariq's tone was clipped, efficient.

"You stay with—" Ford began, but Alariq cut him off.

"My being here will make no difference as to when he awakens," he said simply. "But if we don't get these creatures into the lake, this whole thing has been for nothing."

They jogged over to the ettin who had knocked out Callum. It took all four of them to drag it over to the other bodies, alternatively lifting, pushing, rolling, and pulling.

From there, it was an even harder task, maneuvering the ettins out into the deeper parts of the water. They had to pull them out past the point where they could touch the bottom. Having no need for it, dwarfs were not natural swimmers. Fortunately for Alariq, it was a requirement to advance to any higher rank in the dwarfish army, so he and Ford, as well as Brimir and Blainn, had learned the skill long ago. Asher, who had been taught the basics by Ford, could stay above the waterline, but was of essentially no help. Tianna, on the other hand, was easily the most adept of all of them.

The ettins, consisting almost wholly of muscle, sank, but unwilling to risk them floating to the surface later, Alariq, Tianna, and Ford took turns diving down and tying rocks to their arms and feet. They kept careful watch for the lake creatures on whom the dwarfs intended to blame the attack. The finfiends might not be guilty of attacking the ettins, but that did not mean they were innocent.

Alariq kept glancing over at Brimir and Callum. He watched as the old dwarf tried various tactics: water on the face, pressure points in the hands, even pricking Callum's finger with a knife.

Still nothing.

Alariq focused on the task in front of him, unable to think about the possibility that Callum might not be alright. He'd seen dwarfs much bigger than Callum take hits to the chest like that from an ettin. Sometimes they were fine. But occasionally, their hearts simply gave out, sometimes days later. Even if Callum woke up, Alariq knew better than to let himself be relieved just yet.

Finally, the four of them managed to adequately submerge the ettins. Alariq looked back at Brimir and the old man was waving at him.

For a second, fear gripped Alariq, but then he saw Brimir was smiling. Callum sat, his hand rubbing his chest, coughing.

Alariq turned to the other three. "Can you take care of the rest?"

They all nodded and immediately went to work doing their best to obscure footprints and the trail they'd made dragging that first ettin to the lake.

Alariq jogged back to Callum, pausing to pick up his bow and sword, and knelt once more by his cousin.

"You alright?" he asked.

Callum nodded.

"How does your chest feel?"

"Like I was run over by a horse and cart." Callum looked up and made a weak attempt at a smile.

"And your heart?" Alariq prodded.

"A little funny," Callum responded. "Just...slightly off kilter, you know?"

Alariq nodded. He turned to Brimir.

"Get him back to the treehome."

"No!" Callum almost shouted and then coughed again.

"You can't fight like this," Alariq said, more harshly than he'd intended. Callum probably didn't realize his heart might've been damaged. He didn't realize he wasn't out of danger yet.

Callum looked back stubbornly.

"Fine," he said. "But you don't need to lose another fighter. I'll hide back on the beach with the others and only come out if needed."

Before Alariq could respond (with a resounding and conversation-ending *no*), he heard it.

The signal.

More ettins were on their way.

"Go," he hissed. "Hide behind the trees."

The three of them ran, Callum somewhat awkwardly, until they reached the trees where Tianna and Asher hid. Alariq pulled himself up while Brimir and Callum nestled down in the roots on the other side of the tree.

Alariq turned his attention back toward where the other ettins had emerged from the trees. He once again braced his bow on the branch in front of him.

Then came the grumbling voices of ettins and the crushing of brush. Two gray giants emerged from the trees. Just two. Alariq exhaled his disappointment.

The plan was the same. Wait and draw the ettins out onto the beach.

But the ettins looked wary when there was no sign of their fellow soldiers. The taller one ducked his head and spoke quietly to the other.

Alariq knew they couldn't wait. He gripped his crossbow tightly and pulled the trigger.

It hit the taller ettin in the middle of the chest. The other, much darker, ettin reacted instantly. It pulled its club, which was spiked on one side, from a sling on its back and used it to shield its face and chest. It looked in Alariq's direction for the source of the attack. Asher's arrow struck the club directly where the ettins face would have been.

Alariq put his foot in the stirrup, cocked the bow, and loaded another metal arrow into the groove. Asher had already fired again and hit the taller ettin, who had just drawn its sword, this time in the stomach. Both ettins were backing reluctantly into the woods, clearly wary of an attack to their rear from within the black forest.

Tianna still had not fired her first arrow. Alariq pulled his trigger for a second time and quickly looked over to her tree. He saw no sign of her.

His distraction had caused him to miss his target. He'd hit the tall one again, but in the forearm.

But despite Alariq's poor hit, the taller ettin was in trouble, four arrows protruding from various places on its form, Asher having added yet another to the ettin's chest. It seemed the shorter ettin had realized the impending fatality of its partner, because it drew himself behind the taller one and started to back away as quickly as it could.

Alariq gave the signal for the ground forces to charge, later than he should have, because he was still wondering about Tianna's whereabouts. Asher fired several more arrows, only one of which hit the remaining ettin's club, none finding their true mark.

Things were getting desperate. The ettin had almost disappeared into the forest. The trees were providing it cover now. It had retreated away from the creek, instead of back down it, so Blainn and Gideon would be attacking from the side, instead of from behind, as planned. Alariq leapt down from the tree.

At this point, the ettin realized his (barely) living shield was rapidly becoming a hindrance, rather than a help. Alariq was closing in and he could hear the others behind him. The ettin realized now was the time to run. He shoved his now unconscious partner in Alariq's general direction, hunched down, and made to run for it.

It turned directly into the path of Tianna's sword. She had thrown it from behind a tree and hit her mark exactly. The ettin fell backwards from the force of her throw, dead.

Alariq rushed over to the first ettin to make sure it was dead too. It was. He, Tianna, Gideon, and Blainn converged on the second one at the same moment.

Alariq glared at Tianna, his eyes wide, but his brows furrowed. "That was not the plan," he almost yelled, as the other three arrived.

"No, it was not. But if we had stuck to the plan, he might've gotten away. Or worse," she nodded toward Gideon and Blainn, "what happened to Callum might've happened to one of them."

Was she insinuating Callum's injury was his fault? Alariq's muscles clenched involuntarily. He'd never had his orders defied before. But it was more than just ego. The others had been counting on her being in the exact position she was supposed to be in. What if the ettin had run out on the beach or they'd needed her to cover them? And her absence was what had distracted him in the first place!

Alariq turned his back on her and addressed the others. "We need to get them moved and fast. When yet another group does not return to Dendreya, they will most certainly know something is afoot and come in greater numbers."

The group made quick work of these two ettins, mechanically following the same procedure as before. Callum tried to help, but Alariq ordered him to stay seated.

This time, they unblocked the creek, leaving only traces of debris at the mouth of the creek.

When they were done, Alariq spoke, still ignoring Tianna. "I'm staying to see how the ettins respond. See if our plan to blame the attack on the finfiends worked. I need one more to stay with me. Who's not tired?"

"I'll stay," said Asher immediately.

"Good. Everyone else, back to Tianna's."

Alariq turned and began to look for a place to hide, one farther away from the attack site, the best vantage point from which to see, but not be seen. He turned back just in time to see Tianna's golden hair disappear into the blackness.

12

One Step Forward

There is an old expression you have probably never heard before: *from post to pillar.* It comes from the game of real tennis. (Yes, *real* tennis. You see, the "tennis" with which most are familiar is actually *lawn* tennis, which is one of many descended iterations of real tennis, which is played indoors and whose rules are infinitely more lax and complex.) The expression is said to come from a particular match between a king and a lowly serf who had quite the reputation as a skilled tennis player. The story goes that the serf boy returned the king's pathetic serve so forcefully that it soared over the post supporting the rope dividing the court, hit the pillar behind the king that supported the ceiling, and returned back over the rope to the serf boy once again, who promptly hit the ball a second time, scoring not one, but two points against the king.

Thus the expression *from post to pillar* was born, which means to move about rapidly hither and thither. It does *not* mean, as some ignorant fools with dark thoughts maintain, to go from the playing court to the hangman's noose, although, given the fate of the poor serf boy who so thoroughly trounced the king, I suppose it is understandable how such a misconception arose.

Regardless, you now know what I mean when I say Alariq's mood had yet again gone from post to pillar.

Whish. Thud.

Whish. Thud.

Whish. Thud.

Alariq swung the axe in smooth motions.

He had chopped enough wood to last them a month, considering how mild the weather was in Loraheem, even in the winter. But he kept going because it allowed his mind to go blank.

He could not explain his malcontent. Callum was doing well and their plan appeared to have worked. After the rest of the group had left to return to the treehome, he and Asher waited in the trees for several hours before the ettins finally came. They were out in force and well-armed, but grumbling about their companions. All but the tattooed one. He was silent, and even in the dark, Alariq could see he was taking the missing ettins seriously.

A leader's job, Alariq thought. When he had been First Authority, Alariq could not ignore a potential threat. No matter how unlikely or implausible something might seem, if there was a shred of evidence that his company, city, or mission was in danger, he could not afford to make light of it.

The ettins had searched the beach, seen the signs of struggle by the waterline, and come to the conclusion that something from the lake had dragged their compatriots in. They heard the commander give the order that no one was to go near the water alone or unarmed. Then he told the others to clear the creek quickly, while the rest stood guard, and then they all returned to Dendreya.

Maybe it was the fact that they had only killed six ettins and were essentially in the same place they were before the skirmish on the beach. He and Asher had counted the ettins as best they could in the dark. Alariq counted twenty-nine and Asher twenty-six. Assuming they left a few at Dendreya, that still meant the ettins numbered over thirty. *Still too many for a direct attack,* Alariq thought.

Whish. Thud! Quicker and more forcefully now. *Whish, thud!* Or maybe it was his argument with Tianna.

Whish, thud! The axe split through the piece of wood and buried itself in the tree trunk underneath. He left it where it fell and stood there, chest heaving, shoulders rising and falling, remembering the events that transpired after the attack.

After the ettins had left the beach, he had stayed in the tree for some time. Asher sat beside him, without saying a word. When Alariq climbed down, Asher followed, wordlessly, back to the treehome. The dwarfs had all waited up for him, despite the fact it was almost dawn. Even Callum. He briefly told them the good news and then, without asking where she was, headed up to Tianna's room.

He stopped on the penultimate floor and opened the door without knocking. He scanned the room quickly, his eyes sweeping around the round room. It was her bedroom, as the others had reported, and very like the bottom floor, warm and cluttered, but in a pleasing way. It was empty, though, so he immediately ascended to the top floor of the treehome, again entering without knocking, knowing she would be inside.

He barely had time to take in his surroundings before she started yelling at him for coming up there and barging in without knocking. He did not remember all that was said between them, so loud was the pounding of blood in his ears that night, but he knew he had essentially told her he would do whatever he wanted in order to protect his men. He told her she was never to disobey his orders again because if she endangered his company a second time, he would consider *her* the enemy, instead of the ettins.

She had said a lot of things back, but those words were not the ones that bothered him. It was *his* words that were eating at him right now.

And oh, how he hated it.

Guilt. That's what you feel, a voice deep inside him said.

When he had turned to leave Tianna, he found Asher standing behind him, having silently come up the staircase. At the time, he'd barely registered it. He brushed past and Asher followed him down without a word a few seconds later. But now

Alariq wondered...why *had* he been up there?

Alariq didn't know, but he didn't like it. Or maybe he didn't like it *because* he didn't know. Alariq was accustomed to a clear head, not this mangled mess that currently made up his thoughts.

He sat down, harder than he meant to, bruising his rump. He hooked his arms over his bent knees and hung his head between them, thinking about the person who was most responsible for his current state.

He had, in essence, threatened her. *Do what I say or be on your guard.* While he hadn't said those words exactly, that's what it boiled down to, calling her the enemy.

He shouldn't feel guilty, he told himself. If any of his soldiers in Division Three had defied a direct order, he would have said the same thing. Well, *essentially* the same thing.

But she isn't one of your soldiers, the voice whispered. *And neither are the rest of them. They're here because they choose to be, not on your orders.*

And then there was Callum. His cousin was injured because of him. He was still coughing occasionally and had one of the worst bruises Alariq had ever seen, but it seemed he was going to be alright. But still, it had been much too close a call...

Alariq stood up, unsure of what he meant to do. Tianna had not said a single word to him since that early morning several days ago. The rest of the group, except Callum, had resumed their reconnaissance of the ettins and except for two more large excursions to the beach to search for whatever had taken their companions, their routines remained unchanged. They had been discussing other ideas on how to lure small groups of ettins out, but they kept coming up empty. Tianna had not participated in any of these discussions and Alariq grudgingly admitted to himself they might be further along in their planning if she were still helping them.

He had no choice then. They needed her and he'd have to apologize.

He gritted his teeth, squared his shoulders, and headed back through the forest toward the treehome.

He stopped. He turned and gathered an armful of the wood

he'd been chopping.

Better take a peace offering.

He set the wood down in the wood pile located on the edge of the clearing where two trees were close together. Tianna had hung some kind of waterproof cloth made from seaweed between the trees, which kept the wood dry.

He stood looking up at her room, thinking about what he would say and coming up with absolutely nothing.

He had just headed for the staircase when he heard her voice. It was coming through the open window on the main floor. He heard his name.

His apologetic mood evaporated at the fact that she was talking about him to his own men behind his back. And while guilt had been gnawing at his insides, no less! He headed for the door, but pulled up short, just beside the window. He could see Tianna's reflection in the glass.

"You chose to follow him, even into exile, when his own family did not? I assumed he did not have family." Tianna's voice was cold, but there was also a note of confusion in her tone. "Why did they not come with him too?"

The others had clearly told her of the exile. Brimir probably thought she already knew.

"They have a life in Ishtara. They have safety and security there." Brimir spoke as if he were explaining the way something worked to a small child.

"So did all of you," Tianna responded, her voice quiet.

"We were with Alariq," Ford's deep, distinctive voice said. He was using his "talking-to-his-subordinates" voice that seemed to come so naturally to him. "Blainn and I, the night Haamith said he was meeting with Karxani dwarfs. We know his innocence as fact."

Alariq saw the back of Blainn's head nod.

"And if my brother says he's innocent, he's innocent." Asher's tone was lighter, more good-natured. "But I've also known Alariq for four decades, and fought under him for almost two. He would not do what he was accused of. He would not commit treason. He would not stand against Ishtara."

"All the more reason his family would have stood up for him

as well," Tianna said, her voice filled with doubt.

"He only has two blood relatives left. A brother, Garrin, who lost a leg in the Ettinwar, and his mother, who is the only one left to care for Garrin."

Alariq willed Brimir not to say the words he knew were coming next.

"And then a wife. Rheia."

The words were said matter-of-factly, but Tianna's head snapped in Brimir's direction, as though he had just told her he planned to paint her treehome dandelion yellow.

"He has a wife?" Tianna's tone was carefully controlled. "What happened to her?"

"What do you mean?" Ford asked, puzzled. "Nothing."

Tianna's face did not change, but even in the glass, Alariq could see her amber eyes harden.

"But she's not here." It was a statement, not a question.

The dwarfs left at the table looked around quizzically at one another.

Even her reflection was frightening. It was as if her face turned to stone and her eyes bored, white hot, into Ford.

Before she could open her mouth, Brimir spoke, his voice gentle and knowing. "You must understand, Tianna. Dwarfs are very practical by nature. We don't often marry for love. Marriage is a way to unite families, cement friendships, and secure safety, stability, and if you're lucky, companionship. Rheia's actions were not unexpected, least of all by Alariq."

Alariq watched Tianna's face carefully, trying to discern her thoughts. But, as was so often the case, she was unreadable.

"Technically, he doesn't have a wife anymore," Callum said matter-of-factly.

Tianna simply looked at him, her face still like stone.

Callum shifted uncomfortably and absentmindedly rubbed his chest before he continued, more out of nervousness than a desire to inform. "Exile cuts off all ties with those in Ishtara. Of blood and covenant. He cannot inherit from his family, and his marriage will have been invalidated by now."

But still Tianna continued to stare. When she finally spoke, her voice was strained. "I just...can't imagine living that way.

Where I come from...well, love is the *only* reason people decide to marry. I cannot imagine a marriage, a life..." Her voice trailed off and she turned her head and gazed into the forest. If he were standing a half a pace to the right, she would have looked right at him.

The other dwarfs seemed as surprised as he was to hear her speak so personally. They looked around at one another, seemingly to figure out how they should respond. Only Asher continued to look at Tianna. His intent gaze on her made Alariq angry, though he wasn't entirely certain why. It felt...disloyal. Asher opened his mouth, as if to speak, but at the same moment Tianna rose quickly from the table and walked to the door.

Alariq could have tried to hide or pretended he had just come down the stairs, but instead he stood exactly where he was.

Tianna opened the door and met his gaze.

He scrutinized her face for a clue as to her thoughts. She was looking at him in a slightly different way. As they stared at each other, he replayed the conversation he had just overheard in his head, trying to think of what could have triggered such a change in outlook toward him. But the only thing that stuck out to him was that his family and wife had stayed behind. And why would that make her think better of him?

Slowly, Tianna tilted her head slightly to one side. Then she nodded.

Without understanding what was transpiring between them, Alariq nodded back.

Then, before brushing past him and heading up the stairs, she gave him a small smile. Not of pity, but encouragement. Alariq had no idea why, but he felt much better.

Things in the treehome went back to normal after that. Tianna resumed her place among the group and Alariq treated her return as though nothing had happened.

It had been over a week since the fight at the creek, and so far they had come up with no further ideas. They couldn't block the creek again because the ettins were now expecting it to be an ambush. They would no doubt come to the beach in numbers. And four ettins had resulted in one of them being injured, in what could have been a fatal way. Alariq certainly wasn't willing to take on the entire horde.

"I think we may just have to accept that they're going to know they're under attack. I don't see a way we can trick them again," Gideon finally said, after hours of going round and round.

"No. We cannot give up that easily." Ford slapped his hand on the table. "Once they know they are being systematically eliminated, they will hole up inside the city walls and we'll have no hope."

"But they *have* to come out to get supplies," Callum repeated for the thousandth time.

Alariq was tired of hearing the same arguments over and over. They'd been keeping watch for any sign as to how the ettins might be getting food, but so far had learned nothing. "Tianna said they're getting supplies some other way. We have to assume that if they hole up, they're in there for good."

Tianna, who had opened her mouth, clearly about to say the very same thing, looked at him, eyebrows raised, bemused at his defense of her. He shrugged and gave her a small, half smile.

"What about the forest?" Asher asked. "I mean, it's very difficult to navigate, could we draw them in somehow? Separate them in the darkness?

Alariq shook his head. "It's too risky. We don't know how they will react to something like that. We cannot predict their movements. And if it fails, we are back at a bunch of ettins behind dwarf-built walls."

They continued like that for days. Finally, they came to the conclusion that they needed to wait for an opening created by the ettins. Tianna said they did occasionally hunt or go on village raids, so they decided to wait for the ettins to give them an opportunity.

It occurred to Alariq as he was falling asleep one night that a few weeks ago, he would have simply suggested they give up and move on to Dirnovaria. As he passed into sleep, he briefly registered how unsavory that prospect felt to him now.

That night he had the same dream he'd had over a week ago, where he walked in the woods outside Ishtara, came to a path, and then embraced the king's son. It unnerved him just as much as it had the first time.

A week passed before an opening was presented to them. Instead of being restless, as they had been before, the group seemed to have settled into a comfortable, albeit cramped, state. They all talked and joked frequently. They even played a game called Tiles, in which wooden pieces with dots burned into them were placed end to end in a line of play based on the values on each piece. Tianna showed them another interesting use, however, which was to set them up on their ends in elaborate systems and then knock the first tile over and watch them all fall, one after the other, in rapid succession. On first seeing it, Callum and Brimir found it delightfully funny. It all reminded Alariq of the comradery among his men during patrol of the border around Ishtara. Only now, he actually joined in occasionally.

Then, one mild and breezy day, Tianna and Asher came back from the watch post early, breathless and excited.

"They're going hunting tomorrow!" Asher's words came out between shallow breaths.

"How do you know?" Alariq immediately asked.

"We heard them," Tianna answered. "The guards were talking about it."

"Well, complaining, rather," Asher amended with a smile at Tianna. "Talking about how it wasn't fair they had to stay behind."

"How many are going?" Alariq's eyes moved back and forth quickly from Tianna to Asher.

Tianna shook her head. "They did not say."

Alariq knew this was the chance they'd been waiting for. But he did not like how rushed they were and how little they had to go on.

"We will need to watch them," he said, "see how many go on the hunt. If a large group goes, there will be nothing we can do. Even if they leave a small contingency behind, if we attack them in the city, they will know what's going on as soon as the others return."

"But if a smaller party goes, we can try to draw them into the forest." The words seemed to stumble over each other to get out of Asher's mouth. When they had originally discussed where to settle, Asher hadn't seemed particularly enthusiastic about any of their options, including Dendreya, but lately, he had become the most avid supporter of staying in Loraheem.

"How many do you think we can take?" Blainn asked the group.

"Quite a few if we can draw them in and split them up." Ford stood as he spoke.

Things were moving too quickly. Alariq held up his hands and silence immediately fell.

"We need to slow down." He turned to Tianna. "Do you know where they hunt?"

She nodded. "The southern quarter of Loraheem. They stay fairly close to Dendreya, within a few miles."

"Do you know that area of the forest?"

She nodded again. "The trees are not as thick over there. It does not get dark like it does here. We need to draw them east and north."

Alariq returned his attention to the entire group. "Ideas?"

"Well they would definitely chase us," Callum said.

Gideon joined the discussion. "But assuming it is a smaller group, they would probably send back for the others."

"We could anticipate that, and head them off on their way back to Dendreya," Asher responded.

"Then they'll know what's going on. The point of drawing them into the forest was to make them think the hunting party got lost."

"Do you really think that will work?" Tianna asked. "You don't think they'll be suspicious?"

"Of course they will be, but they'll have no proof. They're clearly not meant to be holed up inside that city, in such close quarters. I doubt they'll be willing to wall themselves in with only suspicions to go on. They might even send out a search party and we can whittle the pack down even further." Alariq was getting that good feeling in his gut that only a solid plan could give him. "You said yourself they avoid the forest out of fear of getting lost. So clearly they've thought it possible."

He continued. "The real issue is how big of a group they'll send out. When we first arrived at Dendreya, all but three had been out."

"That was a raid on the village just south of the Vestri River. They were gone for two weeks. You arrived at just the wrong moment. They always take the whole group for village raids." Tianna's words were hard and clipped. "I've only ever encountered them out hunting a few times, but the parties were always small, five to ten ettins."

"Why didn't you tell us that before?" Alariq demanded.

Tianna shrugged. "You didn't ask and it didn't seem relevant."

Alariq studied her for a moment. "Alright," he said after a long moment, willing (for once) to let it slide, "then we only need to be concerned about how to draw them into the forest. We don't want to leave any signs of a struggle and they can't know it's us, in case any ettins manage to get back to Dendreya."

"Then I'll draw them in."

Every face turned toward Tianna.

No one spoke for a moment. Finally, Alariq asked, "What do you mean?"

Tianna looked at him as though he were a bird repeatedly flying into a clean glass window. "I am not sure how else to say it," she said. "I will be the one to draw them in," she repeated, enunciating every word. "They've never seen me before, and I look like an easy target. They'll follow me in for sure. Plus, I know the forest best."

"And where would we be?" Alariq asked cautiously.

"We'll pick a spot, I think I know a good one. We can go this afternoon to scout it out. Tomorrow, I'll draw them in and you attack."

Alariq studied her face carefully. "Not alone. One of us will stay with you."

"No." It was simply stated and Tianna just looked at him, her gaze even.

"It wasn't a question." He kept his features as schooled as hers and returned her stare.

"You will only slow me down. And if we fail, and they see a dwarf, what then? You will have lost your anonymity. Wasn't that the whole point of this ruse?"

All of the other dwarfs were quiet, their faces moving back and forth between Tianna and Alariq during their exchange.

"And if they catch you?"

"They won't."

Alariq was about to respond, when Tianna grinned mischievously, her eyes twinkling.

"But if you don't believe me, I'd be more than happy to prove it to you."

13

And Two Steps Back

Alariq stood, looking down at the stick in his hand, wondering how he had gotten talked into this. He backed away and Tianna and Asher stepped up to the line he had just drawn in the dirt. They both crouched and perched on the balls of their feet, arms at right angles.

The eight of them were at the edge of the forest near the beach, where the trees were thinner. Alariq stepped away from the line and motioned to Callum, who was almost fully recovered and grinning from ear to ear.

"Ready?" Callum asked, his voice shaking with glee.

Tianna and Asher glanced at each other and, grinning, they looked up at Callum and answered affirmatively.

"Go!" he shouted.

They both took off. Asher managed to keep pace with Tianna for about four breaths, but then she was gone. Alariq had never seen anyone so fast, except maybe ettins, who weren't actually that fast, but whose long strides gave them such an advantage, allowing them to cover significantly more ground in half the time it took a dwarf. Although Tianna was not any taller than Asher, her proportions were very different. She had long legs and a short torso, whereas Asher, like all dwarfs, was the opposite, and much more muscular and stockier in build.

She arrived at the finish line, which Ford had drawn a few hundred paces down the tree line, and had already almost caught her breath by the time Asher crossed it behind her, head kicked back and arms pumping. He immediately collapsed onto his back, dragging in air.

The others jogged to meet them, heckling Asher the whole way. Alariq took his time following, thinking as he sauntered over.

Everyone else was laughing when they reached Asher and Tianna, the former still drawing in ragged breaths and the latter smiling triumphantly.

"Alright." Everyone quieted when Alariq spoke, but the large grins remained. "You're fast."

Tianna's grin turned into an *I told you so* smirk.

"But what we're talking about isn't a footrace. It's a group of ettins, armed, chasing you through a thick forest, trying to catch you and kill you."

The grins faded from all of the faces, except Tianna, who just kept on smiling.

"Fair enough. Let's do that then," she said.

"What?" Alariq asked, confused.

"All of you. Try and catch me." And with that she darted into the woods.

The dwarfs all stood there for a moment, looking around at one another as if to confirm that this was really happening. Then, all at once, they dashed after her.

The seven dwarfs chased the golden blur (because that's all she was in the dimly lit forest) through the trees. Once, Ford and Asher, working in tandem, managed to get her up a tree, but she climbed so high Alariq could no longer make out her face, and Asher, who weighed more than her, couldn't follow. Alariq thought the game was over and he and the others approached the tree. But just when they all reached the trunk, looking up at Tianna and Asher, she leapt from her perch and just managed to grab onto a branch of a neighboring tree. She fluidly swung herself up on top of the branch, balanced, and grabbed another one. In seemingly one motion, she swung over to a third tree and scaled down.

The chase was on again.

After almost an hour, Alariq conceded defeat. Even with their knowledge of the forest, which the ettins wouldn't have, they couldn't catch her. He even had the horrible feeling that she hadn't been trying her hardest either.

"Alright, alright," Alariq said between breaths.

Tianna popped out from behind a tree only a few strides away from him and grinned.

"So we're agreed? I'll draw them in and you'll all be waiting?"

Alariq hesitated only a moment before he nodded once. What choice did he have after that?

They returned to the treehome for lunch and ate quickly before heading back out. Tianna led them in a wide semicircle to the west of Dendreya and then headed south from there.

She pointed out the place she thought the dwarfs should wait. It wasn't a clearing, exactly, but rather an area where the soil was rocky, and the trees were sparser. There were several large boulders behind which some of the dwarfs could hide, while the rest would be concealed in the trees.

They next made their way cautiously to the ettins' hunting ground and Tianna pointed out the route she planned to take back to the dwarfs.

They timed out how long it should take Tianna to get from where she would pick up the ettins back to the dwarfs. They went over the plan until everyone knew it by heart, and returned to the treehome just after sunset, chatting amicably as they walked.

More than once, Alariq caught himself about to ask Tianna where she'd learned to fight. He had to remind himself not to let the newly relaxed atmosphere coax him into too much comfort. They were not friends, he and Tianna, although they may have settled into a partnership. Besides, he was sure she wouldn't answer him anyway.

In contrast to the eve before the last fight, they ate a quick supper and all went to bed, so tired were they from the day's escapades.

Alariq went to sleep that night with a small smile on his face and almost chuckled out loud as he recalled everyone's expressions after Tianna had sprinted into the trees. His sleep was heavy and dreamless.

Brimir roused Alariq and the others shortly before dawn and Alariq felt as if only moments had passed since he'd laid down. Tianna handed them all fruit from the forest and a handful of jerky, wrapped in well-worn cheese cloth. They ate the fruit as they walked and tucked the jerky away for lunch.

They took the same path they'd taken the previous day. Tianna dropped them all off in the clearing. Ford, Blainn, Brimir, and Gideon hid behind boulders, while Alariq, Asher, and Callum climbed into the trees.

Once they were all in position, Tianna said goodbye and turned and headed into the forest. Less than a minute later, Ford stood up from behind the boulder. Alariq nodded to him and he headed into the woods, trailing after Tianna.

If the others were confused by the turn of events, no one said anything. Alariq tried to see Asher, who was in a tree on the other side of the boulders, but couldn't. He thought back to the night before when he, Ford, and Asher had gone up to their room.

He had told the brothers he wanted someone going after Tianna in case she needed help. Asher immediately volunteered. Alariq almost said yes. Asher, although not as strong and muscular as his older brother, was the faster. But then thought better of it.

"No, with Tianna gone, I've already lost one archer, I need you in the trees with me to cover everyone else." He turned to Ford. "You go. Stay out of sight. And that includes Tianna's."

Ford nodded, but said nothing.

"Hang back, so she doesn't know you followed her, but get back to the clearing as quick as you can. We need you in the fight."

Alariq returned to the present and settled into his post.

They had left the treehome incredibly early because they weren't sure when the ettins would leave for the hunt. It was several hours later, but still a fair amount of time before midday, when he heard the signal. He made sure his crossbow was ready and braced on a branch in front of him. He watched carefully for a sign of gold in the trees.

But it was not Tianna who came crashing out of them into the glade.

It was Ford.

He stumbled on the rocky soil, but managed to duck behind a boulder right before three ettins appeared behind him. Alariq hesitated for only a second, glancing around quickly, searching the forest for any sign of Tianna.

Then he fired.

This time, with all the dwarfs gathered around, ready to ambush the ettins, the fight was over fairly quickly. Alariq and Asher didn't even have to leave their trees. He leapt down as Blainn pulled his sword out of the last ettin, an incredibly fat one, who smelled even worse than usual, if that were possible.

Before he could ask where Tianna was, Ford yelled as quietly as he could, "Get back to your positions! Tianna is coming and she's got six more behind her!"

Relief pouring through Alariq, he grabbed the lowest branch and pulled himself back up into his tree and cocked his bow again.

He waited, heart pounding, listening for one sound and one sound only.

He heard it. The signal. He recognized it as Tianna this time, now that he was specifically listening for her timbre.

Moments later the ettins came hurtling into the open. Asher fired before he did. He pulled the trigger on his crossbow and hit an ettin right in the base of the throat, the metal arrow burying deeply.

He started to reload, but movement behind the ettins caught his eye. Tianna leapt down from a tree behind the ettins, sword drawn, standing between the ettins and the way they'd just come.

The others on the ground came out fighting and Callum leapt from his perch.

Alariq fired another shot. Asher had fired several and already brought one ettin to its knees. The one Alariq had hit first was facedown and not moving. *That still leaves four.* Alariq set his bow down on the branch.

Ford was fighting a small, rotund one all on his own, trading blows and dashing around the ettin's feet. Blainn and Gideon were holding their own against a large one Asher had wounded in the calf. Brimir and Callum were battling the largest, who was fighting with a set of long knives. Tianna was darting around the fourth, who was armed with another spiked club, trying to get close enough to take a slash, but also avoid its reach.

Alariq leapt down. It took him a lot longer to reload than Asher, so he could be of more use on the ground. He drew his sword and headed for the closest ettin, the one Ford was fighting. Together, they took it down quickly and Alariq turned his attention to the one engaged in combat with Tianna. She had gotten a few small jabs in, but the ettin was still going strong. Alariq attacked it from behind.

He and Tianna took turns running at the ettin, exchanging a quick blow and then retreating, only for the other to surge forward. Asher hit it with two arrows, both in the neck, and Alariq finished it off. That left the two largest.

Alariq turned just in time to see one of their adversaries rip a large tree branch off the trunk, wielding it like a club, and swipe at Ford and Blainn, which sent them flying backwards several paces onto their backs. Ford managed to hold on to his weapon, but Blainn's shot out of his hand. Gideon, Brimir, and Asher were focused on the only other remaining ettin, which left Callum alone with the largest, cornered against a boulder. Alariq saw, in his mind's eye, the ettin smashing his fist into Callum's chest, just like last time.

Alariq knew he couldn't get to him in time. He threw his sword and hit the ettin in the back of the shoulder. Just then the other one charged him. Unprotected, he tried to draw his knife and dive out of the ettin's path at the same time, but his foot caught between two rocks and he fell backwards.

Asher hit it in the arm with an arrow, but it barely flinched and kept charging.

The ettin raised one knife, having lost the other in the fight, and brought it down. Alariq closed his eyes, but instead of feeling the slashing pain he was expecting, he heard a clash of metal, steel on steel.

Tianna had leapt in front of the ettin and met its blow,

blocking the strike intended for Alariq. The force of it had knocked her to her knees, but she kept her sword raised, holding back the knife, which was almost as long as her weapon, and certainly thicker.

The ettin swiped at her with this other hand, but by then the others had recovered and attacked it from behind, drawing its attention away.

It was all over a few minutes later.

Alariq tried to rise, but his right foot was still stuck. He unwedged it, and let out a grunt of pain. Brimir knelt beside him and started gently prodding it.

"I don't think it's broken." Brimir's face was set. "But it's already started to swell, which isn't a good sign. Can you put any weight on it?"

Ford and Blainn helped Alariq rise and he tested the ankle, keeping most of his weight on his left side. He grimaced and grunted again. "Some," he said, although even the slightest bit of weight caused pain to shoot up his right leg into his hip.

Tianna walked over to them. "You three should start back toward home now. It'll be slow going and we need to get out of here quickly. Just in case," she said. "We'll clean up."

"No, I can manage..." Alariq began.

"Yes, you can." Tianna cut across him. "But not well and not quickly."

"I am not leaving," he said simply.

"Then I sure hope some more ettins do not show up. Because you'll likely get yourself, or worse, one of your company, killed."

Alariq's jaw tightened. Clearly, she felt that him getting killed would be the least objectionable prospect.

Alariq didn't like that. And even more, he didn't like that he didn't like that.

Not fully certain why he was doing it, he conceded defeat.

"What will you do?" he asked her.

"Bury the bodies. I am hopeful the ettins won't be able to track their missing soldiers this far into Loraheem. But if they're left above ground, the bodies will attract vultures and other animals, which would lead them straight here."

He nodded, and with Ford and Blainn's help, hobbled into

the forest back toward the treehome.

After they got out of earshot, he addressed Ford. "What happened?" He didn't need to be more specific.

"She knew I was following her. Seemed to expect it, actually." Ford paused. "She seemed pretty angry about it."

"She thinks I sent you because we don't trust her." The words left Alariq's lips before his head even had time to comprehend them.

Ford nodded, his face slack and his eyes downcast.

Alariq could get the rest of the story later. Instead, he focused his attention on walking, each step more difficult than the last.

It was funny. Well, almost. Tianna was mad because she thought Ford had been sent to keep an eye on her. Ironically, this was the first time Alariq had been thinking no such thing. He'd just been concerned for her safety.

But how did he tell her that? "I was concerned for your safety," didn't exactly ring true, even in his own head. It was the truth, but it felt disingenuous, even to him, after all of the hostility and mistrust between them.

Alariq, his concentration slipping as he thought about Tianna, tripped, and Blainn almost went down with him.

Setting his mind back to the task in front of him, Alariq decided Tianna was just going to have to get over it herself. She'd eventually gotten over everything else. She'd put this behind them too.

He hoped.

The others caught up to them just before they reached the treehome. Tianna went upstairs and did not come down for dinner. Alariq supposed the walk home hadn't been enough time to get past it yet.

Unable to climb the stairs, and unwilling to ask for help, Alariq slept on the main floor that night.

14

The Foul Disposition Returns

Over the next two weeks, Alariq thought about what bad luck he'd had in the last battle. Actually, to say Alariq "thought" about it is a kindness. More accurately, he constantly and obsessively dwelled on it, mostly to try to find a way he could blame his misfortune on someone else, a particular *female* someone else, most preferably. It wasn't just his ankle, although Alariq was very unaccustomed to being out of the action, and he didn't settle well into bedrest. No, it was also this discord between him and Tianna. Alariq's patience with their hostess and her cold shoulder had run out. More than a week previously, in fact. It was for these reasons that Alariq reacted just as you might anticipate to the news Callum brought back from Dendreya one morning during Alariq's confinement.

"Twenty-three ettins left!" Callum announced upon his return from watch duty, Blainn right behind him.

Alariq, laid out in a chair, with his foot propped up on a footrest, barely straightened at Callum's declaration. "How do you know?" he asked, his voice low and indifferent.

"They said it! They said 'only twenty-three of us left,'" said Callum, missing, or perhaps ignoring, Alariq's lack of enthusiasm.

Alariq turned his head slightly toward Blainn for confirmation.

Blainn glanced at Callum, who was positively squirming with excitement, much like a child who needed to relieve himself, and gave a rare smile at the lad. "They were complaining about how they had to patrol much more frequently now that there was only twenty-three of 'em left."

Brimir, who was wrapping Alariq's ankle, looked up.

"Twenty-three ettins is still too many to take head-on."

Alariq nodded, his hand to his chin and lips pursed, finally turning his thoughts away from his own hardships and onto Callum's announcement.

Brimir finished tending to his ankle. "It's healing nicely." His voice took on a stern note. "Just keep off it."

Alariq nodded absentmindedly and waved him off as Brimir walked away.

"Did you tell Ford and Gideon when they relieved you?" Alariq asked.

"Yes, they were—" Callum quieted when Tianna entered the treehome. She was wearing her dark brown doeskin pants and off-white linen shirt. She had her bow and quiver attached to the straps she wore across her back, over a lightweight, dark coat. It was made from an animal skin Alariq had not yet been able to identify, despite the fact that he had seen it frequently now that the mornings were a little cooler. She sized up the room quickly.

"News?" she asked.

Callum looked at Alariq, who answered her. "Yes. We have a headcount. Twenty-three."

She nodded, expressionless, and did not ask how they had come by this new information. Instead, she turned to Brimir.

"There are two rabbits out there."

Brimir gave her a casual salute, grabbed some things off the counter, and headed outside. Tianna headed upstairs without another word, or even acknowledging Alariq's presence.

The room remained quiet after she left. The collective mood had been subdued lately. The others did not ask about the latest reason for Tianna's icy treatment of Alariq, or Alariq's much warmer hostility, but they had all certainly picked up on it.

Tianna hadn't said anything to him about the events and he had followed her lead and gone on as usual. But as the days passed, Alariq grew increasingly unpleasant. His frustration at not being able to do anything more than hobble did not combine well with his growing irritation at Tianna. At first, he'd been understanding of her...moodiness. Alariq had thus far failed to even identify exactly *what* she was. He had seen her angry, and this wasn't it. She wasn't the kind to hold that emotion in.

So what was it then? Frustration, irritation, dislike, what? Alariq continued to walk away from these internal conversations without an answer.

But the more he thought about it, the angrier he got. After all, he *hadn't* sent Ford after her because he didn't trust her. He'd done it to protect her.

He was further incensed by the fact that this should be a time for celebration. They had gotten away with another ruse. When the hunting party did not return, the ettins sent out several search parties, but they were unable to track their comrades into the depths of Loraheem.

Within a few days of the attack, operations at Dendreya had resumed according to their usual routine, with the exception of one thing. The leader of the ettins had started patrolling with random pairs. This new development gave Alariq pause, but did not overly concern him. If he were in this situation, with members of his company disappearing at random, he might do the same thing, just to show his troops he was taking control of the situation and to put their minds at ease.

He tried to use his confinement to his advantage, looking at maps and thinking about their next move, but he was unable to focus, often shoving the maps away in frustration and staring out the window for long periods of time.

The friendly chatter between Tianna and the other dwarfs that he was constantly subjected to did not improve his mood either.

"I don't know what I did wrong." Callum held a pile of mush in his hands.

Tianna rubbed some of the mush between her fingers.

"Too much water."

Callum nodded, his expression glum. He slopped the mush into a bucket and sat down hard at the table. Alariq smiled slightly at Callum's miserable first attempt at papermaking. Served him right, chasing after such ridiculous pursuits. Especially when Ford and Blainn had both offered to give him some training with his new sword.

"Tianna, is this an original map of Dirnovaria?" Gideon approached the table, holding an unrolled scroll in his hands. Intent on the map, he bumped into the table as he made his way toward her. Alariq smiled again. Served him right too.

She glanced at the map in his hands. "Yes. I purchased it from a nomadic trader a few years ago. See there?" she pointed to a place on the map. "That is the library. Halls and halls of books, they say."

A dreamy look crossed all three of their expressions.

Alariq rolled his eyes and returned his attention to the weapon he was sharpening.

"Ooh, I would love to go one day," Callum said, and Alariq had to refrain from pointing out that he'd had the opportunity to do that very thing and had vehemently turned it down less than two months ago.

"Yes, we do not have many books in Ishtara," Gideon said dolefully to Tianna. "Our most prized possession is an old Oryndi history. It is incomplete though," he finished with a sigh.

But Tianna perked up. "You have an Oryndi text? An original?"

Gideon nodded eagerly, happy to contribute something to her scholarship for once. "Oh yes. Callum and I bought a whole collection off a trader and it was in there. It was in the original Oryndi language, which is probably why the trader didn't recognize it for what it was. Or he would have charged a lot more for it."

"How did you translate it?" Tianna asked, her attention completely focused on Gideon.

"Well, Callum did that actually."

Tianna glanced at Callum and he blushed. Alariq gritted his teeth. Did their infatuation know no bounds?

"We didn't have a straight Oryndi to Dirni translation, so I had to walk it through a few other languages," Callum said shyly. "I can't be certain it's perfect, but it's readable."

Tianna nodded, clearly impressed.

Alariq couldn't hold it in any longer.

"What is so special about the text?" he snapped.

Gideon and Callum gave him pitying looks, but Tianna just stared at him like she expected nothing better.

"The Oryndi were an ancient race of men, who once ruled Dirnovaria," said Gideon, and Alariq didn't miss the slight condescension. "They were the first to write down histories, of themselves and the rest of the Continent. Their work is how we still know about events and peoples long since lost to living knowledge."

Alariq just shrugged and returned to his sharpening. After that, he didn't have to endure any more book conversations between their hostess and his two eccentric academics.

A few days turned into a week, and the week into two. They continued to watch the ettins every day and Alariq continued to sulk. So nasty was his mood that the rest of the company had taken to spending long periods outside, despite the cooler weather, even picnicking on the ground for most meals. They always invited him to join them, offered to help him outside. But always he declined. Lately, his refusals had even been reduced from a terse "no" to a mere grunt.

"And then, everyone in all of Dirnovaria laughs at me and all I can do is start conjugating verbs in ancient dwarfish," Callum said after one such meal, as he brought his empty plate down to the kitchen. Brimir, Blainn, and Asher filed in behind him.

"Do you think it means anything?" Callum looked genuinely worried. "It's the second time I've had the dream."

"Yeah, it means you've wasted your life learning things like ancient dwarfish," Blainn said and Alariq couldn't disagree.

Brimir shot a reproving look at Blainn. "No, of course it doesn't mean anything, Callum."

"Maybe it wasn't even you." Asher handed Brimir his plate when he held out his hand for it.

"What do you mean?" Callum asked.

"One time, Ford and I were in the outer settlements and we

saw this dwarf who looked *exactly* like this other dwarf we knew. I mean, indistinguishable. We told my mother about it and she said they're called doeppelgangers. And that everybody has one. Maybe you didn't see *you* in your dream, but your doeppelganger who lives in Dirnovaria."

Alariq couldn't tell if Asher was teasing Callum or not. Apparently, Callum couldn't either, because he just stared at Asher skeptically.

"Are you certain you didn't just see the dwarf you knew in the outer settlements?" Blainn asked and this time Alariq was sure who was being mocked.

Asher threw his fork at Blainn, who simply caught it with a grin and dropped it in the wash basin.

"Is that really true? That we all have a doeppelganger?" Callum continued to look doubtful.

"That's what I have always heard," Brimir said as he dried the dishes he'd just cleaned. "But I think it's just something people say."

"People say that because they do not understand doeppelgangers."

Alariq's head snapped up at Tianna's voice, not having noticed when she came to stand just inside the open doorway.

"What do you mean?" Callum asked for the second time.

"Doeppelgangers are cunning creatures." Tianna leaned against the doorframe. "They are able to insinuate themselves inside a person's dreams, sometimes to observe and sometimes to manipulate."

Callum didn't look skeptical anymore, but rather, was listening with rapt attention. Alariq gritted his teeth.

"So why do they say doeppelgangers look like you?" Brimir asked, picking up Alariq's empty plate from the table.

"Because when doeppelgangers enter a dream, they often take on the dreamer's form. It creates an inherent trust in whatever the doeppelganger does."

Callum opened his mouth to ask another question, but Alariq had heard enough.

"Callum, it is high time you took Blainn up on his offer to

teach you how to fight. Go make a better use of your time than gibbering about fictional magical creatures."

Callum flushed and bowed his head. He got up, retrieved his sword, and followed Blainn silently outside.

No one in the treehome spoke.

Finally, Asher broke the uncomfortable silence. "I'll go see if I can help."

"And I think I will go rest my knees." Brimir shot Alariq a look as he passed him, before heading downstairs.

For the first time in a long time, Alariq was left alone with Tianna. She just stood, unblinking and unmoving, arms crossed, still leaning against the doorframe.

Alariq stared mutinously back.

"What?" Alariq snapped.

He watched her fight for restraint. He felt a small degree of satisfaction that he got under her skin.

She straightened, but didn't approach him. Her eyes flashed. "Look, I don't care how you speak to me, but stop taking your anger out on the others." She started to turn and walk out, but then seemed to decide she wasn't done. "Or better yet, stop having your little temper tantrums altogether."

Which is when Alariq decided he would stick to grunts until his situation improved.

Finally, he was able to put enough weight on his ankle to walk without help. He limped, and badly, but he could make it up the stairs, which meant he could resume sleeping in an actual bedroom.

But on the first night back in his bed, he just tossed and turned. He finally admitted defeat and rose, pulling back the covers and dressing with care, so as not to wake Ford. Asher was on watch duty the first shift that night. Alariq figured he might as well relieve him, being as he was awake anyway. He made his way down the stairs, using the railing for support and stepping gingerly with his right foot.

He had overestimated his recovery. His ankle was sore and swollen and he sat down on the steps halfway down. He was just about to call out to Asher to tell him he'd finish the watch, when we heard movement inside the main floor. He was on the other side of the tree, so he couldn't see who exited.

"You know he hates it when you disappear like this." Asher's voice startled Alariq.

"Do I?" A soft, aloof voice answered. "Because he has never mentioned any such thing to me."

"Yes, you do," Asher answered. "And yet you continue to do it. Continue to head out into the night without a word, or even a sound. Would it really be so terrible to simply tell one of us you were leaving?"

"Yes," Tianna replied simply, but firmly. "And your mistake is in believing his preferences hold sway over my decisions." Tianna's voice was cold, though there was something else in it. "Besides, it is not me who was sneaking around tonight." Tianna paused and then her voice softened. "I did not hear you come down the stairs."

"I didn't mean to startle you," Asher said.

"You didn't." Alariq heard her footsteps on the ground and she came into view in the moonlit clearing. He shrank back into the shadows, flattening himself against the tree.

Perhaps realizing she sounded unconvincing, she shrugged and gave a small, reluctant smile.

"So, now that you know I *am* leaving, aren't going to ask me where I'm going?"

"Would you tell me?" Asher asked lightly. It was the very same question Alariq had just been thinking.

"Yes," Tianna responded quietly.

Alariq almost laughed out loud, so strong was his disbelief, but Asher seemed to take it in stride.

"I don't need to know where you're going. I trust you." Asher paused. "We all do."

Tianna actually did laugh at that.

Asher still had not moved from the post he'd chosen, a hollow created by two partially exposed roots of the enormous tree. Alariq couldn't see him, but knew that's where he was. He had chosen that very spot many times himself when on watch duty. It was a great place to see and not be seen.

"He did not send Ford after you because he does not trust you. He did it because he was worried about you." He paused again, longer this time, as though deciding what to say. The words apparently came to him, but Alariq could not make them out, so quietly were they said. Whatever it was made Tianna turn around and face Asher.

Alariq remained completely still. She was staring almost in his direction, though her gaze was fixed on Asher. She looked at him for several long moments before speaking.

"Why does he still have you watch me then? You say he trusts me, that you trust me, yet here you are."

Asher responded, but Alariq was hearing Tianna's words repeated inside his head. *Why did he still have them watch her?* He would like to be able to say this was a precaution, that they were watching over everyone, not just Tianna, but he could not say that truthfully. He could have given them the order to keep watch over the treehome in general, but he had not rescinded his order to keep an eye on her.

The others had asked him countless times if he thought she was a threat, although less so lately. They didn't ask him much of anything lately. But the honest answer to the question was *no.* The rational part of his brain said she really was on their side. And Alariq considered himself a pretty good judge of character. Tianna, he believed, was an inherently good person at her core. But his gut...his gut told him there was something else, something she wasn't being forthright about. He couldn't explain it, but there was still something about Tianna that felt...*off*...to him. She was too skilled a fighter to be of no importance. That kind of training was hard to come by, except in the militaries. And she spoke so little of herself. He knew nothing about where she'd come from or why she had chosen to live alone in the middle of an essentially uninhabited forest. That alone was suspicious, even if something inside him wasn't whispering doubts in his ear.

Her voice pulled him out of his reverie.

"Just being practical?" incredulous now, was her tone. "Being practical is about recognizing the reality of your situation, the world around you. He doesn't. He refuses to."

Asher did not speak. Tianna turned to leave.

"He's still trying to figure out his life. We all are. It..." Asher hesitated. "It looks very different than we thought it would."

Tianna stopped midstride and turned to face Asher again. She stared at him for a long moment before asking him, "And how did you think your life would look?"

Asher was quiet for a minute and then let out a sound that was half-exhale and half-chuckle.

"I don't know. I never really thought about it."

Tianna stood there, looking at him, as though waiting for a different answer.

Finally, he said, "My grandmother was from Karxana."

Tianna's brow furrowed and her eyes sharpened.

"My grandfather was scouting around Karxana and found her in the woods in the outer settlements. She had run away, fallen down a rock face, and broken her leg. He saved her. Stayed with her in an abandoned house until she could walk and then helped her get back to her people."

Tianna continued to stand in the moonlight, unmoving and silent. She looked unearthly, but strangely, not out of place. She wore a lighter pair of doeskin pants, these coming all the way to her ankles. She had that same dark coat, which Alariq realized was really more of a doublet, now that she actually was standing still long enough for him to examine her appearance. And her hair was tied back with string at the nape of her neck, in a long tail that fell down her back in loose curls.

But most noteworthy to Alariq: she looked interested in what Asher was saying. So often, she seemed nonchalant and barely mentally there, as though she was listening, but also thinking about a thousand other, more important, things at the same time. Not now, though. Now, she looked...invested.

"He was betrothed back home. But when he came back to Ishtara he broke off the engagement. He died when I was really young, in an ettin skirmish in the outer settlements, but I remember him telling me he couldn't marry someone when all his dreams were about someone else."

"So what happened?" Tianna moved out of Alariq's sight. He felt the stairs move slightly, indicating she had sat down on them.

"He went back for her. He looked for her in the outer settlements of Karxana, but never found her. He finally snuck into the city, planning to beg her to come back with him."

"And he convinced her to return with him?"

"He didn't have to." Asher's voice hardened. "They'd somehow found out about her contact with my grandfather and she was imprisoned for treason."

"Why didn't they just kill her? Or send her into exile? I thought that was the usual way dwarfs dealt with such crimes."

Like Alariq. She didn't say the words, but Alariq heard them nonetheless.

"I do not know. I do not know much about their customs. Not all dwarfs are alike, you know. And my grandmother never spoke of her time there."

"So how did she get back to Ishtara?"

"My grandfather rescued her. They were married a few weeks after his return."

"And the Ishta dwarfs, your people? They just accepted her?"

"Some did. Some were understandably mistrustful. But my grandfather didn't care. He loved her and that was all that mattered to him. He would have left Ishtara for her, lived in the outer settlements or even the wild." Asher paused. "But he didn't have to. They accepted her eventually, even if only for my grandfather's sake. Everyone loved him." He paused again. "Especially my grandmother. She died less than a year after he did. Knomic fever."

"I didn't think that was usually fatal."

"It isn't. But she just didn't have the will to fight it."

A pregnant silence followed.

"So, to answer your question, I guess that's how I hoped my life would be," said Asher, more lightly now.

Alariq, uncomprehending, stayed perfectly still, barely breathing, so as not to miss whatever was said next.

"You hoped you'd fall in love with an enemy dwarf and have to risk your life and social status to be with her?" Tianna asked, a small laugh in her voice.

If Asher had been having this conversation with Alariq, instead of Tianna, those were the exact words Alariq would have asked him. But then, he would never be having this conversation with Asher.

Asher chuckled, "No. Well, maybe. I didn't...I mean, I don't really care how it happens. I didn't know my grandfather long, but he was...happy. Beyond happy. He was grateful. Grateful for his life. For every second. That's what I want. To feel that way about my life. I don't know what it will look like for me. But that's what I want."

The quiet stretched out into the darkness.

Alariq knew the story, of course. Everyone did. But hearing Asher tell it made him see it in a different light. Everyone always talked about how unfortunate it was that an Ishta dwarf had fallen for a Karxani. People spoke as though he'd been unlucky in love, a victim of bad circumstances. Alariq heard it differently now though, seeing it through Asher's eyes. Now, it seemed like the luckiest break anyone ever had.

"My parents loved each other too." Tianna's voice made Alariq jump. He held his breath, waiting for her to continue, willing her to continue. "I can't describe what it was like being in their presence."

"Try," Asher almost whispered.

Tianna was quiet. Alariq thought Asher had pushed his luck too far, that she wouldn't answer him. That's why when she spoke, her voice, although so quiet he could barely hear her, startled him nonetheless.

"It was like they thought every single day was the greatest day ever. Even when times were hard." She laughed quietly. "And they smiled *all* the time."

Asher chuckled. It was a low, deep-chested laugh, instead of his usual bark.

Tianna continued, "Sometimes when they smiled at each other, it felt like warm sunlight on your skin on a cool day." She let out another small laugh, though this one was more like a sad laugh. Alariq didn't know such a thing existed until now.

They sat there in silence a while longer, two in friendship and one in secret. As the silence grew longer, Alariq's mind threatened to overcome him. Thoughts battered the inside of his head, one after another, never giving him time to follow any one to its conclusion. Finally, Tianna rose.

"I'll think about what you said about Alariq."

"Thank you."

"Good night, Ash."

Alariq, thinking he was about to be discovered, almost leapt up. But then he saw the back of her golden head stride decidedly away from the treehome and into the forest.

"Good night," Asher whispered to the darkness.

Alariq sat there for a while longer, forcing his mind to quiet, and then got up and silently made his way back upstairs.

He slept soundly, but woke up the next morning with the feeling that he had dreamt all night, though he could not remember any of it.

15

Reassurances

Now, before we continue I hope you will forgive a brief interruption. For I feel compelled to pause at this moment and remind you of what I promised at the start of this tale. I told you Alariq deserved the title of hero which I bestowed upon him. I am worried now, as I think back over what I have told you thus far, that you may doubt my trustworthiness on this matter. I am more worried still that what is to come will make you doubt me further. So I beg you to bear with me (and Alariq) for just a little longer.

Alariq's ankle continued to heal nicely over the next few weeks. They had resumed discussions of their next move. Predictably, they talked in circles, finally settling once again on waiting for an opportunity to present itself.

Less predictable were Alariq's moods. Some days, he was his old self from before his exile, all about business and friendly in an aloof way. Others, he was given to sullen brooding, snapping at everyone and refusing to participate in the social goings-on in the home. This was not helped by the reappearance of what could now only be called a recurring nightmare, the one where he hugged Haamith in the forest outside Ishtara.

He couldn't explain it himself, his moods or the dream, and

felt as though he'd engaged in quite enough self-examination as of late.

Things had improved moderately with Tianna. She was less openly hostile, but no more friendly toward him. Her relationship with the other dwarfs, however, seemed to grow into what Alariq was forced to recognize as friendship, which of course, only worsened his mood. Her relationship with Callum and Gideon was the most annoying, of that Alariq was certain. But the one between her and Asher was more distressing. He couldn't stop thinking about that midnight meeting between the two of them. Alariq wasn't sure what bothered him more. The fact that Tianna offered to tell Asher where she going and he'd turned her down, or the fact that she was willing to tell him to begin with, particularly when she went to such great lengths to conceal just about everything about herself from Alariq.

In the fifth week of Alariq's incapacity, Callum came to deliver the news they'd been waiting for.

The ettins were going on a raid.

Without a word, Ford immediately went to call Brimir and Gideon inside, who were in the forest, cleaning fish Ford and Asher had caught that morning in a small, nearby pond in the forest. Blainn had stayed on watch and sent Callum back alone. Asher followed Ford outside, and Alariq heard the stairs creak.

Soon, all of them except Blainn, but including Tianna, were gathered around the table on the main floor.

"Did you hear when they're going, Callum?" Alariq asked.

"Day after tomorrow."

"A raid means almost all of them will be leaving the city. Do we try attacking them on the road?" Ford asked.

"Twenty or so ettins?" Alariq shook his head, thinking of the fight on the beach with only six ettins, which had almost cost him Callum. "It's too many."

"Maybe not." Tianna joined the discussion. "We would have the element of surprise and could take a decent number out with our bows."

"No. It's too risky." Alariq's voice was hard, his words perfectly enunciated, and Tianna didn't argue.

"So what do we do then? We don't know when we'll get

another opportunity. I doubt they'll be hunting any time soon." Asher gestured in the general direction of the site of their last attack.

Everyone looked at Alariq, who stared intently at the woodgrain of the table, deliberating.

"We attack the ettins they leave behind." Alariq spoke the words slowly, as they came to him. The plan was forming in his mind like a storm rolling in at speed.

"But that'll out us," said Gideon. "The ettins will know they're under attack."

"That's the plan," he answered.

"What do you mean?"

"We're going to attack the ettins inside Dendreya and then fortify the city. We'll put *them* on the offensive."

Alariq looked around as the idea sunk into everyone's minds. Callum and the brothers started to smile. Gideon looked dubiously out the window, pensive. Brimir looked approvingly back at Alariq. Tianna alone looked thoroughly dissatisfied with his plan.

Alariq ignored the prick he felt at her displeasure and addressed the rest. "Let's put *them* in the forest and *us* behind the walls."

The dwarfs nodded excitedly and even cheered a little. Alariq decided that was enough for him. If Tianna didn't like it, well, that was just too damn bad.

They planned for the rest of the afternoon. Alariq's day only continued to improve. Not only had Tianna left the dwarfs alone to plan without her constant comment, but also Blainn had returned with new information when Brimir and Asher relieved him from watch duty that afternoon. Two ettins who would be staying behind were injured.

Alariq smiled. This was a stroke of luck. As long as they could get into the city undetected, they should have no trouble retaking it.

The real issue was getting inside, as presumably all the doors would be locked again. He sent Ford and Gideon to carefully scout out the area around the arena, to see if there was another viable option.

They came back with only one.

"There's a branch of a tree that gets within an arm's reach of the wall. It looks like it would hold our weight." Ford reported the news, while Gideon looked on, his brow furrowed. "If we can figure out some way to secure a rope, we should be able to slide down right onto the roof."

Alariq smiled again. "They've grown sloppy. That's what being out of the action for thirty years does to you."

Then Alariq noticed Gideon's expression. "You don't think it will work?" he asked.

"I think it's possible, but we'll have to go one-by-one." He paused, fidgeting slightly. "And I worry about our ability to fortify the city. It was built to provide moderate protection from things in the wild or possibly hungry, desperate villagers, but not to withstand ettins. The front gate will certainly hold, but I don't know about the rest. Not to mention, the walls are fairly low as far as fortifications go. They might be able to scale them."

"We don't have a choice!" Alariq snapped. "This is taking too long as it is."

For the second time since he'd spoken them, his own words came back to haunt him. *Well it's not as if we have anywhere to be, anyone waiting for us.*

But they did have somewhere to be now. And Alariq in particular had somewhere he *didn't* want to be. The treehome had started to feel suffocating to him. Maybe it was his injury and his resulting confinement, or maybe it was the constant tension with its owner, but the treehome felt more like a cage now.

He took a deep breath before continuing. "Our plan is solid, Gideon. A raid will take at least several days, if not a week or longer. That gives us plenty of time to block the entrances, build up a food store, and dig an exit tunnel."

The exit tunnel had been Brimir's idea, who had been one of the few dwarfs who worked down in the mines after his military tenure, as an overseer and engineer. Dwarfs were excellent at tunneling, and their natural craftsmanship abilities were an asset in building them. A small group of dwarfs could dig and shore up a short exit tunnel in a day or two. If the ettins broke their defenses and made it into the city, the dwarfs should be able to get out quickly and without exposure.

Gideon's face was still strained, but he nodded resolutely.

The most pressing concern, however, was building a supply store. They would need to outlast the ettins. They could use the exit tunnel, but it was risky. They planned to dig a longer tunnel that would reach into the deeper parts of the forest, but that would take at least a couple of weeks. They needed something to keep them fed until then.

So he sent Asher out to hunt. Alariq was hoping Tianna would agree to go too, but no one had seen her since Callum had come back with the news. Gideon set to work preparing campaign biscuits, hard crackers made from only a few ingredients and cooked at high temperatures, which made them almost imperishable.

Asher came back with a large deer. Brimir would be able to make weeks' worth of jerky out of it. Normally that process would take several days, but Tianna had a large outdoor oven, made from stone blocks, which smoked the meat and dried it more quickly than simply air-drying it in the sun.

The day passed quickly, with preparations and plans unfolding in every direction. Dinner came and went and there was still no sign of Tianna, however. She had disappeared for an entire day before, but the timing of this disappearance had Alariq concerned.

The sun had long since set. All the dwarfs had stayed up. Nobody had to ask what was troubling Alariq, but nobody dared to bring up the subject.

Finally, Alariq asked the room, "Does anyone know where she is?"

He couldn't help it, he looked directly at Asher. He tried to keep an accusing look off his face, but his eyes narrowed involuntarily.

Asher returned his stare, but didn't speak. Ford, noticing the silent exchange, intervened before Alariq could address Asher directly, "Who saw her last? I haven't seen her since we first hashed out the plan."

Gideon and Brimir both murmured their agreement.

Slowly, shaking, Callum raised his hand slightly. "I guess I was the last to see her then."

"Where? Did you speak?" Alariq tried to keep his voice even, but it came out gruff.

"It was just outside, in the clearing." Callum's voice was high. "She asked me if the ettins said which village they were raiding." He stopped.

"And?" Alariq leaned forward toward Callum.

"And I told her they said something about the Sudri River settlements."

"What else?" Alariq demanded as he tightly gripped the edge of the table.

"N-nothing. That's all." Callum looked down at his hands, breathless.

Asher's soft voice broke the tension that had built during Alariq and Callum's exchange.

"She went to warn them," he said quietly.

"You knew? You knew she was leaving and you failed to tell me?" Alariq stood up abruptly, wincing at the pain in his ankle. He could put most of his weight on it now and move at about half his usual top speed, but not without mild pain.

"No. She didn't tell me anything."

"Then how do you know she's gone to warn them?" Alariq could feel the blood rushing into his face, pounding in his ears.

Asher considered the question for a long moment before he answered, still seated. "It's just a guess. But it's a guess I'd bet my life on."

"A guess?" Alariq sneered and took a step toward Asher, who finally rose from his seat. "You just *happened* to guess where she went?"

Ford immediately stepped between them.

"No, I didn't 'just happen to guess,'" Asher mocked. "I've gotten to know her. We all have. On your orders, I might add. All of us except you."

Alariq had never seen Asher's eyes flash that way.

Alariq drew himself up to full height and broadened his shoulders. His voice was almost a yell.

"You've been under orders to learn about her, not 'get to know her,'" he growled. "There's a difference."

Both of them stepped toward one another until they each met one of Ford's outstretched hands.

"I thought you'd put those outlandish ideas behind you! Thought you'd finally realized she's one of us now!"

"One of us," Alariq spat. "You are showing your age. Even if she's not a threat, she just wants us to take care of her little backyard pest problem. She saw an opportunity to get rid of the ettins and she's taking it. Nothing more."

Alariq pushed against Ford's palm, and Asher did the same. Callum and Blainn rose from their seats now too, Callum grabbing Alariq's right arm, and Blainn doing the same to Asher.

Alariq pulled free, never breaking eye contact with Asher. "And maybe I wouldn't be so damn suspicious if my soldiers did what they were told, instead of having midnight meetings by moonlight!"

Everyone's eyes turned to Asher, who was slightly taken aback, but no less angry.

"Now I'm the enemy too?" he asked. "First Tia, the person who saved our lives and took us in? The person who saved your life in the last fight, by the way. And now one of the only people who stood by you too?"

Asher stared daggers at Alariq, scorn permeating every angry line in his face. "You know, these last months, I've wondered why it was so easy for Tanith to cast you out. How the rest of Ishtara could watch it happen without so much as a single sound of protest. But now I know." Asher's voice was quiet, deadly.

"Nobody cared enough to intervene. They didn't care whether you were innocent or that you were being sent away." Asher paused. "They just didn't care about you. And why would they? When this is what they'd get in return for their affection."

Alariq just stared back at Asher, color draining from his face and neck, fists clenched.

"Now I know. I know why there are only six of us."

And with that Asher shook off Blainn's hold and strode from the room, slamming the door as he went.

Alariq stood there, his shoulders rising and falling unevenly.

Everyone still stood in exactly the same position, Ford with both arms still outstretched, his left holding back nothing but air, and Callum with his grip on Alariq's forearm.

They all stood, frozen for a moment, before Alariq pulled himself free and walked upstairs.

16

Smoke and Water

Asher didn't return to their bedroom that night and Alariq slept fitfully. He dreamt he was back in Ishtara and that he was slowly sinking into the floor, which had turned to mud beneath his boots. He was begging everyone there to help him, but no one would. They just stood by, some watching his descent, expressionless, and others just chatting away with one another, until only his face remained unsubmerged. He cried out futilely one last time before he was swallowed.

By breakfast, there was still no sign of Asher or Tianna. Alariq began to feel a weight upon him. Guilt at not thinking to warn the settlers himself settled a heaviness in his stomach. And he kept returning to the night before, to Asher's words. Over and over, he heard the sound of Tianna's sword clashing against the ettin's just before it attempted to deal Alariq a final blow.

Finally, just before lunch, Tianna returned, and Asher a few minutes after. Alariq had resolved, in the early morning hours, when the first light had hit the forest, not to ask her where she went. He hoped that would be enough to smooth things over with Asher. This was their opportunity to retake Dendreya and he couldn't risk ill-will between him and his soldiers putting everyone else, and the mission, at risk.

It appeared to work. Asher seemed to be expecting a military-style interrogation on Tianna the minute she returned, and he was clearly ready for a fight, but Alariq's casual continuation of activities, as if nothing had happened, brought Asher out of his highly-strung state.

Tianna also appeared surprised by Alariq's complete disregard of her disappearance, but quickly mimicked him and acted as though nothing were out of the ordinary.

They continued planning. Ford and Asher kept watch. Alariq sharpened weapons as he reviewed the plan with Callum, Blainn, and Tianna, while Brimir and Gideon made provisions.

After trying to climb a tree several times, it became clear, however, that Alariq could not be part of the initial attack. His ankle simply wouldn't stand up to the climb. He reluctantly agreed to keep watch for any returning ettins.

His gut twisted thinking about his men and Tianna going in and fighting while he sat outside twiddling his thumbs. But he would be a liability if he went. And someone did need to keep watch anyway. *Might as well be the one with the game leg*, he thought sourly.

Despite being clearly exhausted, Tianna did not ask for a respite at all during the day. Alariq had to credit her for that. They packed their supplies that night before going to bed. It seemed sleep had eluded more than just Tianna and Alariq, for all of them ate dinner with heavily-lidded eyes and slow movements, and they all retired soon thereafter.

Alariq slept better, but his dreams were still active. That night, for the first time in his entire life, he dreamt of his wife.

He saw her from a great distance, but he could make out the details as if he were standing right in front of her: her ash blonde hair, her strong, but lean build, even her large, gray eyes. He could see her, but she couldn't see him. She was married to a man who looked just like him, but somehow, Alariq knew it was not him. They had a son. Rheia held the quiet infant in her arms, her husband standing over them looking down at the child. Everything seemed off. Even within the dream, Alariq realized it was the color. His vision was less vibrant, everything diminished-looking, all the edges blurred.

When he woke, Alariq dressed slowly, trying to grasp the details of the dream, but they slipped away the longer he was awake. What was it about this place, Alariq wondered, that made him dream so much more than he ever had back in Ishtara. Or maybe it wasn't the place, but rather his new, unstable state. Either way, Alariq didn't like the dreams. They felt like someone teasing him with information that he couldn't quite understand and that they refused to tell him.

He walked downstairs, breathing in the cool morning air, pulling it deep into his lungs, trying to clear away the haze the dream had left behind. They ate a hurried breakfast and Asher and Tianna left to make sure the ettins had left for the raid.

Alariq went over the plan in his head for the thousandth time. The remaining six of them were to head to a prearranged meeting place to wait for word from Tianna that the city had been emptied. They would enter the city using the tree and a rope with a grappling hook at the end. Then, they would take care of the ettins inside and secure the city. All the while, Alariq would keep watch from outside.

Soon after Asher and Tianna's departure, the rest of the dwarfs followed, sitting down in the predetermined spot to wait for Tianna's go-ahead. It came shortly after they arrived. They all followed her through the dark forest toward the city.

The time came for Alariq to bid farewell to the others. He wasn't particularly worried. Alariq had given Asher and Tianna most of his metal arrows to use. The two of them should be able to cause enough injury to the ettins to allow for a safe ground attack by the others. Especially when two of the enemy were injured.

Nonetheless he looked each of them in the eye as they passed him, clasping Callum on the shoulder and giving him an encouraging squeeze. Brimir did the same to Alariq.

And then they were gone, swallowed by the trees.

Alariq took up a spot near where they had first entered the woods all those months ago. From here, he would be able to hear the others if they called for help before they headed over the wall. He would also be able to hear ettins approaching from the beach. He sat down, leaning his back against a tree trunk and placing his bow beside him.

The trees were still thick enough that he couldn't see the walls of Dendreya, but he could glimpse the sky just above it.

He sat there, trying to determine how long it would take them to get up the tree and inside. By his calculations, they should have been scaling the wall at that moment. He listened for the sound of fighting, knowing he probably wouldn't be able to hear it through the thick city walls.

He couldn't help it. His mind returned to the things Asher had said to him the night before. He'd always thought of himself as practical and utilitarian. Like a dwarf ought to be. But the way Asher told it, he wasn't practical, he was suspicious and defensive; he wasn't utilitarian, he was heartless.

It was a line his grandfather had walked with perfection. He was sensible, but full of life. Alariq had never had trouble with the former. But the latter had always escaped him. He'd seen his grandfather be both simultaneously, but it always felt like a choice to Alariq. One, or the other.

Alariq stared into the sky.

They appeared suddenly. Three distinct black puffs of smoke, directly above Dendreya. He straightened. Those were not created by a campfire. They were signals.

A trap.

He grabbed his bow, put his foot in the stirrup, standing and cocking it all in one swift motion. His ankle gave him a twinge, but he kept going, loading an arrow as he went.

Still in the forest, he saw the ettins through the trees, near one of the side entrances.

There were about ten of them, along with the leader, who was wordlessly directing them with hand motions. He saw no sign of the rest.

Alariq ducked behind a tree. How was he going to get to the others in time? And without being seen by the horde of ettins.

There was only one way. He secured his bow to the strap he wore across his back. And he ran.

But he wasn't running toward Dendreya. Instead, he backtracked about a hundred paces. Then he dove.

The creek wasn't very deep and his chest scraped the bottom, but he kept going. He surfaced, the water only coming up to his shoulders. But the creek bed was deep enough, and the water level low enough, that he couldn't be seen, nor could he see out. The water was moving fairly quickly, but not so fast that he could not have stood still if he'd wanted. He swam, chopping through the water with awkward strokes, grateful for the practice he'd had in the calm waters of the lake a few weeks prior.

Thankfully the fast moving water carried him along at twice his normal speed. The creek narrowed and shallowed right before it went under the city wall. Alariq could touch both sides of the bank at the same time.

The waterway had been rerouted by the first dwarfs to arrive in Dendreya, to go under the walls and part of the city, and then through the glassmaking rooms. The problem was, Alariq didn't know how far it was to one of those rooms or how narrow the creek got. If it got too narrow to pass through, he wasn't sure he'd be able to swim back up against the current. Or that he'd have enough air to last him...

Another puff of black smoke appeared in the sky above him.

He braced his arms on the sides of the creek bed to stop himself from going under the wall. He took three deep breaths. And plunged.

The creek bed was very narrow. His fingertips hit the sides with every stroke, but it remained wide enough. It was also very shallow. Several times, he felt his knees brush the bottom. It was completely black. He kept his eyes open, but the blackness was so complete, he might've just kept them closed.

He focused on what had to be done. He didn't know how long he'd been down there, but he must've swam a hundred paces. He was starting to run out of air. His chest squeezed and his lungs screamed. His throat felt like it was collapsing in on itself. His arms and legs refused to move as quickly as he wanted them to. And his brain began to get fuzzy.

But suddenly, the water lightened. He could see his hands in front of him. He shot upwards, bracing his hands once again against the walls to stop the current from carrying him forward and felt his head break the surface of the water.

He'd made it. He was inside the city. He dragged in deep,

ragged breaths.

Alariq listened. He didn't hear anything. That either meant whatever was about to happen hadn't started yet. Or, unthinkably, whatever happened was already over.

He stood there, dripping, frozen to the spot. Still, he heard nothing. He unstrapped his bow to make sure it was still ready and then put it back on his shoulder, opting for his sword instead.

He made his way quietly through the rooms and passages. He didn't know where he was or, more importantly, where he would come out.

The passage turned and Alariq stubbed his toe against the hard stone steps that suddenly appeared around the corner. He could see a shop at the top of the stairs. He climbed and found himself in the largest room he'd seen in the city. It, by all evidence, currently served as the sleeping quarters of an ettin.

He looked out the window. He could see two ettins laying out in the middle of the forum. They did appear genuinely injured. He could see bloody clothes used as bandages on one, and the other ettin's arm hung at a strange angle. They were clearly bait.

Alariq breathed a sigh of relief. If the bait was still there, then the trap had not yet been sprung.

He couldn't see any others. He looked up, searching the ceiling for a trapdoor.

He was in luck, he pulled it down and climbed up, pulling the ladder up behind him and closing the door once more. His ankle protested, but he ignored it.

He still saw no sign of the rest of the ettins or Tianna and the other dwarfs. He was starting to panic. As soon as he exited the room, the ettins would see him, but he had to find the others. He couldn't do either from this tiny bedroom. He looked around the room frantically, not for anything in particular. A pull chain caught his eye. He looked up. There was another trap door!

He pulled it down and climbed, this time not bothering to pull the door up behind him. Below, there had been a larger, single bed, but up here, there was a set of bunk beds. *Children. The dwarfs who lived here had children. That's why there was a second trapdoor.*

Alariq wondered vaguely in the back of his mind whether this had been Gideon's room once.

There was only a tiny window in this room. Through it, he could only see the structures directly opposite him. He tested the ceiling with the tip of his sword. It stuck easily into the wood.

Rotten.

He climbed up on the top bunk and could see it was crawling with woodbugs. He remembered talking with the others about the state in which they might find the city. They'd previously been worried about potential deterioration of the city structures. Well, not only was that true, but it was, quite ironically, also a stroke of good luck.

Alariq thrust his sword upward, through the ceiling. Bits of infested wood rained down on his head and shoulders. He twisted the sword until he made a hole big enough for his arm. He shoved it through, grabbed the exterior of the roof, and pulled. A great chunk of ceiling collapsed downward, but didn't fall. He tossed his sword through the hole and tried to hoist himself up, but more roof crumbled under his weight. The soft rotten wood wasn't making much noise as it hit the bed below, but he knew the ettins were listening for any sound of movement. He desperately hoped the others recognized a trap when they saw one.

Still not hearing any sound of fighting, he tried again, this time closer to the wall. It held! He heaved himself up on the roof, hooking his uninjured ankle over some solid wood and using his arms and one good leg to pull himself over the edge and roll onto the roof.

He carefully raised himself up on his hands and knees. The wood was tenuous at best, creaking beneath him, and he was afraid to stand. He crawled stiffly, trying to keep his weight as evenly distributed as he could, while still moving quickly.

A flash to his left caught his eye, but by the time he looked over, it was gone. He turned back to task, but before he'd moved more than a few paces forward, he noticed something else from the same direction.

Smoke.

Another flash. A flaming arrow landed in the middle of the

smoke. He looked for its source, but the oval shape of the city prevented him from seeing where it originated.

It had to be Asher or Tianna. He'd seen ettins use ground-based archery stations, but never known them to use handheld bows. No, Alariq instinctively knew this wasn't the work of the ettins.

The others know something is not right.

He kept moving.

A few more arrows hit the smoking roof almost directly across from him. He looked up and saw another spot smoking a few hundred paces in front of him. He looked behind and saw more smoke in another spot.

They know it's a trap. That was the only explanation. They were clearly trying to distract the ettins and split them up. A wave of relief washed through Alariq and he let out a breath he didn't realize he was holding.

The wood was getting stronger, but he still didn't believe it would hold his weight if he stood. At least he was able to move a little faster.

Then, like an unexpected thunderclap, came a deafening crash.

The area where he'd first noticed the smoke had collapsed. The second floor crumbled into the first. For a moment, Alariq thought it was the fire that had caused the collapse, but then four armored ettins came spilling out of the wreckage.

He flattened to the roof. From his vantage point, he could see into the collapsed region. The ettins had removed portions of the walls between the adjoined shops, giving them the ability to move around the first floor without having to enter the forum.

They could be anywhere.

Now was the time to throw caution into the wind. Alariq pulled himself up on his hands and knees again, knowing the ettins would be able to see him if they looked up. They were busy searching the wreckage, however, looking up into the sagging third floor above.

Alariq heard another crash behind him, but didn't bother looking back. He just kept crawling.

He heard the third crash he'd been waiting for in front of him and looked up just in time to see six dwarfs and one tiny woman running right at him.

"Stop!" he yelled, holding one hand up.

But it was too late, the roof cracked and collapsed beneath them. Alariq watched them drop out of his vision and into the rooms below. Tianna, who had been in front and weighed the least, managed to catch herself on the edge of the roof. She pulled herself back up and lay face down on her stomach, turning herself back around toward the hole. She reached an arm inside and pulled Callum up, who rolled away from the hole and kept himself flat on the roof on his back.

"Callum!" Alariq yelled. "Crawl to me! Stay near the outside edge!"

Callum obeyed immediately, making his way quickly toward Alariq. Tianna was still reaching into the hole created by the dwarfs.

She pulled Asher up next.

"Asher! Crawl to me!" Alariq yelled again. He could hear shouting down below, but couldn't focus on any of the words being said.

Asher started toward him, but looked back over his shoulder. Tianna was still hanging over the edge, bent at the waist into the hole, half her body dangling down. Asher rolled over onto his stomach and grabbed her ankles, keeping his weight spread out.

Gideon came up next, followed by Brimir. Alariq called out to both of them and they made their way toward him slowly.

"Trap!" Brimir shouted. "There are two groups patrolling the outside. They uprooted the tree we used to get in."

So that was where the other ettins were. Cutting off the dwarfs' escape route.

"We have to use the creek," Alariq said as they reached him, their hands and knees spread as far apart as possible.

"Is that how you got in?" Gideon asked, taking in Alariq's wet clothes and hair.

"Yes. It's narrow, and there's no air as it passes underground, but I think we can make it. Do you know how far it continues under the rest of the city?"

"It just cuts in under two glassmaking rooms and the well

166

room, but then it veers back into the forest and heads east."

Alariq looked up as Blainn made his way shakily over. He felt a lurch under his knees. The ettins were trying to bring down the floor beneath them.

He looked over to Tianna and Asher. She was struggling to pull Ford up, but the roof was becoming increasingly unstable.

It gave one last, shuddering creak, and collapsed. Asher tried to maintain his hold on Tianna, but had to grab the roof with one hand to keep from falling after her and her ankle slipped out of his grasp.

Alariq crawled over to the hole.

Asher was yelling down to Ford and Tianna below, desperately trying to ascertain their condition.

The building lurched again, Alariq turned his head to the others. "Go! I made a hole in the roof. Follow the passage and take the creek. We'll meet back at the treehome!"

The creek was narrow and shallow, so he wasn't too worried about Gideon and Callum. And even if there was trouble, Blainn and Brimir could swim, both having been Third Authorities.

Alariq looked back into the wreckage below. Asher was still yelling down to his brother and Tianna. After a few seconds of stillness and relative quiet, Ford's head forced its way from beneath rotten bits of roof. He wiggled an arm free and pulled his body out. He turned and pulled Tianna free as well.

"Are you hurt?" Alariq called down.

Tianna and Ford looked at each other and then back at him and shook their heads, though Tianna had a cut on her forehead and was holding her right arm, and Ford was rubbing the back of his head.

In addition to the roof, the third floor had collapsed as well and the pair was down on the second floor. There were now two stories separating them from Alariq and Asher.

"Can you climb up?" Alariq asked, cupping his hands around his mouth. "We have a way out if you can get up here."

They looked around. "I don't see anything," Ford called.

"I'm going down," Asher said.

"No." Alariq grabbed Asher's shoulder. "You'll just be stuck down there too."

"Go," Tianna yelled. "We'll find another way out."

Ford nodded emphatically his agreement.

"No!" Asher roared. "I can get you up, you just have to find something to stand on. Alariq, grab my ankles!"

They felt another lurch and the part of the roof behind them where Alariq had just been started to sag.

Alariq looked down at Ford and Tianna. He knew they had no chance of getting them up. If he and Asher didn't move now, all four of them were going to end up falling right onto the ground and into the ettins' hands. Ford and Tianna's only chance was if Alariq and Asher could lure the ettins toward themselves instead.

At least they had the high ground. Though for how much longer, Alariq could not say.

"Asher, we have to go. Come on, we'll draw the ettins away." He pulled at Asher's shoulder.

Asher looked down into the destroyed rooms at Ford. He held his gaze for a moment and then Ford nodded. Asher met Tianna's eyes for the briefest breath and then turned to follow Alariq.

Alariq and Asher made their way over the hole, pieces of roof collapsing all around them. Cracks and thuds, knocks and yells, the sounds which had previously been spread out across the city were becoming more concentrated.

Alariq flattened himself to the roof to let Asher pass him. Alariq grabbed Asher where his shoulder met his neck, forcing Asher to look at him, to focus on his words. The intensity Alariq felt came through in his voice.

"Through the trapdoors and down the passage. Listen for water. Take a deep breath and follow the creek's current. Gideon says it's not far to the next room. Get air and keep going. I'll draw the ettins off Ford and Tianna."

Asher stared at him for a single heartbeat and then disappeared through the hole. Alariq waited for a minute to give him time to get out and then made his way over the edge of the roof, where the ceilings were reinforced. He intentionally stood where the ettins could see him.

There were about fifteen in the courtyard, including the two injured ettins. They were gathered around the area where Ford and Tianna currently hid. There was no sign of the commander. That explained why they weren't attacking yet.

They didn't see the others leave. They think we're all in the wreckage.

He grabbed his crossbow from his back, aimed, and fired, hitting a large ettin in the back. They all turned to face him. He made sure they all saw him and then jumped down into the hole. He scaled down the ladders, his ankle screaming in protest. By the time he reached the stairs, he was limping badly.

As Alariq reached the bottom and turned the corner, he heard the ettins tear into the room above. He made it down the passage and as he entered the glassmaking room, he looked over his shoulder and saw an enormous, muscular ettin fill the hallway, almost to the last square inch.

Alariq staggered into the room over to the rushing water. The ettin burst through the doorway behind him, sending pieces of doorframe in every direction. It snatched out, grasping in the place Alariq's head had been just a moment before.

But Alariq had already leapt into the dark waters below.

17

A Shifting of the Winds

Alariq's feet hit the creek bed hard. The current threw him awkwardly forward, jarring his back. He righted himself and swam as hard as he could. The water was only pitch black for a few moments and then he could see in front of him again. He was passing through another room under the city. He surfaced for a single breath, the current still carrying him onward, and then dove once more.

The next underground segment was longer, but still shorter than his swim into the city. He surfaced a second time in a tiny room that held a water pump. The walls had been destroyed in places. He stood for a moment, bracing his hands on the wall in front of him, the water battering his back as it rushed passed him and under the wall. He listened for a sign of fighting, or Ford or Tianna, but the water was too loud to hear anything. He took two deep breaths and submersed himself again. He focused on getting out of there quickly, not knowing how long the passage would be.

Alariq swam, his strokes getting smoother as the skill came back to him. The creek bent sharply. He almost hit his head on the bed wall, but everything was flooded with light just in time. He'd come out from under the walls. He kept floating with the current, but turned around to see the city.

Ten or so ettins came barreling around the corner to his right, followed by another ten or so on his left.

Alariq's stomach did a somersault. *It worked!* Most of the ettins were following him. Ford and Tianna should be able to slip out of the city.

Only now, Alariq had twenty ettins on his trail.

He turned and kicked out hard, digging his arms into the water. There was no way the ettins could follow him in the creek. It was far too narrow. And soon the creek headed into deeper, thicker woods, which would slow the ettins down considerably. The creek sped up as it headed downhill. He kept going, long past when he could no longer hear their shouts and battle cries.

The creek began to get narrow, shallow, and rocky, with twists and turns every few paces. A small sandbank appeared and he dragged himself out of the water. He saw footprints in the sand and realized he was not the first dwarf to have done so.

Alariq's insides started to shake. He lay on the bank for a moment more, breathing heavily.

A twig snapped and he grabbed for his sword, rolling up onto his knees.

It was Asher. He held out his hand and helped Alariq up. Alariq sheathed his sword and tested his ankle. It was painful to put weight on it, but he could make it back to the treehome okay. With Asher's help.

But Asher stood stock still, his eyes locked on Alariq's, silent.

Knowing exactly what he was waiting for, Alariq gave it him. "The ettins followed. Around twenty."

Asher let out a breath and without a word, switched over to Alariq's bad side and hooked his arm under Alariq's shoulder and around his back. They made their way slowly north.

They recognized the area. Tianna had shown them this part of the forest when they fought the hunting party of ettins, but it took several wrong turns to get them back onto truly familiar territory. From there, they cut west, back toward the treehome.

It started to rain, slowing their pace. At least their tracks would be washed away. They finally reached the treehome around midafternoon. All of the others were waiting inside.

At their enquiring looks, Alariq explained about Ford and

Tianna. Callum got them both blankets and Gideon made them some of Tianna's herbal drink. Then they sat for what seemed an eternity.

Asher had not touched his tea. His face was pale and he stared at the floor, his hands often coming up to his face, running them through his damp, dark-brown waves. He finally threw off the blanket and paced to the window, looking out for long minutes before returning to his seat.

Alariq sat completely still, his tea also untouched, while Brimir tended to his ankle. He kept forcing his brain to think, but he couldn't hold on to a thought. All he could do was sit and wait, expressionless, unthinking and unfeeling. No one spoke.

They couldn't go back for them. They could never stand against that many ettins. And they couldn't risk leading the ettins back to the treehome. They'd gotten extraordinarily lucky with the rain, and Alariq was not willing to tempt fate further unless he had to.

So he sat, trying to reassure himself that he'd made the right call.

Alariq was sure his plan had worked. The ettins inside had followed him away from the wreckage where Ford and Tianna were trapped. And then, according to his, admittedly brief, count, around twenty had tried to pursue him down the creek. Hopefully that had been enough.

But still he worried.

Asher kept pacing the room, his disheveled hair and wild eyes making him look a little crazed.

Alariq knew if he wasn't here, Asher would have strode off into the forest toward the city long ago. Actually, Asher never would have left Ford and Tianna in the first place.

And he would have drawn the ettins straight to them. And they all would have been killed.

Still, Alariq knew how he felt. He was just better at handling it.

It hadn't been so very long ago that it was Alariq in Asher's shoes, waiting for a brother to return.

Garrin had, of course, been under Alariq's command. The divisions divided the city, not just the army. Citizens were free to move between the divisions. It was just a way of organizing the city, especially for military purposes. Still, certain divisions tended to have different reputations. Like Alariq's, which was by-and-large, known as the most-skilled fighting group. His division was known for its good soldiers. A lot of that had to do with him. He was a career military dwarf, uncommon in Ishtara. Ford and Blainn had planned to serve indefinitely too. And Brimir had been in over a century before he finally retired from service.

Alariq's younger brother, Garrin, had always wanted to be just like him. But he wasn't well-suited for fighting like Alariq was. Skilled, but just lacking the ability to emotionally distance himself from what was going on around him. Alariq had tried to convince him to wait to serve his mandatory term, hoping he would harden a little as he aged, but Garrin insisted on signing up the day he was eligible, just like Alariq had.

Alariq remembered that night better even than he remembered yesterday. It was near the beginning of the Ettinwar. They were in the outer settlements, protecting the main road the traders used to get supplies into Ishtara. The ettins had launched a surprise attack. Ford's company, which included Garrin, had gotten separated from the rest of the division during the retreat. The rest of them made it back to the city boundaries and waited for Ford and the others. Alariq sent Blainn and most of the division back for reinforcements so they could resecure the road, but he stayed behind with a small contingency.

The wait had been horrible. He'd been tempted to go back a hundred times. But they'd be headed back to fight the same group of ettins that had just overpowered them. They couldn't go without another division. He'd be sacrificing his soldiers *and* his brother. So he waited that day too.

He'd wondered then, just as he did now, if he made the right decision.

The missing soldiers arrived back just before Blainn returned with Division Seven. Their number had been cut by a quarter and most of the rest were in pretty bad shape.

But worst off was Garrin. An ettin had crushed his leg and dislocated his hip. He was unconscious from the pain and blood loss, his face devoid of color.

They couldn't save the leg.

Alariq had told himself over and over that he did exactly what he was supposed to do. He made the right choice. But he sometimes still dreamed, not of Garrin being missing or returning injured, but of the days that followed. Alariq had always wanted Garrin to grow a tougher skin. Well he did, and then some. Losing the leg, the recovery, it was simply too much for Garrin's gentle soul to manage. Alariq had watched his brother fade away to almost nothing, physically and mentally.

More than once, Alariq had caught himself resenting his brother, thinking that a stronger dwarf would have pulled through. Guilt immediately followed such thoughts.

Now, watching Asher, pacing around, wracked with guilt and worry, Alariq knew why he'd resented his brother: Alariq couldn't forgive himself while Garrin was still suffering.

Garrin had eventually improved. And he'd assured Alariq on more than one occasion that Alariq wasn't to blame. And on a conscious level, Alariq knew that. But the guilt still gnawed at him, just as he knew it would if anything happened to Ford or Tianna today.

Alariq wondered, if Garrin hadn't been hurt, would he be here, sitting next to him in Tianna's cozy kitchen?

His thoughts were interrupted by footsteps outside, and a second later, the door was thrown open and Tianna entered, followed by Ford. Dried blood caked the side of Ford's head, but the wound appeared to have stopped bleeding. Tianna still held her arm and Alariq could see dark bruising through the huge rip in her sleeve. The cut on her forehead slowly oozed blood.

But they were alive. Alariq released a slow, shaky breath.

Asher stared at the two of them, not breathing. Tianna returned his gaze for a moment and then hastily walked over to the stove to warm her hands. Brimir brought her a blanket and a wet cloth to clean the cut on her head. Alariq watched as the old dwarf gave her a gentle squeeze. Tianna looked at Brimir and smiled slightly. For a moment, it looked to Alariq as though she might cry. But then she averted her face and dabbed at the wound.

Asher rushed over and hugged his brother, who returned the

embrace. Asher took the blanket from his shoulders and threw it over Ford's.

"What happened?" he asked his older brother. "How did you get away?"

"The ettins left the city. They all chased after the rest of you." Ford used the blanket to dry himself. "We waited until it was quiet and then snuck out the south entrance."

"So what took you so long?" Asher asked him.

"The injured ettins stayed back. They saw us and called for the others. Most kept after you, but two came back. I think we killed both of them. But then some of the others must've heard the fighting and returned. There were too many, so we had to run for it. We lost them in the trees. Then to avoid the group that was following you, we had to double back, and follow the beach."

Ford looked at Tianna. "I wouldn't have made it out if it wasn't for Tianna. She was amazing." Tianna turned to face him and he gave her a brotherly smile.

"Was she?" Alariq asked quietly. He slowly stood, letting the blanket fall from his shoulders. Until this moment, Alariq had been consumed by worry. There was no room for anything else in his thoughts. But now, now that he knew they were safe, his mind sprang to life again, as the details of what happened replayed in his head.

Alariq turned to look at Tianna, who was eying him warily. "Or perhaps the ettins who came back just weren't expecting she'd attack them?" He raised an eyebrow.

"What exactly are you accusing her of?" Ford demanded, in a voice ill-fitting an address to his superior. Everyone seemed surprised at his tone.

Alariq addressed Ford, but never took his eyes off Tianna.

"We have been here for months, with no problems. Every plan has worked so far. But the day before yesterday, Tianna disappears and does not return for over a day." Alariq felt the muscle in his jaw twitch and clenched down tightly. "And the ettins knew we were coming."

Tianna's face reddened and her eyes flashed, but it was Asher who spoke.

"You're saying she betrayed us to the ettins?"

Alariq ignored him and advanced on Tianna.

"You have clearly lived here for a long time, yet the ettins have never bothered you. Why is that, I wonder?"

Brimir rose and took a step toward Alariq, his voice low and calming. "Son, you don't know what happened in there..."

But Alariq cut him off.

"I don't have to know," he yelled. "She disappears without a word to anyone and then the ettins just happen to figure out what's going on? I find that all a little too convenient."

"Tianna is the one who realized it was a trap." Callum's voice was meek, and it shook. "She's the reason we're all alive."

Alariq rounded on Callum. It was the fear in Callum's eyes, his frame shrunken inward in apprehension, rather than his words, that drained away some of Alariq's anger.

"Don't bother, Callum." Tianna's voice also shook, though hers with a cold fury, rather than fear. Alariq turned to her, unsure what to say.

"He made up his mind about me a long time ago and it's clear nothing is going to change it." She stood there, arms straight at her sides, fists clenched. "It does not matter how much help I give him or how many times I save his ungrateful rear end."

Alariq's anger, which had burned down to a bed of embers, blazed back to life. "Maybe if you didn't go slinking off into the woods or act so secretive, it would be easier to trust you!"

Tianna took a step toward him, skirting the kitchen table. "So it's *my* burden to get you to trust me? Taking you in, helping you, saving your life...that's not enough? I also have to act according to your standards of trustworthy behavior? I didn't ask for a bunch of homeless dwarfs to show up in my forest, needing my help. And I certainly didn't ask for someone to dictate how I live my life."

She took another couple of steps toward him. Either one was close enough to strike out at the other. All of the other dwarfs unconsciously moved closer, tightening the circle they'd formed around the two of them, ready to intervene if necessary.

Alariq looked around at the sea of faces in the room, seeing the expressions bombarding him, but not identifying the dwarfs they belonged to. Some were contorted and red, others expressionless, and the rest pleading, begging him with their eyes to put an end to this.

In that moment, Alariq was suffocated by their condemnation, their accusations, their blame. This was the very reason he'd wanted to go out on his own.

"I did not ask any of you to come with me," said Alariq. "Not one. You all made this choice of your own free will."

"Well, maybe if we'd known how this, how *you*, were going to turn out, we'd've ended up on the other side of this story," Asher said, moving directly between Alariq and Tianna.

Alariq's jaw spasmed as he spoke. "I am sorry exile is not living up to your lofty expectations."

Without another word, he strode out into the rain, an uncomfortable lump in his throat.

He sat in the clearing, rain falling down around him. He stayed that way, hunched over in the deluge, for hours.

The words he'd been dreading, but known were coming. Asher had a knack for saying those lately. *We wish we hadn't stood with you.*

Those hadn't been his exact words, but they were clearly what he meant. What they all felt.

Alariq knew they would all feel that way, sooner or later. Everything happened so fast in Ishtara. He'd been too busy worrying about whether he was about to be executed to try and stop the others from taking his side. If he hadn't been so blindsided, maybe he could have spared them this fate. Told them to stay, *made* them stay.

He remembered the exact moment this fear had first gripped him. It was the very first step outside the city gate. He'd known then they would all regret their decision. The question was simply a matter of when.

He heard footsteps in the puddles and the very last person in the world he would have expected to come after him, sat down in the rain beside him.

Tianna stayed there, perfectly still, staring out into the forest, her shoulder touching his, silent for a long while before she spoke.

"You and I are a lot alike, you know?" She chuckled half-heartedly. "More alike than you realize." She cut her eyes at him and smiled slightly. "More alike than either one of us wishes were true."

Alariq looked down at the grass between his legs and nodded slightly.

"I understand why you are the way you are," she said, her voice soft, but clear.

Alariq met her gaze, about to tell her there was no way she could understand anything about him, but when he looked in her eyes, through the rain, he couldn't say the words. He couldn't say them because he didn't really believe them.

Tianna's sympathetic face hardened slightly. "*I* understand. But those dwarfs inside," she pointed toward the treehome, "they do not."

Alariq continued to meet her gaze. She searched his eyes, as though trying to determine whether he was really listening to what she had to say. "They do not understand why their loyalty is being questioned. Or why their willingness to stand by you is being used as a weapon against them."

She looked away for a moment, as though summoning the courage to say her next words. When she looked back, her face was strained. "They do not understand, because they do not know what betrayal does to you."

Tianna continued to look into his eyes and Alariq looked back, confusion creasing his forehead.

He was just about to speak, when she stood up abruptly. She looked down at him one last time before turning, about to head back to the treehome.

"I am sorry."

The appearance of those words on his lips surprised even him. But he felt better once he'd said them. Ironically, they didn't seem to surprise Tianna in the slightest.

Tianna did not say anything in return. He thought she was just going to leave without acknowledging his apology. And he didn't blame her. He hung his head.

But then he felt a small hand on his shoulder.

Her voice was so soft, but thick with emotion, when she spoke.

"I know."

She squeezed his shoulder ever so slightly, and then walked away.

Alariq continued to sit there until the rain stopped. It had been a warm, gentle rain, but the cooler night air chilled him now.

He thought about what Tianna had said. *Betrayal.* He hadn't identified the emotion he'd been feeling all these months. Hadn't wanted to examine it. But Tianna had identified it for him. And now he had no choice but to confront it.

He felt betrayed by his family, his king, his soldiers, and his kin. He'd defended Ishtara flawlessly and faithfully for decades and the people just forgot all of that the minute he was accused of treason, and only on Haamith's word. As much as he told himself any father would believe his son, he still hated Tanith for believing Haamith without even hearing Alariq's account, or the accounts of Ford and Blainn, whose word also seemed to count for nothing compared with Haamith's. As much as Alariq tried to convince himself he was happy his family had stayed behind in a safe, stable environment, it hurt that they didn't so much as say goodbye. Of his soldiers, only three stood by him. Even then, Blainn and Ford had only defended him because they knew he was innocent. And Asher had faith in his brother's word, not Alariq's. That had certainly been made clear over the last few days.

He shouldn't be so angry. The dwarfs who'd stayed, his king, his family, they made the rational choice. They took the most well-traveled path, the easy one. He prided himself on being like that, sensible and pragmatic. Or at least, he always had before now.

That had always been his plan. Make the right choices, do a good job, don't mess up, and that would be enough. Isn't that what all dwarfs did?

He just never thought the king's son would lie about his loyalty.

He finally asked the question he'd refused to confront, because ultimately, he knew it didn't matter.

Why?

Why did Haamith do it? Had he offended Haamith in some way? Did he just dislike Alariq? Was he threatened by Alariq's position in the military? The king himself was First Authority of Division One, but the king's son was traditionally named First Authority in one of the other divisions, and Tanith had not yet bestowed that honor on Haamith. Was it that? But there were seven other divisions, and within each one, a First Authority. Why Alariq? Why him?

He rubbed his hands over his face in frustration. None of it made sense.

The lump returned to his throat and his eyes began to water. The last time he'd cried was when his grandfather was killed in battle when Alariq was a small dwarfling. He didn't even cry when his father was killed only a few years later.

He refused to allow the tears to spill over. He thought of Brimir, who had been a close friend of his grandfather's and who had become like a father to Alariq. If he was honest, Brimir had always been more of a father to him. Which seemed strange, now that he thought of it, because Alariq was so like his father. His father had also lacked the vibrancy his grandfather had possessed.

All these months, Alariq had purposefully steered his mind away from his exile. But now he examined it fully, looking at every detail.

As soon as he had entered the King's Hall, Tanith had immediately read the charges. Alariq didn't even have time to remove his pack or coat. He remembered how Brimir hadn't spoken a single word. Just walked over and stood next to Alariq, shoulder to shoulder, before Tanith was even finished.

He thought of Ford and Blainn who had tried to defend him to the king, yelling out his innocence to all of Ishtara, Asher standing beside his brother unquestioningly.

Alariq himself had just stood there. It was the only moment in his entire life that he had been truly frozen, unable to act.

And Callum. Brimir's story came back to him too. Sweet, timid Callum, who had called the king's son a liar to the king himself before Alariq and the other soldiers had arrived. He chuckled, picturing the scene.

He felt the hot tears well up again, though this time in

happiness and gratitude. These, he allowed to flow. These were tears worth shedding.

After a time, he wiped his face, and stood. He looked out into the forest for a moment more, then walked back inside and joined the group for dinner. Tianna was already there and everyone looked at her when Alariq entered.

"Hungry?" she asked.

Alariq nodded.

"You should rest that ankle. I'll fix you a plate," she said, rising.

"Thank you," he responded, taking his usual seat at the table.

The other six dwarfs seemed to accept this as an official armistice. Ford resumed giving a blow-by-blow account of his and Tianna's fight with the ettins. Soon after, he told the story of when he'd been called out to settle a dispute in one of the outer settlements. He and another soldier had been checking a barn for allegedly stolen property and a snake had fallen from the rafters onto the other infantryman's shoulders. Everyone laughed at the recount, including Alariq, who, despite the unfortunate occurrences of the day, felt lighter than he had since leaving Ishtara. Asher alone seemed to still be burdened by the earlier events. He laughed only half-heartedly at his brother's tale, his countenance still drawn and pallid.

As they ate and talked and laughed, only one thing continued to gnaw at Alariq. He thought about his conversation outside with Tianna.

He wondered who had betrayed her. He wondered whether he would ever be brave enough to ask her. And he wondered whether she would answer him if he did.

18

Foxholes and Friends

There is a phenomenon in human (and dwarf) interaction that causes imperfect people—and all but the most narcissistic among us will admit to some degree of imperfection—to form a higher degree of fondness for others who are also imperfect, greater even than for those they see as closer to perfection. It is of utmost importance to note, however, that there is a law of diminishing returns in this phenomenon. It is possible to reach such a degree of imperfection that you are no longer likeable in the slightest. It is a fine line, to be sure.

And Alariq seemed to have made that line his permanent home.

Just when you thought he was going to cross over the line, his behavior would change, for better or for worse.

It created a whiplash-like effect in those less familiar with him. But those who knew him better had faith that whenever Alariq flirted a little too seriously with imperfection, that he would redeem himself sooner or later.

For once, in our story, we find Alariq in a period of such redemption.

After a day of surveillance, it became clear that, as feared, the ettins had holed up inside the city. They even discontinued patrols. But despite this unlucky turn of events, Alariq did not sink into one of his usual bad tempers.

Instead, he set himself to the task of determining how the ettins had known to lay a trap. After a brief discussion of the topic, Alariq dispatched Ford, Asher, and Blainn to the site of their battle with the hunting party of ettins. Sure enough, they came back with the news that the graves they'd dug had been disturbed. The ettins must have tracked the party, slipping out of the city unnoticed by the dwarfs, and venturing out into the woods in secret. From there, it must have been clear someone was intentionally attacking the ettins, eroding their numbers.

Alariq didn't dwell on it. It was done and there was no sense devoting energy to it. In lieu of brooding about their mistakes and bad luck, Alariq constantly spurred discussion of their options with Tianna and the other dwarfs at great length. If Ford and Tianna were right, and they killed both of the ettins that pursued them, it would mean there were twenty-one left, two of which were still injured. They were so close. The eight of them had whittled down the ettinhorde from over forty to almost twenty. An entire division of Ishta dwarfs could be proud of that achievement. Despite the new hurdles, Alariq would not admit defeat now and he attacked the task with new vigor.

For over a week, they watched Dendreya, trying a variety of different vantage points. A thickly and intricately woven tapestry of ideas hung constantly over the dinner table. Alariq, Blainn, and Ford, the three soldiers who had fought in the Ettinwar, went over their battles, searching for any weakness or idea.

And most importantly, they continued to try and figure out how the ettins were getting food. They had discussed blocking the creek again, to deny them freshwater, but they couldn't be sure the entire clan of ettins wouldn't come to the creek, armed for battle. And even if they used such an opportunity to enter the city, there was no way to fortify Dendreya in the time it would take the ettins to return from the creek. They reserved this plan as one of last resort, though they revisited it frequently, ultimately coming to the same conclusions.

They also discounted the creek as a potential point of entry. After the dwarfs used it to escape the trap, the ettins were probably watching, or worse, had rigged it with some sort of trap or concealed peril.

Tianna seemed energized by Alariq's new enthusiasm. Ironically, it was she Alariq turned to with most of his ideas, trusting her to find any holes in his plans. But now, instead of being threatened by her criticism, he welcomed the challenge, relishing in their back-and-forth deliberations of strategy. She seemed to enjoy the interactions as well and Alariq finally understood why the other dwarfs had taken to her. When she wasn't giving him the stink eye or speaking in her icy, overly-enunciated tone, her company could be downright delightful.

But while Alariq was reveling in his newfound friendship, the spirits of the other dwarfs began to fall. There was a momentary reprieve from the despair, when Blainn and Callum heard the ettins fighting amongst themselves inside the city.

"They are not meant to stay cooped up like that," Alariq said for at least the third time. "They have to be starving, that cannot help the situation. They cannot continue like this for much longer."

But continue like this, the ettins did.

Alariq set patrols night and day, on either side of the city, but not so much as a single ettin finger breached the boundary of the city walls.

One night, in the early hours of the morning, Alariq dreamt that he was outside the city keeping watch in a tree.

He looked up, and high in the branches was a leaf that was different from the others. While all the others were green, it was a golden auburn, gleaming in the sunlight. He started to climb, all thoughts of watch duty and ettins abandoned. The branches began getting thin and supple, but still he climbed, reaching for the leaf. Just as he stretched out to grab it, he heard rustling sounds. Reason started to return to him and for a brief second he realized how strange it was that he was going to such lengths for something as meaningless as a leaf.

He awoke to Asher climbing into bed, having returned from his watch. Alariq quickly dozed back off, thinking about how funny the mind could be sometimes.

His ankle finally healed, Alariq rejoined the recon rotation. Now that they were watching the ettins all day long, he had everyone working shorter, but more frequent shifts. He was also varying the lengths and locations of the shifts randomly, in case the ettins were somehow watching, so they could not anticipate a shift change and attack or sneak out for food.

One early morning, a fortnight after the foiled attempt to recapture Dendreya, Alariq was on watch with Brimir. They sat, perched in side-by-side trees on the south side of the city, which lay between them and the treehome. They were barely a stone's throw from where they had seen the city for the first time.

Alariq looked over and caught Brimir rubbing his legs. They had been there since midnight. Dawn was still a few hours away. He'd scheduled this as a longer shift, not meant to end until dawn. He made this one long to minimize travel through the forest in the dark, when the blackness was utterly complete. He'd also been giving himself the longer shifts, to make up for all the time the others had to pick up his slack during his confinement.

But seeing Brimir, coiled up tightly on his perch, massaging his old, aching joints, made Alariq regret his oh-so-carefully-thought-out decision.

"Why not head on back to the treehome?" Alariq called quietly over to Brimir. "I'll finish the watch."

"I'm alright." Brimir shook out his arms. "I just need to get down and walk around a moment. Loosen up a bit." He made to climb down the tree.

"Well, you can loosen up on your walk back to Tianna's," Alariq said. "Seriously, that's an order." He gave Brimir a faux-stern look.

Brimir looked back, his face set in protest, but then the frown lines gave way to laugh. He chuckled. "You are just like your grandfather," he said, shaking his head.

Alariq's face softened too. It wasn't the first time Brimir had told him so, but he loved hearing it. His grandfather had been his role model in so many ways. He was practical, but kind, with just the right amount of eccentricity. Typical in so many ways, but just rebellious enough to refuse the trades and spend his working life in the military.

"When he was First Authority, he normally gave orders like a detached, professional leader. But he always seemed to take special delight in telling me in particular what to do." Brimir stretched his lower back.

Alariq chuckled. Of all the things in his childhood, the thing he remembered most was the friendship between Brimir and his grandfather. They'd been like brothers. Brothers who'd chosen to be brothers.

In a way, Alariq guessed they had. Alariq's grandfather had been born to dwarfs living in the outer settlements and his parents had been killed in an epidemic. He'd been found, a baby crying alone in a hut, by the nomads who spent their lives crisscrossing the Continent. The Wanderers, they were called by most people. They had another, more formal name, but Alariq couldn't recall it. They'd taken his grandfather and raised him until he was a young dwarf. That's when he ran away in search of his own people.

As if Brimir could read Alariq's thoughts, he said, "I can remember when I first met him. I was playing outside the city with a bunch of the other dwarflings, while our fathers were fetching food from the outer settlements. I fell down a hill and right into the pathetic excuse for what your grandfather called a camp."

Brimir chuckled. "I took to him instantly, but he took a while longer to warm up to me."

Alariq smiled. That sounded like his grandfather. Slow to warm up to folks. It also sounded like Brimir, who was quite adept at accurately judging people within mere moments of meeting them.

"He came looking for his kin, but then got cagey about actually entering the city. I knew immediately he was just scared of being turned away."

Alariq climbed down from his tree too, stretching once he hit the ground. But really, he just wanted to be closer to Brimir while he told the story.

"He had been starving for so long, living off rats and whatever he could forage, that he was this tiny slip of a dwarf. I could have knocked him over with one finger."

Brimir outright laughed this time. "It sure didn't take long for the tables to turn on me. A little proper food and I was standing in his shadow in no time."

"Is that when he came to live with you and your family?" Alariq asked.

"Heavens no! That boy wouldn't come near the city for months. I had to sneak out to bring him food. We were lucky it was peacetime, or it would not have been so easy to get in and out of the city."

"I never knew you did that," Alariq said, although he wasn't terribly surprised. Taking in a vagabond dwarfling sounded like something only Brimir would do.

Well, maybe Callum, Alariq thought with a shake of his head.

"Sure." Brimir nodded. "Like I said, slow to warm up. But eventually he came up to the city with me. And my mother always wanted another child, so the decision was an easy one."

Alariq nodded. He'd never realized just how much he owed to Brimir. He'd known about the nomads and that Brimir's family had taken his grandfather in when he returned to Ishtara. But not about the rest. Alariq had always known Brimir was the softer of the brotherly twosome, and he'd always thought of it as a somewhat unfortunate idiosyncrasy. But now, now that Alariq knew the role Brimir's open-heartedness had played in his grandfather's story, and in his own, he wasn't so sure.

"Head on back," Alariq said, this time as a friend would talk to another. "Take the long way around the west side. We have seen neither hide nor hair of an ettin in a fortnight, I doubt you'll have any trouble, especially once the forest thickens."

"I can finish the watch with..." Brimir began, but Alariq held up a hand.

"I know. But there is just no need." Alariq paused and looked at the city walls, barely visible in the moonlight.

Brimir nodded. "Alright. If you're sure?"

In answer, Alariq just smiled and pulled himself back up into the tree.

Brimir chuckled quietly again and headed off into the darkness.

For the first time since sitting in the clearing after his fight with Tianna, Alariq was alone. He straddled the large branch he was on, his back against the trunk. He just sat for a while, listening to the forest sounds. Dendreya had been quiet for the duration of the watch.

Soon, however, the hairs on the back of his neck began to rise. He listened carefully for the telltale sound that someone was close by, watching him. But he heard nothing. He pretended to stretch out his arms, unhooking his already cocked and loaded crossbow from the limb it hung upon.

"If I were anyone else, you would be in trouble."

Alariq heard the soft, feminine voice from the tree directly behind him. Without turning, he said, "If you were anyone else, I would have heard you coming."

He heard a soft rustling and felt his tree move slightly. Tianna appeared at his side, golden hair and amber eyes standing out in stark contrast to the green foliage around her. She was on a branch slightly below and to the left of his. She balanced along its surface, continuing much farther out than Alariq would have dared to venture, and sat, her legs both thrown over the same side of the branch, facing him, a broad smile on her face. She clearly recognized the compliment.

"Where's Brimir?"

"I sent him back to the treehome." Alariq kept one eye on the city. "His joints were bothering him, being up in the tree for so long."

Tianna nodded. She removed her bow and quiver from her shoulders and looped them over a small limb. Her hair was in a long, tight braid, but small golden wisps had escaped at her temples and framed her face.

They sat quietly for a few moments before Tianna spoke.

"How badly do you want to ask me where I have been?" she asked with a grin.

For once, Alariq had nothing to say back. He'd just been wondering how long he had to wait before asking that very question without seeming as though he was suspicious. And whether there was a way to work it into casual conversation.

Tianna laughed the laugh that only belonged to her. It wasn't a giggle exactly, more of a chuckle, but combined with a lady-like snort through her nose, if there was such a thing. It seemed to be reserved only for good-natured mocking. Usually of Alariq.

"I walked the beach," she said. "I had a thought about the ettins getting food. I was thinking they might be getting fish from the creek. I have never had much luck fishing in it, but if they're rationing supplies of some sort, every bit helps." She swung her legs slightly as she talked.

"So I made a net out of lakeweed and strung it across the mouth of the creek. Water will still get through, but fish of any decent size should be kept out."

Alariq nodded approvingly.

"What?" she asked.

Alariq looked at her, wondering how she always seemed to know when his mind was working. And how she *especially* seemed to know when he was thinking something he'd rather keep to himself.

He considered carefully before answering. "Are you sure it was wise, going out to the beach by yourself?"

Tianna laughed her laugh again. "You know, I lived alone here long before you and your companions arrived to protect me." Her mouth twitched and her eyes sparkled as she spoke.

Alariq seized his opening. "How long exactly have you lived here?"

"Long enough to feel perfectly safe walking around by myself." The smile remained, even in her eyes, but her tone suggested she did not approve of the direction the conversation was taking.

He'd made an express promise to himself, and an implied one to Tianna and the other dwarfs, that he would be more trusting of her, despite the many questions he had about who she was and where she came from. So he let the matter drop. But he gave her a look to let her know that he was *choosing* to let it drop.

And damn it, if she didn't just grin at him.

"When is your watch up? Dawn?" she asked.

He nodded. "Then I was planning to walk the beach back."

Tianna feigned appalled shock. "All by yourself?"

He couldn't help himself.

He threw a piece of bark at her.

And she just laughed her Tianna-laugh and grinned.

Alariq marveled at her. At them. He'd never seen her so

agreeable—at least not to him. And he'd certainly never gone so long in her presence without wanting to wring her neck.

"I'll finish the watch with you," she said.

Before Alariq could say anything, she already had her bow and quiver back on her shoulders and was swinging down from their tree. He just watched as she scaled another one a few paces away and took up a similar position to his.

They sat silently in their respective trees until close to dawn. When he saw the sun peek at them over the horizon, Alariq sat up and looked over at Tianna. In silent question, he raised his eyebrows and cocked his head toward the beach. In equally-silent response, she swung down from her perch.

They started toward the beach, still in comfortable quiet. Once they reached it, they stepped out onto the sand, and instead of hugging the tree line like Alariq usually would have, they walked along the middle of the beach, enjoying the sunrise.

They didn't go far before two figures appeared further down the shore. It was clear from their statures and hair colors that it was Gideon and one of the brothers. Both Alariq and Tianna had reached for their bows when the figures appeared, but they weren't moving quickly and the taller one raised a hand in a casual salute, so they resumed their mellow jaunt.

When they came within hearing distance, Alariq asked, "Why are you not on the west side of the city?"

Ford and Gideon both nodded in greeting to Tianna.

"We heard you were out walking the beach alone and thought it would be wise to escort you back to the treehome," said Ford.

Alariq gave Tianna an I-told-you-so look.

Tianna rolled her eyes so hard, her head moved right along with them. "How on earth do you all think I survived before you lot came along?"

For once, Alariq got to laugh good-naturedly at her.

Ford and Gideon looked at each other uncomfortably. Ford mumbled something and shifted awkwardly, looking at his feet.

At Alariq and Tianna's questioning stares, Gideon spoke up. "Actually...we were...we were talking about Alariq," he said, looking at Tianna, and by definition, *not* looking at Alariq.

Everyone was silent for a moment and then laughter burst out of Tianna with such force, that Ford and Gideon jumped. Alariq, who had expected no less from her, just glared at the other two.

Tianna looked at Alariq, and seeing the scowl on his face, laughed even harder, grabbing her side and doubling slightly.

Alariq continued to glower, while the other two dwarfs tried not to make the situation worse by laughing too. They looked at Tianna as though they thought she was very much pushing her luck.

"What's that?" Ford asked, his voice suddenly sharp.

Tianna immediately quieted and she and Alariq turned in the direction of Ford's stare.

Six wagons, covered in tan cloth and traveling in tandem, dotted the pasture through which the dwarfs had travelled all those months ago.

They cut a slow, but steady path through the tall grass, making their way slowly toward the small company on the beach.

There was only one possible intended destination of the caravan.

Dendreya.

19

Too Many Familiar Faces

Without speaking, the foursome retreated into the cover of the forest.

"No armed guard," said Ford as he crouched behind some bushes at the tree line.

Alariq knelt beside him in the sand, pulling aside some brambles to get a better look. He turned to address Tianna, but she had disappeared from his side.

"The wagons are pulled by mules," came her voice, and Alariq looked up to find her already a quarter of the way up a tree. She looked down at him.

"Supply trains," Alariq said simply. One mystery was solved. The ettins were being supplied by someone. But the answer only raised the next question: *by whom?*

"Tianna—get the others. Meet us just inside the forest, directly north of the city's front gate."

She leapt gracefully to the forest floor and shot off toward the treehome without a word.

Alariq returned his attention to the caravan. "Can you see the waggoners?" he asked the remaining two.

"No, they're driving the mules from under the wagon cover.

We'll need to get closer and get a direct line of sight into the wagon," Gideon replied.

"Alright, let's move then. Gideon—stay here and give the usual signal when the wagons come into your sight." Alariq stood and led the way into the forest.

They quickly reached the spot where he told Tianna to meet them. They were just inside the forest, at the edge of the clearing in which the city was nestled.

"Do we attack?" Ford asked.

Alariq shook his head. "Not with only two of us." He paused, staring at the city. "I am not nearly as interested in stopping the caravan, as I am in knowing who is behind it."

Alariq looked around. They had a perfect view of the gate, but their angle was from the side. The only way to get a direct look into the wagons was to be inside the city itself. From their current position, Alariq could no longer see the wagons. He tried to determine how long before the caravan made its way across the grasslands and over the beach.

A while yet, he thought, but his palms began to sweat and fingers twitch for his crossbow.

Alariq retreated a few paces into the forest and Ford followed. The possibility that someone was keeping the ettins in rations had entered his mind many a time. It made sense. They were mercenaries, after all. Maybe someone was keeping them on retainer. But why in Dendreya?

It was a ready-made, but deserted city. It certainly had that in its favor. But it was far away from the thick of action, on the opposite side of the continent of Dirnovaria and the Gateway Cities. But maybe that was the draw? Keep the army hidden away until needed?

Alariq crouched at the base of a tree, ready to duck out of sight as soon as he heard Gideon's signal.

The ettinhorde might be here under orders from Ettinridge. But for what purpose?

Every nerve in Alariq's body tingled, completely aware that he was perhaps moments away from knowing who was supplying the ettins, mere breaths from unlocking the key to moving his life forward again. He deliberately slowed his breathing, forcing himself calm.

Three small whistles, repeated twice. There was Gideon's signal. Alariq lay on his stomach, as flat as he could make himself, concealed by a large, gnarled tree root that snaked above ground, Ford to his left.

The minutes crawled slowly by, like a turtle crossing a path. Alariq counted his breaths, just to focus on something else. From his low vantage, he heard the wagons before he could see them. His pulse quickened.

The first pair of mules came into view. They were small and so was the wagon that followed.

Then came the sounds of wood creaking and metal groaning. Alariq turned slightly to see the front gate being opened. No ettins emerged.

They are worried about an attack, Alariq thought. *From us.* He smirked with satisfaction.

From where he laid, he could not see the drivers of the wagons. The front gate opened just enough to allow the caravan clearance and soon all six wagons had disappeared. The gates had just begun to swing closed when he heard sounds behind him.

He rolled behind the tree and sat up to see Tianna jogging toward him, crouching as she approached the tree line. Asher was right behind her, followed by the remaining three.

Alariq addressed Blainn. "Gideon is back toward the beach. Go fetch him."

They all crouched around the tree, looking at the city, even though they weren't likely to learn anything from the closed gate.

Alariq motioned to everyone to lean in.

"The ettins are expecting an attack," he said. "The supplies are already inside and we cannot hope to take on the whole horde, plus whoever came with the caravan.

"What we need," he continued, "is to know who is supplying them and how often, so I think our best bet is to follow the wagons when they leave," said Alariq.

"What about the supplies?" Callum asked.

"Nothing we can do about them," Alariq answered, shaking his head slightly. "But if we can find out who is supplying them and when the next delivery is, maybe we can use that information to our advantage."

"How do we do that?" Asher asked. "Should we try to get closer?"

"No, we'll follow them when they leave the city." Alariq looked over at the gate and then up at the sun. It was not even close to midday.

"Is everyone up for a long walk?" he asked the group and everyone nodded enthusiastically.

"Good. We need to get to the other side of the city. They are probably unloading the wagons as we speak, so we will have to move fast." Alariq looked around to ensure everyone was ready and then headed off at a brisk pace around the walls.

They stayed just inside the tree line as they circled the city, pausing frequently to listen for sounds of the front gate opening or wagon wheels turning. Once they made it around to the front of the arena again, this time on the southern side, near where Alariq and Tianna had been on watch just a couple of hours previously, Alariq held up his hand and everyone stopped, alert for any sound from the gate.

Tianna tucked one of the escaped strands of hair behind her ear. "What will we do once they head into open pasture? They will see us if we follow them."

Alariq had been pondering that very question as he knelt on one knee, listening and catching his breath from the jog.

"We will have to stay far enough back that they cannot see us." He looked up at the scorching sun. "The grass is so tall, shoulder height almost, that we should be tough to see anyway. But once midday passes, the sun will be at our backs and it will be even harder for them to see us looking into the brightness."

Alariq looked at the city. He'd expected the caravan to have left Dendreya by now, but still the gate remained tightly closed. For a second, he panicked, thinking they had missed the wagons leaving while they circled behind the city. But then he looked at the ground in front of the front gate. He could see the mule tracks in the sandy dirt. All led toward Dendreya, and none away from it.

The gate remained still and stalwart until the sun was directly above the city. Alariq was just about to suggest they start taking shifts to get some water from the lake when he heard the gate begin to wail. Again, it opened only wide enough to let the wagons leave, one after the other.

The waggoners remained concealed under the covered portion, reigns popping out through the dark hole. If it had still been morning and the sun had been to the east, shining into the wagons, they might have caught a glimpse of their drivers. Instead, the sun bore down directly from above, keeping the inside of the wagons in shadow.

The caravan took the same route away from the city as it had toward it, following its own tracks perfectly. The mules ascended the hill at the beach, while the dwarfs remained concealed in the trees and rocky foothills to the west. Because the dwarfs had the high ground, they were able to keep an eye on their target, but the rocks and the sun above concealed them from view down below.

Soon, the wagons and Alariq's company were on level ground again and the former headed off through the swampy grasslands, while the latter hunkered down in the last of the rocky shelters to wait for the caravan to gain enough distance that the dwarfs could follow without being noticed.

When they could barely see the wagon tops, the dwarfs and Tianna headed after them. If ever they closed the distance, they sat down in the tall grass and allowed a little more time to pass before continuing.

During these respites, Alariq kept peering up above the grass to check on their target. Whoever was driving the wagons was staying off the beach, but following it closely, not giving the lake nearly as wide a berth as the dwarfs had.

When the sun began to set, Alariq hastened their pace, not wanting to lose their mark in the dark. Just as the sun met the horizon and the ground began to slope slightly downwards, Asher spotted a fire down by the beach. Alariq's keen eyes could just make out the outlines of the wagons down below.

They approached slowly. The object of their pursuit had chosen their campsite wisely. The lake was to the north, the beach to the east and west, and a large flat area of marsh to the south, making it impossible for anyone, including the dwarfs, to get close without being seen.

They got as near as they dared, but still could not make out the mystery wagon drivers. Clouds had covered the moon and whoever was down on the beach was staying out of the firelight. Alariq's boots sunk into the marshy wetland beneath them.

Unwilling to order his men into a fight without knowing the identity of their adversaries, Alariq was just reconciling himself to having to wait until morning, and wondering about how to get food to last them another day, when the clouds shifted.

The dwarfs instinctively flattened themselves to the ground, hiding behind the small tufts of grass and moss. The moon was full and it bounced off the surface of August Sound in every direction, illuminating the campsite below.

A thought had been growing in Alariq's mind ever since he had seen the wagons up close. They were too small to be driven by other ettins. And ettins were not the type to send others in their stead.

That left only four other options: men, knomes, Utu, or dwarfs.

The Utu were a desert people who lived in the northern part of the Continent. They kept to themselves and would have no reason to ever have dealings with ettins, much less provide them supplies in a dead dwarfish city hundreds of leagues away.

And the two cities of men, Prienne and Lysette, were situated north of August Sound, which meant anyone traveling from those cities would likely take the northern route around the lake, not the southern one this caravan had traveled.

The route we traveled, he thought grimly, his palms starting to sweat again.

Even with the direction his thoughts had taken, Alariq would have been surprised to discover that he was right in guessing the identities of the campers on the beach.

He was utterly shocked to discover he was wrong.

Instead of the small Karxani dwarfs he expected to find sleeping around the fire, he saw twelve even smaller creatures.

Around him, every member of his company made various sounds of disbelief as they struggled to reconcile what they were seeing with what made sense.

Knomes.

"What are they doing?" Ford asked, his eyes wide and his mouth ajar.

A thousand theories raced through Alariq's mind, each more unlikely than the one before it. An ettin deception designed to trap them, Knaba betraying Ishtara, renegade knomes.

Tianna looked from Alariq to Ford with her perceptive eyes narrowed slightly.

Before Alariq could respond, an icy shiver shot down his spine. He turned back to the campsite just in time to see the first ripples appear in the water.

20

The Short of It

There wasn't even time to give an order. Alariq leapt from his spot and charged the campsite, trusting in the others to follow. The moon disappeared behind the clouds again, leaving only the campfire for illumination. Before he had even covered a quarter of the distance between their hiding spot and the knomes, he heard the first cries.

He yelled, hoping to distract what he instinctively knew were the finfiends, or turn their attack away from the knomes. His bow was useless in the dark, so he drew his sword. The knomes continued to scream, shadows dancing everywhere. But the finfiends stayed away from the fire and out of the light.

Alariq could hear the others right behind him. The clouds shifted yet again and permitted the moon to reveal the scene on the beach. He barely took in the tiny bodies littering the ground before he jumped right into the middle of the largest group of finfiends, slicing his sword through the air. Then the other dwarfs were around him, twisting, jabbing, parrying, punching.

Alariq dove through the fire, grabbing a burning log as he went, and wielded it in his left hand, just as though he were fighting with two swords. He saw in flashes of his periphery that some of the others had followed suit. The beach was alight with fire and flashing steel, the air filled with a mixture of dwarf yells, knome cries, and finfiend screams.

Suddenly, Alariq was face-to-face with a familiar foe. The white-haired finmaid recognized him immediately, and her mouth contorted into a half-smile, half-snarl, and Alariq had the inexplicable feeling that she'd been hoping to meet him again. She bore two long, thin knives, one of the few finfiends armed with modern weapons. Alariq wondered briefly where she had obtained them. Or from whom.

She was much taller than Alariq and quicker, but not nearly as strong. His blows drove her backward and his burning club kept her at a distance. But still she sought to advance, her knives ever-cutting through the air.

A scream, a real scream, not an unearthly finfiend cry, distracted him for a moment, and the finmaid's knife sliced across his forearm. Searing pain shot up from the wound into his neck. He struck out with the burning log and felt it connect with her stomach. He did not check to make sure she was incapacitated and instead searched for the source of the scream.

To his right, near the water's edge, he saw three finmen dragging Tianna into the water. Blainn had come to her aid and delivered two quick blows with his sword to the back of two of her captors' calves. Tianna was able to shake off the other, though how, Alariq had no idea. The finfiend was the most enormous creature Alariq had ever seen, other than an ettin.

Alariq started toward them, but caught a flash of white out of the corner of his eye and raised his sword just in time. The finmaid had charged him yet again, but he blocked her blows.

"Together!" Alariq yelled. "Stay tight!"

The dwarfs drew inward toward the original campsite, forming a semicircle that curved outward toward the lake. Some of the injured finfiends had already retreated and the eight who remained were cornered, with no choice but to back slowly into the lake, their faces all contorted in hatred.

The last finfiend disappeared, the muscular, chiseled finman who had tried to grab Tianna, but escaped Blainn's blade. They watched as his black hair disappeared into the black water.

Ford immediately turned his attention to the knomes.

"We cannot stay here," Alariq called, as Ford bent down over a tiny body. "We have to move."

"We can't just leave them!" Ford yelled back, moving on to another knome.

Ford was right. "Alright. Brimir, Gideon, Callum—check the knomes." Alariq patrolled the water line. "The rest of you—stay with me. Keep sharp!"

Ford reluctantly moved away from the campsite and joined Alariq as he watched the water's edge. Tianna was shaking off Asher's questions of concern and retrieved her weapon, having lost it in the fight.

Alariq heard a small groan and turned to see Brimir and Callum converge on a small body near the fire.

"This one's alive!" Callum called. "But he's hurt."

"Any others?" Alariq asked, keeping one eye on the water.

"Not so far," Gideon replied, his tone doleful.

Alariq looked at the lake, but the water's surface was utterly calm once more.

Gideon and Callum checked the remaining knomes and searched the area for a minute more, while Brimir tended to the one they'd found alive. The rest continued to patrol the beach.

Gideon walked over to Alariq and said in a quiet voice, "The rest are dead. And I think the finfiends might have taken a few. It seems like some are missing. They were armed with tiny knives, more for cooking than for fighting. They had no chance."

"And the other one?" Alariq asked.

"He is in bad shape, I do not think he is going to make it. And I am not sure we should move him." Gideon wiped some blood from his lower lip and shot a look over at Ford, who was peering with concern at the only surviving knome, and then leaned in close to Alariq. "If you want to talk to him, now is the time."

Alariq started to walk over to Brimir and the knome, but paused, and then turned to Ford. "Ford—come here. Callum, take his place."

Callum immediately took up Ford's position between Tianna and Blainn, while Ford joined Alariq as he approached what was left of the fire. They knelt in the sand on either side of Brimir, who was applying pressure to the wound in the knome's stomach.

"Fordinand..." The knome's voice was so tiny and childlike.

Alariq looked at Ford. "Do you know him?"

But Ford was reaching out to take the knome's outstretched hand.

"It's alright," said Ford, his voice strained.

"The others?" asked the knome.

Ford stared at the toddler-sized creature for a moment and then shook his head.

The knome's eyes closed for a moment and when he opened them once more, a few tears leaked out.

"They said in the mines that you were exiled...," the knome let out a cough and a tiny groan of pain, "...for treason." He searched Ford's face. "But I knew that couldn't be true." He coughed again and this time, a little blood tinged his lips.

"No," said Ford, his voice cracking. "It isn't true, but that doesn't matter right now."

"Yes." Another cough. More blood. "It does. You are a good dwarf. You were so kind to all of us. Always asking about our families, making sure we were eating enough."

Ford smiled kindly at the knome, his eyes watery.

"Yes, you are a good dwarf," the knome repeated. "And you did not deserve what happened."

Ford shushed the knome softly. "That is not important now."

"Yes," the knome raised his head, trying desperately to pull himself toward Ford. "It does. Because the dwarf who did it to you is not a good dwarf."

Alariq, who had been caught up in the emotion of the moment, snapped back into his head, remembering that this knome held the information they so desperately needed.

"What do you mean?" he asked, a bit more harshly than he intended, angry not at the knome, but at himself for letting emotion get the better of him.

Ford shot him an angry look, but the knome hadn't seemed to hear Alariq. He only had eyes for Ford.

"Your king," said the knome. "He is not honorable..." Another cough and the knome lay flat again. "...like you." The knome spoke in broken, halting sentences, his voice growing fainter by the word. "We make this trip, to the old charter town, twice a year, to deliver supplies to those horrible creatures."

"For how long?" Ford asked, lowering his face close to the knome's.

"Since the war." His voice was barely a whisper now.

"Thank you for telling me." Ford's voice caught and his eyes welled up.

"One more thing..." Blood leaked out of the corner of the knome's mouth. "I was sent, with a few other knomes, five months ago..."

Alariq leaned in as well, trying desperately to hear the words the knome was trying to say.

"We delivered a message to the leader. I...I don't know...what it said..."

The last words were barely audible. He drew one last rattling breath and then his eyes closed and his hand went slack in Ford's.

Ford hung his head over the knome's tiny hand, which he still held. Brimir stopped applying pressure to the wound and gently covered it with a blanket.

Alariq pushed himself up from the ground and backed away, looking at the tiny creature's body for a moment, trying to memorize every precious word he'd said. He backed away slowly, his mind replaying the scene he'd just witnessed over and over again, in broken flashes of memory. Finally, he turned away.

The others were still by the water. They hadn't heard the story, so quiet were the knome's words. They all looked expectantly at Alariq.

Alariq rubbed his hand over his jaw.

"You're hurt." Tianna strode over to him and took his arm to examine the cut. "It's not deep, but it's long." She looked at him when he winced from her ministrations. "Callum—get me one of those blankets." She nodded toward the campsite.

Tianna looked up from his arm to his face, studying his eyes, as if she could see the scenes dancing through his head too. She raised her eyebrows ever so slightly, her eyes widening in question.

Alariq wanted to blurt out everything he had just heard. Wanted her, or the others, to make sense of it, so he didn't have to.

But then Callum was next to him with one of the blankets the knomes had slept on, and Tianna was ripping it in half, using one half to wipe away the excess blood on Alariq's arm, and the other to tie up the wound. Alariq just stood there and allowed her to tend to him, letting his mind go blank.

His thoughts refused to order themselves. Alariq willed his brain to focus, his mind to quiet.

Every year. Since the war. Not honorable...

The knome's words circled like a vulture above its meal. They ate at Alariq, tearing away so many things he'd thought he'd known, like flesh from bone.

He felt like some of his soldiers after bloody combat. Battle shock, it was called. They would just stare with hollow eyes and you could see their minds shutting down, to delay dealing with the memories.

Alariq fought to stay present. He couldn't shut down. Not now.

Ford and Brimir joined them at the lake's edge.

"We shouldn't stay by the water," Brimir said gently.

"We have to bury them first," Ford replied, his voice hoarse.

"No." Alariq's tone was hollow, but clipped.

"What?" Ford turned toward Alariq. "You want us to just leave them here like this? For the animals?" Ford's eyes flashed, even in the moonlight. His nostrils flared and his hands curled into fists.

"We'll put them in the lake," said Alariq quietly, still looking out over the water.

"No, I'm burying them." Ford turned and started to walk over to the body of the knome he'd just left.

"Leave him!" Alariq barked. "That is an order."

Ford turned, shock and fury in his eyes. He advanced on Alariq.

Tianna got between them, but none of the others made a move. None of them had been like Ford, who was kind and friendly to everyone. No, they'd all kept away from the knomes. Not out of dislike or scorn. Just because there was never a need for much interaction between dwarfs and knomes. But despite this, they all looked at Alariq now, disbelief on their faces.

Tianna turned, facing Ford, her back to Alariq. Ford continued to look past her for a moment, kept his eyes on Alariq, his mouth in a thin line. Tianna moved her head into his line of sight and he finally met her gaze. She placed her hand lightly on his arm, just above his elbow.

"Alariq is right," she began and Ford tried to shake off her grip, but she held on to his shirt. "No, listen." She forced him to meet her gaze again. "If anyone comes looking for them and they find them buried, it would raise suspicion. Who else do you know that would bother to bury knomes?"

Ford's face softened slightly.

Tianna continued. "If anyone knows you were here, they will assume you know what the knomes were doing—supplying the ettins. And that puts all of you in danger."

She gave him a hard, but sympathetic look. "These are the kinds of secrets people will do anything to keep."

Alariq watched the situation unfold, but more from a distance, as if it wasn't happening a single pace in front of him.

Tianna kept talking, something about still giving the knomes a proper sendoff, and then the others went to gather the bodies. Alariq walked to the knome farthest away. It looked like he had tried to run, but a spear hit him in the back. Alariq removed the spear and brought him to the water with the others.

Ford spoke for a minute about the knomes back in Ishtara and about how grateful he was for the final gift this one had given them. And then, carefully keeping watch over the surface, they eased the knomes into the water and pushed them to float out into the deep.

The eight of them stood for a moment, shoulder to shoulder, along the water's edge, silent and unmoving.

Then they all turned and silently headed back the way they'd come. Alariq walked behind everyone and they all seemed content to leave him alone. He knew the others were wondering what the knome told him, but no one was speaking, not even Ford. They were probably all wondering what Tianna had meant by her words. They all saw the knomes, but had they put the pieces together, like she had?

Alariq quickened his pace until he caught up with Tianna,

who was also walking alone.

"How did you know?" He did not need to be more specific.

"It is well-known that the knomes are under Ishtar control." She cut her eyes over at him. "There is only one possible person who could have ordered them to keep the ettins supplied."

Alariq nodded. Yes, there was only one person.

Tanith.

21

A Proposal and a Rejection

People often talk about life and emotion in terms of *stages*. They define periods of time by varying standards, such as age, maturity, and focus of priorities. They describe the emotional progression as one of steps, as though we travel through them one at a time, moving on to the next as soon as we are finished with the prior.

Real life, however, simply does not work that way.

Real life is a continuum. There are no clearly-defined stages, no perfect little boxes, no successive and sequential phases. Emotions are a spectrum of feeling, feeling that is often difficult to pin down and impossible to define.

No, the real thing is infinitely more complex...

Thirsty. That's how Alariq felt as they made the long journey back through the grasslands. His tongue stuck to his teeth and the roof of his mouth.

He was also suddenly very aware of his boots. They were heavy. Had they always been this heavy?

They walked all night without stopping. The silence was as thick and suffocating as the hot smoky air in the furnace rooms of Ishtara. No one spoke, all lost in their own thoughts about what had happened. All were exhausted, physically and emotionally, from the day's battering events.

They reached the treehome just after dawn, but instead of going up to bed, they all went in silent agreement to the main room.

The fire they usually kept burning in the stove had burned out and Alariq walked straight over to it to get it going again, using the wood and tinder Tianna kept stocked beside it. Brimir started to fetch water and the dried herbs for the tea they had all grown so fond of, but Tianna laid a hand on his shoulder and cocked her head toward the table. He smiled gratefully and sat down, rubbing his knees. Tianna started preparing their drinks and Callum fell in to help. The others sat around the table.

After the fire was going, Alariq took the pot of water from Tianna and placed it on top of the cast iron stove, and then took up his usual position at the table.

When everyone was seated, he nodded to Ford, who understood he was to recount the knome's story. Everyone listened without interruption. The room was utterly still and quiet, except for the sound of Ford's deep, velvety voice and the fire crackling inside the stove.

"And then he said that he and some other knomes were sent to Dendreya five months ago to deliver a message to the ettin commander," Ford finished.

"What did it say?" Asher predictably asked.

"He did not know." Ford braced his elbows on the table and clasped his hands together, interlacing his fingers, and rested his head against them.

Silence.

Alariq looked at Ford, transfixed. His chocolate brown hair was short, shorter than Alariq's. It followed the shape of his head, and wasn't wavy like his brother's. He must have been cutting it, Alariq realized, or it wouldn't still be so short.

He raked his fingers through his own hair, realizing it now fell almost to his shoulders. If he was still in Ishtara, he never would have let it get this long. Long hair wasn't uncommon, on males or females, but it got in the way of fighting, so he always kept it somewhere near his jawline.

Alariq continued to stare at Ford. He would have been First

Authority someday. Ford had sometimes said he only stayed in the military to protect his younger brother, until he'd served his mandatory term, but Alariq had always suspected Ford would continue. He was just that type, the type to serve and lead at the same time, the kind to command, but with concern for those he commanded. Alariq had always felt lucky to have Ford in his division, and until now, he'd felt lucky to have him at his side.

But in that moment, having seen Ford's reaction to the knome's pain, having listened to the empathetic retelling of the events, and watching him now, head bowed and shoulders hunched, Alariq felt a great sense of unease.

He looked over at the stove. Steam had begun to rise from the pot of water.

"This does not make any sense," Asher said, as he hunched forward, mirroring his brother.

Ford didn't move. Alariq's unease grew.

"Unfortunately, it does." Brimir's voice was calm and steady, much steadier than Alariq's would have been. "We just do not want it to be true."

"The knomes have been coming to Dendreya for thirty years," Brimir continued. "We all know what that means."

"Is there any other explanation?" Callum asked timidly, his eyes pleading.

Still Ford did not raise his head. And no one answered Callum.

It was as though the silence was impenetrable. Alariq heard the first bubbles start to break the water in the pot on the stove. Everyone sat, locked inside their thoughts, unable, or perhaps unwilling, to say what they were thinking.

Why don't they just say it? Just ask what they want to know? Alariq thought.

They are afraid, a little voice said.

Afraid. Afraid of what it all meant. Afraid of what it would mean.

You are not saying anything either, the voice whispered to him.

It was the kick Alariq needed.

He forced himself to say the words none of them wanted to

hear. "Tanith did not defeat the ettin army. He ended the Ettinwar with a bribe, not a battle."

He thought he would feel better once he said them. But looking at the top of Ford's still-bowed head only settled the unease lower in his stomach.

"How?" Blainn asked simply, his voice hoarse.

No one answered him, so he continued. His face flushed deeper with every word, and with every word Alariq's stomach tightened. "Did Tanith meet them in battle and then, when the division was defeated, beg for his life and those of the dwarfs still alive?" His fists clenched. "Or was is prearranged?"

"Think of what you are saying Blainn!" Brimir looked at him sharply. "Do you really believe the king would lead an entire division into battle, intending them to be slaughtered? Ishtara lost some of her best soldiers that day."

Blainn did not respond, but the anger did not recede from his face.

"We cannot know for certain." Alariq kept his voice even.

"Yes." Ford lifted his head from his hands and lowered them onto the table. "We can."

Every face turned to him. Every face, except Tianna's. She sat at the other head of the table, next to Ford, who was at the end of the bench. Alariq could see her clearly in his periphery. She never looked up, but closed her eyes and ever so slightly and slowly, shook her head.

And then he saw on her face, what he knew must be in his.

Dread.

"What do you mean?" Alariq asked, not really needing to.

"We defeat the ettins and make them tell us!" Ford stood up with such force that the bench moved backward a few inches, despite being weighed down by both Asher and Brimir.

Alariq was numb, numb to all but the sense of foreboding that had spread throughout his torso. The only thing that penetrated his mind was the sound of the rolling boil of the water in the unattended and forgotten pot.

"And then we return to Ishtara and expose Tanith for what he really is: at best a coward and at worst, a murderer."

And there it is. Alariq closed his eyes and exhaled slowly, struggling to keep it steady.

Asher thumped his fist down on the table in agreement and Blainn and Callum nodded enthusiastically. Brimir and Gideon shot glances at Alariq. When Alariq opened his eyes, Tianna was staring directly across at him.

Ford and the others clearly realized not everyone was passionately in support of the idea, and they all turned to look questioningly at Alariq.

"No."

Alariq said it slowly, in his deepest voice. Looks of shock turned to outrage on the faces of the soldiers in his company. Callum just continued to stare at him, his eyes begging Alariq to explain. Brimir and Gideon both appeared as though this was the answer they expected. As usual, Tianna was unreadable.

"What do you mean, 'no'?" Ford's eyes glinted dangerously.

Alariq had always found Ford's perfection a bit irritating. But now he found it absolutely loathsome. Why, he could not say.

Alariq simply stared back at him, unblinking, letting his silence stand for itself.

"You would just let our people, our families, live under Tanith's control? Knowing what you know?" Ford's body started to positively vibrate.

"What proof do we have?" Alariq asked, trying to stay calm. "You fought ettins, Ford, you know they are unlikely to betray whoever is paying them." He placed his hands on the table, pressing down hard, the pressure stopping them from shaking. "And even if they did, how would that help us convince those back in Ishtara?"

"We have to try!" Ford yelled.

Alariq held Ford's gaze. "It would be our word against the king's. What makes you think it would be any different this time around?" Alariq felt a twinge of pity for Ford. His nobleness and desire to see the best in others blinded him to the fact that others were not as honorable as he. "They would kill us all on the spot."

"I do not care! It is wrong to do nothing." Ford's voice trembled in rage. "How can you be so content to leave those we care about in danger?"

Alariq finally stood, barely managing to maintain control of his temper. It was only the sorrow he felt on Ford's behalf that kept him from striking out with his words. "The citizens of Ishtara, our families, our soldiers, they made their choice. It was not just me they chose to walk away from, Ford. You gave your word in front of all of Ishtara. You said I never left camp. But they chose Tanith." Alariq's muscles relaxed. "Now they must live with the consequences."

The last was said, not with anger, but with direct simplicity.

Ford did not respond, his smooth, chiseled face unmoving, except for the tiniest twitch in his jaw. Alariq was unsure whether Ford was going to attack him or break down into tears.

He did neither. Instead, he spun away abruptly and strode decidedly from the room, his hands in fists and a look of utter and complete disenchantment on his face, as if he were seeing Alariq clearly for the first time.

Fine, Alariq thought. *Maybe he will be a little less naïve about the world around him. Even if it means he thinks less of me.*

The room remained fixed for a moment, and then in turn, Asher and Blainn rose from the table and followed Ford out the door, similar, though less pronounced, looks on their faces. And then, to everyone's surprise, Callum rose and exited too.

The remaining four sat there uncomfortably.

The water finally decided it had been patient long enough and spewed over the edges of the pot and onto the hot stovetop. Tianna rose and removed the pot from the heat, before fixing them all cups of her herbal tea. She distributed them around and both Brimir and Gideon gave her small smiles of thanks.

She fixed four more mugs and put them on a tray and Gideon offered to take them to the others.

Once Gideon was gone, Brimir stood and gently squeezed Alariq's shoulder before heading downstairs to his bedroom.

Alariq was left alone with Tianna, who had resumed her seat directly across from him.

He could feel her gaze on him, so he raised his eyes to meet it. "You think I am wrong." It was a statement, not a question. He lowered his eyes again.

And then she did the most frustrating thing she could have done.

She laughed.

Alariq looked up at her, startled.

"Please let us not pretend that my opinion of your decisions counts for so much as crow's feather," said Tianna, smiling kindly, her lips gently curving upward.

The aura of the room changed. He felt like he'd just been hugged at a time when he needed it most. He felt like he'd found an ally.

Alariq had the insane urge to smile at her. Ford was out there, crying over knomes and the citizens of Ishtara, and Alariq was the one who'd essentially said to let them rot. But there she was, smiling at him. And he wanted to smile back! What was wrong with them?

Alariq didn't say anything in response, but he was grateful for the slightly more relaxed atmosphere.

"Do not make this more than it is," she said, her smile disappearing and concern creasing her brow.

He looked up at her sharply. "What do you mean?"

"This is about them, their sense of nobility, their innocent ideas about the world."

Alariq studied her, taking in her slightly-narrowed amber eyes, the small crease above her nose, and her understanding expression.

"I know," he said simply, realizing how foolish it sounded a moment too late.

She smiled, but this time it didn't make him feel good. It was a knowing smile, a smile that said she knew why he'd dreaded this conversation. This was a smile that made him feel exposed and predictable, two things a soldier should never be.

She didn't push him, but he could tell she was going to wait for him to speak, even if it took all day.

"Why not just tell me what you are getting at, instead of smirking at me like that?" he lashed out.

And damnit if she didn't have the nerve to laugh again.

"You do *not* know," she said, still smiling, but something else tinged her expression. "You think this is about you. Their wanting to return to your city."

Alariq recognized the look in her eyes.

Pity.

At the realization that she cared enough to pity him, the words jumped out of his mouth without permission.

"They have wanted to return since the moment they left with me."

He thought he would regret saying it out loud, the fear that had haunted him since the moment the gates of Ishtara clanged shut behind them. But then Tianna nodded, the smile gone from her lips, and Alariq could tell she understood. She looked out the window for a moment, her expression downcast.

When she looked back at him, there was something new in her eyes, something Alariq couldn't pinpoint, except to say that it looked painful.

"At least they came with you."

They looked at each other for a moment, until she broke the connection.

"Unless you need me," she said as she stood, her voice and countenance back to usual, "I am going to get some sleep." She didn't wait for an answer and instead headed for the door.

She paused, one hand on the latch.

"There is one good thing to be said about all of this," she said, a little too innocently, a grin hiding behind her eyes.

Alariq raised his gaze to meet hers once more, lifting his eyebrows in question.

She looked at him, her eyes wider than he'd ever seen them, her lips twitching faintly.

"For once it wasn't you who threw a fit and stormed off."

22

An Even Fouler Disposition

The passage of time is a funny thing. Usually when one experiences positive emotions, it passes quickly. Conversely, when one experiences negative emotions, is passes slowly. But, as with all rules (including this one), there are exceptions.

One such exception is when you are experiencing a multitude of differing emotions, some good, some bad. Another exception is when you yourself may feel one way, but those around you are in another mood entirely. Moods, like water into wood, tend to seep, pervading into every crevice.

I bring it up because at this point in our story, the treehome was, both literally and figuratively, wood soaking up the water and emotion that battered it.

Ford was in a mood that put Alariq's to shame, refusing to sleep with Alariq in the main bedroom, and instead taking up residence in the basement, as if in a show of solidarity with dwarfdom. On top of that, it was raining almost constantly. Unseasonably so, to boot.

Asher, surprisingly, did not follow in his brother's stead and remained in the bedroom, but he had not spoken to Alariq in the week that had passed since the grand exodus from Tianna's table. Alariq often caught Asher present in physical form only, his mind clearly lost in thought.

Blainn and Callum had both tried to persuade Alariq to change his mind, Blainn with talk of military strategy and Callum with a poorly attempted appeal to Alariq's sensibilities. When Blainn failed, he accepted his commander's decision, but made no attempt to hide his disagreement, nor his displeasure. Callum, on the other hand, became more determined, and often ambushed Alariq when he was least expecting it with a new plea, or a more-impassioned rehashing of a previous argument. It was getting so Alariq was afraid to turn a corner or walk in the woods, for fear of Callum popping out in a doorway or from behind a tree.

Brimir and Gideon tried to carry on as usual, but it was clear the tension was affecting them too. It was one thing when there was conflict between the dwarfs and Tianna. But it was quite another when they found them*selves* divided. Each of them had only six links left to their old life and none of them wanted to lose a single one.

Tianna, quite unexpectedly, seemed almost cheerful. She uttered no criticisms and offered no advice. Instead, she chatted and joked with everyone, including Alariq, and seemed utterly unconcerned when everyone's participation was less than enthusiastic.

Alariq himself went, once again, from post to pillar, although the speed at which he moved from one to the other had greatly increased. On the one hand, he understood Ford's sense of morality. As a soldier, it was bred into him to do what was best for Ishtara, and he had to consciously and constantly fight the instinct to do his duty.

On the other hand, the day he'd always known would come, had. He knew the others would regret leaving their lives for him. And the fact that they now did, that they wanted to return to the city they missed so dearly, brought with it its own cadre of emotions. He'd known this day would come and he had the urge to tell them all "I told you so." And then, when he thought about how they'd convinced him to try to retake Dendreya, his fists and jaw would clench involuntarily. It was a little late for their regret.

But he was also curious. He *wanted* to know the truth, the

answer to Blainn's question, but not for the utility it held for him, because really, what could knowing do to improve his situation? No, he simply wanted to know because ever since leaving Ishtara, nothing but unsolvable puzzles and uncertainty had plagued him. Nothing but unanswered questions, like open doors he wasn't allowed to go through, encircled him.

And finally, there was something else, something Alariq did not want to examine too closely, because it felt something like happiness. And that felt all wrong.

All of this had a downright dizzying effect on Alariq and how time passed. Some moments, like those when he was falling asleep with Asher in the same room, felt like an eternity. But others, like the time he spent walking alone in the woods, went by much too quickly for his liking.

He sought out the company of Tianna (and the irony did not escape him), who alone seemed unaffected by the moods swarming around her. They had spent almost all day, every day, together since they tracked the knomes.

Alariq did not want to give orders he was not sure would be obeyed. So he had decided to keep watch over Dendreya on his own.

He had been quite surprised when Tianna showed up at the base of his tree shortly after he'd settled into it. They kept watch together during the day and took shifts at night. Tianna seemed to be holding up well under the rigorous schedule, but Alariq was wholly exhausted. Although, he was sure his tiredness was caused by more than simple sleep deprivation. Constant vigilance of mutiny or Callum's surprise attacks was wearing on him too.

The eight of them ate dinner, split evenly, half dining inside and half dining outside. Alariq would have liked to have eaten outside, but did not want to impose his company where it was clearly not wanted.

On the fourth night after their discussion at the table, Alariq, Brimir, Gideon, and Tianna ate dinner quietly. Tianna seemed content in the silence, but the three dwarfs shifted around in their seats and made various half-hearted attempts at conversation.

After dinner, Tianna silently left. Neither Alariq, nor Tianna had spoken of their arrangement to anyone and no one had asked

Alariq about their comings and goings. She was to take the first shift and Alariq was supposed to relieve her later that night, so he went up to bed and tried to get some sleep.

Surprisingly, he fell asleep quickly. One second, he was thinking about whether the rain was ever going to let up, and the next he was standing next to Callum in the clearing outside, bright sunshine shining down on them.

"Are you sure?" Alariq asked Callum.

"Absolutely," Callum answered, smiling an unnaturally wide smile that distorted his face.

"Well where is it?" Alariq asked, vaguely aware in the back of his mind that he had no idea what it was.

From there, Callum proceeded to give him very complicated directions that took him deep into the forest. Once his cousin was finished, Alariq ran into the trees, shouting a quick "thanks" over his shoulder as he ran.

In his head, he had the perception that he was running quickly, but everything, even his thoughts seemed to move in slow motion. He followed Callum's directions, but time and again, he lost his bearings, having to retrace his steps, and go back to where he last recognized.

He fought to remember the complex instructions Callum had told him, but they slipped from his mind's grasp.

Alariq started to panic. He was alone in the forest without his bow or sword.

I'll climb a tree, he thought frantically. Maybe he could see the treehome from up higher. But try as he might, he could not attain any height. Every time his feet left the ground, he would just slide back down the trunk, as if it were greased.

He let out a guttural sound of frustration, which echoed all around him.

And then there were other sounds: cracking twigs, rustling leaves, and...

Laughter.

Giggles and whispers, snickers and murmurs.

And then he caught a flash of gold and a blur of brown. Faces and eyes peered out from behind trees and from within bushes.

It was the others. They were watching him, watching as he struggled.

Then they were all out in the open, clapping Callum on the back, *looking at Alariq, mocking him with their words and their eyes.*

He went from asleep to awake just as a quickly as the reverse had happened. He looked over to see Asher sitting on the edge of his bed on the other side of the room, taking off his clothes, his back to Alariq.

Alariq lay there, remembering the dream. The details slipped away, but the feelings remained. Fear, panic, abandonment, a vague sense of betrayal.

Alariq shook them off, but he felt worse than when he'd laid down. He readjusted the bandage on his arm that had moved in his sleep. He winced, the bandage tugging at the wound.

At least it has stopped raining, he thought, fighting to pull himself out of the miasma of emotions trying to pull him under.

Based on the fact that Asher had just come up to bed, Alariq judged he'd only been asleep a few hours, but he was unable to go back to sleep. He waited until he heard Asher's deep, even breaths and then dressed and set out to the spot in which he and Tianna had been keeping watch lately. He walked slowly, savoring the quiet.

In the week they'd been keeping watch together, the ettins still had not emerged. They had no reason to, Alariq supposed, given that they'd just been delivered a half-year's-worth of supplies. He had not brought up the topic with the others and unlike before, no one pestered him for the next step.

But he began to wonder as he walked if he should broach the subject. Maybe a new plan would remind them of their desire to stay in Dendreya.

Alariq paused, midstride.

What if the others decided to leave for Ishtara? He'd been a commander for so long, the thought that his decision might not be obeyed had not occurred to him until now. What would he do? Going back to the city was suicide for him, but did he not owe it to these dwarfs to protect them? And he couldn't protect them from Loraheem if they chose to leave.

He started walking again, a little faster now.

If Ford left, Asher would surely follow. Based on their recent behavior, Blainn and Callum would probably go, too. That would leave him with Brimir and Gideon. They couldn't retake

Dendreya with only three. Well, four, if he counted Tianna.

Alariq stopped again.

He *did* count her. He counted Tianna.

He had the silly urge to laugh out loud. What was wrong with him lately? Was he coming unhinged?

He shook his head, trying to clear it, and continued through the forest.

There was no guarantee Brimir and Gideon would not join the others if they decided to return. Alariq supposed they might think they all had a chance if they returned without him. After all, none of *them* were accused of treason. Maybe they thought the king would let them return, if they swore they were rid of Alariq.

Maybe the king would really do it. There was that rumor about Ford and Tanith's daughter. Maybe Tanith would allow them to reenter the city for his daughter's sake.

Alariq watched, in his mind's eye, as the six of them walked back through the front gate. Then, as if pulled backwards at super speed, from a bird's view, Alariq's vision swept out of the mountains, across August Sound, into Loraheem, and settled onto himself.

What would he do? If all of the others left?

Stay in Loraheem, a voice immediately whispered.

He shoved the thought away. It was ridiculous. He'd only come to this place because the others wanted to make Dendreya their new home.

He supposed he would go to Dirnovaria. Isn't that what he'd wanted from the beginning?

But the idea didn't hold the same appeal it once had. It sat in his stomach, like something unpleasant he'd just eaten.

Yet again, he shook himself. All of this was mere speculation. No one had said anything about leaving without his say-so.

But like a boomerang, his dream returned to him, and the unease returned along with it.

He finally reached the watch post and Tianna leapt down, even before he said anything. They were closer to the edge of the forest and the moon was bright, but he could still barely see her outline.

"Something on your mind?" she inquired.

"Why do you ask?"

"You're early."

Alariq weighed his words carefully. "I was just thinking about whether we should...whether I should...well...begin discussing the next step."

Tianna was silent, her outline perfectly still.

"What?" he asked her.

"I do not think they will let this go."

"I can only control my actions." Alariq meant the words, although they were hard to say, in light of everything he had just been thinking about.

"What will you do?" She leaned against the giant trunk. "If they are determined to return to Ishtara?"

She had obviously been having similar thoughts.

"I...do not know."

He barely saw her nod in the blackness.

Alariq smiled slightly, grateful for the darkness. He liked this, he realized. This easy conversation. The comfortable silences. In the last few days, his time spent with Tianna had been effortless and organic. So different than it was before he'd made up his mind to trust her. And definitely different from his interactions with his fellow dwarfs at the present.

Alariq was thankful, he realized, that she was here. And that she wasn't falling in with the others. For some reason, he wasn't surprised. He didn't know why, maybe it was the look in her eyes, or the conversation they'd had out in the clearing after their failed attack on the city, but her failure to jump on the anti-Alariq bandwagon felt true to what little he knew about her. At least in this instance.

They stood there, but still she did not move out of the way, to let him take up the post.

All of a sudden, the silence felt a little less comfortable.

"Something on your mind?" he parroted back at her.

She laughed her Tianna-laugh, but did not speak.

This felt strange and familiar at the same time. Their interactions felt natural, but that it felt natural, felt strange. Being as she was his only friend at the moment, Alariq decided to just

221

go with it.

He walked over and leaned against the same trunk as she, facing her, although he could still make out little more than a shadow.

He nudged her foot with his own. "So what is it?"

But she pushed away from the tree and started off for home.

He sighed and just stood there. He supposed he should be used to her secrecy and abrupt departures by now.

But then he heard her stop. He didn't turn, sensing it might scare her off, and instead waited for her to make the first move.

"I just..." She took a deep breath. "You asked if I thought you were wrong." An owl hooted and he heard her dig her foot into the soft, wet earth. "I don't. I don't think you're wrong."

Still Alariq did not turn, suspecting there was more.

"I wouldn't go back," she said, "if it were me."

Finally, he turned to face her, although they could not see one another.

"Why not?"

He didn't know where that question came from, but it was the first thing that came to mind and it slipped through his lips before he could give it any thought. The answer was so quiet he almost missed it.

"Because they deserve it."

The words had barely registered when she spun on her heel and walked determinedly into the forest.

Because they deserve it.

The words kept playing over and over again in his head.

Because they deserve it.

Like a punch, that happy emotion he'd been feeling hit him again. Only now, Alariq recognized it for what it was.

Because they deserve it.

It wasn't happiness, not really. It was...what? Vindication? Retribution? Comeuppance?

Because they deserve it.

No. It was fair. A sense of pure, unmitigated justice.

None of the dwarfs in Ishtara had come to his aid when Tanith had accused him of treason, why should he come to theirs now?

The wave of guilt welled toward him, but he refused to get pulled under.

It wasn't as if Ishtara was in any danger. It was peacetime. The ettins were clearly in Tanith's pocket and Karxana hadn't been a threat for generations. A coward for a king didn't mean a lot in peacetime.

Because they deserve it.

Alariq scaled the tree to finish the watch, wondering how Tianna, once again, had pinpointed his feelings before he had. He felt as though he learned new information about her every day, but none of it made sense, or fit together in any logical way. He settled himself into his usual spot, trying to resign himself to living with the enigma.

Dawn broke and he realized he'd dozed off. It was the first time in his life. He'd never slept on a watch before. Tianna was supposed to relieve him at dawn. He waited a little longer, but by the time the sun was visible over the horizon, he'd begun to worry.

The ettins weren't going anywhere, so he headed straight for the treehome.

He heard them before he saw them.

"You cannot be that naïve, Ford." Tianna's voice wasn't difficult to recognize. "Tanith will kill you. Before you can tell any of your kin."

"What am I supposed to do? Nothing?" Ford's voice dripped with indignance.

Alariq crept as close as he dared. He could just see Tianna, who was facing him. Ford's back was to Alariq. They stood near the edge of the clearing, Tianna's face inscrutable as usual, and although Alariq couldn't see Ford's face, he recognized his stance. The other dwarfs were all gathered around the arguing pair.

"There is nothing you *can* do. Look at the facts. If you do not act, the dwarfs of Ishtara will remain in the dark about the Ettinwar. If you return, you will be stopped, and the dwarfs of Ishtara will *still* remain in the dark about the Ettinwar." Tianna gave him a sympathetic look. "The only difference is, you will be dead."

"Would you really do nothing, Tianna, if you were me? If you had family there? Others you cared about?"

Alariq could tell from Tianna's expression that Ford had caught her off guard.

But she quickly recovered. "Yes," she said. "I would do nothing."

"I do not believe that." Asher stepped toward Tianna, his eyes set fixedly upon her face, urging her to meet his gaze. "That is not who you are."

She locked eyes with him, her face hard. "You do not know who I am."

Asher looked as though she had punched him.

She turned back to Ford. "The stakes do not change the reality of the situation. Your motives are noble, but they are misplaced, and they are leading you down a path you cannot follow to its end."

Alariq could see Ford's shoulders rising and falling, slower now.

"But if honor and duty are nonnegotiable for you," she continued, taking a step toward Ford, "then you are still in luck." Ford's head perked up slightly. "Tanith has a small battalion of ettins at his disposal." She gave him a challenging look. "Now *that*...that is a problem we can do something about."

Alariq smiled, marveling at her brilliance.

Everyone stood still, looking at Ford.

Ford looked around at the others, lingering on his brother, and then on Blainn, who had been his own second-in-command, just as Ford had been Alariq's.

Finally, he looked back at Tianna and gave a single curt nod.

Alariq felt it would be wrong to pretend he had not overheard, so when Ford turned toward the forest, he stepped into view. Ford paused, taken slightly aback.

But then he appeared to steel himself and he walked toward Alariq, passing him, but then pausing.

"I will take the next watch," he said over his shoulder before striding into the forest.

Asher shot a look at Tianna, his face tight and his eyes hollow, and then followed his brother, meeting Alariq's gaze and nodding slightly as he passed.

Alariq looked around at the others, who were staring at him, their expressions less angry now than in the last week. But he only had eyes for the person he currently owed everything to.

He bowed his head to her, almost imperceptibly, and she smiled gently in response before turning and heading up the stairs.

"Breakfast?" Brimir asked him.

Alariq nodded and followed him inside. He sat down at the table and Brimir sat a plate filled with fruit and nuts in front of him.

Just as he started to eat, the other dwarfs filed in the door and sat down around the table too.

They ate in a comfortable quiet, Gideon and Callum making a few remarks here and there about their first attempt at making a leather-hide book cover, and Brimir's occasional comments on how the sudden downpour of rain was likely to affect the food supply in the forest.

Alariq was just thinking that things might go back to normal when he heard a shout from outside.

He was up and nearly to the door when Asher wrenched it open, his chest heaving.

"Ettins," he said between ragged breaths.

Alariq grabbed Asher's shoulder. "They've left the city?"

No," Asher responded, still fighting for air. "In the grasslands. Three of them. Headed for Dendreya."

23

The Long of It

The eight of them all stood, side-by-side, just inside the tree line on the beach, in the very spot where Alariq and the others had watched the knomes approach the city. From there, they could see the three ettins making their way across the grasslands. They were moving slowly, but steadily, cutting wide paths in the tall, pale green grass.

Alariq turned to the others. "We do not have long. We must stop them before they get close enough to the city to call for help." He paused, giving his soldiers a hard look. "But listen—we need them alive. They may have information we need."

"I thought you said ettins would not give up their employer?" Callum asked.

"It is worth a try when there are only three of them. They pose much less risk than the whole ettinhorde. But more importantly, we don't want three more ettins inside that city."

The others all nodded gravely.

Alariq led the way. They sprinted to the rocky outcropping that marked the gateway to the grasslands beyond.

Alariq, Asher, and Tianna took up positions in the rocks that surrounded and overlooked the path below. The rest hid on the ground behind boulders or in crevices. They were just in time.

No more than a few minutes after they got into position, they heard the ettins approaching.

Alariq waited until all three ettins entered the narrow alley. The largest one filled the path to the brim, its shoulders rubbing both sides of the rock face as it walked.

Now was the time.

Alariq carefully aimed and fired an arrow low to the ground. His wooden arrow hit the lead ettin in the calf, just above the ankle, exactly where he'd intended it to fall.

"Another ambush!" shouted the largest ettin, who was in the middle. "Run!"

Before anyone could act, including the other two ettins, the large one barreled over the smallest ettin behind him and made for open pasture.

"Leave him!" Alariq yelled to the others. "Focus on the other two!"

It was pathetically easy. Asher and Tianna's arrows both hit the first ettin directly on the top of its feet, one arrow in each foot. Those on the ground jumped out and disarmed both of their foes. Ford and Blainn kept the uninjured one pinned to the ground with their swords.

Alariq stood up on the rock he had been hiding behind, resting his reloaded crossbow on his knee. He looked out over the grassland, watching the largest ettin running farther and farther away from the city. He turned his attention back to the two below.

"We do not intend to harm you further," he said in his most authoritative voice, looking down at the ettins. "As long as you cooperate."

"I'm done dealing with dwarfs!" the injured one spat in its deep, gravelly voice. It made to strike out at Callum, the closest dwarf to him, but Tianna put an arrow in its forearm and it recoiled, howling in pain.

Tianna glanced over at him and although her face was inscrutable, he could see a small smirk in her eyes. He felt his lips twitch.

Alariq had to remind himself he was in the middle of an interrogation with dangerous enemies. He schooled his features once more.

"We only want information," Alariq continued, as though nothing had happened. "Identify yourselves."

Neither spoke. The ettins just glared back mutinously.

"Alright. In that case, you—" Alariq pointed at the injured one, "—will be Ettin Number One. And you—" he pointed at the smaller, uninjured one, "—will be Ettin Number Two."

He paused and tilted his head to one side. "And in case you were wondering: that *is* the order we'll kill you in if you don't cooperate."

He watched as fear crept into their eyes.

He reassumed his talking-to-a-subordinate voice. "Who sent you to Dendreya? Who is supplying you?"

Still nothing.

Alariq relaxed his stance slightly and forced his tone to match it.

"We know you came here after the war with Ishtara."

The ettins exchanged glances, but remained silent.

"Did Tanith bargain with you in exchange for his life at the end of the war?"

The two ettins looked at one another again, more uncertain now.

"You...you are not with Tanith?" Number Two asked. Its voice was softer, but still raspy.

Alariq considered a moment before answering. "No," he replied slowly. "We are not."

The ettins exchanged awkward looks again.

"You will spare us?" it asked again. "If we tell you?"

Alariq gave a single, decisive nod. Then a thought occurred to him. "You must return to Ettinridge, however," he said. "There is a small army of us and we have retaken Dendreya." He thought of the lie as he said it. "You must leave these lands if we let you live."

"Fine!" Number One yelped. "We don' care. We were on'y comin' back to warn the others."

The detached acceptance of the knowledge that their comrades had been killed by a fictitious army of dwarfs didn't even phase Alariq. Death, even of their own people, seemed to have no effect on ettins. He'd learned that lesson long ago.

"The other ettins? Warn them of what?"

"That Tanith betrayed us!" Number One pulled Tianna's arrow from his forearm, grunting in pain.

"Betrayed *you*?" Ford yelled, incredulous.

Alariq shot him a warning look. "So it *is* Tanith who is supplying you? How was the deal struck?" he demanded.

The ettins looked nervous now. Number Two opened his mouth several times to speak, before finally managing to get the words out.

"I don' know the particulars, but it happened at the end of the war. Gerrack, our commander, disappeared for half a day, an' when he came back, he told us the dwarf king wanted an ettin army on his side, that they'd worked a deal."

The ettin paused. Alariq did not dare to breathe.

It was prearranged. Alariq steeled himself against the shock that Tanith willingly led his division into a trap. Shock was the archenemy of focus. And Alariq needed to focus now more than ever.

When no one spoke, Number Two continued.

"We got into position an' ambushed the dwarfs," it said, looking fearfully at Ford and Blainn, both of whom were shaking with rage.

Alariq forced his mind to keep moving. He'd let the emotions settle in later. Right now, he had to push past it.

"And then what?" Alariq said in his deadly calm voice.

"An' then nothing." Number One yelped as he pulled another arrow out of his foot. "We came here. An' the dwarf-rats come twice a year with supplies. That was the deal."

Ford twitched at the ettin's insult to the knomes, but he held his composure.

"So why do you say Tanith betrayed you?" Alariq asked.

"Part of the deal was we were to fight if called," Number Two said. "Well, Tanith called a few months ago. Sent the dwarf-rats with a message, and Gerrack told us Tanith wanted ten of us."

"What for?" Alariq demanded.

"Apparen'ly, to ambush us!" Number One sat up quickly, but

shrank back when Tianna and Asher both tightened their still cocked bows.

Alariq simply looked to Number Two for a better answer. He knew they were so forthcoming only because their employer had betrayed them. For once, Tanith's treacherous nature was falling in their favor.

"Gerrack told us we were supposed to meet some dwarfs at the foothills of the Brackish Mountains and get further instructions. All we know is we were supposed to take care of some dwarfs who Tanith wanted dead. Some dwarfs who would be coming out of the mountains."

Suddenly, the image of an elk with a crushed hip surged into Alariq's vision. Blood pounded in his ears.

"When was this?" he demanded. "When exactly?"

Ettin Number Two shrank toward the ground, eying Alariq's hand on his crossbow.

"I...I'm no' sure. Five months, I think."

Every eye turned to look at Alariq. He knew their thoughts must mirror his own.

He shot them all a look, warning them not to reveal anything. It was a battle he was fighting with himself too. *Five months.* He was exiled almost exactly five months ago.

Alariq didn't believe in coincidences. At least not ones that worked out so perfectly for the king. A king with a lot of secrets.

"Who were they? The dwarfs you were supposed to kill." Alariq asked calmly, though he heard his voice shake a little.

"We don' know. Gerrack just said they posed a threat to the king," Number One bleated. "But it don' matter because it was all a trick. We made camp the day before we were s'posed to meet the dwarfs and then we were ambushed by a bunch of them in the middle of the night!" It pulled Alariq's arrow from its calf, yowling as it yanked.

"They killed five of us an' another two died from injuries on the way home," Number Two finished.

"So what took you so long getting back here?" Alariq asked.

"Well, all of us was injured, so we holed up in the mountains for a while, an' then we couldn' decide if it was safe to break cover, or even if Dendreya was still safe to return to."

"An' then it was slow goin' with the two who was injured bad," Number One added.

Alariq was quiet for a moment, studying the ettins, going over everything in his mind, trying to think of anything he'd missed. He was just about to give the order to the others to let them up, when a thought occurred to him.

"The ettins in Ettinridge," he directed at Number Two, "are they part of this agreement?"

"No," the smaller ettin responded. "That was part of the deal. That we couldn' tell the others back in Ettinridge."

Alariq nodded, believing him. If the other ettins knew, they'd probably want in on the deal, and Tanith couldn't support the entire ettin population. There was at least one break in their favor.

Now, he just had to get rid of these two.

"Tianna—take their weapons and run them far out into the field, at the edge of the beach."

She nodded, putting her arrow back in her quiver and looping her bow over her shoulder. She took the weapons from Gideon and sprinted off.

"Remember—Dendreya is our territory now. If you ever return to the city, we will kill you."

The ettins both nodded.

They sat there in silence until Alariq could see Tianna headed back along the beach. Alariq refused to allow himself to think about what the ettins had said. He didn't trust himself not to shoot them if he did. He'd only promised to let them go to make them talk. But they'd held up their end, and Alariq wasn't about to let ettins be the more honorable ones.

"Alright," he said to the others. "Let them go."

The dwarfs kept their weapons brandished and backed slowly away from the ettins. The grey giants rose, their stances hunched and guarded, and backed out of the path, before turning and walking away as quickly as Number One's injuries would allow.

Alariq could not look at the others. So many thoughts and feelings vied for his attention.

"Everyone back to the treehome. I will stay here to make sure the ettins do not double back."

The other dwarfs all nodded and headed silently down the path. Alariq climbed up the rocks, sitting down where he had a clear view of the ettins cutting through the tall grass, following the same paths they'd made earlier. He rested his back against another rock, which was warm from the sun. He wasn't really worried about the ettins coming back. He was pretty sure they were done with anything remotely related to dwarfs, even if they didn't believe his lie.

No, he stayed for another reason.

Alariq could not explain it, but there was only one person whose company he craved right now. Only one person who he felt would understand what was going on inside him at the moment.

He smiled slightly when Tianna leapt lightly up on the rock beside him.

He never took his eyes off the ettins, still visible in their massive size, but he felt her studying him.

She sat down next to him and they sat in one of their comfortable silences for a while. He watched the ettins pause and bend over, he assumed to pick up the weapons Tianna had left for them.

"Did you have any idea?" she finally asked him.

He let out a bark of angry laughter.

"What? That my king, the dwarf I've served for almost a century, was the kind of person who would lead over a hundred of his own soldiers into a trap?" Alariq looked out at the ettins, expecting to feel a seething fire at the sight of them. But he didn't. No, his hatred was reserved for someone else. "Or were you referring to the fact that the same king trumped up false charges against me, exiled me, and then planned to have his ettin mercenaries kill me?"

His lips curled. Just thinking about Tanith drained every positive emotion from his body, leaving nothing but hate and disgust.

Tianna remained silent, letting him vent.

But he was done. Because rage would do him no good right now.

"No," he said, his voice was sad now. "I had no idea."

She leaned over ever so slightly, so that her shoulder rested against his. It was such a small gesture, but the warm comfort it gave him nearly brought tears to Alariq's eyes.

"The others will want to return to Ishtara again," he said in a low voice.

"Not necessarily," Tianna responded. "The situation has not changed."

"Has it not?" he asked quietly, looking down.

She turned her head to look at him. "No." She sounded irritated. "Knowing the truth does not change the fact that if you go back, you will be killed."

He nodded, raising his head to watch the ettins continue along the beach.

"And it does not change the fact that those who stayed in Ishtara chose to stand with Tanith instead of you," she reminded him quietly.

He was silent for a moment. He had the strangest urge to lay his head on her shoulder. For some reason, it felt like doing so would make all his problems fade away.

She was right, of course. His family, the soldiers he'd commanded, they still hadn't come to his defense, or left with him like the others back at the treehome. None of that had changed.

But something else had.

"No," he finally said. "It does not. But it does change how I see it."

"How you see it? She stood up. "There is only one way to see it."

He remained seated, looking up at her. He suddenly felt cold without her warm presence next to him. She looked annoyed, but there was something else in her expression.

He longed to talk with her about this. Hash out all the options, like they did when they talked of attacks on the ettins. But right now, all he could do was try to make her understand.

"No. Before...before, I felt as you did. That they deserved it. But now..."

"Now what?"

His eyes searched hers, darting from one to the other.

"I was fooled by him too."

She let out a derisive half-laugh, half-snort.

He stood and faced her. For once, her features were unschooled, revealing the thoughts currently shaping them. There was anger and frustration, yes. But deeper down, there was something else. It couldn't be disappointment. He had to be misreading her.

"I never believed he would lead an entire division to be killed by ettins," he said, willing her to see it the way he did. "I just thought he lost the battle and begged for his life,"

"All the more reason you should not return," she answered back. "You know for certain now that he will not hesitate to kill you."

Everything she was saying made sense. It was logical and practical, all the things Alariq prided himself on being. But for some reason, they just didn't fit now.

"I know," he said simply.

"You just do not care."

She looked at him, that same disillusioned expression on her face.

He couldn't explain why it bothered him so much to see her look at him that way. Hadn't Ford given him that very look only a week past?

He took a step toward her, only inches away now.

"I cannot let this stand. You heard what the ettin said. 'Five months.' And they were supposed to kill some dwarfs who 'posed a threat.'" He searched her gaze for any sign she was coming around to his side again.

"It never crossed my mind that Tanith fabricated the charges against me on purpose. I thought his son did it out of, I don't know, jealousy maybe, and Tanith simply believed him."

"But what does that matter?" she demanded.

"It matters because I justified not returning to Ishtara because my kin made their choice. But I was wrong. It wasn't a choice. Not an informed one, anyway. How can I blame them for something I, myself am guilty of?" He saw nothing but her amber eyes.

"Tanith fooled me too," he repeated, knowing he'd lost. She

wasn't going to be on his side this time.

Or maybe he wasn't going to be on hers.

"And what about me? What about this mess here you would leave behind? You poked the hornet nest in my backyard and now you are just going to leave me to deal with it alone?"

Guilt flooded his chest. He hadn't even thought about the ettins in Dendreya. He didn't respond. How could he?

She stood looking at him, her eyes narrow and her lips pressed together in a thin, pink line.

"So you are decided, then?" she asked.

Honestly, he wasn't. But he realized how naïve he'd been to count on this quasi-friendship they'd struck up recently. Clearly, this wasn't newfound harmony. Instead, it was no more than the calm between two storms.

"I...I do not know. As you said, knowing does not change the challenges we would face, if we returned."

Some of her anger seemed to drain away. She could have asked him anything in that moment: how would they enter the city, how would they convince the citizens of Tanith's treachery, what would happen if they failed. Alariq was prepared for those. He was not prepared for the one she actually asked.

"What do you want?"

Alariq knew his surprise must have shown on his face.

"I...I want to do the right thing," he answered lamely.

Now she looked at him with something dangerously close to revulsion.

"No you don't," she said and every word was coated with derision. "That is Ford's game, not yours."

Alariq was caught completely off-guard by her reaction. Why was she so angry? What difference was it to her what he wanted?

"You are not looking to do the right thing. You want vindication." She took a step toward him. "And you're not wrong for wanting it. But revenge won't give you what you think it will. It won't give you your life back."

Now it was her turn to search his gaze. He stared back into her unguarded eyes, transfixed.

"Even if you succeed, even if you convince your kin that you are innocent—they will always be the people who abandoned you when you needed them the most."

Alariq bristled. Who was she to tell him how he would feel or what he wanted? And why was he suddenly so high up on her list of priorities? Her sudden display of emotion felt so out of character for her.

But then Alariq remembered he really didn't know her character, and his resolve hardened.

"I was not aware I owed you justification for my decisions."

Something flashed quickly in her eyes before her features returned to their usual, well-controlled state. Without a word, she turned and leapt down from the rocks, disappearing down the path.

Alariq looked at the empty trail. What did she care whether they stayed or left? He conceded she had a point about the ettins in Dendreya, but she'd lived with them there for however long she'd been in the forest, probably her whole life.

And yes, she'd struck up friendships with most of his company. But they had just discussed the possibility of them all leaving against Alariq's wishes. The thought of that hadn't angered her like this. Or had it, and she'd just done a better job of hiding it?

It couldn't be this strange arrangement they'd established lately, him and her, could it? Did it mean something to her?

He dismissed the thought immediately. Until a week ago, they'd barely gotten on at all. And a week didn't change anything.

He repeated that last thought several times before turning back to look at the ettins, barely visible now in the distance.

He turned his eyes to the lake. The sun was setting. It seemed like the light was coming from within the lake, instead of a mere reflection. For a moment, he just stared at it.

What do I want? The question popped unbidden back into his head. As if that wasn't bad enough, he kept hearing it in Tianna's soft voice.

It was a question he'd never asked himself before. His whole life had been about what he *didn't* want. He didn't want to work the furnaces, so he became a career military man. He didn't want to go against the grain, so he'd gotten married. He didn't want to die or his family and those loyal to him to suffer, so he'd taken his sentence of exile with barely a protest, and walked away from his home forever. Even now, he'd come to fight for Dendreya because he didn't want to disappoint the other dwarfs.

"What do I want?" He spoke the words aloud, hoping someone else would answer him.

As if the universe knew how much he needed help, so desperate was his plea, the answer came to him.

He wanted what Asher wanted.

To be happy.

He let out a bark of almost hysterical laughter, not because he didn't believe it. Rather, because he knew it was true, and simply saw the great irony of it all.

Happiness was an emotion for the oddballs like Callum and Gideon. Or the romantics like Asher and Brimir. But it wasn't for the average dwarf. And it certainly wasn't for the solider.

You kept your head, you made the right choices, you did what you were supposed to. That's what a dwarf did. That's what Alariq had always done. What he thought he'd do until his time was up.

But look how far it got you, he thought, shaking his head.

No, chasing the whimsical notion of happiness was not what he'd envisioned for his life.

It seemed so simple when Asher had said it to Tianna that night, like such a humble wish, a basic desire, if a little naïve. But now that he was faced with the prospect of achieving this vague "happiness," it became an insurmountable obstacle.

It was as though a huge black mountain materialized out of the ground in the middle of his path. He was relieved, because it was what he'd been looking for. But now...now he was faced with climbing it.

So what do I need to be happy?

24

A Reversal of the Winds

"We are going back to Ishtara," Alariq announced.

The rest of the dwarfs were gathered around the table, except Gideon and Callum, who were cleaning the dishes. Tianna was nowhere to be seen.

When Alariq had entered the treehome, everyone quieted and turned to face him. He'd walked to the head of the table and, still standing, made his pronouncement.

There was silence for a moment. Followed by an outburst of cheering.

Ford and Callum grinned widely. Blainn smiled and crossed his muscled arms over his broad chest, nodding appreciatively. Gideon gave a half smile and continued wiping the dishes. Brimir rose and clapped Alariq on the shoulder, giving him an approving look. Asher looked pleased, but Alariq saw him shoot a concerned glance out the window.

Alariq looked around and his eyes caught on Ford, who was looking at him intently.

You were right, Alariq tried to say with his eyes, giving Ford a small conciliatory nod. *It just took me a while to get here.*

Ford smiled and nodded back.

I knew you'd do the right thing in the end, he seemed to say. Or at least that's what Alariq hoped he was saying.

Alariq returned his attention to the group and held his hands up to quiet everyone. "Listen—we must do this very carefully. We cannot just go marching up to the front gate and declare ourselves unexiled. We will have to be stealthier than that."

Do you have a plan?" Callum asked.

"Nothing in stone. I think we should see which division Tanith has put on patrol. If we know any of the soldiers and think they might believe us, we can try to separate them from the group, convince them a few at a time."

Brimir sat back down. "And what if it is his own division patrolling?"

"I do not know," Alariq answered honestly. "That is why I am warning all of you now that this may not happen quickly. And it certainly will not be easy. But if we do this, no one can rush in recklessly, even if Tanith is putting the city in danger." He looked specifically at Ford. "We are of no use to the city if we are dead."

He locked eyes with Ford again, this time giving him a silent command.

We do this my *way.*

Ford nodded, showing Alariq that he understood this was the compromise he must make for them to return.

"When do we leave?" Asher asked, his face now more solemn.

"A few days. We need to prepare supplies. We do not know how long we will be stranded in the mountains outside Ishtara."

"What do you want us to do?" Blainn, in usual form, wanted a direct order.

"Nothing tonight," Alariq said. "Tomorrow, Asher and I will hunt so we can prepare jerky, and then we need to make some more arrows. Ford and Blainn—sharpen our weapons. The rest of you can make campaign biscuits."

Everyone nodded.

After a moment of quiet, Callum spoke tentatively, "Why do you think he did it?"

No one needed clarification that he was referring to their king and Alariq's exile.

Everyone looked to Alariq. "I do not know," he answered slowly. "I have been turning it over in my mind, looking at it from every angle." He looked out the window. "I cannot imagine why he was threatened by me. He is not well-liked, as far as kings go, but his right to rule is absolute. No one in Ishtara has ever stood against the king before. And I do not believe I ever gave him reason to fear that I would be the first."

"Would he have reason to suspect you knew of his pact with the ettins?" Brimir asked wisely.

Alariq hadn't thought of that. He tried to think of anything that might have given Tanith that idea. "Not that I know of," he replied, coming up empty.

Blainn sat down too. "Did you ever defy one of his orders?"

Alariq shook his head.

"Did you ever..." Ford paused, thinking. "Is it possible you did, or said, something to offend him?" His words stumbled out awkwardly.

"I suppose that is possible," Alariq responded, not at all surprised the question had been posed. "But what, I have no idea."

Everyone looked around at each other, asking silently with their eyes if anyone else had any thoughts. No one spoke.

"Ultimately, it does not really matter, does it?" Alariq shrugged his shoulders. "What matters is that Tanith knew I was not guilty of treason, perhaps even fabricated the lie himself, and then intended for ettins to ambush me on my way out of the mountains."

The others looked back at him, afraid to speak.

He shrugged again. "But that is not why we are going back. We are going back because he led an entire division of our kin into a trap, like lambs to slaughter." He looked at Ford again. "We cannot let that stand."

Ford smiled back, his eyes a little watery. Silence fell once more.

After a few moments, Alariq addressed the room. "Has Tianna come back?"

"Yes, she went straight upstairs," Asher answered.

Alariq nodded and headed for the door. He ascended the

stairs quickly, but paused before continuing to the upper levels.

What am I going to say?

He took a step up, only to pause again, one foot on a stair and the other still planted on the landing.

He knew what Tianna would say if he asked her that question. She'd say there really wasn't anything to be said.

And she'd be right.

Alariq slowly stepped down from the stairs and stared up through the leaves and branches to her quarters above.

There really wasn't anything to be said.

He'd like to tell her that if they were successful, that would mean the payments to the ettins would stop and they would probably leave and return to Ettinridge. Or that he would make sure the city sent a division of dwarfs back to remove them.

But all of that was conditional. Conditional on a success she already stated she did not believe to be possible.

So, there really wasn't anything to be said.

Alariq turned and headed back downstairs.

"Did you tell her?" Asher asked, as soon as he entered.

"Was she upset?" Ford added.

"I did not tell her," Alariq responded, slowly sitting down at his usual place. "But I think she already knows."

At everyone's confused looks, he added, "We spoke at the grassland path. I think she guessed my decision."

Brimir sat a bowl of stew down in front of him and Alariq smiled slightly in thanks.

Blainn turned to Ford. "Why would she be upset?"

"Because she gave us her help to get rid of the ettins and now we are leaving with the job left unfinished." Ford looked at Blainn as though it were obvious.

"Well, she's better off now, isn't she?" said Blainn, a little indignant. "We cut their number in half for her."

"I suppose..." Ford answered.

Alariq ate his stew without comment and then ordered everyone to turn in early.

"No need for anyone to keep watch," he said, "just get some sleep. We have busy days ahead of us."

They all retired, Ford returning to the main bedroom with

Alariq and Asher. Alariq tossed and turned, constantly trying to make his body understand that he needed to sleep.

But it wasn't his body that kept him awake.

He couldn't stop thinking about Tianna and her reaction. She had let slip her so carefully maintained wall. Why? It seemed so arbitrary. He'd accused her of betraying them more times than he could count. Hell, they'd all accused her of trying to poison them. Sometimes she'd gotten a little angry, but nothing like this.

He thought back to something Callum had said when they first arrived. He said he thought Tianna was lonely. Was that it? Did she dread going back to her solitary life?

Well what the hell was he supposed to do about that? She chose to live by herself after all, unprotected in the middle of nowhere, with ettins and finfiends on her doorstep.

Alariq realized his pulse was raging, so he took several slow, deep breaths.

How Tianna chose to live was not his concern, he told himself.

And with that, he shut off his brain, thinking only of blackness whenever a thought requested an audience with his mind.

The next two days passed quickly. At first light on the first day, Alariq and Asher rose and went hunting. When they'd killed a deer and two squirrels between them, they headed back to the treehome, and then set about the task of making more arrows.

Alariq's arm was healing nicely. The wound was mostly closed and he appeared to have avoided infection. He couldn't wait to be rid of the bandage. He hated having anything that felt constricting on him.

Alariq still had most of his starmetal arrows from Ishtara, but he needed to keep the rest of his store high. Besides, he really only needed the iron ones against ettins or an enemy wearing armor. And he expected to use his bow more for hunting than for fighting in the coming weeks.

Soon after their first fight with the ettins, Tianna had shown them how she made her arrows with the materials indigenous to Loraheem, so he and Asher set about making them that way. Asher had already made a few using Tianna's method, but it was foreign to Alariq. He kept looking around for Tianna to ask her a question, but she was nowhere to be found. The others said she had told them goodbye while he and Asher were out hunting, but he had not seen so much as a flash of her golden hair.

In fact, she was nowhere to be found for the rest of the day or the next. As Alariq lay in bed the night before they were to leave, he wondered if she was going to say goodbye. He had not told her they were leaving the next day, but if she had been anywhere near the treehome this evening, she would know. Their supplies were laid out and ready to go. All that was left to do was wrap up the jerky and the last batch of campaign biscuits tomorrow before leaving.

He rolled over in his bed and stared at Asher's empty one. He still had not come up for the night. Ford had come up only recently and fallen straight to sleep. Alariq knew because he was snoring. Snoring was essentially Ford's only flaw. Alariq had listened to that on many a night, here and on campaigns back home.

Home.

It still felt surreal. The idea that he was going back to Ishtara. He had worked so hard to make himself stop thinking of Ishtara as his home that now it felt a little stiff and wooden, referring to it that way.

He knew this was the right decision. He was a soldier of Ishtara and he owed his city his allegiance. Tanith was clearly a master manipulator and, as Ford had said all long, it was his duty to unmask him to the dwarfs who trusted him with their lives.

He could never live with himself if he did nothing. But more than that, he refused to let his destiny be decided for him.

That was what he needed to be happy. To be in charge of his life, not some puppet in another dwarf's schemes.

It had come to him while he sat on the rock, looking out at the lake, red and fiery in the sunset. Alariq knew he could never be happy if someone else was deciding his fate, if he was letting someone else choose his destiny.

And that's what Tanith had done. For some unknown reason, he had chosen Alariq's destiny for him. Alariq wasn't sure exactly what he wanted his life to look like, but he knew he'd never be able to see beyond the fact that Tanith, not Alariq, had been the one holding the reigns.

He flopped over, punching his pillow.

The treehome was silent, the leaves whispering quietly in the gentle breeze. He heard a tiny thud on the landing just outside their door and then a stair creak.

Tianna.

He quietly got out of bed and dressed, glancing over to make sure Ford was still asleep. He exited the room, creeping out on the balls of his bare feet. He barely made it down a few steps when he heard voices.

"I didn't realize you were upstairs." Alariq was unsurprised to hear Asher's voice. He had suspected as much when Asher did not come to bed.

"I went up this evening," Tianna answered casually.

"You mean you snuck up," Asher said, "while we were eating dinner."

Tianna said nothing. Alariq edged down another step, his back hugging the trunk of the tree.

"You know we are leaving tomorrow?" Asher's voice was harder and colder than usual.

"Yes," Tianna responded softly.

"Were you planning to say goodbye?"

Alariq heard Asher rise.

"I said goodbye," said Tianna stiffly. "I told Ford to pass it on to you as well."

"He told me," Alariq heard Asher moving around.

Neither spoke for a long time. And then Asher said something Alariq could not make out.

Suddenly, this felt like something Alariq should not be overhearing. Even more, it felt like something he did not want to overhear. He started back up the steps but Tianna's voice stopped him.

"You are all senseless," she said, her voice trembling slightly. "This will end well for no one."

"You cannot know that," Asher answered. "You underestimate us, I think." His tone was light, joking.

"I have lived with you for months, I know your skills and I know your limitations." Her voice took on an almost pleading quality. "You cannot stand against an entire army."

"And we won't," Asher said reassuringly. "We are going to try to convince any dwarfs who leave the city."

"And if you cannot? What then?"

"Then we will try something else."

She laughed, that half-exasperated, half-incredulous laugh.

Another whisper.

One in return.

And then Tianna's golden head came into view as she strode decidedly into the forest.

Alariq watched the blackness swallow her up, knowing this was his last chance to see her before they left.

But he let her go. He was not sure what he had meant to say to her tonight, but he knew he wished he could walk away from this place on better terms.

He heard Asher move below, so he quickly re-entered the bedroom, undressed, and got back into bed. Asher came up shortly thereafter.

Alariq slept fitfully that night, waking up often. He heard Asher tossing and turning all night as well and knew he would not be the only dwarf who would dread the long day in front of him.

He had the same dream he'd been having since coming to Loraheem, the one where he embraced Haamith. Except this time, when he pulled away from the embrace, he saw Tanith's face instead.

He awoke with a start. It was finally morning. He was glad to put the restless night and that incomprehensible dream behind him.

He rose and dressed before the others. On a whim, he decided to walk up to Tianna's rooms, to see if she was there, knowing she wouldn't be. He stayed up on her top floor landing awhile, just looking out at the forest around him.

As he reached the landing, Ford and Asher emerged from their room, their packs loaded on their backs. Alariq went back into the room and finished preparing his own pack. He looked around one last time. He looked out the windows that he himself had unboarded and cleaned. He carefully inspected each corner, telling himself he was checking for things he or the others might have missed while packing. Seeing nothing, he looked out the window one last time and then turned and walked over the threshold.

When he got to the bottom of the stairs, Ford and Asher had removed their packs and were sitting in the grass.

"We need to wrap up the jerky," Alariq reminded them.

"It's already done," Ford said. "Tianna must've done it early this morning. Biscuits are done too, Brimir said."

Alariq nodded, having nothing to say. He set his pack down with Ford and Asher's and walked into the main room. Brimir was putting already-wrapped jerky and biscuits into the pack Gideon had brought. Gideon and Callum were lovingly wrapping up the books they'd each finally managed to make.

"Oats were on when I woke up this morning," Brimir said, looking up from the supplies.

Alariq looked at the table, thinking back to when they had all tried to cram in on one side of it that first day in the treehome. For some reason, the thought of eating his last meal here made his chest tight.

"Let's eat outside," he said instead.

Brimir nodded.

Alariq went back and sat with the brothers. Blainn joined them shortly, bearing two bowls of stewed oats, with nuts and berries mixed in. The other three followed, also bringing breakfast for everyone with them.

They ate in silence. It was a hearty meal. It would hold them most of the day.

That was, of course, assuming Alariq could finish it. His throat was tight now too. He stared at the enormous trees around him, the lush greenness. He'd thought that after a time it would all seem more commonplace to him. But even now, he was still astounded by all the wonders of Loraheem.

He managed to finish his breakfast and Brimir and Callum collected their bowls. Alariq wished he'd kept his so he had a reason to go back inside one last time.

He wondered what was taking the others so long and realized they were washing the dishes. He decided to go back inside anyway.

"Almost finished?" he asked, walking through the door.

"Drying the last dish now," Callum said.

Brimir was closing up the pack. Alariq walked around the room, looking for anything of theirs. But there was no sign they had ever been there. It looked exactly as it had the night they'd arrived. It was as if they had never come to Loraheem at all.

"Ready?" he asked the other two, and they both nodded. Callum put the last dish on the shelf and strapped the food pack on his back.

Alariq let the others exit ahead of him. He took one last look around the room and then he closed the door behind him. He'd never noticed the click the latch made when it closed before.

"Ready?" he asked again, this time to everyone.

They all nodded assent and slowly rose from the grass. Alariq, the brothers, and Blainn strapped on their packs and the dwarfs all fell in behind Alariq.

Alariq looked back at the treehome before entering the forest. He thought of the first time he had seen it. Had it really only been five months ago? He remembered the way it looked to him then. Strange. Unfamiliar. He had felt anger at the treehome at first. It was a constant reminder that he wasn't where he was supposed to be. A tree is, after all, about as far from a dwarf's normal habitat as he could get.

It looked so different now. Now that he was leaving it. He noticed things about it that he never had before. Like the way the branches naturally parted, as if the tree had grown that way on purpose, intentionally calling out for someone to make it their home. He tried to picture the tree without the manmade structures. The mental image of the naked tree left him feeling hollow and lonely.

His chest tightened and his heart fluttered anxiously at the thought that he would never see it again. He quickly shoved away the feeling and made himself relax. Of course he would never see it again. This wasn't his home. He didn't belong here. That he might never set foot in this spot again was supposed to feel good, right.

It didn't. But neither did staying. And he'd made his decision. So without another thought, he turned his back on the treehome and strode purposefully into the forest. But not before noticing that each of his companions looked as conflicted about leaving this place as he was.

They took their usual route to the beach. Once they reached the tree line, they turned north, heading into unfamiliar territory. They were taking the northern route around August Sound this time in order to avoid the finfiends, who so far seemed to stay in the southern part of the lake. They followed the forest until they reached the northern beach of the lake, a journey that took them three days.

On the fourth day, they said goodbye to Loraheem and turned east. They kept directly off the beach, just in case, but stayed within sight of the water. Although the mood had been somber upon leaving the treehome, the majority of the group had perked up considerably as the journey wore on. But Ford and Asher had had some kind of row when they were fetching water one night because instead of the usual light-hearted comradery, they walked separately and barely spoke to one another.

Alariq's chest had ached when they left the forest, but with every step he took east, he grew one step closer to Ishtara. Which meant he was one step closer to revenge, to vindication, to justice. Every step was taken with one of these purposes in mind. Yes, he definitely felt better the more they traveled, but there was still a hollow feeling in his stomach.

Probably just the fare, he assured himself. He was used to good, healthy food at the treehome. The biscuits and jerky did not exactly fill the hole left in its absence.

"Let's fish tonight for supper," he announced to hearty agreement.

"What about the finfiends?" Callum asked.

"The lake is enormous, we are unlikely to encounter them by chance again. Besides, both attacks occurred on the southern beaches. And we will be vigilant." Alariq adjusted the straps on his shoulders to a more comfortable position. "Besides, we will not make camp on the beach. We will fish and then camp farther away."

Callum nodded agreeably. They were all missing the good food back at Tianna's.

Alariq pushed the thought away. He focused on Ishtara. On

the dwarfs there. Over the past few days, they had been coming up with a list of dwarfs from each division who they thought could be convinced of either Alariq's innocence or Tanith's treachery. They had come up with at least one from every division. Every division except the king's.

When the sun kissed the horizon, Alariq called a halt for the day. They found a good campsite and Brimir and Callum stayed behind to start a fire and heat the pans so the fish would cook faster once caught.

The other five headed down to the lake. Gideon was somewhat of an expert in fish-catching. He'd brought fishing line and iron hooks with them from Ishtara, they just hadn't had much cause to use them before now. When Alariq had mentioned fishing, Gideon had started looking for good candidates for poles and by the time Alariq called an end to the day, he had four. Soon, they had ten fish between them.

"Asher, run these up to Brimir and Callum to get on the fire." Alariq handed him the two sticks speared with fish. "We'll catch a few more and then follow you."

As soon as Asher was out of earshot, Alariq side-eyed Ford, "You two are not your usual selves," he said casually.

Ford merely grunted in response, uncharacteristic of him to be sure. But then again, so was rowing with his brother.

"Anything I have to be worried about?" Alariq asked.

Ford shook his head.

Alariq gave him a piercing stare.

Ford relented. "No, really. It's my fault. He's been surly ever since we left Loraheem and I've been trying to get him to buck up, and," he paused. "I just pushed too hard, I suppose."

Alariq nodded and returned his attention to his fishing. He had guessed as much.

He felt something tug on his line. It felt big. He tugged hard to set the hook. The others grinned appreciatively.

Out of the corner of his eye, he saw Blainn's wrist twitch too. They'd be done in no time, at this rate.

Then Ford and Gideon's lines went taunt as well.

Alariq let go of his pole a second too late. The thing on the other end gave a mighty pull and although he avoided getting pulled into the water, he was yanked off his feet and face-planted into the wet sand. He heard the others yell out and the sound of splashing water.

He pushed his palms into the sand and heaved himself upward. He saw a flash of white, then of brown, and then nothing but black.

25

The Fly in the Honey

For those of you who do not know, there are essentially three basic states of unconsciousness. The first, which I like to call "only-just" unconscious, is the state in which you are cognizant of the things going on around you. You can usually hear and feel, and sometimes even taste and smell, too. You are aware of all of these senses, but your mind is incapable of either focusing on any of it, or making sense of it. The second state, we shall call it "mostly" unconscious, is one in which you are not aware of anything going on externally, but things are still firing internally. It is in this state that people claim to see bright lights or hear voices of far away or deceased people. Finally, there is what ought to be called "basically dead" unconscious, which is the third state. This is when there is only darkness.

Often these states progress sequentially. From the first to the third when a person is falling unconscious, or in reverse order when a person is waking. But the mind is a tricky thing indeed...

Alariq was aware of his body, which hurt. And of his head. Which hurt. And of the wound on his arm. Which hurt. And that his wrists were bound. Which hurt.

And then he was aware of nothing. Which felt quite wonderful, actually.

Then he heard voices. Some of the voices made him feel scared, while others comforted him.

He fought against the darkness, but it engulfed him once more.

Some time later, Alariq felt hands on his body and sensed someone close to his face. Fingers on his head poked and prodded, cool air stinging his skin.

This time, he embraced the black when it called for him.

Finally, Alariq felt cold. He hated the cold. He was used to the dark, but not the cold. Cold felt like a violation. It breached the boundaries of his body and reached deep inside, to the very core of his bones. It was a pain like no other.

He tried to curl up to warm himself, but he ached all over.

"I think he is waking," he heard a small voice whisper.

More hands on his head.

If the effort it took was any indication, opening his eyes was the greatest accomplishment of his life.

It took a moment to focus on the four, no, two, faces above him.

He blinked, trying to clear the fog in his vision and his mind.

"Alariq," a familiar voice said. "Are you alright, son? Can you hear me?"

Finally, Alariq's eyes and head started speaking to one another again and he recognized the face above him as Brimir's.

He nodded and tried to speak, but his mouth was too dry.

"Get him some water," Brimir said.

Alariq recognized Callum too as he handed Brimir a bowl.

"Hold his head up a little."

Alariq felt hands on the back of his head and then a bowl pressed to his lips. Cold water spilled into his mouth and down the sides of his face. He coughed a little and the bowl was removed.

He tried to sit up.

"No." Brimir put a hand gently on Alariq's chest. "Not yet. You need to get your bearings first."

The hands under his head were replaced with something soft and lumpy.

Suddenly, the events at the lake came back to him.

"The others?" he said in an unrecognizable rasp.

"Everyone is alright," Brimir answered calmingly. "You got the worst of anyone."

"Where"—cough—"are we?" Alariq asked.

"Somewhere on the lake. A peninsula, I think," Callum replied.

"Finfiends?" Alariq asked, not really needing an answer.

Brimir nodded. "We heard yells and by the time we got to the beach, they had already pulled you and Gideon into the water." Brimir tipped some more water into Alariq's mouth. "Ford and Blainn were in the shallows, with four finfiends each pulling them in. We tried to help them, but by the time we got there, they were too deep. That's when the rest came for the three of us."

"And you're certain everyone else is alright?" Alariq reached up to feel the source of pain on his head, wincing when he found the wound.

"Couple of bumps and bruises, Ford's ankle is a little tweaked, but he walked here well enough."

"Walked here?"

"They dragged us all into the water, disarmed us, and tied us up. But then they pulled us back out and walked us here. They had to carry you and Gideon, who they kept underwater too long." Brimir put the bowl to Alariq's lips again. "He's fine now. He woke up shortly after we arrived."

"Where are they?" Alariq asked.

"Blainn and Gideon are in the cell to our left." Callum pointed to the wall behind him. "And Ford and Asher in the one to our right." He indicated the wall behind Alariq.

Alariq sat up, grimacing. Brimir helped him turn so his back rested against the wall. Alariq looked around at the tall stone walls. There were no windows, except a small one in the door, through which a gray light shown. On the dirt floor, there were three piles of straw, on one of which Alariq currently sat.

"What is this place?"

"It is some kind of prison," Callum responded. "There is a courtyard out there, surrounded by a semi-circle of cells. A huge stone wall, at least two stories high, separates us from the rest of the land. The lake surrounds us on the other three sides."

"How long have I been out?" Alariq asked.

"Two days," Brimir answered. "You need to eat."

He turned to Callum and nodded, who reached over to the one corner that did not have straw in it and pulled over one of the packages Tianna had wrapped for them.

"They've been doling out our own supplies to us," Brimir explained, his tone biting.

He handed Alariq a biscuit. "If you can keep that down, you can have some jerky."

Alariq ate it slowly, taking small bites and chewing them well before swallowing. After the third bite, the nausea started, but he managed to keep it down. He refused the jerky Brimir offered him, but took the water. He didn't think his stomach could handle anything else.

"Are we able to communicate with the others?"

Callum nodded. "Through the windows in the doors. The others can hear us, but so can anyone else close by out there."

"Are there guards nearby?" Alariq drank some more water.

"Four are always posted at the gate, and two more at each end of the wall." Callum nodded at the door. "They come around and check our cells several times a day."

Alariq wanted to look through the window, but it was high off the ground, at a human's eye level, and he was not sure his stomach and head could handle it yet.

"Have the finfiends said anything?" he asked instead.

"Not much," Brimir replied.

"So we don't know what they are planning? What is next?"

Both Brimir and Callum shook their heads.

"How did they find us?"

"They've been looking for us," Callum answered, and this time, his voice will filled with fear.

Alariq looked at him sharply, which made his head throb.

Brimir pressed some more water on him. "It's true. Some of them were mocking Ford and Asher, who were fighting back pretty hard. They said they've been keeping an eye out for us ever since that first night all those months ago. It's why they attacked the knomes. They thought they were us. When we showed up, so close to Dendreya, they assumed we'd taken up there. So they started patrolling the western edge of the lake. They tracked us from the beach at Loraheem."

Alariq nodded. His words to Callum came back to him. He'd told his cousin their odds of meeting the finfiends by chance again were small. Well, this meeting hadn't been by chance.

Alariq looked at the window again. He could barely see the sky through it, gray and pregnant. "What time of day is it?"

"Around dusk," said Brimir. "Although it is hard to tell. It has been storming all day."

Alariq nodded.

"I think you should sleep now, son," Brimir suggested gently.

Alariq wanted to refuse, but his head was pounding and the blackness calling him once more. He nodded and both Brimir and Callum helped him lay down again. Within seconds, he was asleep.

When he awoke, the light outside looked exactly the same. He sat up gingerly, waiting for the nausea to roll in. But surprisingly, it did not come.

"Morning" said Brimir quietly. He nodded over at Callum, who was still curled up in a tiny ball, asleep.

"Is that what it is?" Alariq asked.

Brimir nodded. "Just past dawn."

"Anything new?"

"Just some more biscuits and water." Brimir passed him the bowl of water as he spoke.

Alariq drank and then handed the bowl back, taking the biscuit and slice of jerky Brimir passed him in return.

He ate them slowly again. The biscuit went down fine, but each bite of the jerky was an effort. He felt listless though, so he forced himself to finish it.

Callum stirred soon after and ate breakfast too. Just after he finished, a finfiend appeared in the window. A massive male, still handsome, with hair the blackest black Alariq had ever seen, and those same silver-ringed eyes the attractive ones had. Alariq could only see his chest and arms, but it seemed like every muscle was straining against the confines of his perfect and unmarred skin. A tug of recognition pulled at Alariq's mind, but his head was still too fuzzy to think about it. The finman looked around for the briefest of seconds and then moved on.

"They do not seem overly concerned about us," Alariq remarked resentfully.

"They know they've got us good and cornered," Callum answered, his face flat and his tone glum.

"Then they do not know dwarfs very well," Alariq answered, smiling slightly at Callum's confused look. "How long before the guard comes round again?" he asked Brimir.

"Noonday," he answered. "Why?"

Alariq stood carefully without answering. He walked to the window. He had to stand on his tiptoes to see out. He saw exactly what Callum had described. A courtyard ringed to the left, right, and rear by connected cells, shaped in a large crescent that extended all the way to the water. A straight wall, that ran from beach to beach across the width of the narrow peninsula and extended a few paces into the water, blocked everything on the other side of it from view.

He looked at the other cells. He could only see a few on the edges of the semi-circle. Alariq realized they must be somewhere near the middle.

"The walls," he said, turning to the others. "They are about an arm's length thick."

Brimir nodded. "And solid stone."

"I am not proposing we go through the walls." Alariq smiled. "But under them."

Brimir shook his head. "We already discussed that. It's no good. We are on a beach. The earth will be too wet; it will collapse on top of us."

"I don't think so." Alariq returned to the window. He gestured for Brimir to join him. "Look there, where the wall meets the beach. Do you see why they put the wall there?"

Brimir did not answer, his brow creased in confusion.

"Look at how the ground is level, but just after the wall on our side, it starts to slant upward. Steeply." Alariq pointed to the grading of the beach.

"I do not think we are merely on a peninsula," he said, turning once more to Callum and Brimir. "I think we are on a cliff."

Comprehension dawned on both of their faces.

"Look at what we are standing on." Alariq dropped to one knee, touching the ground with his hand. "It is sand on top, but look—" He dusted away the top layer. "Clay underneath. It will be hard work, but we can tunnel through that."

Callum and Brimir smiled. "Should we tell the others?"

"No, we cannot risk being overheard. We can dig under the walls fairly quickly." He grinned again, surprised at how much he was smiling lately, given their current predicament. "We will surprise them."

Alariq looked around. Dwarf hands were made for digging. Their fingers were tough-skinned and their nails incredibly hard. They could dig quite well without tools through loose soil, but clay would be much more difficult without something harder to loosen it. He found a few fist-sized rocks, one of which was pretty sharp. They'd have to do.

It was only about two paces over to Ford and Asher, but it took them nearly two hours to get through the clay and under the wall. They took turns digging, while one kept watch. They tried to spread the dirt they brought up evenly over the floor of their cell. Finally, Alariq felt the dirt loosen above his head and pushed with the hand of his uninjured arm. He hit something soft and heard a yelp. Then he felt a hand grab his.

A little more digging and he was through. He emerged, dirt showering down from his head onto his shoulders. Ford and Asher were both grinning ear to ear, Ford rubbing his rear end.

Alariq dragged himself out of the tunnel, which, for all the time it took, looked very much like a hole dug under a fence by a mischievous animal.

"Here, help me with some of this dirt." Alariq started scooping out the loose dirt and clay from the tunnel and Ford and Asher began patting it down on their floor.

"How's the head?" Ford asked.

"Better," Alariq replied. "Listen—it is almost noon, which means the guards are coming. Cover this tunnel back up with the straw. We'll start digging one over to Blainn and Gideon after the guards do their checks. One of us will come get you when we're through."

Both of them nodded curtly, accepting their orders. Alariq

returned to his cell and kept watch while the others covered the hole. Then he sat with his back against the wall and his legs over the straw covering the opening.

The guard made another pass, this time a shorter male, with pale blonde hair. He too gave the cell a cursory glance before moving on to the next. Alariq got up and looked out the window. The guard paused at only one other cell that he could see. One near the very end on the right.

We're not alone. Alariq wondered who else the finfiends had managed to ensnare.

As soon as the finfiend returned to his post on the wall, Alariq gave the order and the others started digging. They followed the same approach, this time with the opening to the tunnel in the back left corner of their cell.

Alariq emerged in Blainn and Gideon's cell to similar surprise, though this time without molesting any of his companions.

They helped him finish the tunnel on their side and he told them he'd send for them after the next guard sweep. He returned to his side and the three of them ate what was left of the biscuits and jerky, their mouths dry, having finished the water during their digging.

When the guard came by, this time a tall, reed-thin red-headed female, she threw another package of jerky through the window.

"Bowl," she said.

It was the first time Alariq had heard one of them speak. It was strange, unearthly. Breathy and higher pitched than seemed natural.

Brimir passed her the bowl through the window, which she filled and handed back. Her hands revealed only a hint of webbing between the fingers. Her skin glimmered like she had just emerged from the water, but Alariq could tell from her completely dry hair that it must just be their natural state. They were beautiful, both the males and females. But it was a cold, lifeless beauty.

The finmaid studied the cell a little more carefully than the finmen had, but seeing nothing that caused her alarm, moved on.

Brimir took a sip of water and then passed it to Callum, who likewise took a gulp and handed it to Alariq. Brimir stayed at the window, watching the guard make her rounds.

"She's back at the gate," Brimir said, bending over to pick up the packet of jerky.

"Good." Alariq rose and began to uncover the tunnel to the right. "Callum, go get Blainn and Gideon. I will call Ford and Asher."

"It is going to be tight squeeze," Brimir said quietly, returning to the window.

It was. There was barely room for them all.

"First things first," Alariq began. "Does anyone know what their plan is?"

Six heads shook from side to side.

Alariq exhaled in defeat. Without knowing the finfiends' plan, it was difficult to make one of their own.

"Then we only have one choice," he said. "Tunneling."

The others nodded solemnly. They all knew what they were getting into. Digging a couple of paces under a wall was easy enough. But real tunneling was dangerous, even in good conditions. And without knowing the terrain or the soil conditions, it was even worse. Unable to take measurements above ground, they would be best-guessing as to where they'd come out.

"What lies on the other side of the wall?" he asked the room.

"Nothing much, a few rocks and some sparse trees," Ford answered. "But it was dark when they brought us here. We couldn't see much of anything."

"So nothing to use for cover," Alariq said, more to himself. "What about our weapons? Does anyone know where they put them?"

"In the first cell on the left," Blainn answered, his fingers twitching, as if anxious to grip his sword. "They dumped them in there before leading us to our cells."

"That's too close to the beach," Brimir warned.

"We have no choice," Alariq snapped, a little too loudly. "We cannot make a run for it in the open with nothing to defend ourselves," he said lowering his voice. "Blainn, Gideon—get started on a tunnel in that direction. One of you keeps watch, always. If you hit wet sand, stop and report back."

They nodded. Alariq turned to Ford and Asher. "Your cell is closest to the middle of the cellblock, so we'll dig our escape tunnel from there. We'll get started tonight." He clasped Ford's shoulder. "You must stay straight. We have to stay as close to the middle as possible and away from those beaches."

Ford nodded.

Alariq removed his hand and looked at the others. "Keep your ears open for anything from the finfiends that might give us a clue as to their plan or what they want from us."

Everyone's heads bobbed slightly.

"Alright, Callum, go with Blainn and Gideon. Brimir and I will work with Ford and Asher."

His voice took on a stern quality. "Be mindful of the time. Everyone must be back in their cells with their tunnels covered before the next guard sweep. Understand?"

Everyone nodded their understanding and they disappeared into the tunnels, three to the left, and four to the right.

Alariq ordered Brimir to keep watch while he and Ford and Asher took turns digging. It soon became clear, however, that they were producing far too much earth to simply spread around their cells. So Alariq set to work digging through to the cell to the right, hoping it was empty.

It was. They started excavating the dirt into that cell too, hoping the guards would continue to simply pass over the empty cells.

They made decent progress. They'd dug down to the necessary depth to protect against collapse and leveled off. The clay had already changed mostly to dirt by the time they finished, which meant it would go even faster from then on.

Alariq and Brimir helped cover the holes and then returned to their cell. Callum was already there, his hole covered, standing by the door keeping watch. Alariq felt a surge of pride. The kid was turning out alright.

"Progress?" Alariq asked him, while Brimir covered the tunnel to the right.

Callum moved away from the door and took up his spot over the tunnel to the left. "About four paces. But we're having trouble concealing the dirt."

"You'll have to dig into the cell beside you," Alariq answered. "We did."

Callum nodded. "I'll tell them when I go back over."

Brimir passed everyone the jerky that had been forgotten and they all ate and drank what was left of the water. "They do one pass around midnight and then not again until dawn, when they bring more food and water," he said.

"You two get some sleep," Alariq said. "I will wake you after the guard comes round."

They nodded gratefully and immediately laid down. Within minutes, Alariq could hear Brimir's quiet snoring and Callum's deep, even breathing.

Alariq laid down too, making sure he could still see the window. The guard came by after about half-an-hour. He let the others sleep a little longer before rousing them. Then they each went their separate ways again.

Ford and Asher were both asleep. He roused them both and they set to work again. They formed an assembly line of sorts, with Brimir at the bottom, Ford in the middle, and Asher at the top. They constantly moved in and out of the tunnel opening. Air movement. That was the key to avoiding asphyxiation in tunnels. Alariq's head was pounding, so Brimir insisted he keep watch this time.

"Digging tunnels is not to be done with a hazy head," he'd said.

They were slowed at various intervals when they had to move the dirt over to the other cell and spread it out, but when it got close to dawn, Alariq was pleased once again with their progress.

Once more, he and Brimir returned to their cell. Callum appeared moments later.

"We dug into the next cell and got rid of our dirt, but didn't get much farther than that."

Alariq nodded. He didn't have his best diggers over there, but that was fine by him. It would take them longer to dig out of the prison than it would to the other cell. He'd send them Brimir if they fell behind or things got dicey. He was the expert tunneler, after all.

Callum offered to keep watch this time and Alariq accepted

appreciatively. He had just closed his eyes when he heard the commotion outside. He immediately rose, as did the others, and strode over to the window, peering out into the soft light that precedes the day.

He did not see anything in the courtyard and the gate remained closed. He looked up and saw the guards staring west, into the water. He craned his neck, but he could not see the object of their attention. Soon, however, it came into view.

Eight or ten finfiends cutting through the water, two of them dragging something with them.

They pulled whatever it was ashore and gathered around it. Alariq recognized the incredibly tall and broad, black-haired finman shoving the others back.

He lifted the thing off the ground and threw it over his shoulder.

Three things became apparent to Alariq all at once. First, the thing was a person. Second, the black-haired finman had clearly laid some sort of claim to it. Third, Asher had been right: Tianna was not the sort of person to do nothing.

26

In Good Company

Even wet, that golden hair was unmistakable. Alariq felt the blood drain from his face.

She is alive, he said to himself. *They didn't kill us, and they won't kill her.*

He searched for any sign of movement, but saw none. He was aware that Callum was talking to him, but all he could focus on was Tianna and any sign that the finfiends hadn't drowned her.

He heard Asher yelling threats at the black-haired finfiend, who turned and snarled in their direction. Alariq could hear Asher pounding futilely against the door.

But still his eyes remained locked on Tianna, looking for any clue as to her state. The finfiend carried her into one of the cells to his right, three or four down from Ford and Asher, by his guess.

She must have followed them and gotten captured on the way, just like them. Maybe at the very same place they had. Or had she been captured back at Loraheem and brought all this way?

He heard the cell door close and the black-haired brute strode back to the others. They all disappeared into the lake once more, this time, completely below the surface. The only sign that they had ever been there was the wet spot on the beach.

"Tia!"

Asher's shouts broke through Alariq's terror-induced torpid state. He saw the guards at the gate turn toward them. He could not risk them entering the cells.

"Quiet!" he hissed through the window, but Asher continued to call for Tianna.

"Keep watch!" Alariq snapped to no one in particular and quickly threw the straw covering the tunnel to Asher's cell aside. He pulled himself through, less careful than he should have been.

Asher was at the door, still yelling for Tianna to answer him. Ford was tugging at his shoulders trying to quiet him.

Alariq strode over and pushed Ford aside. He seized Asher by the shoulder and wrenched him around to face him.

"Listen to me!" he growled.

Asher's eyes were wide, his face pale.

Alariq was close, their noses were almost touching. "She is alive. Do you hear me?" He shook Asher's shoulders. "They would not have brought her here, would not have locked her up, if she were dead."

He watched as reason returned to Asher's eyes and felt the fight go out of him. Asher nodded slightly, breathing heavily.

Alariq held his grip for a moment more to make sure Asher was really finished. Then he released him and headed back for the tunnel.

"Keep him quiet!" he snapped at Ford as he disappeared into the hole.

Alariq had just gotten back into position when the face of the pale-haired male appeared in the window. He tossed in a packet of their campaign biscuits and refilled their bowl.

Alariq held his breath as it moved on to Asher's cell, only releasing it once he heard the finfiend move on.

He went to the window. He waited for the guard to appear in his vision again, but still he did not. The finman must have paused at Tianna's cell. Only he wasn't moving on quickly, like he did with the dwarfs. Alariq could almost feel Asher's rage and anxiety through the wall. Or was that just his own?

But then the guard came into his sight once more. The breath whooshed out of Alariq's lungs. He hadn't even realized he'd been holding it.

He watched the guard continue around the walkway, pausing at that same cell near the end. The finman tossed some of their supplies inside and a hand emerged from the window, holding out a bowl, confirming Alariq's suspicions that there was, in fact, another prisoner.

"What are we going to do?" Callum asked, his eyes filled with worry.

"We will tunnel over to her," Alariq answered without hesitation.

Callum let out a sigh of relief.

Alariq stared at him for a moment. Had he really thought the answer would be anything different? Of course they would include Tianna in their escape. He thought that would be a given. It stung a little that Callum would worry otherwise.

They ate quickly and then Alariq dispatched Callum once more with orders to the others to keep going. Then he and Brimir headed next door.

"What do you reckon, Brimir?" Alariq asked. "Do we dig a separate tunnel over to Tianna or make an offshoot of the one to the spare dirt cell?"

"An offshoot, definitely," Brimir replied.

"Sounds good to me. Get started." He turned to Asher. "You keep watch."

Asher instantly obeyed and glued himself to the window. Alariq knew that's where he would want to be, but more importantly, he didn't want Asher digging any tunnels while he was in this state of mind.

Alariq and Ford continued to work on the escape tunnel, slower now that it was longer and there was only two of them.

They paused again at midday, careful, as always, to get back into their cells before the guard made rounds. He had planned for them to get some sleep during the day, but now that they had to dig over to Tianna too, that was out of the question. At least until they made sure she was unharmed.

He and Brimir slept for about an hour over lunch. When Alariq awoke, his head ached, pain shooting into his eyes with every pulse of blood. He sent Brimir over to the others to make sure they were digging toward the right spot and enlisted Callum to help Ford with the escape tunnel.

He set Asher to watch again and kept working on the tunnel to Tianna, forcing himself to be careful, despite his pounding head and concern. When he emerged with some dirt, Brimir had just returned from Blainn and Gideon's cell.

"They're about halfway there," he said. "I needed to correct their path a little, but they should be good now."

"How long until they are through?" Alariq asked.

"With just the two of them, at this pace? A full day."

Alariq nodded. "How long until we reach Tianna?"

"Let me take a look." Brimir descended below the wall, returning soon after.

"You've made good progress. Tonight, I think."

"Good, now go get some rest," Alariq ordered.

"I'm fine." Brimir waved him off.

"Brimir..." Alariq began.

"Not until we get to her," Brimir said quietly.

Alariq looked at him for a moment before nodding. Maybe Tianna had become a more important part of the company than he'd realized.

Brimir headed back into the tunnel and Alariq excavated the dirt behind him. They surfaced once, but the cell was empty. They had to pause again for the next guard sweep, but then immediately set back to work.

About an hour after dusk, they surfaced again.

Alariq heard Brimir's voice, but couldn't make out the words.

Then Brimir called over his shoulder. "I found her. She's alright."

The tightness in Alariq's chest loosened. He backed out of the tunnel and found Asher staring questioningly at him, his eyes wide and hopeful.

"She is unhurt," Alariq said softly.

Asher nodded and turned quickly away to face the door.

Alariq descended into the escape tunnel to tell Ford and Callum the good news and help for a bit while Brimir finished Tianna's tunnel and brought her over.

But when he emerged with some dirt, Brimir was at the door and Tianna was nowhere to be found.

"She would not come," he said at Alariq's questioning stare.

"What do you mean?" he demanded.

"She is afraid of the tunnel. The tight space. Asher is over there with her now."

Alariq made for the tunnel. As he crawled, he remembered Tianna being uneasy when they had discussed tunneling out of Dendreya if necessary. And he had heard of people being afraid of close quarters before, but honestly never thought Tianna would let fear get the better of her.

When he emerged, she was sitting on the bed, arms wrapped around her waist. Asher was nearby, on one knee, a look of concern on his face.

Brimir had told him she was alright. Alariq hadn't realized how much he'd needed to see the truth for himself, however. At the sight of her there, shivering and scared, but apparently unhurt, it felt like the tunnel was falling out from underneath him.

She looked up at Alariq as he climbed out of the hole.

"Brimir says you will not come through the tunnel," he said gruffly.

"I am pleased to see that you are alright, too," Tianna bit back.

Asher rose and crossed over to him. "She is afraid of the tight space," he murmured.

"It's a small cell. I can hear what you are saying." Her face was pale, but her eyes less filled with fear now.

"Well this is your only way out," Alariq said without remorse. "You will either crawl through the tunnel or we will leave you here."

Asher shot him an angry look, but Alariq ignored him.

"I do not have time to coddle you." He stared unblinkingly at her until she finally nodded.

"Asher, you are needed in the tunnels." When Asher did not move, he added, more forcefully, "Now."

Asher shot a quick glance at Tianna and then disappeared into the tunnel.

"I am serious," Alariq said looking back at Tianna, their gazes locked together. Then more gently, "I don't know what these creatures want from us, but it cannot be good. If there was another way, I would give it to you."

And he realized it was true. If he could spare her this pain, he would.

Tianna nodded again, taking a deep breath and rising. She took a step toward the tunnel.

But Alariq stepped in front of her.

"Not now," he said, taking pity on her. "The escape tunnel will not be ready for at least another two days. And there is no reason you cannot just wait here."

"You do not need my help?" she asked.

He laughed and to his surprise it came out sounding quite a bit like that one of hers he had grown to uniquely associate with her.

"Look at you—you would only be a liability down there."

She nodded and sat back down weakly and looked at the dirt floor.

"I will send for you when we are ready." Now that she wasn't looking at him, he let his gaze scrutinize her more carefully, looking for signs of injury. She wore her dark, long doeskin pants, and a light tan, long-sleeved shirt he'd never seen her wear before. One of the sleeves was ripped and he could see scratch marks through the tear. Her hair was a mess. But on the whole, she did look physically sound.

Emotionally was another thing. He'd never seen her like this. More importantly, he'd never *expected* to see her like this. The fear and vulnerability that creased her face was difficult to look at, though Alariq wasn't sure why.

She rubbed her arms. He had the insane urge to go over and warm them. He settled for collecting the dirty blanket in the corner and, after dusting it off as best he could, handing it to her.

She took it from him with a murmured thanks.

But still Alariq did not back away. Her clean face and hands contrasted starkly with his, filthy from the digging. It made her look over-exposed. He took the blanket back from her and draped it around her shoulders, dropping down to a crouch so that they were eyelevel.

She smelled like the lake. But underneath it, was the scent he'd come to associate with Loraheem.

"Why did you come?" he whispered.

She searched his gaze. Her fear, whether of the tunnel, or the finfiends, or the unknown fate that awaited her, stripped away the wall she usually kept to mask her thoughts. For the first time, Alariq felt like he was getting a glimpse of what lay beneath the carefully controlled surface. She looked like she desperately wanted to tell him something, but couldn't get the words out.

She opened her mouth to speak, but then closed it abruptly and stood, almost knocking Alariq on his rump in the process. She walked over to the door and looked out.

"Because we both know your plan is a terrible one and you clearly need someone with a more sensible disposition," she quipped.

He chuckled. There was the Tianna he recognized.

"More sensible than a dwarf?"

She turned to face him.

"More sensible than *some* dwarfs."

She gave him a pointed look and then a half smile.

Satisfied that she was as back to her usual self as she was going to get, Alariq headed for the tunnel, a small smile on his lips.

But something stopped him from leaving. He paused at the mouth of the tunnel and looked back at her. She held his gaze and a hint of emotion crept back into her features. He looked at the ground and said softly, "I *am* glad that you are alright."

Then he descended into the darkness below.

He called a halt to the tunneling when he returned and ordered everyone to sleep for the night. They slept until morning and then got back to work after the guard delivered breakfast. Alariq knew their supplies must be running low. He wondered what they'd feed them then.

He sent Brimir back over to Gideon and Blainn and he came back with excellent news. One more shift and they should be through to the weapons. The ground was getting sandy and damp, but so far everything was holding.

That evening, he sent Asher over to check on Tianna. Alariq

wanted to go himself, but something about their previous exchange held him back. To his surprise, Asher returned only minutes later.

Asher poked his head out of the tunnel. "She needs to see you." He disappeared back into the tunnel without waiting for an answer.

Alariq gritted his teeth. He was not accustomed to being summoned. But he followed Asher through the tunnel. He emerged ready to chastise her, but just as he opened his mouth to do so, she cut across him.

"Do not bother. I knew you wouldn't appreciate being beckoned. But I have something important to tell you."

He simply stared at her and when she did not continue, he cocked an eyebrow. "Well? What is it?"

"There is someone else here," she said.

"In the third cell from the end," he replied casually. "Yes, I know."

She was slightly taken aback by his tone, but quickly recovered.

"Yes, well, he may be able to help us."

"He?" Asher asked. "How do you know the prisoner is a male?"

But Alariq was more concerned about the last half of her statement.

"How?" he asked, skeptical.

"He has information," she replied, holding Alariq's gaze unwaveringly. "About this place. About the finfiends."

"How do you know?"

"He visited me last night," she said, her eyes still locked on his.

Alariq saw Asher twitch out of the corner of his eye, but he kept his own vision on Tianna.

"What do you mean?" Asher demanded.

"How?" Alariq asked again, still ignoring Asher.

Tianna gave him a hard look.

"In my dreams."

27

In Bad Company

Have you ever noticed that people—and, of course, I include dwarfs in this category—are not always very good at judging themselves? It always seems to me that this paradox occurs most often when a person is at their best or their worst. It is in those highs and lows of life that we tend to shy away from self-reflection, and therefore, impartial assessment of ourselves. In these moments, another's perspective is usually much more accurate.

Unfortunately, it is in these moments that the universe has a nasty little habit of sending us someone from whom we'd rather hide our true selves. It is a reminder, I think, that what we want and what we need are not always the same...

Alariq's jaw began to ache from the constant grinding of his teeth. He massaged it and then continued to dig. The present cause of his frustration was that progress on the main escape tunnel had once again slowed. What's more, now he had also called a halt to Blainn and Gideon's tunnel to their weapons in order to have them help Brimir dig yet another tunnel.

A tunnel to the man of Tianna's dreams.

Alariq had to consciously force his jaw to unclench.

He could not believe he was doing this. He'd almost quit a hundred times. This was taking time they could not afford and

271

with no guarantee of a payoff.

And yet he continued to dig.

A doeppelganger. Tianna had been adamant it was a doeppelganger who was being held with them in the prison. And she had insisted further that he could be of use.

Alariq could afford to pull Gideon and Blainn away anyway. The tunnel to the weapons was almost finished, while the main escape one was still over a day away from being done. Alariq was currently digging at the fore of that tunnel.

He carved out a chunk of earth above him. He felt the distance between his head and the curved roof of earth above. He had not given any order to make the tunnel a little roomier, but had simply started carving out a little extra room himself. Apparently, Asher or Brimir had told the others of Tianna's fears, because the other diggers had followed suit.

Alariq thought back to what Tianna had told them in the treehome about doeppelgangers. Something about being able to enter the dreams of others. And that they take the dreamer's form while in there. Alariq tried to remember his own dreams over the past few nights, searching for any sign of an outside presence in them. But what few dreams he'd had had been broken and nonsensical. Either this prisoner wasn't a doeppelganger at all, or he had only entered Tianna's dreams.

Alariq was grinding again. He took a deep breath and decided to call it quits for this shift. He backed slowly out of the now quite-long tunnel. By his (and more importantly, Brimir's) calculations, they should be just past the gate. He called out behind him and heard Ford do the same.

As he climbed out of the hole, he almost collided with Callum, who was helping Brimir out of the opening of the tunnel that now led to the third cell from the end.

"Just about through," Brimir said, seeing Alariq.

"Good work," he replied.

He consulted Gideon, who was keeping watch. "How long until the guard comes back?"

"A while, yet." Gideon looked at the sun in the west. "At least an hour, maybe two."

Alariq turned back to the others. Uncharacteristically, all

seven of them were piled in the tiny room. "Everyone back to your cells. Get some sleep. After the next guard check-in, Gideon and Blainn—finish that tunnel to our weapons."

They all went back to their cells and slept until the sun had fallen below the horizon. Upon waking, they drank some water and then got back to work. Alariq set Brimir and Callum back to work on the escape tunnel. He, Ford, and Asher gathered around the tunnel leading east. It went to Tianna's, but they had built another offshoot to reach the alleged doeppelganger.

Alariq went first, but instead of taking the offshoot, he continued straight to Tianna's cell. Once they were all topside again, Alariq turned to Tianna and gave her a hard look.

"We are going over to your doeppelganger now. A few more minutes of digging and we should break through."

Tianna looked back at him warily.

"You are coming with us."

This caught all three of the others off guard.

"Why?" she asked and her voice trembled. Perhaps she realized it, because she cleared her throat and spoke more strongly. "You do not need me."

The quiver in her voice threatened Alariq's resolve. He felt bad for her, yes, but he felt even worse that it was he, Alariq, who was causing her this pain. He forced his spine to straighten into an unyielding rod.

"This was your idea. You are the one who claims he is a doeppelganger. You are the only one who has noticed anything amiss in your dreams."

He stepped closer to her and forced her to meet his gaze. He knew no matter how quietly he spoke, the others would still be able to hear him, but he couldn't help lowering his voice to a near whisper, wishing suddenly they were alone.

"You need to prove to me that you can do this." He looked deep into her bottomless amber eyes, unblinking. "Before we are all counting on you."

She looked back for a moment and then nodded tersely.

Alariq turned to Asher. "Give us enough time to get to the end and finish the tunnel. Then you two follow us."

Asher gave him a look of surprise, but nodded, a strange

expression on his face. Tianna on the other hand looked like she'd just been told she was going to be executed and had to sit on her hands waiting for it.

Alariq gave her one last look and then nodded to Ford to indicate he should follow him. They crawled through the darkness until they reached the end. The loose earth started to drizzle down as he neared the surface. He had to get through this quickly. The person in the cell would be able to hear them and he could not afford him getting scared and calling for help. He dug hard and fast, felt Ford pulling the dirt and spreading it behind him. He pushed his head upward and through the dirt above.

He came up almost directly in the middle of the cell.

Damn! They'd overshot. A hole in the middle of the ground was a lot harder to conceal than one in the corner.

Nothing to be said about it though; it was too late now. He pushed the earth up and out around him. Once he was sure the opening wouldn't collapse on top of Ford below, he turned searching for the purpose of all this effort.

He found him sitting on a blanket on top of some straw in the corner. Sitting. Not standing, or cowering in the corner, not even sleeping. He was sitting completely upright, facing the hole that had just materialized in the very center of his cell, legs crossed beneath him.

And he didn't look scared. Or even surprised. In fact, he looked...*bored.*

Alariq hated him immediately.

He climbed out of the hole and Ford followed. Long moments passed and no one spoke. The man just sat there, eyeing their dirty clothes and skin. Alariq had a feeling the man was waiting for something, but for what he did not know. It was a bright night and there was just enough light to make out the man's features.

Or, there would have been.

The man was the most nondescript thing Alariq had ever laid eyes on. Every time Alariq thought he could describe a feature, it seemed to shift or slip from his mind. It was as if he were one of the faceless people Alariq sometimes saw in his dreams. One of those figures he knew had a face, but he couldn't quite focus on it or describe it.

It set Alariq ill at ease.

Then a flash of blonde below caught his eye and he looked down to see Tianna emerging from the tunnel. Her face was strained and pale, and she was shaking. He immediately went to her, and pulled her out of the tunnel, asking her with his eyes if she was okay. He did not release her until she nodded.

They moved aside and Asher came through the hole. Ford walked over to the window and peered out.

"You did great," Asher whispered to Tianna.

"Oh my," the man in the corner said, looking from Asher to Tianna to Alariq. "This is an unexpected twist." His voice was silky smooth. It felt to Alariq like his words slipped into Alariq's ears and wound gracefully into his mind.

Alariq narrowed his eyes, but didn't speak.

"I thought you would be here sooner," the man said.

"You were expecting us?" Alariq asked, unconvinced.

"Told you," muttered Tianna from beside him.

The man turned his attention to her. "I was expecting dwarfs. I was not expecting her." He looked her over from top to toe, his gaze lingering long past decency. "I am rather surprised you made it through the tunnel, actually."

"What does that mean?" Asher demanded, stepping slightly in front of Tianna.

The man smiled slowly, his eyes taking in everything about Asher now.

"Simply that she is terribly afraid of the tunnels. She dreams about them endlessly. Stopping at a dead end. Collapsing on top of her. Filling with water." It was said casually, but Alariq saw something more in the man's eyes.

He was baiting them.

Tianna paled, but Alariq recognized the look in her eyes. A small smile played across his lips.

"You clearly know why we are here," she said, her voice tinged with contempt. "Can you help us or not?"

That cutting tone of hers was a whole lot more pleasing when it wasn't directed at him.

"Not so fast," the man said. "First, we must have a meeting of the minds, so to speak." He looked at Alariq. "You will take me with you, naturally."

Alariq hesitated.

The man's eyes bore into Alariq's. "If you do not, I will alert the finfiends to your plans." He raised an eyebrow.

Alariq cursed silently to himself. And at Tianna. He had no choice now.

"Alright," he bit out.

"Lovely!" the man said, uncrossing his legs and reclining comfortably. "Now, we can discuss business."

"Who are you?" Alariq asked him.

"Nyeven is the name and dreams are my game," he answered in a singsong voice.

"So you *are* a doeppelganger?" Asher prodded.

The man gave a small bow with his head and a flourish with his hand. "At your service."

Alariq's dislike for him intensified. "Where are we?"

"Right to the point, are we, Sunshine?" The doeppelganger seemed to be delighting in their annoyance. "Fair enough. We are in Loraporth. The lone port city of the finfiends. And the only gateway to Eynhallow."

"The island where the finfiends live?" Tianna's voice was back to normal.

Nyeven tilted his head toward her exaggeratedly.

"So their plan is to take us to this island?" Alariq probed.

"Exactly so, dear sir." The doeppelganger lounged casually in his corner, talking as if he were explaining the game of lawn darts.

"Why?" Asher asked. "What do they want from us?"

Nyeven considered Asher for a moment before responding.

"As even you must have guessed by now, finfiends are lake creatures. They live on an island out in the deeps of August Sound."

"Yes, we know that much," said Alariq impatiently.

The doeppelganger turned on him now, still smirking.

"They are born beautiful creatures who can transform their bodies to suit life on land or in the lake."

Alariq remembered back to the two attacks and how some of their webbed hands and feet seemed to disappear the longer they stayed on the beach.

"But they must ensnare a non-finfiend spouse before they reach a certain age. If they succeed, they remain in their current form and live long lives."

Alariq had to fight back revulsion. The finfiends planned to make them their unwilling mates? They had known from the beginning that the finfiends wanted them alive. Now they knew why. Out of the corner of his eye, Alariq saw Asher move slightly toward Tianna.

"And if they fail?" Alariq asked.

"They become hideous water monsters who cannot survive on land for long periods of time. And their lifetimes are drastically shorter in this form," said Nyeven, as though this information did not concern him in the slightest. "That is why they are taking us to Eynhallow. The marriage ceremonies must be performed on the island for them to have their desired effect, you see."

"I told you they wouldn't attack ettins," Tianna muttered out of the corner of her mouth.

Apparently, Nyeven also possessed excellent hearing.

"Ettins?" He snorted. "Of course they would never attack ettins. An ettin spouse would not transform a finfiend. Finfiends draw their continued beauty and life-force from their spouse. Given the general repulsiveness and short lifespans of ettins, I cannot imagine they would ever be a target of the finfiends."

Tianna shot Alariq a look before turning her attention back to the doeppelganger.

"What do you know of the area around us?" Tianna asked.

Alariq was glad he'd brought her with them. In his distaste of Nyeven and disgust at the fate that awaited them all, he'd forgotten to ask about that.

"I know there are eight guards posted on the wall at any given time." Even his voice was slippery and indescribable.

"Yes, we can see that for ourselves," said Asher scornfully.

"Yes, well, can you also see the three finfiends posted underwater on each side of the wall?" Nyeven mocked back.

Alariq and Ford exchanged glances. That put their enemies up to fourteen. A minimum of fourteen.

"The others go out on hunts. They patrol the beaches constantly looking for victims." Nyeven continued to glance back and forth between them, his shrewd eyes overlooking nothing. He lingered once again on Tianna. "They have been particularly successful this time."

"We are tunneling about a hundred paces past the gate," said Alariq.

"That will not be far enough," Nyeven replied.

"We will go at night, when visibility is low." Alariq's tone was annoyed. "And we have tunneled over to our weapons. We can handle fourteen finfiends, as long as we stay away from the water."

"But you cannot handle fifty." Nyeven casually flicked a stray bit of something from his sleeve.

"Fifty?" Asher interjected. "You said eight on the gate and six in the water. That's fourteen."

"I daresay I am a bit more accomplished at mathematics than a dwarf." Nyeven's tone wasn't irritated. No, Alariq realized he was intentionally inciting their emotions, pushing them to see how far they'd let him. Asher's eyes flashed, but he didn't respond.

Nyeven smiled ever so slightly before continuing. "The rest of them sleep in the shallows by the beach below the cliff. It is just a short swim to cut you off. You might get lucky and they may be out hunting." He looked up at them and held his hands out to the sides. "Or not."

"So what do you propose?" Alariq had grown tired of this constant mental game of chase.

"There is a rocky outcropping about three hundred paces past the gate and another fifty to the right. After you have gotten far enough out, tunnel east until you hit wet sand. You should come out behind the rocks. We might be able to get out of here without them knowing until the guard checks our cells."

Alariq didn't like it. And not just because Nyeven had suggested it. It would add several days to their time and take them into dangerous soil conditions.

"But you must hurry," Nyeven said, as if reading Alariq's thoughts. "The finfiends are waiting for flood season to take us to the island. It is only accessible above water during that time, you see." He looked up at the roof. "And in case you haven't noticed, it has been raining quite a lot lately."

One thing nagged at Alariq. "You are a doeppelganger," he said simply, crossing his arms over his chest.

"I have already indicated as much," Nyeven replied.

"If you were expecting us, you have clearly been in our dreams and you made it clear you have been in Tianna's. I thought doeppelgangers had the ability to manipulate those whose dreams you enter. Bend their will to yours." Alariq narrowed his eyes. "If you can, in fact, do such a thing, why are you still imprisoned here?"

The doeppelganger's casual smile froze and a muscle in his face ticked. He looked at Alariq, his nostrils flaring slightly. Alariq thought for a moment he was not going to answer.

"Finfiends only speak the trade language to ensnare their spouses. Among themselves and in their dreams, they speak finspeak. I do not. The minute I speak in Dirni, their subconscious knows something is not right and they begin to awaken. I can observe their dreams, but I cannot manipulate them."

Alariq considered him for a moment before deciding to believe him. Not that he had any choice. He nodded.

"Alright. We will do it your way. Ford—go tell Brimir we must dig three hundred paces past the gate and then east until we hit wet sand. Asher—take Tianna back to her cell."

Ford immediately obeyed. Tianna seemed dazed at having no time to prepare for her next trip into the tunnel. She had just gotten ready to drop into the hole when—

"Just don't think about those dreams, Buttercup," Nyeven mocked.

Asher took a threatening step toward the doeppelganger, but Alariq put a hand on his chest. Asher shot Nyeven a look and then turned to help Tianna into the tunnel, giving her hand an encouraging squeeze.

They disappeared one at a time below.

After Alariq was sure they were out of earshot, he turned to face the doeppelganger.

"Stay out of our dreams." His voice was a low growl.

Nyeven laughed. It was an unpleasant sound.

"Of all of you, only the girl knew I was in her head." Nyeven leaned toward Alariq and dropped his voice. "You would not know me if I spoke directly to your face in your dreams tonight."

He rose from his spot and took a few steps toward Alariq, who tensed. Nyeven was a full head and neck taller than him, of average human build.

"The girl. She is of value to you." Nyeven said slowly, looking at Alariq for confirmation.

Alariq looked at him sharply. What was he playing at?

"That is none of your concern."

"I beg to disagree," he responded in his smooth voice. He fixed on Alariq with an unblinking stare. "She puts us all at great risk."

"What do you mean?" Alariq asked, staring intently at the doeppelganger.

Nyeven ignored him. He narrowed his shrewd gaze on Alariq. "You would be unwilling to leave her behind, I take it."

"Of course," Alariq answered immediately. "Why?"

Alariq studied the doeppelganger, trying to determine whether this was just a game designed to get a rise out of him.

"As I said, she puts us all at risk," he responded coyly.

Alariq clenched his fists to stop him from throttling the shifty charlatan. He couldn't explain it, but the thought that this trickster might know more about Tianna than he did made his blood boil.

"That is not an answer."

Nyeven sat back down, leaning his back against the wall. "Yes, well, I suppose not."

Something instinctive told Alariq this wasn't just a game. Nyeven knew something about the secretive woman he and the others had been living with these past months. The allure of learning more about her was too tempting to pass up.

"What is it you know?" Alariq demanded, unwilling to let the matter drop.

Nyeven shot him a knowing look, smiling slightly. "Mysterious, isn't she?" he asked quietly, playing with a stray string on his threadbare pants. "Very few people are able to sense a foreign presence in their dreams." Nyeven seemed to be talking more to himself now and Alariq could tell he was lost in his own thoughts about the cryptically bewitching air that surrounded Tianna.

"Tell me now, or I will leave you behind," Alariq growled.

"No you won't," the doeppelganger replied quickly, his tone filled with snark. He pulled the string abruptly, breaking it off where it met the fabric and began twirling it around his finger.

"But it doesn't matter. I do not know anything about her." He gave Alariq a look of mock apology.

To hell with it! Alariq started toward the tunnel. "I am tired of your games!"

"Temper, temper," Nyeven chided. "Do you want to know what I know or don't you?"

Alariq stopped and slowly turned to face the doeppelganger again, dislike creasing every line in his face.

"That's better," said Nyeven in a voice like a parent speaking to a child. "It is not her I am concerned with. It is the finman. The largest one, with the soot-black hair."

This caught Alariq off guard. "The one who carried her to her cell?" he asked, perplexed.

"Yes. He is determined to marry her himself," Nyeven said.

"And?" said Alariq, fully nonplussed. He could have guessed as much on his own.

"No, you misunderstand." The doeppelganger locked his pale eyes on Alariq's. "He is obsessed. More so than any other finfiend. Normally, they do not care who they ensnare for a spouse, just so long as they do ensnare one."

Alariq simply raised an eyebrow, waiting for further explanation.

"But this one is different. There is something about her that draws him. He is not just interested in ensnaring *any* spouse. He is determined to take *her*, and only *her*, as his wife. I believe he will pursue us with all that he has to get her back."

"Why?" Alariq asked, skeptical. He'd gotten the feeling that the white-haired finmaid had some sort of preoccupation with him, but what Nyeven was describing unsettled him in a much more primitive way.

"I am not certain. But he dwells on something in his dreams. He dreams of it over and over again." The doeppelganger continued to wind the string around his finger.

"I thought you said you could not see their dreams." Alariq's tone was more suspicious than ever and if his eyes were any narrower, he would not have been able to see.

Nyeven rolled his eyes. "No, I said I cannot *manipulate* their dreams. But I can *observe* them. And what I have observed is this finfiend dreaming of the same thing, night after night. Even before they brought all of you here."

"And what is that?" Alariq was concerned now.

"It is a memory, I believe." The doeppelganger closed his eyes. "It is nighttime. He is in the shallows of the lake. He and two other finmen are dragging the blonde one into the water. There are sounds of fighting all around."

Alariq was paying careful attention now. For Nyeven was describing the fight on the beach the night his company failed to save the knomes.

"He uses one hand to grab her hair, just at the base of her neck," the doeppelganger continued, "and the other, the scruff of the back of her shirt. The moon shifts and shines down directly on them and he sees something."

"What?" Alariq urged. "What did he see?"

"A mark. High on her back, between her shoulder blades. A downward-pointing, diagonal trident." He opened his eyes and looked at Alariq. "Branded into her skin."

Something clicked in Alariq's mind. "Draw it," he ordered.

The doeppelganger complied, drawing the mark in the dirt.

Alariq stared at it for a long moment, forcing his eyes to check and double check that they were seeing what his brain thought they were. Finally, he tore his eyes away from the symbol and returned his attention to the doeppelganger.

"Is that all?" he demanded, his tone brusque.

"For now..." Nyeven answered mysteriously.

Alariq shot him a look of loathing. "Be sure to cover up this hole behind me."

Then he climbed into the tunnel without another word.

He encountered Asher on the crawl back, coming out of the tunnel leading to Tianna's cell. He waited for Asher to pass and then fell in behind him.

Upon emerging, Blainn happily announced that they had made it into the cell that held their weapons. They'd left them there, he'd added ruefully, so as not to tip off the finfiends.

Well at least that was done. Alariq ordered everyone but Ford and Asher to bed for the night.

"We have a long few days ahead of us. We will start digging in shifts. You two take the next one after the guard comes by at midnight."

After he, Callum, and Brimir had returned to their cell and covered the passages, he waited to hear the telltale breathing that indicated his young cousin was asleep. While he laid there, he thought of the symbol Nyeven had drawn. The downward-pointing, diagonal trident. He had seen it before. He was sure. And he thought he knew where.

When he was certain Callum was asleep, he crept over to Brimir and gently woke him up.

"What is it?" he asked, instantly ready.

"It's just me," Alariq whispered. "I need to ask you something."

Brimir sat up. "What is it?"

"Come with me to the door," Alariq helped him up. "Into the light."

Brimir followed him over to the square of moonlight that shone through the window in the door.

Alariq bent over the patch of light on the ground and drew the symbol that Nyeven had drawn for him. He straightened and looked directly at Brimir, who was staring at the symbol. In that moment, Alariq knew he was right.

But he had to be sure.

"Brimir, where have I seen that symbol before?"

Brimir looked up from the ground and met his gaze. "You know where."

When Alariq remained silent, Brimir answered, "On your grandfather's arm—when they brought back his body."

28

Sidetracked

Alariq slept fitfully that night. His nerves were completely shot. He was constantly on guard against an attempt by the doeppelganger to invade his dreams. He kept falling asleep only to jerk back awake moments later. His conscious thoughts would slowly melt into dreams, but then he would realize he was dreaming and jolt awake yet again.

It was more of the same for the next two days.

Alariq's anxiety was not alleviated by the fact that he had started having thoughts of finishing the tunnel in secret and leaving the doeppelganger behind. He constantly worried those thoughts would somehow show themselves at night in his dreams. And that the doeppelganger would sense Alariq's desire to leave him behind and alert the finfiends out of spite.

And it continued to rain. A slow, but steady drizzle, that continued to get heavier as the rainy season approached its full swing. But the storms that would flood the lake and allow the finfiends to transport their prisoners to Eynhallow had so far remained at bay.

Alariq dwelled constantly on the symbol Nyeven had described, desperately searching for a link between Tianna and his grandfather. His mind circled it like a vulture above its prey.

He thought back to the only time he had ever seen it. He was just a dwarfling. It was during the Knomic Wars, when Knaba was under attack from men seeking the wealth within the city. The surviving soldiers brought back the bodies of those killed in combat. His grandfather's was among them. Alariq was sure at first it was a mistake. His grandfather seemed all-powerful to him at the time. But when they brought back the body and Alariq looked at his grandfather's pale face, there was no more room for wishful doubt.

Then, as they were carrying his body inside, Alariq saw something through a tear in his shirt. There, on his left bicep, was the slanted trident, pointing downward. It was a faded, black tattoo. It had stuck in his mind because tattoos simply did not exist in Ishtara. They served no utilitarian purpose.

He'd never seen his grandfather without a shirt on, which was strange now that he thought about it. Was the tattoo why he'd always remained covered?

What the doeppelganger had described on Tianna was a brand on her back, however. But the symbols being the same could not be mere coincidence. There must be a link somewhere. But Alariq knew he was in over his head.

On the third morning, after the red-headed female guard brought them breakfast, he sent Callum and Brimir over to the right, knowing Ford and Asher would return in their stead to get some sleep in Alariq's cell. Alariq crawled through the tunnel over to Blainn and Gideon.

"Watch out for Ford and Asher coming through to my cell," Alariq said, as Blainn headed for the tunnel.

Alariq stepped in front of Gideon's path, however, waiting to speak until Blainn had gone.

"I have need of your expertise."

Gideon's eyes narrowed in confusion and interest.

Alariq was hesitant to reveal too much. This was something he wanted to work out on his own before he divulged any secrets. His grandfather's or Tianna's.

But over the last two days he had watched the black-haired finman. He returned to the prison often, usually just to check Tianna's cell and then return to the water. None of the other finfiends were behaving that way. And there was a look in his eyes that made Alariq see red. The intense fixation of the finman on Tianna was something he could not ignore. For all of their sake's.

Alariq bent down and drew the symbol in the dirt.

"What can you tell me about that symbol?"

Gideon studied it for a minute. "Not much, I'm afraid," he said, his brow creased in concentration. "It is familiar, I know I have seen it before. But I cannot place it."

Alariq exhaled his disappointment.

"It is not an Ishta symbol," Gideon continued, "Of that I can be certain."

Alariq nodded, already knowing as much.

"You might ask Callum," Gideon said casually. "My area of knowledge is really more Ishta and Dirni history, but he studied quite a lot about other regions and people of the Continent."

Hope surged inside Alariq once more.

"Will you send him to me?" he asked.

Gideon nodded and headed for the tunnel. If he was at all curious as to why Alariq was asking about some random symbol, he did not convey it.

For the hundredth time, Alariq went over everything he knew about Tianna, looking for any clues that might explain this unlikely connection. Always, he had felt there was more to her story. He felt the pressure of the blood in his face increase. He shouldn't have to devote time to this, damn it! He should be focusing on their escape!

Just as his mental rant started to gain traction, Callum appeared through the tunnel. Alariq forced his emotions into submission. He needed information right now, not feelings.

"Gideon said you needed my help?" Callum looked even more mystified than Gideon had.

Alariq nodded and then cocked his head toward the symbol in the dirt.

"Have you ever seen this symbol before?"

"Oh, yes," Callum said, recognition sparking in his eyes.

Alariq's pulse quickened. "Where?"

"Only in books," Callum answered, looking up at Alariq's

tone. "Why do you ask?"

Alariq grabbed Callum's shoulder. "I need you to tell me whatever you know about this symbol."

Callum, continuing to look confused, said, "It is the symbol of the Zingari."

"The Wanderers?" Now it was Alariq's turn to look confused. "The nomadic people? How do you know?"

"When I learned our grandfather had been raised by them, I scoured the scrollroom for information on them. They're a fascinating people."

Callum's desire to know anything about everything was finally paying off.

"So this symbol, it is the mark of their people?"

Things were starting to add up. His grandfather had been raised by the Wanderers. That was when they must have marked him. And Tianna being a Zingari made sense too, with her living alone and fighting prowess. Although it didn't explain why the black-haired finman was fixated on her.

"Yes, although they only appropriated it," Callum answered.

That stopped Alariq's thoughts midstride.

"From where?"

"From the ancient slave trade. It was how they branded the slaves. You can see why," Callum pointed at the symbol.

Alariq looked at it and realized, positioned between the shoulder blades like the doeppelganger had described on Tianna, it looked like a trident being pressed against a person's back, holding them down. Yes, he could see why the slave traders had chosen that mark.

"So why did the Zingari adopt it?" Alariq asked, still holding on to Callum's shoulder.

"Because after the Great Uprising, when the slaves revolted, those who were born into the trade, who had no families to go home to, they became the first Zingari."

Alariq spoke slowly, carefully thinking through each word first, so as not to reveal too much. "I have seen this symbol before. But it was not a branding. It was a tattoo on the upper arm."

"Yes," Callum said, half in answer, half in question.

"Does that mean anything?" Alariq prodded, exasperated.

"To my knowledge, that's how it is always done," Callum answered, still puzzled.

Alariq rubbed his hand over his face. "You said it was a branding."

"No, I said they branded the *slaves* that way, long ago. I do not believe the Zingari ever marked their people that way."

Now Alariq was completely lost. His grandfather bore the mark as a tattoo, as was apparently normal for a Zingari. But Tianna's mark was a brand. Like the slaves. What had started to come together earlier was now falling apart once more.

"Are you certain?" Alariq stared intently at his cousin. "The Wanderers never branded their people? Below the nape of the neck, between the shoulder blades?"

Callum nodded. "I cannot imagine the Zingari would ever want their children to endure a branding like that. Tattoos are much less painful, and not nearly as barbaric." He pointed at the symbol again. "On their back, you see, it was a symbol of subjugation. But on their arms, willingly put there, it was a show of solidarity and a reminder of their shared past."

Alariq stared at the symbol. Was he understanding correctly? The Zingari used tattoos on the arm. Only slaves from ancient days were branded. That couldn't be right. There must be something else Callum didn't know.

Suddenly, something the doeppelganger had said burst into the forefront of Alariq's mind. He heard Nyeven say the words as if he were standing right next to him, whispering them in his ear.

"They draw their life force from their spouse."

Finfiends chose spouses who lived longer than them. Their spouse's life force kept them young, strong, and beautiful. So if a finfiend found someone who looked young, but who he believed to be very old...

"When did the slaves revolt?" he demanded. "How long ago?"

Callum paused, his expression mingled with bewilderment and mild panic now. It was all Alariq could do not to shake him to make him answer faster.

"About five hundred years—"

"And what happened to the slave trade after that?" Alariq grabbed Callum's shoulder once more.

"Nothing. Nearly all of the traders were killed in the uprising."

Alariq's mind was whirring. Everything started to fit together again, this time perfectly. Only the picture it formed was one that simply could not be real.

Callum continued, eyeing Alariq with great interest. "Dirnovaria had outlawed slavery some time before that, so the trade had already started to die out. It never picked back up after the uprising."

Alariq released Callum, nodding slowly, his eyes open, but not really seeing.

If a finfiend found someone he believed to be over five hundred years old—well, Alariq imagined that was a spouse a finfiend would do anything to ensnare. In fact, he knew it was.

This is why the finman wants her so badly, he announced silently to himself. *He believes Tianna is immortal, or at least very old.*

Only one question remained to be answered.

Was he right?

Before Callum could ask him again what his interest was in the symbol, Brimir's head emerged from the tunnel.

"Sorry to interrupt, but I thought you should know." He smiled. "We hit wet sand."

"That's great news!" Callum exclaimed. He turned to Alariq. "What does that mean?"

"It means," Alariq answered, looking from Brimir to Callum, "We go tonight."

Callum and Brimir both nodded, smiles on their faces, but trepidation in their eyes.

Alariq squared his shoulders. The mystery surrounding Tianna would have to wait.

"We need to tell the others," Alariq peered out of the window in the door. "But it is getting close to noon. The guards will come round soon."

The three of them returned to their cell. Alariq shook Ford awake, while Callum tickled the back of Asher's neck until he finally slapped himself in the head. After swearing at Callum, Asher headed down the tunnel, Ford snickering behind him.

But just as Gideon's head emerged from the tunnel leading to Ford and Asher's cell, Brimir hissed from the window.

"There are only three guards at the gate," he whispered loudly.

Alariq looked through the window at the sky. It was impossible to tell what time of day it was due to the weather. Had they misjudged the time?

He leaned down and helped Gideon out of the hole.

"Hurry!"

Gideon didn't even bother to stand but simply belly-slid into the other hole to his cell. Blainn emerged a second later.

"Get back to your cell, quickly! One of the guards is missing from the gate!"

Without a word, Blainn likewise dove headfirst into the tunnel leading to his cell. Alariq hastily covered one hole, while Callum covered the other.

Alariq had just leaned casually over the straw-covered opening when Brimir sat down against the wall abruptly.

"I can hear him coming," Brimir breathed and had the cell not been so small, Alariq would not have been able to hear his words.

They all waited, trying to look unconcerned, but all strung tighter than a bowstring, hoping the others had covered their tunnels in time.

Alariq listened with bated breath as the guard paused by Blainn and Gideon's cell. His heart beat in every part of his body. A single moment felt like a thousand.

But the footsteps continued and a head came into view. The finfiend looked around their cell and then moved on. Alariq didn't relax until he heard it move on from Ford and Asher's too.

They all looked at each other in relief. Alariq's muscles unclenched. No one spoke for a long time.

"Take some rest, you two," Alariq said to his two cellmates. "It will be a long night."

They both nodded gratefully and laid down on their beds of straw, Callum curling into his usual ball and Brimir tugging his hood over his face to block the light.

Alariq did not sleep, though this time on purpose.

If he was right in his suspicions—and his gut was telling him he was—Tianna was not what she seemed.

The doeppelganger wanted him to leave her behind.

That was out of the question. Even if Alariq wanted to, they would need her if it came to a fight. And besides that, he didn't want to, he admitted to himself, gritting his teeth again.

What he wanted, was some damn honesty from her. She knew everything there was to know about him, about all of them. He was risking a lot to get her out. They could have been out days ago. He even widened the cursed tunnel to make it easier on her! Was it really so unfair to expect her to be upfront about herself in return?

Alariq was not convinced the branding on Tianna's back was in fact a slave's mark. Rationality ruled out that possibility. But he was at least certain that is what the black-haired finman believed it to be. If the finfiend was right...well, that would mean she was over five hundred years old. And she looked like she had only just reached her majority.

Except in her eyes, Alariq thought.

The treehome jumped into Alariq's mind. The top two floors, which Tianna said she'd added herself. The stacks of homemade books and paper. Her detailed maps and extensive knowledge of the forest.

And the ettins.

She'd known all about the ettins' arrival in Loraheem over thirty years ago.

It all made perfect sense. Except that it didn't.

He ran through the list of the races he knew on the Continent: men, dwarfs, ettins, knomes, finfiends, and Utu. That was all. To his, albeit limited, knowledge, none of them attained such an age.

One question kept plaguing him. If all this was true, if she had been branded half a millennium ago—

What is she?

It seemed like so crude a question, but it was all he could think. He had never heard of such long life, except in the old dwarf kings. And they at least aged normally, just more slowly. What he was currently contemplating was something very different indeed. Something that looked a lot more like immortality...

He wanted to go to her cell this very minute and demand answers. The doeppelganger was right. She was placing them all at risk. Her lies of omission were putting them, him and his companions, who were risking everything to rescue her, in danger. But he didn't trust himself to be alone with her right now. Alariq's blood pounded in his ears and behind his eyes.

He had always sensed there was something not quite right about her. That there were things she purposely kept hidden.

And I was right. He clenched his jaw so hard, he sent it into spasm.

Rubbing it, he got up and checked the door. He neither saw, nor heard the guards. He crawled halfway through the tunnel.

"Ford, Asher!" he whispered loudly.

"Yes?" Asher called back quietly.

"Tell Tianna and the doeppelganger that we go tonight. Tell them one of us will come and get them when we are ready to go."

"Got it," Asher answered.

Alariq returned to his patch of straw and stretched out on it. He had only laid down for a quarter hour when Ford returned, out of breath.

"What is it?" Alariq demanded, alarm lacing his voice.

"The doeppelganger, I went to his cell and he was gone," Ford answered between huffs.

Alariq sat upright. "What?"

"I found him," Ford said quickly. "He is in Tianna's cell."

"What?" Alariq repeated, this time even loud and angrier.

He didn't wait for Ford to answer, just pulled him out of the tunnel by the back of his shirt and crawled through it himself, passing through Ford and Asher's cell, and continuing on to Tianna's.

He emerged to find Tianna and Asher on one side of the cell and Nyeven on the other, sporting a quickly-swelling eye.

"Asher!" Alariq barked. They couldn't afford to be fighting. The guards might hear.

To Alariq's great displeasure, Asher was smiling. Alariq advanced on him, about to give him a dressing down.

But Tianna stepped in front of him.

"Asher did not hit him," she said quietly. "I did."

Asher snickered behind her, looking at the doeppelganger and making no attempt to hide his mocking.

"Oh," Alariq said simply, taken aback.

He looked at Tianna for a minute. At the sight of her face, all the anger and mistrust and frustration at her lies bubbled up inside of him. As if she sensed it, she took a half-step back.

Then a thought occurred to Alariq. He turned on Nyeven. "What exactly did you do that caused her to feel the need to hit you?" He gave Nyeven the most threatening look he possessed.

"Well this just gets more interesting by the second," Nyeven said cryptically, massaging his face.

Alariq covered the distance between them in two long strides and grabbed the doeppelganger by his shirt, pulling him down to his level.

"Answer me!" he said, too loudly.

Tianna put a hand on his arm, exerting just enough pressure to get his attention.

"He did not try to harm me," she said, her face a little red. "I let his provocations get the better of me." She turned to Nyeven, eyes narrowed, her voice hardening. "It will not happen again."

Alariq glared at him a moment more before releasing him. He went to the window and peered out carefully, to make sure his outburst had not been overheard. Eight guards remained on the wall, four at the gate and two on each side. Alariq relaxed.

He had to get himself under control. He could barely keep track of who he was most mad at. His anger randomly shot from one bull's-eye to another and he wasn't sure where it might land next. The next person to say something that irritated him, he supposed.

He turned back to Nyeven, completely unapologetic. "What are you doing here?"

"My face felt a little too perfect." The doeppelganger gently probed his cheek, wincing.

Alariq took a step toward him.

"I needed to speak with you," Nyeven said hastily, holding his hands up.

Alariq forced his breathing to even.

"We can talk after I have escorted you back to your cell,"

Alariq growled.

The doeppelganger gave him a conciliatory nod and Alariq held out his hand toward the tunnel entrance in a mock gesture of courtesy.

"How kind," said Nyeven, sarcasm dripping from his tone. "Always a pleasure, Buttercup," he said as he passed Tianna. He nodded at Asher. "Lover-boy."

Then he fluidly slunk into the tunnel and out of sight.

Alariq wasn't sure why, but he gave Asher a hard look. "Back to your cell," he said before following the doeppelganger.

He stayed just behind Nyeven on the trip back, giving him much less room than he would anyone else. It wasn't that Alariq was afraid Nyeven would try to pull something. Where could he go? No, it was more out of spite.

"Well, I guess it's true what they say," Nyeven said, brushing himself off as Alariq climbed out of the tunnel. "You never really notice just how small dwarfs are, until you've crawled through one of their tunnels."

Alariq stared stonily back.

Nyeven pursed his lip. "If you were an ettin, you would be rolling on the floor right now."

"Ettins do not laugh," Alariq replied, his voice deadpan.

"Perhaps you are just not the jester you think you are, Sunshine."

Alariq refused to get pulled in. "What do you want?"

"Always to business," Nyeven taunted. "Is that how you handle the ladies?"

Alariq simply stared at him.

"Fine." Nyeven folded up his blanket and sat down on it. "I want to ensure our understanding remains...intact."

"As much as I would like to be rid of you, I have no intent of going back on our agreement."

"Well, not *no* intent," Nyeven drawled, giving Alariq a knowing look.

Alariq shook his head and made for the tunnel.

"But—" Nyeven snapped. "Just to be sure you do not...reconsider, I have something else that might be of value to you."

Alariq turned slowly, looking at the doeppelganger, his eyes sharp.

"But I will only tell you once we are safely out of here."

Alariq nodded. He didn't really care if Nyeven was telling the truth, as he'd already resolved to get him safely through the tunnel.

"And—" Nyeven half-smiled, only one corner of his mouth turning up. "—you escort me safely to Dhema, a small port on the Vestri River."

"No," Alariq said simply.

The doeppelganger looked as though he was very much unaccustomed to hearing that word. He quickly recovered and the nonchalant look returned to his face.

"I promise it will be worth your trouble."

"Yes, but will it be worth the trouble you bring with you?" Alariq shot back evenly.

Nyeven just smiled his crooked smile and looked at Alariq as though he knew all the secrets of the world.

Alariq simply stared back, thoroughly convinced he didn't.

"It is about your king."

Alariq's cavalier attitude quickly evaporated. He straightened.

"What do you know of Tanith?"

"Tsk, tsk, tsk." The doeppelganger wagged his finger at Alariq. "You really must learn to pay attention. I said I would tell you when we reach my destination."

For at least the thousandth time, Alariq ground his teeth together so hard, he felt it in his still healing head.

"How far up the Vestri?" Alariq asked through his clenched teeth.

"A ways..." Nyeven picked up a piece of straw and started to chew on it.

Alariq shook his head. "That will take us too far out of our way. And into the wild."

"Yes, which is exactly why I need your escort."

Alariq considered him for a moment, weighing his options. None of them seemed particularly appealing. Outside of strangling him. But finally, he nodded. A chance to learn more about their traitor king was not one he could casually pass up.

Nyeven smiled, his lips cutting a wide line through his cheeks. "Excellent. I am sure you are looking forward to it as much as I am."

Alariq just glared back. "Be ready. We will come soon after sundown."

Alariq returned to his cell to find everyone crammed inside.

"What did he want?" Ford asked.

Alariq decided honesty was called for here. "He wants us to escort him to a port on the Vestri River."

"That's ridiculous." Ford looked indignant. "We do not have time to play his bodyguards."

"He says he has information."

"What kind of information?" Callum asked.

"He says he knows something that would be of value to us. About Tanith."

Everyone was quiet for a moment.

"He's lying," Blainn said.

"Probably," Alariq agreed.

"Actually," Gideon said very slowly. "I think there is a possibility he may be telling the truth."

29

Fears and Faults

It was one of those moments when you wonder if you actually just heard what you think you did, where your brain has to play catch up to your ears. They all simply stared at Gideon.

"What do you mean?" Alariq finally asked, too surprised and curious to be suspicious.

Gideon looked around and shrank back a little. Whether he was just uncomfortable being the focus of so much rapt attention or he regretted saying anything, Alariq wasn't sure.

"Well," Gideon began, "I...I have suspected that things are not quite...right, so to speak, with our king for some time."

"Why?" Alariq did not take his eyes off Gideon, though he could tell the others were glancing at one another.

"Well, it started when I was younger, quite some time ago. Tanith had recently become king, and at quite a young age, relatively speaking. He came to me in the scrollroom one day, asking to be shown around."

Alariq waited for him to continue. He'd never known a king to express much interest in scholarly matters, but the request did not seem overly suspicious to him.

"I gave him a tour, showed him how we categorized things. I asked if he was looking for anything in particular and he said that

he just wanted to know how things worked in his kingdom."
Gideon nervously cleaned his spectacles.

"None of that seems out of the ordinary." Alariq tried not to
sound as though he thought Gideon had just wasted his time.

"Right, of course," Gideon stammered. "But he came back.
That night. Late that night. I had fallen asleep in my office,"
Gideon paused, looking embarrassed, "as...as I often did."

Gideon wasn't telling Alariq anything he didn't already know.
Gideon's oddities had not gone undiscussed in Ishtara. It's how
Alariq had known Callum would fit right in.

"He removed a bunch of texts and never returned them."

"What texts?" Alariq asked.

"All kinds. There did not seem to be a rhyme or reason to it.
Various texts on dwarfs, Ishta, Karxani, and the ancient tribes, the
various accounts of the Dwarf Wars, the king's ancestry, a few
maps, and..." Gideon paused, now looking quite nervous. "And a
scroll detailing ettins."

Alariq rolled his shoulders and rubbed the back of his neck. It
made sense. Although the fact that it started so long ago was
unsettling. Alariq wondered if the secret the doeppelganger
intended to share was the one they had already uncovered. When
they arrived at Dhema, would Nyeven reveal Tanith's bargains
with the ettins, thinking it was new information to them?

"There is more," said Gideon, and Alariq looked back at him.

"About ten years ago, it happened again. Well, sort of. I...I'd
fallen asleep again..."

Some things never change, Alariq thought, barely restraining
himself from rolling his eyes.

"...and voices woke me up. It was the king and his daughter."

"Lenya?" Ford interjected.

Gideon nodded. "I crept to the door. Tanith was angrier than
I had ever seen him. And the poor girl looked scared out of her
mind. She was saying that she found the texts in his room and
thought he'd forgotten to return them, so she was bringing them
back. Tanith started yelling at her never to go into his chambers
and never speak to him about this again."

"Then what?" Ford's eyes were wide and he leaned toward
Gideon, urging him with his stance to continue.

"Then he took the texts from her and left."

Ford relaxed a little, his shoulders falling and his features slackening.

Looking over at Ford's expression, Alariq realized the rumors about him and the king's daughter must have been true. He felt the familiar tug of guilt. Ford had given up even more than Alariq had originally believed to follow him into exile.

Alariq returned his attention to Gideon. "So what do you think it was about?"

"I do not know, but it seems pretty suspect. At least to me," he added nervously.

"It does seem suspicious," Alariq conceded. "Why did you wait until now to say anything?"

"Because I wasn't sure it meant anything. At the time, I tried to brush it off as the eccentricities of a king. But it never sat right with me. It was not until we discovered Tanith was supplying the ettins at Dendreya that I realized it might be important. And even then, I didn't see how the information would be...helpful."

Alariq nodded, giving Gideon a small half-smile to tell him he understood. Gideon had kept quiet about it because the situation back at the treehome had been difficult enough. Had he revealed what he knew, the others probably would have wanted to return even more and used it as leverage against Alariq. Based on the way Gideon had said it, Alariq also had the sneaking suspicion that Gideon hadn't wanted to add to Alariq's distress during that time.

Alariq made a mental note to thank Gideon in private later.

Alariq looked at the old dwarf's aged, yet still childlike face. When Gideon had caught up to them in the foothills of the Brackish Mountains, he'd assumed Gideon was fond of Callum and was coming along in support of the kid. But now Alariq wondered if Gideon's experiences with Tanith hadn't played a part.

"Is it possible that there is, perhaps, more to this story?" Gideon continued hesitantly. "And that the doeppelganger knows about it?"

Alariq considered it for a moment. His money was personally still on bluffing, or that Nyeven simply knew of Tanith's treachery in the Ettinwar. But then a thought occurred to him.

"Maybe there is more to the story, or maybe not. But Nyeven might know something that can help us convince the others in Ishtara. Some way for us to get proof. Even if the secret he knows is about the ettins in Dendreya, how did he find out in the first place? There must be a trail somewhere."

The others glanced around at each other.

Alariq looked to Ford, knowing if he agreed to help Nyeven, there would be no opposition from anyone.

Ford held his gaze for a long moment and then nodded.

"It is worth a try," he said.

"Then we are agreed?" Alariq looked at the others. "After we escape, we take the doeppelganger west?"

They all nodded.

"Brimir, where are we with the escape tunnel?"

"Ready to dig through to the surface. Quarter of an hour at most," Brimir responded.

"Good, then we are ready. Everyone get back to your cells. As soon as the guard comes by, I will send Callum and Brimir over to you—" he looked at Blainn and Gideon "—to collect our weapons. Ford will get the doeppelganger and Asher can get Tianna. I will keep watch."

Everyone nodded, their faces solemn.

"Get some sleep, all of you. After we get out of here, we cannot stop until this cursed lake is far behind us."

Everyone went back to their cells, but Alariq remained awake and alert, waiting to hear the telltale footsteps of the guard.

Before long, his thoughts turned, not to Tanith, but to Tianna. The mark on her skin troubled him greatly. He saw it everywhere now.

He was sure he had guessed correctly in that the finfiend believed her to be immortal, or at least possessing an extremely long life. That certainly explained his obsession with her. But the truth of it, he just could not believe. It seemed too fantastic.

He wanted to get up and pace, but the cell was too small. He had to remind himself the others needed their sleep.

If it *was* true, she clearly could not be an ordinary human. Did she possess other powers? There were tales of sorcerers and potion masters who could do incredible things, but Alariq had never believed them. Or at least, he believed the truth was really some tiny version of the tall tale that was told.

Curiosity and anger constantly fought for the center stage of his mind. Why couldn't she just have been honest? Did she think they would burn her at the stake like the witches of ancient times? Would he even have believed her if she had told him?

His thoughts turned to Asher and he got angry again. The boy clearly cared about her and she was lying through her teeth about herself.

Lover-boy, Nyeven had called him.

Dwarfs did not fall in love, at least not usually. And they certainly didn't fall for non-dwarfs. Alariq had never even heard of such a thing.

Maybe that was why Tianna kept her secrets. Did she return Asher's feelings and was afraid he would wash his hands of her if he knew the truth?

Alariq didn't know why, but that thought made him angriest of all.

He punched the straw behind his back to get the lumps out. He felt the pressure of his blood in every vein in his body.

He forced himself to calm down. He could not dwell on this now. He would have to deal with Tianna and her secrets after they were all safe.

For the remainder of the afternoon, he went over the plan again and again. When Brimir and the others came back with the weapons, Alariq would send Brimir and Blainn down the tunnel, Brimir to complete the last bit of the tunnel and Blainn for protection. They were to wait just inside the tunnel until the rest of them arrived. Callum and Gideon would go next, followed by the doeppelganger and Ford, who was to keep an eye on Nyeven. Then Tianna and Asher. Alariq would bring up the rear.

Ideally, he'd want his archers up front to cover everyone as they exited the tunnel in case there was trouble. But he was hesitant to let Tianna go near the front. If she got scared and lost control, she might cause the tunnel to collapse. So he wanted as many others out as possible first. And, as inexplicably bitter as it made him, he felt Asher would have the best chance of keeping her calm and moving forward.

And he would've gone last no matter what. Just to make sure everyone else got out alright.

Soon, the cell started to darken. Alariq got up and went to the window. The sun was almost touching the horizon.

It wouldn't be long now.

He scanned the area, but all looked like business as usual. Eight guards on the wall, no unusual activity. So he returned to his seat and tried to get a little rest.

Soon, darkness fell. Not long thereafter, the guard came around. It was a new one Alariq didn't recognize. But he filled the water bowl Alariq held out, tossed in the jerky just as usual, and then moved on.

Alariq watched carefully as the guard paused at Nyeven's cell. There did not appear to be any exchange between them other than the usual water. Alariq didn't move until the finman returned to his position at the gate.

He continued to watch the finfiends for a few minutes more and then woke the others. Brimir and Callum shook off their sleepiness and headed for the tunnel to the left. Alariq crawled down the opposite one, waking Ford and Asher, who roused much more quickly, and then immediately left to get their respective charges.

Brimir and Blainn returned first.

"We couldn't get it all in one haul," said Brimir. "Callum and Gideon went back for the rest."

Alariq nodded. They'd discussed that possibility.

Blainn handed him his crossbow.

"Your sword's on the way," he said apologetically.

They set down the weapons and headed for the escape tunnel. Blainn stopped at the opening to allow the older dwarf to go first, but Brimir paused, a small smile tugging at the corners of his mouth. He turned back to Alariq.

"Thank you," he said, resting one hand on Alariq's shoulder.

"For what?" Alariq asked, completely bewildered.

"For getting us out of here." Brimir smiled in earnest now.

"We are not out yet," Alariq replied, blushing slightly. "And anyone here could have done what I did."

Brimir shook his head, still smiling. "I know you really believe that, son. But whether you like it or not, you're an outside the box thinker. I thought these lake creatures had us good and cornered on a beach. I didn't realize we were on more solid soil and I certainly never would have believed we could tunnel out. And do you think Callum and Gideon would have stood a chance without you?"

"Maybe not, but the soldiers would have kept them safe. Ford—"

"—is an inside the box thinker." Brimir gave him a hard look. "Ford is a great dwarf, kinder than any I've ever met. But when it comes to war, he plays by the rules. He never would have risked everything to get us out of here. He would have played it safe. And you know where that gets you in situations like these."

Alariq studied Brimir's lined face.

"But that's not the kind of dwarf you are." Brimir hugged him then and Alariq surprised even himself when he returned the embrace. "And I couldn't be happier about that—" Brimir pulled back. "—or more proud."

Alariq couldn't say anything in response. But Brimir just smiled again before disappearing into the tunnel.

"Take care of him." Alariq gave Blainn a look that said he was serious.

Blainn gave a curt nod in response and followed Brimir into the darkness.

Alariq was left alone only for a moment before Tianna emerged from the tunnel to his right, in slightly better condition than she had been the last time he'd seen her emerge from underground.

He helped her up and then immediately released her and walked back to the window. Just seeing her, all he wanted to do was yell at her. Tell her he knew she was keeping things from him, from them all. Tell her he was tired of it. But he held onto his temper. He heard her and Asher talking quietly, but blocked out whatever they were saying.

It wasn't long before Ford and the doeppelganger appeared as well.

"It smells terrible in here," Nyeven said matter-of-factly.

Alariq gave him a look that clearly said he was not in the mood.

Just then, Gideon and Callum emerged from their tunnel. It was a tight fit once again.

Gideon handed Tianna her bow, but Asher reached out and took it.

"I'll carry it," he said, looping it with his own on the leather strap he wore across his body. He slung both their quivers across his back too.

She smiled gratefully and then took her sword from Callum, which the finfiends had taken from her, sheath and all. She strapped the thick leather around her waist and looked at Alariq. She smiled and nodded slightly, but at his stony expression, her eyes clouded over and confusion flitted across her features, replaced quickly by her usual unreadable mask.

Once everyone was armed, Alariq sent Callum and Gideon down the tunnel.

They had to leave their packs behind. There was no hope of getting them through the tunnel without risking collapse.

Alariq gave them a few minutes and then sent Nyeven and Ford. All still looked well in the courtyard. Finally, he gave Asher a nod, who gently steered a pale, but resolute Tianna toward the hole. Tianna went first and Asher followed.

Alariq gave the guards one last look and then crawled after him.

The tunnel was naturally completely dark. After the first twenty paces or so it widened and Alariq would have been able to move much more quickly if he hadn't been behind Asher, who was softly encouraging Tianna to keep moving.

It was slow going. By Alariq's count, they should be crossing under the gate. Their pace was steady, at least. Finally, after what seemed like an hour, they reached the spot where the tunnel turned right. The dirt started to feel damp beneath his hands.

Alariq could hear voices ahead. He knew they must be getting close to the others. He breathed a small sigh of relief.

But then, voices were not the only thing he could hear.

Rumbling. The hollow rumbling that signals earth moving.

"The tunnel!" he shouted.

But it was too late. He felt a wall of air hit his face, followed by a splattering of dirt.

The air immediately felt denser. Alariq could no longer hear voices up ahead. The tunnel must have collapsed somewhere between his position and the exit. But where, or on whom, he had no way of knowing.

His part of the tunnel was intact. That much was obvious. He reached out and felt Asher's leg.

"Asher!" he yelled. "Are you two alright?"

Instead of an answer, Asher pulled his leg from Alariq's grasp. At least he was alive.

"No, don't move!" Alariq called.

But Asher kept going. Alariq could hear struggling, Asher speaking softly, and Tianna's rapid breathing. Alariq realized he had crawled up to Tianna, and was trying to keep her calm, to stop her from causing the tunnel to collapse fully.

Alariq remained motionless for a moment, reigning in the reflexive fear he'd felt when he sensed the collapse. More whispering up ahead. He could hear Tianna starting to panic.

He had to get her out of there. Alariq gently prodded the walls beside him. They seemed solid, so he tested the ceiling. It held tight too.

He inched forward.

"Asher—I need to know where the tunnel collapsed."

"Just ahead," he called back. "Part of it came down up here, but I can hear Ford digging to us."

Alariq breathed a heavy sigh of relief that the others were alright. But then he remembered he also had to worry about their air supply. Alariq tried to decide if he should start digging upward. If the tunnel collapsed on top of him, Asher and Tianna would be trapped on both sides. He decided to wait a little longer. The real question now was whether the finfiends had seen the tunnel collapse. There had been heavy cloud cover all day, but there was no guarantee that had continued. Alariq pressed his ear to the tunnel wall, but heard no sound of movement on the ground above.

Up ahead, Asher continued to whisper. What he was saying, Alariq couldn't make out, but it appeared to be working. The distressed whimpers had subsided and they both were staying still now.

Questions raced through Alariq's mind. How much of the tunnel had collapsed? Were the others exposed? How long before their air ran out?

"Asher!"

Alariq heard Ford's voice and exhaled his relief.

"Get her out!" Asher shouted.

Alariq felt some dirt come down on his head and he started crawling forward. He could hear Asher digging, could feel more dirt dusting his back.

"I'm through," Asher said finally, and Alariq heard him dragging himself.

Suddenly there was light in the tunnel. Alariq could see the hole through which Asher had just crawled. The tunnel had only partially collapsed, the wall on their left having given way from the weight of the wet sand. The light was coming from the hole created by Ford and Asher.

Alariq had to flatten himself and belly crawl to get through the crude, misshapen opening. The light was coming from the top of the tunnel about ten paces in front of him. He caught a glimpse of Asher's feet as they were pulled out of sight through the opening.

Alariq was able to get back on his hands and knees and quickly made it to the exit hole. It was bigger than it should have been. As soon as he pulled his torso out, he could tell the others had widened the exit hole considerably, digging it out in an effort to stop the tunnel from collapsing further.

Everyone was hunkered behind the rocks. Alariq let out a thankful breath. They had come out where they should. Ford offered him a hand and pulled him the rest of the way out of the tunnel.

Alariq looked up. The moon shone down all around them. He could see each of his companions clearly.

"So what now, Sunshine?"

Without even looking at the doeppelganger, Alariq addressed the others.

"The finfiends?"

"I don't think they heard—" Callum began.

But what the finfiends *heard* was suddenly the least of their problems. Like Tianna's game of falling tiles, the tunnel began to collapse. They all turned and watched as the tunnel caved in on itself, seemingly in slow motion, starting at the weak spot and continuing until they could no longer see it behind the wall. It carved a deep ditch in the earth.

In the darkness, it looked like a narrow path.

A path leading straight to them.

30

Choices

Yells from the gate and the ground below, splashes of water, cell doors slamming closed. The sounds of the finfiends discovering their escape were amplified in the darkness.

"Run!" Alariq bellowed.

Everyone started to move.

"Bow," Tianna said, holding out her hand, but Asher was already pulling the bow and quiver from his shoulders and passing them to her.

"Tianna, let's go," Alariq ordered.

But Tianna shouldered her quiver and leapt up on the rocks, firing her first arrow the instant her feet steadied on the highest boulder.

"Do not waste your arrows!" Alariq shouted, looking at the distance from them to the wall.

But Tianna was not firing at the wall.

Already, six finfiends were emerging from the water on each side of them, less than a hundred paces away. Tianna's arrow struck the red-headed female, who had been one of their guards, burying right at the base of the ribcage.

Already, Asher had started to climb the rocks as well. Alariq took a single step toward them, before he felt something tug on his arm. He turned to find Nyeven inches from his face.

"Leave her," he hissed.

Alariq tried to break free, but the doeppelganger held tight. "If she stays in the company, they will hunt us. We will never make it off the peninsula and up the river alive."

What happened next troubled Alariq for years. He was never sure if his mind ran free for a moment, or if the doeppelganger somehow showed him something. Either way, Alariq saw it as clear as if it was happening in front of him.

They were running along a beach, the finfiends in pursuit. They were gaining ground away from their hunters. But then the black-haired finman and a dozen others leapt from the shallows of the lake beside them and converged on the dwarfs. The finman fought his way toward Tianna with an obsessive fury, while the other finfiends caught up and surrounded them. The black-haired one reached for Tianna. Asher tried to intervene, but the finman grabbed him by the throat. Tianna screamed, but several other finfiends were between her and Asher. The black-haired one clenched his other hand on Asher's throat. He squeezed and Alariq knew Asher's windpipe had been crushed. The gigantic finman released him and Asher lay on the ground, fighting for breath that would never come. And then the rest of the dwarfs were all swallowed by the swell of captors descending on them.

Alariq held Nyeven's gaze for an instant, realizing what he must do.

He ripped his arm from the doeppelganger's grasp and turned. He scaled the boulders that divided them from their captors and came to stand beside Tianna and Asher.

They had already taken down four of the six, but Alariq saw disturbances in the water on either side of the wall.

More were coming.

Alariq pulled the release on his crossbow, hitting one of the remaining two at the same time Tianna did. The finman went down immediately.

Asher took care of the last one, the pale-haired male who had been another of their frequent guards.

"Go," Alariq barked to the others.

Asher started to climb down, but Tianna didn't move. Alariq grabbed her arm just above the elbow.

"You have to go now!" he said, shaking her slightly.

She hesitated, looking back at the water.

In the second that she scanned the lake's surface, her eyes searching, desperate and fierce, Alariq knew she was looking for the black-haired finman.

She knows, Alariq realized. *She knows of his obsession.*

Alariq watched as she frantically searched the water. For once, her face betrayed her. The fear in her eyes revealed it all. Like a bolt of lightning hitting him, the realization struck Alariq. It could only mean one thing.

The finman was right. The truth Alariq's rational mind had rejected was exactly that: truth.

Shock quickly gave way to betrayal. She knew she put them all at risk, yet she had kept it to herself. She knew the finman would stop at nothing to recapture her. That she sought to prevent the finman from following them was of little consolation to Alariq in his hurt and anger. Why hadn't she just trusted him? Why hadn't she been honest? Didn't she know he would not have left her behind?

Another lie of omission. Another betrayal.

Alariq whipped her around to face him, forcing her to meet his eyes.

Because none of that changed what he had to do to save the others. To save Brimir, who he loved like a father. Callum, who Alariq felt most responsible for, more so than anyone else in the entire world. Ford, who was twice the dwarf he was, no matter what Brimir said. Asher, who was in the most danger because of Tianna's lies. Or Tianna herself, who, despite everything, he couldn't bear to think of imprisoned by the black-haired finman.

"I will stop him," Alariq said simply.

Tianna stared at him, unable to hide the astonishment she felt.

He looked deep into her eyes and knew he was making the right choice.

"Go! Now!" Alariq's tone must have conveyed his resolve, because she finally relented and leapt gracefully from the rocks to join Asher on the ground. She looked up at him from below, fear, confusion, and gratitude all shining through her eyes.

Alariq cocked his head at Asher and he pulled Tianna away

from the boulders. Alariq turned back to the lake, watching as the smooth water filled with bubbles. He stood, transfixed, as the massive, muscled shoulders of the black-haired finfiend rose up from the dark water.

Other bodies were emerging from the water, but Alariq kept his focus on the one that mattered. As long as he killed the black-haired finman, the others would be safe. As long as they made it out, the other finfiends would not hunt them like the black-haired one would. If the finman was dead, then what Alariq had seen inside his mind could not happen. Tianna and the other dwarfs would be safe.

Or that was what Alariq hoped.

Alariq pulled one of his starmetal arrows. These shots had to count.

He put his foot in the stirrup, cocked his bow, and then loaded the bolt. His target was out of the water now, wielding both spear and sword, advancing quickly, the rest of the finfiends not far behind him. But Alariq saw the scene in slow motion. Normally, he was thinking ten steps ahead, trying to find his next move. In those times, everything passed at super speed.

But not now. Now, there was no next step. Kill the finman. That was the only thing Alariq must do. Because that was the only thing that would save the others.

Alariq waited a second more, to give himself a better shot. Then he fired.

His arrow struck his target in the shoulder. But the finfiend simply ripped the arrow from his skin and kept coming.

Alariq recocked his crossbow and loaded another metal arrow. The finfiend had already covered half the distance between them.

The scene that had appeared in his mind when the doeppelganger had touched him flashed inside his head again. The black-haired finman reaching for Tianna, the fear in her eyes, Asher crumpling to the ground, desperately fighting for air.

Alariq focused on the black and silver eyes of the colossal foe coming toward him. He took a single deep breath, aimed, and pulled the trigger.

31

The Crossroads

It was one of those shots that Alariq knew, as soon as the arrow left his bow, would find its mark.

And find its mark, it did.

Alariq watched as the finfiend, only paces away on the ground below, fell to his knees, Alariq's arrow in his chest. His adversary fell, face forward, onto the wet earth, Alariq's metal arrow protruding from the finfiend's chiseled back. It had gone all the way through his body, straight through his heart.

Instincts took over. Alariq turned and jumped, hitting the ground hard. He ran, shouldering his crossbow and drawing his sword as he went. He heard the unearthly screams behind him and chanced a glance over his shoulder just as the finfiends climbed over the rocks that had been his cover only a moment before.

They were less than fifty paces behind him. He knew he'd be overtaken in less than a minute. A smattering of trees lay ahead, but nothing thick enough to lose them in. He pumped his legs as hard as he ever had, his grip on his sword tight enough to snap a bone. He made it to the trees and looked for the others, but saw no sign.

He only hoped their absence was because they had managed to

get off the peninsula alive. And not because the finfiends had dragged them into the black water that bordered him to the left and right.

The finfiends were right behind him. He could hear their breathing.

A cracking sound rent the air, followed by a crash just a few paces behind him.

Alariq turned. A huge branch from the tallest tree lay on top of the five or six finfiends closest behind him. Arrows from above hit two others.

Before he could even move, five dwarfs dropped down from trees and leapt over the fallen branch, swords and knives drawn.

Alariq followed, having no time to think about what was happening. He leapt over the branch and used the momentum to deliver his first blow into the chest of a large finman.

Finfiends were all around him. He parried the blow of a spear and the stab of a knife, his blade flashing through the air.

Arrows rained down from above. Dwarfs yelled and finfiends screamed. Metal clashed against wood and sharpened bone.

Alariq spun and took out three at once. He stumbled.

And found himself face to face with the white-haired finmaid.

She snarled and brandished a jagged knife, at least as long as Alariq's forearm. She came at him, knife raised, but he blocked her blow. Another female came at him from behind, leaping on his shoulders, clawing at his neck.

He slammed his back into a tree and she crumpled off him. But the white-haired one was on him again, knife slicing through the air.

Another finfiend crashed into his side, and he turned to defend himself, but it lay still on the ground, Ford standing over it. His lapse in attention gave the white-haired one the opening she needed and she sliced the back of his hand, causing him to drop his sword.

She swung her knife backwards at his head. He watched the blunt end rush toward his temple.

An inch before it found its mark, he grabbed her arm and twisted. He heard a crack and she dropped the knife, screaming that awful scream that pierced deep into his brain.

He picked up his sword and looked around. All five of his companions on the ground were fighting.

And they were winning.

Then from above: "More are coming!" Tianna loosed an arrow. "Another thirty or so."

So these had only been the first to respond. Alariq gritted his teeth.

"Let's go!" he yelled, slamming his fist into a finfiend as he turned.

He let the others on the ground go ahead of him and then trailed after them, hearing Asher and Tianna hit the ground behind him and fall in with the group.

The dirt beneath his feet turned to sand, and in the white moonlight, Alariq could see where the peninsula connected with the beach, the lake curling away on either side of them. They were close. He ran harder, willing the others to keep moving forward.

Tianna, fast as she was, had gotten ahead of them, and she turned and fired two arrows while they caught up. He heard the finfiends yelling to each other and they seemed to fall back a little. Alariq looked back and saw a few finfiends disappear into the water.

They reached the end of the peninsula and ran up the beach, stumbling in the sand. As his feet hit grass, Alariq realized they were one short.

"The doeppelganger—where is he?" he demanded of the others.

"He took off," Blainn said. "When we stopped in the trees to cover you."

Alariq cursed.

"This way," Tianna shouted, heading west.

"No." Alariq looked behind him, but now he saw no trace of the finfiends. He didn't like how abruptly they had disappeared. "We need to go east."

"Nyeven is headed for the Vestri. That's west," she said, continuing to move away from them.

Asher made to follow her.

In his mind's eyes, Alariq saw Asher crumpling to the ground, the life quickly receding from his terrified gaze, the cost of Asher's naïve loyalty to Tianna.

"Stop," Alariq said and everyone, including Tianna, turned to him.

"We are not following the doeppelganger," he said. "And we are not following you."

Everyone looked from Alariq to Tianna, sensing there was more going on.

Splashing water made the dwarfs turn toward the lake. But Tianna kept her eyes on Alariq and he kept his on her.

He moved toward her, while the others brandished their weapons toward the water, looking for any sign of their pursuers. He strode over to Tianna, who didn't even flinch when he got right in her face. But he saw the fear in her eyes. He thought for a second she was afraid of him, but then her gaze flitted to Asher, who was turned away, patrolling the lake.

She knows I know and is afraid I will spill her secrets to Asher. Her continued intentional concealment of the truth was his breaking point. He put his face a hair's width from hers. The others were busy searching the water for any sign of their foe and didn't notice the exchange going on between Alariq and Tianna.

"If you think I am trusting you after your lies put all of us in danger, then you must think I am as foolish as he." Alariq jerked his head in Asher's direction. He warned her with his eyes that he would happily unburden himself of her lies.

Tianna paled.

"Yes, I know of your secrets." Alariq could feel her breath on his face. "I do not know exactly *what* you are, nor do I care at this point. You had your chance to be honest with me a hundred times." He lowered his voice even further. "Do not forget that I could have left you behind." She tilted her chin up and her lack of apologetic attitude broke his control.

He grabbed one of her arms. "Maybe I should have," he spat.

The others finally realized what was going on and hands appeared on his shoulders, wrenching him away from Tianna.

"What the hell is wrong with you?" Asher spun Alariq around to face him.

Out of instinct, Alariq pushed out, sending Asher to the

ground. Ford stepped between them, his hands on Alariq's chest.

But Ford should have been restraining his brother.

Asher dove from his knees around Ford's legs and upward into Alariq's midsection, both of them landing in the sand.

Alariq rolled on top of Asher, hitting him squarely on the jaw. Asher returned the blow, only to Alariq's stomach instead.

Someone yanked him backward and he flew off of Asher. Alariq landed hard on his rump and looked around, his muscles tensed and ready for a fight, expecting to see several of the other dwarfs, but instead, he just saw Tianna, fury furrowed in every line of her features.

Everyone stopped and stared, their faces frozen in shock. Alariq lay several full paces away from Asher. Tianna strode toward him until she was as close to him as he had been to her moments ago.

But instead of hitting him, as Alariq expected, her eyes filled with tears. Her gaze searched his.

When she spoke, her voice was filled with more emotion than Alariq knew she even possessed. "Please do not make the same mistakes I did," she whispered.

She crouched beside him and lowered her voice so that only he could hear her words.

"Do not steel yourself against those who have earned your trust...like I did." She looked at him hard and he saw in her eyes that she meant him, her failure to trust him.

She continued to search his gaze and Alariq couldn't have moved even if a thousand finfiends had rushed out of the lake at the very moment. She laid a hand on his shoulder.

"Do not dwell so much on the crimes in your past, that you cannot see the gifts of your present," she breathed.

She rose and took a step back and gestured at the other dwarfs. "These dwarfs stood by you, when no one else would. They have earned your trust and then some. They have risked their lives, just now and a dozen times before, on your behalf. They left everything they knew for you." She was almost pleading.

"Yet, here you are, risking everything to return to your city, to win back those who did *not* stand with you, those who betrayed you." Her voice begged him to listen. "I do not pretend to agree with your decision to return, and you have made it clear my opinion is not wanted on the subject, but please, *please*, listen to me about this: do not let your desire for vindication make you forget those who are the most deserving of your allegiance." She was on the verge of tears now. "Or your friendship."

She stepped even further away from him. Except for Asher sitting up, no one had moved.

"They have earned that from you a thousand times over." She quieted. "And so have I." She glanced at Asher and took a deep breath. "Despite what you think you have learned."

Alariq simply stared at her, wishing he didn't believe all of this was genuine, wondering if he really was as naïve as Asher because, despite everything that had just transpired, he did.

Tianna squared her shoulders and lifted her chin.

"So say what you will, and think what you want about me. Right now, all I care about is what you *do*. And what I need you to do—" her eyes pleaded with him, "—is trust me."

A battle raged in Alariq's heart. He looked in her eyes. Even in the moonlight, he could see clearly their rich amber color. Faces flashed before him. His mother, his wife, his brother, his soldiers. They passed through the vision of his mind's eye, perfectly preserved in their most idealized states, calling out to him.

And then, slowly, like iron melting over the furnaces, they dissolved into something else entirely.

Seven other faces sharpened in his sight around him, more vibrant and crisp than anything his mind could conjure.

Brimir, the dwarf who taught him it wasn't a weakness to feel love, even if it wasn't a utilitarian emotion. Callum, his innocent cousin, who he realized now he'd be proud to have as a son. Gideon, who had surprised them all when he followed them into exile. Ford and Blainn, the best brothers-in-arms he could have ever wished for. Asher, who he envied more than he could ever admit, even to himself. And Tianna, who by far exceeded, in character and beauty, any of the strange beings he'd heard about in the tall stories.

The gifts of his present.

He stared at them all in turn and something crumbled inside him.

A lump in his throat threatened to choke him. He tried to speak, but words wouldn't come. All he could manage was a single nod.

Tianna looked at him, her eyes filled with unshed tears. And then she smiled. She looked around at the others and then back at Alariq.

"There is a path," she said, and her voice was steady. "It is used by those who know of it, to pass between the Vestri and the Nordi rivers. To cross undetected through the Wayward Hills into the wild." She paused. "But it is concealed."

"We are on solid ground now," Blainn said. "We can outrun the finfiends."

Tianna looked at him and then at Alariq, her eyes filled with meaning. "But not the doeppelganger."

She took a step back toward him, this time in confidence, rather than anger, and spoke softly, her words meant for Alariq alone. "He is your only hope," she whispered.

Alariq searched her eyes, wondering how she was so certain, knowing that there must be a reason.

She looked back, her eyes pleading. "Please do not lead us down a road that will only end in death." She looked down, her long lashes sweeping over her cheeks. "And heartbreak."

Alariq studied her carefully. She had made it clear she did not believe they could succeed in their mission. But this seemed more certain, more concrete. Like she knew something he didn't.

If you go to Ishtara now, you will die. She hadn't said the words, but Alariq had seen them in her eyes, heard them in her tone.

There was no time for questions, although he longed to ask her how she was so certain he and the other dwarfs would die if they continued with his plan.

But then she looked at him once more and her words played over in his mind. She'd said do not lead *us* down a road. She said *us.*

Alariq knew then that she would follow him if he asked her to, even though she thought it would be their end. Just like he would have done if the others had decided to go back to Ishtara without him. And because of that, Alariq didn't care how she was so certain his quest would end in death. He only cared that she was.

And that she was willing to go with him anyway.

So Alariq did the one thing he could do to repay her for her fidelity. He trusted her.

He looked around at the others and knew, in spite of everything he had done since leaving Ishtara all those months ago, they would follow him too.

Their loyalty, their friendship, freely given and undeserved, made all the difference in his decision.

"Alright," he said to Tianna. "Lead on."

32

And Then They Were Eight

So you see, dear reader, underneath all the sullenness and sulking, hiding behind the suspicion and the short temper, was a hero after all. A man, in every meaningful sense of the word, who would risk his life for others, despite doubts and uncertainty. A man with courage, the courage to do what he feared most, and give others power over him, even after that power had been abused by others before them. A man who had the strength to take his life in his own hands and refuse to let events outside his control determine who he was.

This hero, and his seven devoted friends, set out from the beach where he made the most important decision of his life, up to that point or after it: the decision to trust, and trust completely.

And set out they did, and not a moment too soon. Not seconds after they fled the beach, their enemy returned in force, with others they had called from the depths of the sound.

The eight made their way west until they reached a rock face, slanting upward. The Crag, it was called. Alariq and the other soldiers had seen it before, for it ran right through the Wayward Hills, where they had fought many battles in the Ettinwar. It was as if the entire continent had a giant step running through its middle, the high side on the north and the low side on the south.

Tianna had led them to a fissure that ran from the ground to the top of the plateau above. It created a ladder of sorts that could be carefully climbed to the top. And sure enough, along the rock face, but below the ground above, was a stone path, created by nature and worn by man.

It was narrow, but there were tables and caves along the way. They had no supplies and their ability to hunt was limited to birds and the errant squirrel.

But they were together, bound by a common purpose, resolute in their intentions. They would find the doeppelganger. They knew where he was headed and would get there first. He could not know of the path or he would not have asked for their protection.

So when Nyeven arrived in Dhema, they would be waiting. And whatever it took, they would get the information they needed to return to their city and reclaim their lives.

Never before had Alariq been so vulnerable, both physically and otherwise, but he had also never felt so secure. He knew that whatever came, they would face it together, side by side as one.

Eight, they were, determined and united.

Elsewhere...

He knocked on the door. The house was shabbier than he'd expected. There were signs the home was once much nicer and better-cared-for. The crumbling fountain, the stone around the windows, the wrought iron across the peeking window in the large front door; they all spoke of the kind of wealth that was rare in the less civilized areas of the Continent.

The tiny peeking window opened and an eye stared out. Then the lock slid and the door opened. A man stepped into view. He was also shabbier than expected, his clothes well-worn at the seams, frayed at the edges. His hair was slightly thinning and his loose skin suggested he had once been wider and more muscular.

Nyeven silently scoffed. People were so weak. They told themselves the lies they needed to hear, even in their dreams. When he'd spoken with the trader in his dreams last night, the house had been restored to its former glory and the man was young, handsome, and strapping.

Wish fulfillment, Nyeven thought to himself. What had his mother always said? "Fears and wishes. That is where doeppelgangers live."

Recognition crossed the man's face. "I know you, don't I?" he asked Nyeven.

"Jeram, of course you know me," Nyeven said, a smile pasted on his face. "You used to trap with my older brother, Laaghan, out in the edges of Loraheem. It's Wren, remember?"

None of that was true, of course. But Nyeven was hungry and tired of sleeping on dirt. So he'd entered Jeram's dreams the night before and coaxed the information he would need out of him to gain entry to his life.

"Oh yes!" The man slapped his leg. "You used to follow us in the woods, but you would always turn back when it started to get too dark."

Nyeven forced himself to chuckle. "Yes, well, as you can see, I am not opposed to traveling in the dark now." He gestured behind him.

"What are you doing out this way?" Jeram asked, leaning against the doorframe.

"I've just come from visiting my brother. He is back living outside Prienne now. I'm headed back to Loraheem, where I have a small cabin." Nyeven faked a smile. "My brother said I should call on you on my way and see how you are."

"Well come in then," Jeram said, throwing the door wide open.

Nyeven crossed the threshold, smiling in earnest now.

A few hours and some wine later, and Jeram was practically begging Nyeven to stay the night.

"Well, if you insist," Nyeven said, inclining his head toward his new host.

Jeram waved him off. "Of course. You were a good kid, if a little faint-hearted. And your brother was a good friend of mine all those years ago." He took another swig of wine, spilling a little down himself.

"Living in Loraheem," he continued, as he clumsily wiped himself off. "That has to be a lonely life."

"Well, actually, I do not live there," Nyeven said smoothly. "I have a cabin where I stay occasionally, to trap during the off-season back in Prienne."

"Oh well, feel free to call whenever you're passing though!" Jeram guffawed.

"Oh, I will," Nyeven said, his usual crooked smile on his face.

Jeram gulped down the rest of his wine. "Well, I think I will call the day done now."

"Of course," Nyeven replied smoothly. "Please don't let me keep you. I'd like to finish my wine here by the fire if that's alright."

"Fine, fine," Jeram said good-naturedly. "You can find an empty bed in any of the rooms on the left side of the hall. I'm not fussy about which one you take."

Nyeven nodded.

"Well g'night," Jeram said.

"Sleep well..." Nyeven said, a genuine smile creasing his face.

Nyeven sat by the fire, sipping his wine and thinking about how easy this had been. Frankly, he was a little disappointed. Some people were so weak-minded, so easy to manipulate. He almost wished it had been a bit more of a challenge.

Like the little Buttercup, he thought, slowly swirling the wine in its glass. Yes, she had been very interesting indeed. Nyeven doubted he would have even been able to enter her mind at all, if she hadn't been so afraid.

The dwarfs had been easier. He had settled into their dreams effortlessly and observed all he wanted, though he'd sensed they'd be more difficult to manipulate. But not impossible.

He thought back to the dream conversation he'd had with the good-looking one, the one who'd escorted him out of the tunnel. Ford, he thought they'd called him. Nyeven recalled Ford telling him, without realizing it, of course, why they were out wandering the countryside.

He wondered if the dwarfs and the girl had made it out of Loraporth, if they'd escaped the finfiends. He doubted it, frankly. It was a shame, really. They would have been a pleasant diversion, an interesting game to play on his journey to Dhema.

If they had made it, though, they would be heading for Ishtara, according to Ford. The handsome dwarf had been so proud, honored even, to go defend his city-state from the evil king. Nyeven rolled his eyes and finished his wine.

"Heroes," he muttered. "That's a good way to end up dead."

He watched the fire dance in its box and his thoughts drifted to Alariq. Nyeven didn't like him, with his sharp eyes and his guarded mind. His dreams had been difficult to intrude upon. They were jumbled and hard to navigate. A sign the dreamer was conflicted, that he hid thoughts and feelings, even from himself.

Nyeven chuckled. His forays into dreams had taught him that conflict within was always worse than anything going on outside a person.

Although, maybe, just this once, the reverse would be true. Nyeven thought about Alariq's king and the secret he knew, the secret he'd gotten completely by chance, the secret that he was going to use to change his fortunes.

He spoke quietly to the flicking flames. "Sunshine—you haven't even scratched the surface yet..."

57521156R00206

Made in the USA
Charleston, SC
15 June 2016